strangely normal:

the (mostly) true tales of an incurable oddball

strangely normal:
the (mostly) true tales of an incurable oddball

J. Kevin Morris

Hegemony Press
An imprint of Cedar Fort, Inc.
Springville, Utah

© 2011 J. Kevin Morris

ISBN 13: 978-1-59955-914-8

Published by Hegemony Press, an imprint of Cedar Fort, Inc., 2373 W. 700 S., Springville, UT 84663
Distributed by Cedar Fort, Inc., www.cedarfort.com

LIBRARY OF CONGRESS CATALOGING-IN-PUBLICATION DATA

Morris, J. Kevin (James Kevin), 1951- , author.
  Strangely normal / J. Kevin Morris.
    p. cm.
  Summary: The author's own coming-of-age story that is for kids of all
ages.
  ISBN 978-1-59955-914-8
  1. Young men--California, Southern--Fiction. 2. Brigham Young
University--Students--Fiction. 3. Mormons--California, Southern--Fiction.
I. Title.

  PS3613.O7725S87 2011
  818'.603--dc23

2011023820

Cover design by Brian Halley
Cover design © 2011 by Lyle Mortimer
Edited and typeset by Kelley Konzak

Printed in the United States of America

10 9 8 7 6 5 4 3 2 1

Printed on acid-free paper

This work is lovingly dedicated to ten dear friends of my youth and adolescence, each of whom has remained true, right to this day—friends who have taken a licking in the telling of these stories or may yet take a licking in future efforts: (in alphabetical order) Bonnie, Chuck, Dave, Jeff, Jeralyn, Jim, Jody, Lucy, Maeta, and Scott. I write in celebration of all the incredible adventures of our youth and in anticipation of all those yet to be shared.

Acknowledgments

I acknowledge with appreciation those members of the Cedar Fort production staff, especially Shersta Gatica, Kelley Konzak, and Mariah Overlock, who helped put in order the mechanics of a personal dream.

A most special thank you to my courageous father, J.C. Morris Jr., my noble mother, Mildred Ruth Hamblin Morris, and my incomparable siblings, Deborah, Ricki, and David, for helping me not only survive but also enjoy my youth. Except for the time I spent in closets.

To Dale, Joanne, Jim, Jeff, Mark, Mike, Doug, and Joni: Thanks for letting me swipe your daughter and sister.

To Chris and Marc: Thanks for inspiration that pointed the way.

Last, but most certainly not least, I gratefully acknowledge the love, support, and long-suffering of my sweet wife, Dianne, and of my children, Anne, Kristopher, and Jeremy, each of whom has given a special measure of encouragement as I've tried to accomplish an important life goal. And a special note to Jackson, Kaleigh, John, Ashton, Kaden, Brianna, Belle, and Ryan, my most special grandchildren: When you read these stories, please pay close attention to your Pappy's youthful escapades. Reflect the good that you see in them and avoid the bad, and your lives will shine with your own amazing adventures.

Introduction

"I'm beginning to wonder if being young is all it's cracked up to be. We dream of youth. We remember it as a time of nightingales and valentines. And what are the facts? Maladjustment, near-idiocy, and a series of low-comedy disasters—that's what youth is. I don't see how anyone survives it."[1]

Barnaby Fulton, *Monkey Business*

Unlike Barnaby and others like him who *escape* their youth and eagerly leave it behind, I look back on my younger years and smile. I am in constant awe at the length and breadth of my silly choices, lack of common sense, and apparent eagerness to embrace stupidity. But I'm not bothered by that kind of history because I happen to believe it's a common one shared by all—even those who refuse to admit it.

In the telling of these stories, I've consciously, sincerely, and strenuously tried to avoid accusing, insulting, belittling, or incriminating anyone except myself. As an added precaution, I've changed the first names of some characters and never used last names except in the case of a public figure. If I've offended despite my best efforts, I apologize in advance. It is absolutely not my intention to do so. The truth is that *everyone* stumbles through youthful years, to some degree. Most survive it, though, and move beyond its inherent silliness to turn into decent, law-abiding, spiritual, faithful, community-minded, integrated, family people who look—lovingly and probably even longingly, whether they admit it or not—back at those years of mistake and discovery, and hold them to have been very important, even essential, to adult success.

So, dear Reader, I welcome you to my world. I encourage you to have a good time reading about these youthful adventures and getting to know the people with whom I shared them. Life is far too serious far too often, but it can be funny and, in fact, usually is, in retrospect. Please consider these two statements, the first from comedian Mike Meyers in a speech he gave as he accepted the 2008 Legacy of

Laughter Award during the TV Land Awards:

"Making people laugh is something I learned from my father, who always said, 'There's nothing so painful in life that couldn't be laughed at—eventually.'"

And the second from the late Marjorie Pay Hinckley, gracious wife of the venerable and deceased president of The Church of Jesus Christ of Latter-day Saints, Gordon B. Hinckley:

"The only way to get through life is to laugh your way through it."

If you haven't already discovered such value in laughter, I hope these stories will help get you on your way.

Note

1. Spoken by Cary Grant's Barnaby Fulton character in Howard Hawks's *Monkey Business*, written by Ben Hecht, Charles Lederer, and L.A.L. Diamond, 1952.

I take puppet lessons

It's 1961. I'm in the fifth grade at Baldwyn Elementary in Baldwyn, Mississippi. Miz Wood's my teacher.

I say *Miz* Wood instead of *Mrs.* Wood because in Mississippi we don't bother with syllables that aren't absolutely necessary to get the point across. So *Mrs.* is *Miz*, just like *Mississippi* is *Missippi*, and *you want* is *y'ont*. Very economical, this southern dialect.

Miz Wood's a lovely, gray-haired lady who's been teaching for more years than I can even imagine living. She's kind, but no push-over, that's for sure. And although she's a stalwart, dependable, capable woman, she's not what we fifth-graders would call a pin-up girl. Not at all like Miss Marshall last year.

Miss Marshall was something else.

Like all the other boys in my fourth grade class, I had a steaming crush on Miss Marshall. The screamin' warmies. The warm scorchies. She wasn't like most of the other teachers around here. She was younger. She was prettier. She smiled more. She let me get naked in class.

Like that one day.

"Boys, if yawl are too hot todaiy, it'll be awright for yawl to take awf yawl's shirts while we do 'rithmetic," she said, and I figured that meant everybody. So as quick as you can say, "Lawdy Miss Clawdy," I shed my shirt and hung it on a coat hook in the back of the room just like the other boys did. But when I got back to my desk at the front of the fourth row, something just didn't feel right. The room was way quieter than it oughta be. Odd.

3

It took me perhaps just a little more time than the average bear to realize that this sudden, unusual, stifling quiet might have something to do with me. I may be slow, but I'm eventual. The actual revelation came when I began to feel holes being drilled into me by whole bunches of eyes. And I could see that Miss Marshall's eyes were fixed on me too, with what I'd call *especial* interest. Not to mention bewilderment.

Because there I sat at my desk, with no shirt at all.

Nekked as a jaybird from the waist up.

I guess Miss Marshall had presumed that everyone would be wearing an undershirt, and a nekked little kid sitting at the front of the class wasn't at all what she had in mind when she invited us boys to take off our shirts.

Yeah. Like I was supposed to know that she was talking only to boys who were wearing undershirts. There's no way I could've known that. She never set forth any prerequisites. Never stated any givens. No conditions. Never said, "yawl can take awf yawl's shirts if yawl are wearing a T-shirt." *Never* did. And I'm no mind reader, after all.

But almost without skipping a beat, and with great calm and dignity, Miss Marshall said, "Well, boys, I thaynk that's just about anuff time for yawl to cool awf jus' a little, so why don't yawl go ahead and put awn yawl's shirts agin."

Which we did.

It would be years before I'd realize I should've been embarrassed.

Miss Marshall left the employ of the Baldwyn Separate School District before the end of the school year. Probably because of all the unexpected nudity in her classroom. But I can't prove it.

But back now to the fifth grade and Miz Wood.

One day Miz Wood says, "Boys and girls, I've got a vis'tor here todaiy, and she wawnts to tawk with yawl for a minute." Well, we're thrilled. We just love visitors. Grade-schoolers almost always love anything out of the ordinary—anything unexpected.

Except tests. Or vaccinations.

Like that filthy small pox vaccination we'll get in May just before school lets out for the summer. This creaky old nurse with a granite face more suitable for Mount Rushmore than for a school will poke about a gazillion little holes in my upper left arm with a weird-looking needle, like I'm some kind of pin cushion. Then, a few days later, this icky, drippy, painful blister will sprout on my arm like a mushroom on a warm, moist pile of . . . something or other. And then, of course, you *know* that thing's doomed to get popped because there's no *way* a young'un isn't gonna fiddle around with a lovely blister like that. And then comes the scab—something to be fiddled with even more than the blister, thus encouraging the lovely scar that'll still be visible fifty years later.

But there's neither nurse nor needle in sight at the moment, so I'm guessing there's no vaccination today. And Miz Wood isn't passing out any papers, so chances are there's no test. What we do have is another lovely, gray-haired lady stepping bravely in front of the class. Standing right next to Miz Wood's big ol' oak desk that could house a family of four if you left the dog outside, the visitor introduces herself as Miz Garner and, with dignified but wide-eyed excitement, advises us that she'll be giving puppet lessons beginning immediately. And if any of us would like to take puppet lessons, then we need to ask our mama or daddy to call her and sign us up, she explains.

Puppet lessons. Wow. *Puppet* lessons. Now I, for one, am extremely excited about this. Who'd have thunk it? How could I have ever imagined that here in the rural deep South I'd have an opportunity to take puppet lessons.

Now, for out-of-doors-open-spaced-play-till-you-drop opportunity, Baldwyn in the fifties and early sixties is just *the* best place in the world to be a kid. No doubt about that. But the truth must be faced, and the truth is that, otherwise, there's just not that much shaking in this little town of about fifteen hundred.

OK. We do have the Ritz Theatre on Main Street, where pretty much every youngster in town can be found on Saturday afternoon. Little fellas like me only have to pay twenty-five cents to see great double features of westerns and Elvis movies, complete with serials and cartoons. And for a dime, you can enjoy a snowball—most of the world calls it a snow *cone*—with enough juice on it that you can actually taste it. *Drink* it, for that matter. Plus, you can sit next to your girlfriend *du jour* to let everybody know who's whose. That's pretty fun. It is.

Then over on the east side of town, there's Latimer Park, where you'll find the local baseball-slash-football field, a covered pavilion for the occasional birthday party, and our summer haunt: the public swimming pool, a length of a hundred or so feet of water so chlorinated that no self-respecting germ would even *think* about it, with two diving boards and a recently installed slide that's about . . . oh, say, a *thousand stories* high. During the summer months, we're in that pool more than we're not. Rain or shine, unless there's lightning. You don't wanna be chest deep in water with Mississippi lightning flashing around you. Trust me.

And just outside of town, in the lovely community of Bethany, there's Brices Crossroads Civil War Memorial, marking the site where nearly a hundred years ago General Nathan Bedford Forrest bravely withstood and routed the Yankee hoards. Here you'll find a lovely cannon that you can crawl on and spooky-but-interesting really old graves and headstones, including those of more than ninety Confederate soldiers who died during the battle at the Crossroads on June 10, 1864. Plus, there's always the possibility of stumbling onto a mini-ball or other Civil War relic like we sometimes do, then donating it to Mr. Claude Gentry's Civil War museum on Highway 45. Pretty much every locally discovered Civil War relic ends up there sooner or later.

Then, of course, there's the public town drawing that's held on Main Street every Saturday at midday. That's when a pretty nice little chunk of change is given away to the lucky holder of the winning ticket. See, when you buy groceries or other goods in any Baldwyn store, you get numbered drawing tickets—like, one for every five dollars you spend or something like that. Then if the number of a ticket pulled at the drawing matches the number on one of your tickets, you win the pot. Of course, the more money you spend in town, the more tickets you get—and the better your chances of winning the jackpot. This is how local merchants encourage local shopping and keep everyone from driving to Tupelo or Memphis to buy their goodies. But even though the whole town literally closes down for the drawing, it's mostly for old folks like my grandmother who'll move heaven and earth to be there. You won't find me or my friends there unless we're being held hostage by a parent or grandparent. After all, it's not what you'd call front-row excitement for the grade school set.

There are ball games too. Baldwyn's got 'em, that's for sure. Football in the fall, basketball in the winter, baseball in the spring and summer. If there's a high school ball game of any kind being played on any reasonably near court or field or diamond, pretty much everyone in town turns out for it. And every Bearcat victory's just like winning a world championship, as far as we're concerned.

Now, little fellas who aren't in high school yet are just out of luck when it comes to basketball or football because 'round these parts, you can't play those games until you're in high school. Well, that's not entirely true. My backyard's seen some *pret-tee* awful bloody football contests between my big brother and me. Just stuff two or three rolled-up socks underneath the shoulders of your shirt and knock heads like mountain goats for a couple of hours. Awesome.

These backyard battles are the best we can do for football, and we're just out of luck altogether for basketball because there aren't any organized football or basketball programs for the young'uns around here. But baseball—that's another story. Baseball we get to play. And I play it. I'm too little for the peewee team, which is for the *little* guys; but being about two-foot-nothin', I'm just right for the peanut team, which is for the *itty-bitty* guys. Sometimes I play in the outfield, but I also get to play hind catcher, as we call it. And, for a little shaver, I'm just not that bad at this hind catching stuff. I mean, I can snag pretty much every ball the pitcher chucks my way, even when the batter swings and misses—and if you've ever tried this, you'll know it's not as easy as it sounds.

All the baseball teams are coached by Mr. Coggins, who, when he's not coaching baseball, puts in time as mayor of Baldwyn. He's got a stiff-legged limp that he picked up during some heroics in Europe during World War II, but it never gets in his way when it comes to coaching.

We play home games on the field down by the high school, but we also travel to neighboring towns to play on their fields—if they have a peanut team. Some towns don't, but most do. Now, the peanuts ride to the game in the bus right along with the high school and peewee teams—and this association with the older set provides opportunities for us peanuts to learn a lot about life at those away games. A *lot*.

Oh. One other fun thing around these parts is the National Guard armory. I know a lot about this place because it's where my daddy goes to work every day in his olive drab fatigues with pant legs bloused at the top of totally cool GI boots that lace—it seems to me—nearly to his chin. And it's my good luck that Daddy sometimes lets me go to the armory with him.

Now, the actual building where Daddy works is a fabricated metal

Quonset hut that looks like a big ol' metal pipe buried halfway into the ground, long-ways. Surrounding this Quonset hut are all kinds of military vehicles that are just *pret-tee* darn attractive to a little fella. From time to time, I get to ride in a Jeep, a command car, or a pickup truck—and occasionally even in a two-and-a-half-ton transport truck, usually called a deuce and a half. More often than not, these trips are just up and down local dirt and gravel roads, but once in a while, Daddy takes my brother and me along with him to Camp Shelby down in Hattiesburg, about two hundred fifty miles or so from us. And perhaps most fun of all, sometimes I get to climb up on the M4 or other tanks out back, even sliding down inside them from time to time for a look-see and a moment of marvelous pretending.

Inside the Quonset hut are whole bunches of other fun and interesting stuff. Helmet liners. Canvas pup tents. Canteens. Anglehead flashlights. Duffle bags. Little folding shovels that you can use to either dig a foxhole or swat fifteen-pound Mississippi beetles, I guess. Neat stuff like that—pretty much everything in the standard GI olive drab.

And then the bonus. The best part of this whole magnificent deal. That inner sanctum where lie the most wonderful things to fuel any young boy's imagination.

The munitions room.

M1903 bolt-action rifles encased in perfect order along the walls. Colt M1911 semi-automatic handguns. Maybe the odd M1917 or M10 revolver. Bayonets. Scabbards. Ammunition stacked here and there in olive drab metal cases that unlock from the side and open from the top. Just about anything a young boy could imagine in the way of antipersonnel equipment.

Except hand grenades and flame throwers.

Dang it.

Now, I get to visit this paradise from time to time and even handle—under strict parental supervision, of course—these marvelous implements of warfare that, at this moment in my life, represent nothing evil or destructive but only help me imagine for a moment that I'm actually *in* those incredible worlds that I see on television and the big screen. Yep, that's me right there—fighting for the American way of right and freedom alongside the likes of John Wayne, James Cagney, Henry Fonda, and Lloyd Nolan. Overcoming unbeatable odds to triumph over the foe with Robert Taylor, Robert Mitchum, and Charles McGraw. Looking right square into the eyes of death and emerging a hero with Gary Cooper, William Bendix, Robert Mitchum, and Preston Foster. Securing freedom for this and future generations with Audie Murphy, Richard Jaeckel, and Jack Palance. Boy, oh boy.

So, as you can see, we don't really have that many things in Baldwyn to . . .

Well . . . all right. You've caught me. I've lied just a little. We *do* have a *few* things to do around here. OK. We have *lots* of things to do here. Things that, in fact, make growing up in this little Mississippi town a lot of fun for a kid my age. And the absolute truth of it is that, even though in just a short time I'll leave this place forever—well, there'll be periodic visits from time to time throughout my life—I'll carry the memories of small-town life with me to the day I die and be grateful for such an incredible childhood.

That said, it's still true that, by any big city standard, you couldn't call Baldwyn a *happening* place during the years of my youth.

So puppet lessons just seem like a *pret-tee* darn big deal to this nine-year-old.

Now, what in the world I'll ever *do* with puppets once I've learned how to use them's anybody's guess. To be truthful, I guess I'm not all that sure what it even means to *take* puppet lessons. But that's not the point. The point is, this lovely lady here's *offering* them—what-*ever* they are. And frankly, I'm a little surprised that some great cheer hasn't broken out across the classroom at the very mention of this great opportunity. On the contrary, I look around to see who's sharing the excitement that's nearly making me shake, and not one of my class-mates seems mildly interested, let alone excited.

Well, tough toenails for them. I'm still gonna ask Mama and Daddy if I can take puppet lessons. If no one else wants to, then that'll just be so much more time Miz Garner can give *me*.

So when Miz Garner writes her telephone number on the black-board, I'm all over it. Like a hog on a turnip. Like white on rice. Like black on coal. Like a chicken on a June bug. With eyes stretched wide and tongue poking out the side of my mouth, I pull out my Nifty Note-book, which is a sort of vinyl-slash-plastic-coated clipboard. Except it doesn't have a clip. Instead, it has two little pegs for your special two-holes-punched-at-the-top paper, and a magnetically-held-in-place

plastic flip-lid-thingie that secures the paper. And your paper's protected by a jointed top cover that you flip up and over and tuck neatly
against the back of the whole thing when you wanna write. [*Conscience
Note:* I only have this Nifty Notebook because I lied and told Mama
and Daddy that Miz Wood said we *had* to have one, and I'll feel guilty
about that lie for the next fifty years. I mean, that's a buck-and-a-half
the family budget could've used for something more important. But as
long as I've got the thing, I guess I might as well enjoy it.] I pop open
the magnetic pencil holder and unsheathe a yellow-orange number
two Eberhard Faber pencil that needs to be sharpened, but I won't
sharpen it because when it's blunt like this, I write more like Tim, my
best friend, writes. [*Style Note:* Sometimes I use a Scripto mechanical
pencil, but at the moment, I'm partial to the regular wooden kind.]
And as quick as you can say, "Winchell and Mahoney," I've got Miz
Garner's telephone number written neatly across the top of a fresh
sheet of lined paper. And then, right below the phone number, I write
the words *puppet lessons* so I won't forget why I wrote the number in
the first place.

Not that I would.

Well, the day clocks right along, and the rest of it's pretty quiet
except for the few minutes when Miz Wood excuses all the girls from
the classroom and lectures us boys about why we shouldn't have pee-
ing-for-distance competitions at the urinal trough in the bathroom.
Heaven only knows which Peeping Tom pervert in the class told on
Tim and me for this. And when, at last, the day ends and Miz Wood
says, "Yawl can go ahwn howme now," I hop on down to Miz Shirley's
sixth grade room to meet David, my big brother. The two of us go
outside together to meet our grandfather, Daddy Morris, who always
drives the two of us—along with Kay, Alvin, and Dot—home in his
black '41 Chevy coupe with a three-on-the-tree, a heater that works
only sometimes, and no windshield defroster.

Every trip to and from school, especially during the winter months,
is sheer adventure.

Now, we live on Kilpatrick Hill, just up the path a piece from
Daddy Morris and Mama Morris, my daddy's parents. Kay, Alvin, and
Dot live a little farther up the hill in a rickety, old, weather-worn plank
house that they rent from Old Lady Kilpatrick, who owns pretty much
this whole hill—hence, the name. So Daddy Morris carries the bunch

of us to and from school every day. He carries David and me for free, but I think he charges the others a little something for the gas. Next year, only Alvin and Dot will ride with us because Kay, sadly, will be taken in an automobile accident this summer.

Anyway, all the way home, I can hardly stand the excitement of thinking about puppet lessons. I'm just sure that when I break the news to Mama and Daddy they'll be thrilled and start feeling proud of me in advance, imagining all the neat things I'll be able to do with puppets once I learn to use them. They'll say, "You bet, Kevin, 'at sounds like jus' the ticket fer you, son," and I'll give 'em the phone number, and they'll call Miz Garner, and that'll be that. Puppet lessons, here I come.

So, when Daddy Morris's Chevy crunches onto the gravel-and-rock driveway between the house and the garden plot fenced in by honeysuckle-covered chicken wire—where he sometimes plants and harvests a small crop of one thing or another with the help of a plow and a mule or two—I pile out. With little legs pumping like Green Bay's Paul Hornung sweeping wide, I haul my diminutive buns past the storm house that stores Mama Morris's bottled jellies and protects us during thunderstorms and tornadoes. I scamper on through the pine trees scattered about in the fifty-or-so yards between our house and Daddy Morris's, past the black nineteen-thirty-something Ford resting on flat tires and blocks under the pine tree near the trash incinerator, and through the basement door of our house. Screaming past the twelve-inch-thick concrete block wall of our fallout shelter on my left, I skip-hop up the stairs and pretty much fall through the door at the top, spilling onto the hardwood floor in a fit of unbridled and uncontrollable excitement.

I can't remember ever having felt a rush of adrenaline like this . . . well, except maybe for this one day last summer when my friend Skeeter and I disappeared into the thick woods behind my house for a little routine adventure, prepared to be gone until dark. Not unusual. That's the way we play around here. Carefree and fearless and without regard to the clock. There are no kidnappers stalking us in these woods. No one's worried that we'll get lost or stranded and have to be rescued by Search and Rescue at a cost of thousands of taxpayer dollars. The possibilities of getting a slap in the face by an errant tree limb or toppling over a rotten log lying in our path or brushing up against a little poison ivy or facing the painful snags of saw-briar thorns hanging across the path—even kicking up an uninterested snake or picking up a hitch-hiking chigger or tick—none of these possibilities is of any concern to us or to our parents. Bruises, scratches, bumps, cuts, rashes—whatever. We just ain't a-skeert. When we play, we *play*—in a way that'll be utterly and completely foreign to our grandchildren.

More's the pity.

But today, this is *our* world, not the world of our grandchildren. Today, we'll play with total abandon. Today, we'll get dirty and bruised and probably even a little bloody. Today, we'll yell at the top of our lungs and no one but squirrels and snakes and tadpoles will be close enough to even know we're making a sound. And they won't care.

And today, we'll love every minute of it.

So on this one day, with shoes worn out from the countless foot-steps of other grand adventures, and raw potatoes—for snacking purposes—in the pockets of jeans that look like they've just about seen it all, we set out for adventure. Wonder where it'll be found today.

Just a little piece into the woods behind our house is a lake. Well, maybe not so much a lake as a pond. OK. Not so much a pond as a really big mud puddle with some grass and reeds growing in it. But it's water, and it's wet, and it's just deep enough. We've no idea whose property this water's actually on, but that's not such a big issue 'round these parts. And even if it *were* an issue, it wouldn't matter much to us today.

Because today, it's our adventure.

Today we swim.

Obviously, we can't swim with our clothes on, and we didn't bring swimsuits, so this calls for a little discussion. As it turns out, Skeet's a veteran skinny-dipper—or so he says—and "it ain't a-gonna hurt nuthin' if'n we swim nekked," he says, and darned if I can think of a valid argument against his obviously well-thought-out philosophy. Even though I've never skinny-dipped before, I'm persuaded that it's the right thing to do today, so off come the clothes. Right down to the nekked skin. Little bare butts shining right there in front of heaven and everybody. Wade on out a little ways with mud squishing between our toes and water burying our legs and rising toward our chests with every step. Deep enough. Take a little jump and swim.

There's no diving board here and no slide, and the water's too murky to see anything if you open your eyes underwater—so by way of creativity, there's not much to recommend this little puddle for recreational swimming. But it's an adventure, and that's enough. And things are going swimmingly, as far as I'm concerned. We're splashing, yelling, dunking each other. Having a great time.

And then we hear The Voice. It's distant yet, but headed our way. And it sounds kinda familiar.

"Kevin! James Kevin! James Kevin Morris! Where are you! Hoooooo!"

Mama.

Closing in fast.

Now, like I said, Mama's just *pret-tee* darn liberal when it comes to adventures. We can roll down gullies or build a tree house or swing from tree limbs. We can shoot BB guns or get dirty or tear our clothes or chase frogs. We can catch lizards and snakes in the daytime and lightnin' bugs at night. We can be gone for hours at a time and not get in any trouble for it as long as Mama knows roughly where we are.

It's unusual for Mama to join us in the woods. In fact, I can't remember the last time she came hunting for us before we were ready to come in.

Be that as it may, here she comes, just the same.

I figure it must be something pretty important that brings Mama out among the trees and the gullies and the dirt and the fallen logs and the squirrels. I mean, this is kids country, not mamas country. They had their day in the woods but chose to become grown-ups, so now they usually stay in their own world and out of our woods. For whatever reason, though, Mama's challenging the unwritten order of things today and braving the deep dark woods and its denizens to find me.

Now, I have no earthly idea just how she'll take to the notion of the two of us skinny-dipping in this hole. I can't remember a single time when the subject of clothes-optional water sports was ever broached at home, so there's no way for me to know Mama's opinion about this particular type of adventure. Just to be safe, I guess we'd better pull our little nekked butts out of this mud hole and get our clothes on before she gets close enough to see what we're up to.

Adrenaline kicks in, big time.

We are the wind. We're out. We're dressed. And just in time too, 'cause there's Mama just now visible at the edge of the trees—which means we're also visible to her. "Yawl come awn now," she yells and waves us in with a wide, swooping, over-the-head arm motion, kinda like she's pulling the starter cord of a lawn mower that's sitting on a shelf at about shoulder level.

Mama doesn't wait for us to catch up to her. Certain we've seen and heard her, she turns and heads back up the path toward the house—a lucky break for us because it gives us a few minutes to stop looking like we've just been swimming. By the time we get back to the house, we're pretty much dried off—well, as dried off as you can get in deep-woods Mississippi humidity—so Mama's never the wiser about our little swim. Oh, I'll tell her about it later. Like when I'm about fifty-seven or so. By then, maybe she won't be of a mind to scold me for it.

By the way, it turns out that nothing in particular had brought Mama out into the woods to find us. She just decided she should. Chalk it up to mother's intuition, maybe. I don't know.

Anyway, Skeeter and I will never skinny-dip in the lake-slash-pond-slash-mud-hole again. Who knows why. Maybe we figure we're lucky not to have been caught the first time, so why press our luck. Maybe we've never been such good friends, anyway, and just never hook up again for another adventure. Maybe an advanced-beyond-our-years sense of morality and decorum suggests to us the impropriety of such scandalous behavior.

Or maybe it's because of "post-exposure coincidence."

Don't bother to look it up because you won't find it in any book I know of. It's the term I use to describe the phenomenon that, once you've read something or seen something or somehow been exposed to something new, you'll suddenly start seeing and hearing all kinds of things that relate to it.

Like when you read about jets in the encyclopedia and then for the next month everything you see or hear seems to be related to jets.

Here's where I'm headed with this. See, after our skinny-dipping adventure in this little whatever-kind-of-body-of-water-it-is, all of a sudden everybody in the world—or so it seems to us—is talking about ponds and lakes and skinny-dipping.

And about how these slithering, poisonous, mean, chase-you-down-and-bite-you water mocassin snake critters like to inhabit murky little lake-slash-pond-slash-mud-holes around here. Seems like everybody we know all of a sudden remembers a time—and coincidentally shares the memory with us—when he swam in a mud hole and then the next day saw a dozen or so cottonmouth water moccasins swimming around right there where he'd been swimming just yesterday.

Granted, there's a lot of exaggeration around here. Nobody ever caught a fish that wasn't at least as long as an arm up to the shoulder, with a mouth as big around as the tale-teller can demonstrate with both hands together. Every tale involves a close call or danger or grandeur of some kind, and one's never sure just how much of that tale bears even the slightest resemblance to the truth of the matter.

Nevertheless, we young'uns believe pretty much everything we're told because everything's told believably. So we figure that somewhere in that lake-slash-pond-slash-mud-hole where we skinny-dipped, there *must* have been water moccasins that we just didn't see.

Now, Skeeter and I aren't all that bright, truth be told. In fact, if you added our smarts together, you'd probably have to round up just to get a single IQ point. But we do know *some* things.

We know not to wade in a ditch with green, slimy stuff in it. We know not to mess with mean boys named Butch or Lefty or Booger. We know not to sass Mama or Daddy.

And we know not to swim with water moccasins.

With that, my skinny-dipping days are over.

But back now to my more current adrenalin rush. As you may recall, I'm crashing through the door and spilling out onto the hardwood floor at the top of the stairs.

Now, Mama can't figure out whether I'm being chased by the devil himself or just really, *really* need to go to the bathroom. She's curious to know, though, so she says, "James Kevin, what in the world is yer hurry?" and without so much as taking a breath I say, "I wawna take puppet lessons, and I got Miz Garner's phown number, and yawl gotta cawl 'er and tell 'er I can."

Well. I guess *that* was an alternative explanation for my hurry Mama hadn't really considered.

Mama patiently gives me a couple of seconds to catch some breath and then starts a little Perry Mason investigation into this puppet lessons thing. Kinda *grilling* me, from my point of view. Trouble is, I can't answer her questions very well. Even though I thought I was paying real good attention when Miz Garner explained everything to us, I apparently wasn't. Frankly, though, I'm surprised that Mama needs to know anything more than that puppet lessons are available and I've got a number for her to call. That should be all there is to it. But she's a little confused, and I've done nothing in the way of clearing things up for her, so she says she'll be doing just a little more checking on this puppet lessons thing.

I wonder if you've ever thought about how similar the words *puppet* and *public* sound. I mean, if you were a nine-year-old boy with one ear and one eye on a gray-haired lady making an announcement in your fifth grade classroom and your other ear and other eye on Peggy, Bobbie, Emily, and Rosemary, you could easily mistake the word *puppet* for the word *public. Sure*, you could. You *know* you could.

And I guess that's just what I did, because the very disappointing news I'm getting from Mama at the moment is that Miz Garner said she's giving *public* lessons, not *puppet* lessons.

Dang. No puppet lessons.

And just like that, the possibility of a life spent performing impressive feats of puppeteering disappears before me in a flash of reality—a flash of reality that's absolutely heartbreaking.

At least I *think* it's heartbreaking.

But then I don't know what *public lessons* are.

I know what public *restrooms* are. I know what public *telephones* are. I even have some rough idea of what public *opinion* is.

But I don't have a clue about public *lessons*.

Not to worry. Mama clears it up for me faster than you can say, "Liberace likes jewelry." And the answer to the mystery turns out to be something even better and more exciting than the thought of puppet lessons, if you can imagine that.

It seems that when Miz Garner announced that she'd be giving public lessons, she left out one little word. Well . . . either that or else she said the word but my easily distracted neurology saw no reason to trouble itself with anything that followed the word *puppet*, so I just didn't accept delivery on the next word which, as it turns out, was a pretty important five-letter word.

Piano.

Public *piano* lessons.

Hmmm.

Maybe if Miz Garner had mentioned that she's actually a music teacher over at Baldwyn High School, I'd have known that she was talking about piano lessons and then I wouldn't be so confused and surprised right now. But she didn't, so I didn't, so I am.

But now, at last, I've got it straight. Miz Garner's a high school music teacher. She aims to give public piano lessons. She's recruiting students for said piano lessons.

Whew.

Now, this public piano lessons thing's just altogether different from puppet lessons, but never mind about that. I'm just fine with it. And I'm still glad I wrote down Miz Garner's phone number because if there's one thing I'd like more than to take puppet lessons, it'd be to take piano lessons. Public or otherwise.

I love music. Just about any way you can serve it up. Well, except for the stuff Mama listens to on her brown plastic clock radio that's got a clock on one side and, on the other, a speaker that produces a sound that kinda brings to mind Ethel Merman sucking up a little helium and then singing through a Brillo pad. When I say, "the stuff Mama listens to," I'm talking about that hard-core country stuff from singers like Hank Locklin, Hank Snow, Patsy Cline, Jim Reeves, Ernest Tubb, and the like. Right now I'm just not quite ready for this kind of . . . this kind of . . . well, I guess I'll have to use the term *music*, even though I don't want to. And I won't get friendly with it until many years from now. Even *then*, I suppose I'll mostly like it just because it'll remind me so clearly of my childhood.

OK. When I say I hate the stuff Mama listens to, I'm lying just a *leet-tle* bit. There's one exception—one artist that Mama listens to that fits the country-western genre but doesn't sound like his shorts are being extracted through his nose.

Not long ago, Mama got a new record from the Columbia Record Club. A record with an orange and white cover that looks a little like a Creamsicle. A record of great songs. Great ballads. Like "El Paso," "The Streets of Laredo," "Big Iron," "Saddle Tramp," and—my personal favorite—"The Ballad of the Alamo." A record entitled *More Greatest Hits by Marty Robbins*. Even though this album's technically country-western, it is, in a word, terrific. Personally, I think of it as more western than country, and nobody sings a western song like Marty Robbins.

Anyway, except for that really twangy, nasally, hard-shell country fare that I hate, I just love music. I listen to the radio whenever I can, enjoying the incredible, soon-to-be-legendary talents of Bobby Darin, Buddy Holly, Elvis, Perry Como, Jack Scott, Frank Ifield, Brenda Lee, the Everly Brothers, Connie Francis, Johnny Tillotson, Lloyd Price, the Platters, Nat "King" Cole, and on and on. And I like to sing along with the artists, dance along when nobody's looking, and even play along on the drums.

Now, I don't have a set of drums, or even *a* drum, per se. What I do have is an empty cardboard box that Mama's new iron came packaged in, and after poking a hole in each end and sliding a small rope through them and tying the ends together, I hang this puppy around my neck like a snare drum. Then, using a couple of table knives, I play along with anything I hear.

I even like *movies* about music. The first time I saw Clifton Webb's John Philip Sousa directing a big brass band in *Stars and Stripes Forever*, I got so inspired that I just jumped right up and directed the band right along with him. Using that same inspiration, I also direct the big brass band belting out march songs on another record Mama just got from the Columbia Record Club—when I'm alone, of course, and sure nobody's watching.

So, because of my love for music, the thought of piano lessons effectively salves the sting of lost dreams of puppeteering. And what makes it all extra nice is that I don't even have to beg for the lessons. Mama and Daddy are happy to give me this opportunity to develop my music talents even though the family budget can't ordinarily handle much more than essentials. But my mama and daddy won't let anything so insignificant as a little budget challenge interfere with such an opportunity for me. Not today. Not ever.

And before you can hum a chromatic scale, I'm sitting on the piano bench next to Miz Garner every week, learning how to play "Tommy's New Drum" and other masterpieces on our big ol' pretty-much-antique upright piano with the top ivory piece missing from the middle C key.

Miz Garner quickly learns that I'm a careful and hardworking student. The only problem she has is keeping me slowed down to the pace she thinks is right. Now, don't get me wrong. I don't aim to be disobedient. I just happen to think it takes Miz Garner *way* too long to pencil a "K—OK" at the top of each song—which means I've passed it off and am ready to move on to the next one—so I just move ahead at my own speed and beat her to the end of every book. By a *long* stretch, I beat her. Which means that, by the time we start working on a new song together, I already know it. By the time Miz Garner signs me off on the last of the songs that we'll work together on in the blue, grade 1½ *John W. Schaum Piano Course* book, I've already learned every one of the thirty-two songs in it, and I'm just waiting for her to bring me up to where I already am. And I'm patient with her as she signs me off on songs one, two, three, four, five, and six.

But I'll never see "K—OK" written over song number seven. Shortly after Miz Garner signs me off on "The Harpsichord Player" in my last lesson with her, The Day rolls around.

That would be December 27, 1962, when my family leaves our Mississippi home and moves to Southern California to begin the most wonderful adventure of my life—even without puppets. An adventure that'll keep me connected in one way, shape, or form to music at almost every turn for the rest of my life. An adventure that'll literally bend the course of my future.

It'll always feel very satisfying to me—and even somehow ironically fitting—that such a grand and life-changing adventure would begin on my birthday.

2

I stand on the roof and blow

Heaven knows I want to. I really, truly do. And I try. Again and again and again. Honest. I do. If there were Olympic events for wanting and trying, I'd be gold in both.

But finding a place to stand outside the gigantic shadow of an older brother's just a really, really, *really* hard thing to do. And all the more so when you're about two-foot-nothin' and your older sophomore brother, just one grade ahead of you, is nearly six feet tall, three-sport athletic, handsome, intelligent, popular, and generally a BMOC— that would be a Big Man On Campus.

And when I enter Troy High in Fullerton, California, in 1965 as a freshman, I understand in the blink of an eye that the odds against me ever living up to the mark Dave's already set here are very, very long. *Long.* No. That's too optimistic. Let's try the word *insurmountable*. At thirteen years old, I'm my big brother's perfect antithesis. Short, wimpy, plain-looking, so-so academic abilities, unpopular, and not even in the *vicinity* of BMOC status.

My inadequate—read *nonexistent*—social rep has a number of problems associated with it, not the least of which is the harsh truth that girls don't generally groove on a guy who's too small for any sport from football to javelin hurling to tiddlywinks and everything in between. Now, I like girls *pret-tee* darn well. No getting around it. And I have my dreams. Boy, do I have my dreams. But short and nonathletic equals unattractive and unpopular. I guess it's nature's way of culling the herd so that only the strongest DNA gets perpetuated.

Clearly, in the battle for evolutionary dominance, my DNA isn't in the thick of things.

But even though no girl alive wants to help perpetuate my DNA and I've no social image whatsoever, I bravely imagine that there must be *some* purpose to my life. Something I can do that'll be worth *something* to *some*body. Even if I can't reach the mark set by my big brother.

So. OK. Let's just think about this for a sec. Consider my assets and options, as it were.

Brains. Well, I'm not completely without intellectual skills. Then again, I'm not *that* smart, either—so brainiac associations like Chess Club, Forensics, and Genesis are outta the question. Not that they'd be my cup of tea, anyway.

Artistic flair. Nope. Couldn't draw a recognizable stick figure.

Student politics. I don't think so. Too shy. Too insecure. Too unknown.

Practical arts. Mechanical drawing, drafting, wood shop, metal shop. Fuggidaboudit. Couldn't design a toothpick, and if I could, then I couldn't build it.

Music.

Hmmm.

What about music?

Well, I did bring my trumpet to high school with me. I've been playing the little critter for two years now, and I'm not all that bad, I say humbly. Maybe I could use it to some advantage.

Maybe music can be my cup of tea. My bag. My thing.

I am, after all, in prep band.

Now, I didn't sign up for *prep* band. Back when we were all registering for high school classes I signed up for *concert* band. But when I got my freshman class schedule I discovered that I'd been *assigned* to what they call the *prep* band.

Assigned.

To *prep* band.

Not *concert* band.

Prep band.

Where they put kids who aren't good enough to play in concert band or orchestra.

Now, I'm just a tad surprised by this since I was first-seat trumpet, at least for a time, in the Ladera Vista Junior High concert band last year. But apparently the competition here among the high rollin' high schoolers is just a tad stiffer, so now I get to be brought down a notch or two.

Like I really needed that.

But undaunted, I accept my prep band assignment and make up my mind to move beyond it as quickly as I can. I'll practice. I'll practice till my lips are bloody. I'll play every chance I get. I'll pretty much move into one of the soundproof practice rooms in the music building and stay there till they either throw me out or make me pay rent. I'll take advantage of every performance opportunity available, and I won't turn down anything. If I do this, then I'm just *sure* that my great talent will be recognized—and as soon as that happens, I'll get transferred into concert band or orchestra or both, and then I'm bound to be more popular. If I'm good enough, this thing may compensate at least in some small way for my other obvious shortcomings.

It never occurs to me that my game plan might have a glitch or two in it.

See, one of the extra things I decide to do to turbo-develop my skill and secure some kind of social status is to play in the marching band. I figure if I can't be on the field as an *athletic* Troy Warrior, I'll be on the field as a *musical* Troy Warrior. Shouldn't have any trouble making this happen because the marching band's sort of an open enrollment thing and anybody who wants to join's allowed to join. Well, sure . . . I mean, you've gotta be alive and breathing, and you've gotta be able to play an instrument or carry a flag or heft a baton. But within those parameters, anybody's good to go.

Now, the marching band's gotta be ready to go when football season starts—and since football season starts when school starts, the marching band starts practicing before the first day of school. Just like the football team does. We meet every day on the practice field behind the school, learning how to march in formation. How to make clean and crisp right-face, left-face, and about-face turns. How not to run up the tuba player's tail pipe when he stops in front of you. How to play exciting march songs like "Minnesota Rouser," "On Wisconsin," "Mr. Touchdown USA," and the "Notre Dame Fight Song." How to play with reasonable quality despite the fact that your mouthpiece is moving up and down and up and down against your lips while you're marching.

Kinda like your rookie season playing post office.

Just before school starts, we all get fitted for our new marching band uniforms. The tall hat with the lovely white plume and the shiny braided bill. The stiff-necked jacket that crushes your goozle and wouldn't let you lower your head even if your life depended on it. The tuxedo-like, shiny black pants with the shinier-black stripe down the side of each leg. The white plastic shoes that can be wiped clean after a brisk march through mud holes. From head to toe, all red and black and white and silver and new and groovy.

Dang, we're gonna look outasight.

Now, I guess if I were to think about it—I mean *really* think about it—I'd figure out that I'm on the wrong road here. By wrong road, I mean that if I've any hope of achieving my big brother's social status, this is the wrong venue. I mean, check it out. There are no football players marching beside me. No wrestlers marching beside me. No basketball players or baseball players marching beside me. No BMOCs of any description marching beside me.

Don't get me wrong. Marching band's fun. I like the involvement and the marching and the music and the chance to improve my music skills. And to tell the truth, I make some *pret-tee* darn good friends in this group. I mean, it's not like everybody here's a total loser—a couple, maybe, but certainly not everybody. And it's not that there's anything *wrong* with being in the marching band. It's just that it probably won't do much to build the image of a wimpy, pathetic, four-foot-tall freshman to the point that someone wearing a dress might show some kind of interest, or someone of some social stature would say, "Oh yeah, hey, there goes Kevin. What a guy."

To get *that* little thing done I'd have to associate with different people. And the different people I'd have to associate with aren't marching with me. Nope, they're out on the football field, being cheered on by cheerleaders. Or in sixth period PE, waiting with other off-season athletes for their sport's season to start. Or hosting a poster party in preparation for a run at student office. Or nestled into a recessed doorway on campus, making out with the prom queen.

They're not in the marching band.

So I find myself in the midst of a group of essentially good but not necessarily popular people, many of whom in future years will ride the unpopular-at-the-moment-but-eventually-profitable label of nerd-slash-geek-slash-dork to incredible wealth and even fame.

Yeah. I know. You'd think I'd draw the proper conclusion at this point about what this says about *me*. But it's just *pret-tee* darn incredible what kind of defenses the human psyche can put in place to protect itself from collapse under the weight of a depressing truth. And my skills in rationalization, repression, and denial are strong. I'm talking Olympic strong.

But they're about to have to work even harder, if you can believe it.

See, Mr. Howard, the band director, suddenly gets this terrific idea. Since we're the *Troy* Warriors, he observes, our marching band should have *some*thing—something *exciting*, something *innovative*—that reflects a more vivid Homeric image. *Wouldn't it be cool*, he thinks, *if a few select trumpeters played long-belled herald trumpets with lovely banners hanging from them to identify us as the Troy Warriors so no one could mistake us for Sunny Hills or Fullerton or Valencia or Kennedy or Lowell or any other local high school. And they'll be in uniform, these herald trumpet players. Incredible uniform.* Roman *uniform. Now* that *would look groovy*, he thinks. *Just the image we want*, he thinks. *What a majestic sight it would be*, he thinks, *when these herald trumpeters lead the band onto the field.*

So Mr. Howard throws his weight around a little and gets the school to purchase six herald trumpets. *L-o-n-g* suckers. Four-footers. Then he selects some unsuspecting simpletons to be herald trumpeters. Dolts who have no idea just how goofy they're actually gonna look with these *l-o-o-o-o-n-g* herald trumpets sticking out of their faces, and by the time they figure it out, it'll be way too late.

Here stands one of the unfortunates.

Now, the length of this herald trumpet isn't the only component of the image problem I'm about to experience. But it *is* a big *part* of the problem. Let me just remind you that I've got a four-feet-eight-inches-tall body, and this here trumpet that's sticking out in front of me's about four feet long.

Pretty sexy, huh.

But in addition to the trumpet that's nearly as long as I am tall, picture—if you dare—a Roman toga skirt cinched at the midriff by a shiny gold belt, a flowing red cape attached at the shoulders, a lovely headband, and shiny faux boots that are actually more like spats that fit over the shoes and then run about halfway up the shins. Or, in my case, about up to the kneecaps.

Some mental pictures from our youth just cry out to be erased. But then there'll always be those yearbooks that just won't let them go gentle into that good night.

I guess if it were possible for us to launch ourselves years ahead of where we are at any given point in time and look back from that point to see what we are at this present moment, we'd do just a whole bunch of things differently. But it's not, and it never will be, so we can't, so we don't.

But don't worry. I'm happy as a clam. Yep, I am. My defense mechanisms are handling all this just fine. As far as I know, I'm looking just about as cool as any thirteen-year-old boy could ever look. And I'm convinced that nothing in this world will be able to restrain the entire female population within a mile radius from attacking me with aggressive hands and lustful hearts when I step out onto that football field at our first home game.

Now, if I were drawing this story in cartoons instead of writing it in text, this is where you'd see a picture of Mr. Howard with one of those thought bubbles over his head—you know, with little circles going from the thought bubble to his head. And that's because this is where Mr. Howard, who seems more and more dead set on ruining my life with every passing moment and with every new idea, gets *another* great idea.

This new idea has to do with the grand flag ceremony that'll be held on the first day of school. The entire student body will meet in the quad, where the flag will be raised and the Pledge of Allegiance will be recited in magnificent unison. *Wouldn't it be lovely*, Mr. Howard thinks, *if a trumpeter were to stand on the roof overlooking the quad and bugle "To the Colors" as the flag runs up the halyard. It'd be amazing*, he thinks. *Awe-inspiring. Heroic, even.*

If only he could get someone to do it.

Sometimes, before I really give it the forward thinking it needs, I commit to a decision with an unbending passion. Not subject to change or reconsideration. Nonnegotiable. Set in stone. Now, pointed in the right direction, this kind of determination can be a terrific quality. But pointed in the wrong direction, it can be the source of unique and marvelous disaster.

Take, for example, the decision that I shared with you earlier when I set my mind to the notion that I'd "take advantage of every performance opportunity available, and I won't turn down anything." Now, on the surface, this may sound like worthy commitment to accomplishment. Principled determination to succeed. Iron will.

But look deeper. Just below the surface, it's sheer social suicide. At this age it is, anyway, if it's pointed in the wrong direction.

It's about to get pointed in the wrong direction.

"Of course, Mr. Howard. I'd be happy to do that, Mr. Howard. Glad to help, Mr. Howard. You bet, Mr. Howard."

I'll never win a lottery. I'm certain of it. Having the incalculably good fortune to be selected as one of the Troy High Warriors marching band herald trumpeters and then again as the rooftop bugler for opening day flag ceremonies has surely used up all my luck.

So. It's determined that on the appointed morning, I'll slip into my pleated Roman skirt with cape and associated garb, assemble my miles-long herald trumpet, attach the lovely banner to said trumpet, climb up to the roof using the top-secret ladder hidden in one of the band room utility closets, wait for the flag to start its journey up the pole, and then blow.

If this gig doesn't get me the recognition I need to improve my social status—not to mention get me into concert band or orchestra— I just don't know what will.

Yeah. Mmm hmmm.

The day arrives quickly. Go to the band room. Change into my skirt and stuff. Take out the trumpet case. Assemble the trumpet. Attach the banner. Enter the closet and climb up the top-secret ladder to the roof, carrying said trumpet with said banner flowing.

As I step off the top rung of the ladder and out onto the hot, flat roof with pipes and vent covers poking up out of it here and there, I can see that I'm in the back-center area of the roof. I know I'm supposed to go over to the north edge of the roof facing the quad and get as close to the edge as I can—so everyone can see me—but there's this little matter of *heights* that I forgot to mention. Usually if I only just stand on my tiptoes, little fishies start swimming around in my head and I enjoy a panic attack that would stop a train. Now here I am, up on this roof about, oh, say, five *thousand* feet high, looking down at the entire Troy High student body and wondering what in the world was I thinking when I said, "You bet, Mr. Howard. Climbing up on that roof and bugling's just the thing for me."

I can see the color guard in crisp military garb, standing by the flagpole on the other side of the quad and getting ready to run the flag up the halyard, so I know it's just about time for me to blow. I inch forward a baby step at a time toward the edge of the roof, certain that if I get one centimeter too close to it then I'll fall to a screaming, gory death below and probably take out a handful of unsuspecting Warriors while I'm at it. So I stop, oh, say, two *hundred* feet or so from the edge, raise the bannered instrument to my lips, and begin bugling "To the Colors" as the material symbol of the world's greatest nation begins its ascent to the top of the flagpole.

Oh, it's all so majestic.

At least, it probably *would* be if anyone knew I was up here. I'm standing so far away from the edge that I'm almost completely invisible to the Warriors below me. On top of that, the flagpole's clear over on the other side of the quad, forcing the majority of the crowd to face that direction, with backs to me. Plus, there's this little problem with amplitude. See, although I'm blowing my itty-bitty lungs out, the loudest noise I'm able to generate can't come *close* to the racket arising from the multitude assembled below. I'm not sure what the total student enrollment of this grand institution is, but it must be somewhere near a million, and every single one of those students must be here today—yelling, laughing, talking, or fighting with a neighbor.

Not listening at all to the dork in the Roman skirt on the roof with the trumpet.

The irony here is that this anonymity could've been the greatest blessing of my day. If I'd climbed up on the roof, blown my trumpet completely unnoticed by the madding crowd below, and descended to earth having never been heard or recognized, it would've been good. It would've been oh so *very* good.

But no such luck. Remember? I already told you. I've used it all up.

Over on the other side of the quad, just to the right of the flag and about halfway up the auditorium steps, a short, squinty-eyed, blonde-haired sophomore just happens to shift her gaze from the flagpole to the southern skyline. Who knows why. Maybe she's a bird watcher who just caught sight of a rare Greater White-fronted Goose flying low on the horizon. Maybe she's scanning the sky for potentially dangerous, low-flying aircraft. Maybe she's got a nervous twitch in her eye that forces it involuntarily skyward. Maybe she's dreaming of a future day when she won't have to stand in the midst of four gazillion unruly high schoolers to watch the flag roll up a flagpole.

Whatever. The girl looks southward and upward.

And a glint of reflected light catches her eye. A reflection coming from the roof of the building on the south side of the quad. She hasn't a clue as to what this reflection might be, but it catches her interest, so she keeps looking.

Then she sees it.

A long, shiny, brass-looking thing that may be moving slightly but mostly looks fixed in space. Almost like it's hanging there in midair of its own accord. No. Wait. It's not hanging there by itself. There's something attached to the back of it. Look a little closer. Not sure because it's so small but it . . . could . . . be . . . Yep, it is. It's a person. More or less. Human-oid, anyway. Kinda looks like a guy but with a really short weird dress and even some kind of a . . . some kind of a . . . well, it looks *like a Super-man cape, but what in the world could that be about? And what's this little critter* doing *up there, anyway? Oh. Hey. That shiny thing's coming out of his mouth. Hey, wait. I think it's a trumpet. A really, really, really lo-o-o-o-ng trumpet. By darn, I think there's a little guy in a dress and a Superman cape standing on that roof blowing on a long trumpet,* the co-ed finally decides.

But why in the world would a little guy in a dress and a Superman cape be standing on that roof blowing on a long trumpet? she wonders.

In just a few years there'll be these great shampoo commercials on TV advertising Faberge Organics. In one of the spots, Heather Locklear will tell us about how she tried the shampoo and liked it, so then she told two friends, and they told two friends, and so on and so on and so on. And the image of Ms. Locklear's face on the screen and the audio of her voice will double with every "and so on," depicting the speed at which information spreads as contacts multiply in geometric progression.

That principle's about to apply here.

See, this sophomore on the auditorium steps thinks to herself, *Well, I just can't keep this to myself,* so she punches her neighbor on the arm, points toward the roof, and says, "Hey, look up on the roof. There's some kinda small person in a skirt and a Superman cape with a big long trumpet. What in the world do you think he's doing?" and the neighbor says, "Well, I dunno. He's probably playing that trumpet, but darned if I can hear anything," and then she, too, points toward me as they agree that there's a small humanoid on the roof in a skirt and a Superman cape with a long trumpet that's making no sound. Then they pass their observations on to their neighbors.

Now some other doofus just across the way sees these people on the auditorium steps pointing upward, so, of course, he's just *gotta* look over there to see what they're pointing at, and he finally sees the small humanoid in the dress and Superman cape with the trumpet too. Then he pokes his neighbors and says, "What in the world's that?" and then *their* arms point toward the roof, and then this whole process of look, point, advise your neighbor rolls through the throng faster than a rumor about boys getting caught in the girls' gym. And pretty soon there are more arms pointing toward the roof than Carter has little liver pills.

And she told two friends, and they told two friends, and so on and so on and so on.

When a mob combines its collective curiosity with its collective stupidity, you get to see the perfect expression of the sheep syndrome.

So finally, pretty much all the little sheep on the ground have averted their attention from the national symbol running majestically up the halyard and are looking toward the roof of the building on the south side of the quad where stands a small humanoid in a skirt and a Superman cape, blowing on a long trumpet.

As I've tried to point out, I'm not exactly what you'd call popular. Outside of a few close friends, my brother, two sisters, parents, grandparents, and a cousin or two, I think I may very possibly be the most unknown person in the world.

In fact, to most of the people who know I'm alive, I've even got no name.

I'm simply known as Morris's little brother.

So even if every single person in the entire crowd were to see this little humanoid up on the roof, and if every single person in the entire crowd took the trouble to wonder who in the world would be so stupid as to climb up on the roof to do this silly gig, and if every single person in the entire crowd got the biggest laugh of his or her life from watching it—well, *none* of this should do my image any damage because, first of all, no one will know it's me because no one *knows* me, and second, even if they do happen to know it's me, it's still OK because I don't *have* any image to *damage*.

Unless it's possible for an image to decline into negative status.

Nah. Zero is zero is zero.

But there is *one* person who *has* some image to protect. A person who's connected to me and who has friends that just might possibly recognize me because of my relationship to him.

My big brother, Dave.

Who's in the crowd.

And before you can sing a chorus of "Blowin' in the Wind," the "and so on" has reached the people in Dave's quadrant. Now he and his friends are looking skyward just like everybody else.

Then the worst happens.

"Hey Morris, that kinda looks like your little brother up there on the roof in a skirt and Superman cape blowing on that big long trumpet," one friend says. And another says, "Ya know, I think that *is* your little brother up there on the roof in a skirt and Superman cape blowing on that big long trumpet." And Dave says, "Are you kidding me? There's no way my brother's up on that roof in a skirt and Superman cape blowing on a big long trumpet." But then another friend says, "Oh yeah, that *is* your little brother up on that roof in a skirt and Superman cape blowing on a big long trumpet."

Then the words "Morris's little brother" make their way across this great sea of people like a wave rolling unrestrained toward the destined shore.

"And she told two friends and they told two friends and so on and so on and so on."

em•bar•rass•ment (em bar′ əs mənt), n. 1. a state of being embarrassed; perplexity; impediment to freedom of action; entanglement; hindrance; confusion or discomposure of mind, as from not knowing what to do or to say; disconcertedness. 2. the shame you feel when an inadequacy or guilt is made public. (1670–80; < F embarrassement. See EMBARRASS, -ment)

The dictionary could've saved a lot of words by just posting next to the word *embarrassment* a photo of my big brother looking at his little brother standing on the roof of Troy High School on this late-summer day wearing a skirt and a cape and blowing on a big long trumpet.

That'd say it all, I guess.

But life goes on. Both Dave and I will endure the inevitable ribbing that follows this grand performance, and I'll survive to play my trumpet for years to come. I'll make it into concert band next year and develop my talent to the point that I'll get a music scholarship offer—which I'll decline—from the University of the Pacific at Stockton.

And although I'll continue to pursue and enjoy all things musical, I'll discover, too, that even a small person can excel in certain sports that don't require so much in the way of physical size and mass. Sports like wrestling, where the importance of those things is negated by matched equality. And sports that require skills unrelated to physical size—like tennis. Handball. Even a little golf.

Anyway, I won't remain four feet tall forever. I'll grow enough to enjoy a year of high school football before I graduate and many years of church-league basketball and softball after that. And I'll take tennis and golf with me throughout my life.

I'll never surpass my big brother in any of these sports, that's for sure. I could never do that. But I'll enjoy them all the same.

Now, in the midst of the disaster of this day, I've learned a number of things about myself and some things about my big brother. But one *really* important thing.

See, of all the great things I ever observed, knew, or imagined of Dave, it turns out that the greatest thing of all about him is that he loves me. Go figure. He has great compassion and respect for me, even in 1965 when there's not much to justify it. Oh, he thinks I'm a wimp—that's true enough. This I know because he reminds me of it on a regular basis. That's OK. It's in a big brother's job description. Besides, he's right. At least for the moment. But he's the only one allowed to say it. If someone else dares to send a flippant *wimp* or *wuss* remark in my direction, Dave defends me valiantly. Now, you can challenge him if you want, but be advised that you may end up drinking your Thanksgiving dinner through a straw.

Unfortunately, I won't truly understand the full depth of this less-visible part of my big brother today. It'll take some years and a lot more life experience to help me understand in retrospect what I can't see at the moment.

In that retrospect, I'll see that Dave's looks, athletic skills, mental agility, and popularity weren't *really* the things that made me wanna be like him. Oh, don't misunderstand. I admired and envied those things. I'll aspire to them for the rest of my life. But what I'll come to understand is that the part of him that *really* made me respect him and wanna be like him was that he loved me. He protected me. He defended me.

And one day many years from now, when we're both fat and old and gray, each of us with children and grandchildren, my big brother and I will be reminiscing on the phone about this 1965 day, separated at the time of the conversation by two thousand miles of geography but standing right next to each other emotionally. To his great credit, my big brother won't even remember the embarrassment he felt when his little, wimpy brother stood on top of Troy High School dressed like Spartacus and blew on a big ol' trumpet that was as long as he was tall.

Or if he does remember, he won't say so. Instead, he'll try to persuade me that it was *he* who was envious of *me* during those years.

After so many years, still defending me. Even against myself.

That's when I'll take a serious look back at my life and realize that on this particular day I should've felt a little larger than the reality of my physical stature. I'll realize that I should've been a little prouder of my talents and courage to try, even though the trying put me in public view in a way that was momentarily embarrassing. And I'll realize that I had more things going for me in 1965 than I gave myself credit for.

On that future day, I'll understand at last that the greatest of all my big brother's many, many qualities was that he loved me and respected me, even when I stood on the roof and blew.

That'll be a great day.

I offend
Walt Disney

Had you told me just a few years ago that in 1967 I'd be living in Southern California, I'd have said, "You're nuts, kid."

Had you added as a parenthetical oh-by-the-way that I'd be living only about seven miles from Disneyland . . .

*Disney*land.

No way, José.

But I am. Oh, yeah. I am.

The great blessing of living seven miles from Disneyland is that I get to go there a lot.

Ironically, the great *curse* of living seven miles from Disneyland is that I get to go there a lot.

No doubt about it. Disneyland's a great place, when I'm in the proper mood—a place that can make fantasy real and reality, fantasy. But whenever *any*body comes into town to visit, it seems a foregone conclusion that I'll go with them to Disneyland. By the time I'm out of high school, I'll have visited the park so often that the sight of mouse ears or big ears on any random stranger will send me into some kind of anti-fantasy seizure.

To be truthful, though, much of this overdose is of my doing. I mean . . . yeah, out-of-town visitors always wanna go to Disneyland, so this accounts for many visits. But I have to confess that my friends and I actually choose to go there frequently. And why not. It's a great place.

And there's also that special deal with my older sister that contributes to our frequent visits to the Magic Kingdom.

See, Deb works at Disneyland in the Bell Telephone "America the Beautiful" exhibit. To be accurate, she's actually an employee of Bell Telephone, not Disneyland; but in any case, it's true that she works inside the park, and her regular travel to and from there makes it possible for her younger brother and his friends—who are too young for a driver license—to get to and/or from there whenever we want.

Cool.

Mostly.

I say "mostly" because those days when we take advantage of Deb working at the park are arguably the longest days of my life. Marathon days, as it were.

Here's the scenario. Deb's shift begins at four p.m. and ends at midnight when the park closes. Jim or Dave or Jeff or Scott and I think, "Oh, won't it be great to have someone drop us off at the park when it opens and then we'll go home with Deb at the end of her shift? Stay there for the whole day. Sweet."

I wonder if anyone who's never done it can understand just how *dead* a body can be—even a fifteen-year-old body that can reap a new crop of energy about every six minutes—after fifteen uninterrupted hours of full-speed-ahead fun at Disneyland.

Let me just try to paint a picture in your mind.

Two or three young men, sitting on any available bench in Disneyland at eleven p.m., staring with perfectly flat affect into the Disneyland-lit darkness of a California summer night. Arms hanging limply. Shoulders sagging. No one talking or making any voluntary movement whatever except for the every-ten-minutes-or-so glance at the watch and a subtle movement of the head to the left or right—only as much as is absolutely necessary—to see if the friend on that side's still there and alive. Each one praying for the second hand to break its one-second-per-tick habit to move faster and bring that midnight hour just a little sooner.

Trust me when I tell you that this is tee-eye-ar-eee-dee with a capital exhausted. Seriously. You look up *tired* in the dictionary and you'll see a picture of Kevin, Jim, Dave, Jeff, and/or Scott sitting catatonic on a bench at Disneyland at eleven o'clock at night.

And it's on just such a marathon day that a should-have-been-uneventful visit to the Magic Kingdom takes a turn for the interesting.

On this particular visit, Jim, Scott, Dave, and I have deployed the usual get-delivered-when-it-opens-and-come-home-with-Deb plan for the day. We enter the park with a zeal that's illegal in twelve states and being considered for legislative action in two others. Once we're through the gate, we don't have to talk about any plan for our visit or discuss which ride we'll go on first. We know. In fact, no existing machine has the precision to measure the infinitesimal amount of time it takes us to decide that the Matterhorn's our first destination. It's just the way it has to be. So we head there, and our day begins.

After our first ride on the Matterhorn Bobsleds, the day unfolds like any other day at Disneyland. We use our E tickets first, then our D tickets, and then—moving on down the enjoyment continuum—we decide which of the C, B, or A rides we'll lower ourselves to take. I mean, you can spin on the Mad Tea Party or maybe even cruise around Tom Sawyer Island on the Indian War Canoes, and that's cool. But it's *pret-tee* darn risky to go on the Dumbo Flying Elephant ride or Mr. Toad's Wild Ride or the Storybook Land Canal Boats. At least it's risky until you're actually *on* the ride because if you run into a friend while you're standing in line for a ride like that, you're gonna have some serious explaining to do, bub. Unless, of course, that someone's *also* standing in line. You're OK then because he can't point a finger at you without fessing up to his own silliness.

If we happen to use all our tickets—right down to the A—we know what to do then: Monsanto Adventure Thru Inner Space. It's a new ride this year, with a half-moon shaped passenger car running slowly along a track through cool, moist darkness. The premise of the rider and car shrinking to molecular size creates visuals and sensations that are almost even a little interesting. Best of all, the ride doesn't require a ticket. We can shrink and expand as many times as we have to until midnight rolls around or until we're sitting on that bench waiting for midnight, whichever the case may be.

Uh-oh. It occurs to me that anyone who never visited Disneyland before 1982 won't have a clue what these A, B, C, D, and E tickets are all about. Here it is in a nutshell. From 1955 to 1982, you get a book of tickets when you pay for admission to the park. For example, in 1967, four bucks will get you a junior admission and ticket book containing five E tickets, four D tickets, three C, two B, and one A. Now, from the teenage point of view, E rides—rides that require an E ticket—are the best. D rides are not the best, but good. C rides are OK. B rides are for the desperate. And A rides are . . . well, the A ride ticket usually goes home with you.

Now, on this particular day, we go through all of our tickets—right down to the A—at a particularly brisk pace and are somehow bummed out by the thought of several straight hours of the Monsanto thing. So Jim and I—the two more rebellious and party-hearty of the four of us—get this grand idea that'll completely change the way this marathon day's gonna turn out.

Here's our thinking.

First, we surmise that many Disneyland visitors are from out of town. Second, we conclude that these visitors will have no need for unused tickets after they've left the park and will likely even toss them into a trash barrel on their way out. Finally, we convince ourselves that these out-of-towners would certainly be happy to give these unused tickets to us as an alternative to the trash barrels, if only they understood our desperate plight. I mean, heck. We're *almost* cute and *completely* pathetic. Of *course* they'll give them to us.

And thus is born The Plan. We'll stand near the exit gate and ask people leaving if they'll give us their unused tickets.

Now, let me explain something about Disneyland in the sixties. This is one strict place. What's considered proper and acceptable while you're visiting this family entertainment center's just *pret-tee* darn conservative. Mr. Disney expects that not only his employees but also visitors to the park will represent a wholesome, all-American image. In fact, there's an actual dress code for visitors. Yep, that's right, Ringo. A *dress code.* Check out the recommended dress for a lovely day of relaxation and fun at Disneyland in the early to midsixties:

> Ladies, you should wear a patterned dress with the hem well below your knees—or you may prefer to wear a skirt and blouse. Please avoid tennis shoes, sandals, flip flops, or other inappropriately casual or revealing footwear. Halter tops are not acceptable and should not be worn. And please—no shorts. Gentlemen, you should wear pressed trousers, a collared shirt, leather shoes, and perhaps a nice sweater on cooler days. As for *tee shirts*—please remember that tee shirt is another name for *undershirt,* and the use of an undershirt as outerwear just cannot be allowed. All shirts must be tucked into the pants at all times. Hats are always acceptable at Disneyland, both

for men and for women. Excessively long hair as well as facial hair [men only on this one, I guess] of any description is inappropriate.

Now, I know you probably think I'm making this up. I'm not. Check it out.

I shudder to think what this Disneyland of the sixties would make of the semi-nudity, tattoos, and body piercings that'll be walking around inside the park fifty years from now. Wow.

Of course, Jim, Dave, Scott, and I have all been in this park about a gatrillion times, so we *know* about this dress code. We've all felt the club-like paw of a park guard on our shoulders and heard his gruff reminder to "tuck in your shirt, young man. We're a family park here, you know." We know that Disneyland has other strict ideas, too, about how we should behave while we're here. I mean, this place has security guards that cruise the parking lots, inspecting the way cars are parked and actually ticketing those that are parked too crooked between the lines.

Ess-tee-ar-eye-cee-tee. Strict.

Knowing all that we know, it still never occurs to any of us that there could be any problem with The Plan.

So here we are—Jim and I—standing at the exit gate, begging tickets from departing guests like Yogi Bear begging for pick-a-nick baskets at Jellystone Park. We don't know where Dave and Scott are—they didn't think so much of our idea and opted out—and frankly we don't care and won't take the time to worry about them because things are going pretty well here. Lots of friendly people want us to have a very happy night at Disneyland and are forking over their unused tickets with a smile. Most of what we're collecting are A, B, and C tickets, to be sure—but once in a while we're hitting the jackpot with a D or even an E ticket. We're ecstatic. Just a few more minutes—if our luck holds—and we'll have enough tickets to get the bunch of us through the rest of the day and night without even one visit to Monsanto.

Life's good.

I'm not sure which of us goes down first. I don't really have much time to worry about Jim, though, because quicker than I can say, "It's a small world after all," I'm struggling against my own demise at the hands of some unseen monster that's attacked me from behind and secured a lovely grip on the back of my neck. I feel another grip on my arm—or on my shirt sleeve, to be more precise—and I'm not sure what that tearing sound is. As I'm ushered menacingly toward some unknown destination, I'm learning that gravity can actually be out-run, with the help of a monster-claw grip pushing you along from behind.

I can hear some form of language moving along with me, and I believe it's coming from the general direction of the monster-claw grip—but in the midst of the sudden chaos, it's hard for me to be sure of anything. The more I hear, though, the more I believe it to be Eng-lish, or at least—as Allen Ludden says on the game show *Password*—roughly a form thereof, but I can't make out anything in the way of complete sentences. I think I can make out a few *words*, though, like "what the" and "not here, you don't" and "think you're doing" and "outta here."

When I can block out the pain in my neck—remember when your dad grabbed that little muscle between your neck and shoulder and pinched it between his finger and thumb—I'm lucid enough to notice some *pret-tee* excellent examples of sheer terror on the faces of people around me who are watching this whole thing happen. And I realize that their terror comes from looking at this . . . this . . . this *whatever* it is that's got me in its claws. That epiphany brings sudden discourage-ment about this thing ending in any positive way.

I can see a small, white, shack kind of thing just up ahead, and I guess we're headed there. As we get closer to it I know that Jim went down first because I see him standing against a wall inside that little shack. I'm pretty sure now that it's a security building, probably where all the wonderful park guards hang out and swap stories about the teenagers they've courageously scolded for flagrant shirt-tail violations. And I've tentatively concluded that what I've got behind me here's a *pret-tee* darn upset park guard who's taking me to his lair with no love at all in his heart. That thought and the look on Jim's face as he endures the verbal abuse and flailing arms of a seemingly psychotic guard in his face—well, let's just say that none of this does anything to relieve that feeling of discouragement I had just a moment ago.

With one final and brutish shove, I find myself inside The Build-ing, closer to Jim than I usually care to be and getting my first look at what brought-slash-shoved-slash-dragged me here: a behemoth of a guard with a face the shade of a lovely ripened tomato who tosses me aside like a fish too small to keep and continues toward a desk on the other side of The Building. Now, while *my* guard's picking up a phone on that desk, *Jim's* guard's still in his face explaining—at the approximate decibel level of a jetliner taking off—various interesting nuances of the Disneyland code of conduct. I can tell it's interesting and that Jim's paying strict attention because he's opened his eyes as wide as they can go—in fact, they may actually be *wider* than they can go because I can see parts of his ocular cavity that I don't usually notice.

From this point, everything's a bit of a blur. My guard makes a call and says something to someone somewhere about somebody he's got at the gate and should he hold 'em or let 'em go or what should he do. Maybe I hear the word *execute*, but that's probably just my nerves talking, which by now are just this side of shredded. The overall noise level's dropped a bit, but there's not much change in the tension, and Jim and I are still staring blankly straight ahead, avoiding eye contact with each other—like maybe if we don't look at each other the guards won't know we're together on this thing—and waiting for some unspeakably horrible gavel of judgment to drop squarely on top of us.

I guess the guard's got his answer when he hangs up the phone, goose-steps over to Jim and me, takes us by the arms—one of his claws for each of us—and briskly moves us to the door that we entered just hours ago . . . well, it seems like hours to us, anyway. And then out the door and right on over to the exit gate where we get one last expression of well-wishing from this gorilla—something on the order of "if you ever come back here and pull a stunt like this again . . ." something, something, something. The words aren't clear, but the message is: We should go away and disappear forever.

And with one last push, we're past the exit gate and headed—with excellent momentum—into the parking lot.

"Wow . . . What the . . . Where the . . . Wha' hap . . . Are you OK? . . . What in the holy heck . . . Sue the rotten . . . Can you believe . . . H-o-o-o-l-e-e . . . What're we gonna . . ." blah, blah, blah.

OK. Our pulse rates may have us about twenty seconds from stroke or death, but for the moment, we're still alive. *Still . . . ALIVE.* We've survived the attack of the Disneyland security guards and will live to tell about it. We're fine. We're good. We're OK.

And we've just been thrown out of Disneyland.

Geez.

Scott and Dave are still inside the Magic Kingdom somewhere, and they've no way of knowing what's happened to us, and we've no way to get word to them, and we fear we can't get to the employees' parking lot to get our ride home with Deb and . . . well, we're just nailed.

Maybe The Plan wasn't so good, after all.

Oh, well. We're still alive and we've still got each other and, gosh darn it, we're smart enough to think this thing out—our stupidity in devising The Plan notwithstanding.

We've been walking since the guard gave us that final loving send-off and are now out of visual range of the exit gate and The Building which will be forever etched in so loving a way on our memories. From where we are now, we can see Disneyland Hotel. And we can also see, leading up to and away from the hotel . . .

. . . the Monorail.

Now, we just happen to know that you can buy Disneyland admissions and tickets at the hotel and then ride the Monorail into the park—without going through the general park admission gate where certain ill-tempered guards are lurking about.

Hmmm.

Ordinarily Jim and I couldn't buy even a snow cone without taking out a loan, but on this occasion we actually have enough moola between us to take care of this. Not enough for each of us to buy a four-dollar ticket book, but enough for the two-dollar junior general admission for each of us and seventy-five cents each to ride the Monorail from the hotel to Tomorrowland. With the extra tickets we begged before we got tossed—the Cro-Magnon park guards never thought to make us pay for the error of our ways by confiscating them—we oughta be able to make it through the day.

Hotel. General admission. Monorail. Tomorrowland. All righty then.

OK. We wracked our brains to figure out this brilliant piece of subterfuge that brought us undetected into the Magic Kingdom. But until this very moment we've given no thought whatsoever to the problem of finding Scott and Dave among the quadratrillion people roaming the world's biggest amusement park.

Not a good notion between us.

A cell phone would be nice, but the development of that technology will take more time than we have. An announcement over the park PA system might work, but even if we knew where to look for a PA-announcing-station-thingy, with our luck, our new friends, the park guards, would be on duty there, just praying for another round with us. So we figure we'll have to rely on sheer luck or divine fortune to find our friends.

And with some walking and a Skyway Tram ride, one or the other of those is just what we get, because there they are.

It takes just a few quick minutes to catch the guys up on our adventure. And are they ever impressed—first, that Jim and I survived the attack of the security guards, and second, that we actually managed to pool enough IQ between us to come up with The Re-Entry Plan. A plan which, unlike our first plan, actually worked.

Come to think of it, though, it turns out that our first plan actually *did* work. Well, it went the long way around, to be sure, but in the end, here we all are in Disneyland, with enough scavenged tickets to take us right up to that eventual park bench moment.

That is, if we don't get recaptured by the Gestapo Unit.

Bummer. Hadn't thought about that till now. *We could actually run into those lovely fellows again.* I mean, maybe the beasts don't spend all their time at The Building. Maybe they only do *some* of their shift there. Maybe some complex system of personnel rotation allows for their bestial need to wreak havoc on improperly clad, rebellious adolescents all throughout the park. And while *we* probably won't recognize *them*, surely *they'll* know *us* the moment they spot us. After all, some indelible image of us must certainly have been imprinted on their brains during those lovely moments of bonding.

What to do.

What to do.

Got it.

In all of Disneyland, there's one place that we can always depend on in these tricky transitional teenage years to provide a somewhat acceptable release for our childish pretending without risking peer ridicule. A place that's as much to us like Mr. Peabody's Way Back Machine as it is a park attraction. And a place, to boot, where we can physically disappear from the main flow of Disneyland traffic and protect ourselves from that chance second meeting with our friendly guards until the safety of sundown.

Tom Sawyer Island.

We'll never be found there. No way. In all our visits to Disney-land, none of us can remember ever having seen one park guard on Tom Sawyer Island. If we want, we can engage in all manner of she-nanigans there without ever having to account to our friends in The Building. Yep, The Island. The smart thing, for sure. We've gotta make it to The Island, and we've gotta make it there undiscovered.

So it's decided, so it's done.

Now we're to the happy ending of this story—an ending that a little earlier in the day couldn't be imagined.

We stay on Tom Sawyer Island until it closes at dusk. Then, under blessed cover of darkness, the four of us return to the mainland and enjoy some of the tickets for which Jim and I paid so dearly. And we've plenty and to spare. We'll not run out of tickets or see the inside of the Monsanto Adventure Thru Inner Space this night.

But we do find that bench at eleven o'clock.

And as Disneyland's lighted darkness settles on us, pacifies us, soothes us, we quietly ponder the remarkable events of a day that might've been but wasn't just another marathon day in the Magic Kingdom and pray silently for the second hand to break its one-second-per-tick habit to move faster and bring that midnight hour just a little sooner.

4

I work at a service station

In 1967, one of the truest measures of a young man in Southern California is how much he knows about cars. He doesn't have to know about math, really, or history, or human relations—or how to build cabinets, make girls happy, draw pretty pictures, or do landscaping. All that stuff's for losers.

A *real* man knows about cars.

At least, that's what every male high school student seems to believe.

Which is why *any*one who's *any*one works, has worked, will eventually work, or wants to work at a service station.

Now, keep in mind that service stations in this day and age are actually *service* stations. They're not grocery stores that just happen to have self-serve gas pumps with a two-way audio setup and an automatic credit card scanner and a non-English-speaking attendant locked inside a little cage with a drawer that slides in and out from one side of the glass to the other between him and the customer so there's no funny stuff when the coin or the credit card changes hands.

Yeah, that's what you'll see trying to pass as a service station forty years from now. But that's not a *service* station.

When you drive up to the pump at a *real* service station in '67, you might see as many as three men—usually young men if it's after five p.m. or older guys during school hours—come hustling out from the lube bay to serve you. One starts checking the tires, one starts washing the windows, and one comes to your window and greets you with a lovely "Yes, sir" or "Yes, ma'am" or "Can I help you?" Or he might say, "Fill 'er up for you, sir?" or "Will that be regular or ethyl?" Once he knows what you want, he scrambles around to find your gas cap— and no matter what model car you're driving, he knows *exactly* where that gas cap is if your car's made in America or Japan or Germany or Sweden. Could be behind the license plate, on either side of the car in front or back, under the hood if the motor's in the rear, or even behind a taillight. And after he finds the cap and removes it, sticks the nozzle in, and starts pumping the gas, he comes back to the window and asks if you'd like him to check under the hood for you or sometimes—if it's a fill-up and he knows you're gonna be there for a few minutes—he might just pop the hood and check the oil for you without asking. Usually the radiator too. He'll do this even if he knows you're not gonna buy oil today no matter *how* low on oil your crankcase is, and you let him go ahead and do it because it feels great to get such good service and anyway you're paying thirty cents a gallon for this dang stuff so you by darn *oughta* be getting something for free. When he pulls the dipstick—and he knows where to find any dipstick in any car made in America or Japan or Germany or Sweden—wipes it off with the blue or reddish-brown oil rag that's always in the right hip pocket of his brown service pants or Levi's, and shoves it in your face with the immortal words "Looks like you're about a quart low," you go ahead and say, "Thanks anyway. I've got some oil at home," and he's not even bothered because it's his job and he loves doing it even if you don't buy the oil.

All this, even as the other pump rats are washing every window on your car to within an inch of its life and checking the air in all four tires. And actually putting air in the tires if they need it. At no cost, of course.

This impressive array of service is just what you get at the *pumps*. There's also a lube bay with one or two hydraulic lifts and a mechanic on duty during the day who knows pretty much *every*thing about *any*-thing you could possibly need that's in the slightest way akin to auto mechanics.

Maybe you need a tire. Or a fan belt tightened. Maybe you need an oil change. Or a lube. Maybe you'd like a tire balanced or a radia-tor flushed. Brakes adjusted. Rattle checked. Tires rotated. Hand held. Hair washed.

They'll do it all.

If you need something done on a little larger scale, the lube bay's where that happens too. Oil pump. Fuel pump. Water pump. Radiator. Head gasket. Alternator. Belts. Tune-up, major or minor. Even a complete engine rebuild.

No job too large or too small.

And when you pay for any service or product, you get a wad of S&H Green Stamps or Blue Chip Stamps that can be saved and traded in for all kinds of goodies at the Redemption Center. Plus, you may even get a nice piece of glassware or other promotional goody at absolutely no cost, just to make you wanna come back again and again. On top of all that, sometimes you get other neat things, like a little orange Styrofoam Union 76 ball that you can poke onto your car's radio antenna. It'll get stolen, of course, but it sure looks good while you've got it.

Now *that's* a service station.

So if you're a young man in high school and wanna learn about cars, a gas station's where you can do it. Which is, as I said, why every male high school student works at one or has worked at one or will eventually work at one or wants to work at one.

And which is why I'm willing to lie to work at one.

Here's the deal. My good friend, Ron, works at Bill and Jerry's Union 76 on State College Boulevard here in Fullerton. Ron knows that Bill and Jerry need some part-time evening help, so he recommends me for the job. We both know I don't know diddly-poop about anything mechanical beyond taking my trumpet apart to clean it, but Ron assures me that, in the evenings, I'd mostly just have to pump gas. That doesn't sound so hard, so I jump at the chance.

Turns out that you're supposed to be sixteen years old to work at Bill and Jerry's. I know I'm only fifteen-and-a-half, but I need some spending cash and this is a service station job for crying out loud, so let's just go ahead and give it a shot. Maybe Bill and Jerry will just be overcome by my powerful charisma and say, "Hey, what an impressive figure this young man cuts," and just plain forget to ask how old I am.

I have to come in and talk with Bill and Jerry—Jerry does most of the talking—and they wanna know a little about me, like how I'm doing in school and have I ever worked at a service station before and will it be a problem for me to work on Saturdays or Sundays. *So far so good*, I'm thinking, although I'd prefer not to work on Sundays. But life can't always be just how you want it to be, and this is by gosh a *service station* job we're talking about, so back off.

But then comes—gulp—The Question. The one I've been hoping they'd just skip right over.

"How old are you, Kevin?"

Now, I've been raised in what I consider to be an exceptional home in which moral training's been provided for me since I was old enough to know someone's talking to me, and adherence to certain basic— certain *many* basic—moral principles is expected. I'm a church-going boy, active in the church usually referred to as the Mormon Church, the more common name of The Church of Jesus Christ of Latter-day Saints, sometimes also referred to as the LDS Church. Much of my out-of-school time's spent doing Mormon things. Most of my best friends are Mormons. And just as they all do, I believe it's wrong to behave improperly with young ladies or use drugs, tobacco, alcohol, coffee, or tea. [*Rationalization Note:* You shouldn't infer from this that I'll never make any *mistakes* along the way with regard to this lifestyle. I will.] I attended Primary classes from age three to age twelve and got baptized when I was eight. I've attended Sunday School and priest-hood classes since I turned twelve and seminary classes since I turned thirteen, and focused for all my fifteen-and-a-half years on the goal of serving a two-year proselyting mission for the Church somewhere in the world after I turn nineteen.

And the most basic, most essential of the principles I've learned during all those years—the spine of the moral body, if you will—is that a good person doesn't lie. No matter what the consequences may be for telling the truth and no matter what advantage may be gained from lying. You tell the truth, no matter what the outcome. You just simply, absolutely, unequivocally do *not* lie.

"I'm sixteen, sir."

And I don't even blink.

I guess I'm figuring that during my fifteen years, I've saved up. Saved up all those lies that I could've told down through the years but didn't. Saved up all the little, piddling lies that were easy to avoid so that when the time came I'd have some credit against That One Lie. That single, solitary, never-done-it-before-never-do-it-again lie that's due me.

This is what I've saved up for.

And it works.

So now I've got this great job at Bill and Jerry's Union 76, and I just can't wait to get started. I don't have to wait long, either—after school the next day, I'm pulling my first shift. It's a five p.m. to eleven p.m. shift, and I get to work it alongside Ron, who shows me the ropes. Stuff like how to find gas caps and dipsticks on different cars and check tires and wash windows. How to run credit cards and make change and recognize quick-change artists. How to put oil in the crankcase from a new can or from the bulk oil drain and how to wash down the islands and the lube bay and how to shut down the whole shootin' match at closing time.

It turns out that I learn all these things pretty fast, and before you can say, "Peace, brother, peace," I feel like I'm actually *earning* that buck twenty per hour.

I learn other things too. Real important things. Like, how a pair of steel-toed work boots can keep me from going to the hospital when I drop heavy things on my feet. Like, how yummy Gaucho cookies taste toward the end of a shift. And like, how warm and cozy and tasty a thermos of hot chocolate can be on cool, wet, Southern California winter nights.

There's more stuff to be done at Bill and Jerry's than Ron teaches me, though. Stuff, I guess, that he thinks either I'll never *have* to do or I shouldn't *try* to do.

If it's the *second* thought, Ron's right. If it's the *first*, he's got another think coming.

Now, up to the point when I *prove* Ron's got another think coming, I have a really fun time at this job. My buddies find out faster than oil moves through a goose that I'm working at a service station now, so here they come with their cars and their motorcycles after Bill and Jerry have gone home. My guys like to visit because . . . well, because they *like* me, of course, but also—and probably *mostly*—because there's this nice little lube room where they can work on whatever heap they're driving at the moment, and there's all these tools lying around just begging to be used. Even if they don't have a mechanical project at the moment, the guys can still sit around with me in the lube bay waiting for the *ding-ding* of the bell in the lube bay that sings out whenever a car drives over that long black rubber rope thingy strung

out across the driveway by the gas pumps and tells us we've got a customer. Sitting around in the lube bay, my buddies get to smell gas and
oil and see all the neat cars and just have a generally great time. As a
bonus to me, they get to watch me work my magic on those gas tanks
and dipsticks, and my stock with all these guys just goes *way* up. I'm
cool, and there's just no denying it now.

Once in a while, I get to work an hour or two with Bill and Jerry at
the end of their day, which is a good way to learn things, for sure—but
I've gotta confess that they make me more than a little nervous at first.
I mean, these guys are just *pret-tee* darn tough. Both of them grew
up in East Los Angeles and have stories about fights and gangs and
whatnot that would make great Sunday night movies. And Bill's got
the scars on his face and the crooked nose to prove what he says. So I
believe him. Even if I didn't, you can bet the farm I'd never dream of
saying it to his face.

Despite how tough Bill and Jerry are, they're just really nice people.
Basic, good, friendly-if-quiet people. Patient, polite, happy to teach,
and—to go along with the proverbial big stick they carry—soft-spoken.

Still, sometimes I get nervous around them. Like the other day,
right after I started working here. I was just standing by the work
counter in the lube bay, talking to Jerry. A car *ding-dinged* out on the
island. I paused a beat, figuring that Jerry would get it because he's
the boss—but he patiently reminded me that he's paying me to go
out to the island when I hear the *ding-ding* and actually *work* for him.
Hmmm. Kinda made sense. So I got all flustered and nervous because
my boss had to correct me and I was all of a sudden afraid I'd let him
down and there wouldn't be any points for me on this one, that's for
sure—so I took off with a jolt to see how fast I could get out to the
island and *splat*. Stepped right square into a pan of oil. Black, dirty,
gritty oil *every*where.

I was nearly to the office, figuring to grab the phone book and
look up the number for the unemployment office, when I heard Jerry
start to laugh. Just a chuckle at first but then long, loud guffaws. There
I was, sweating bullets and feeling kinda sick to my stomach, and Jerry
was laughing. "Don't worry about it, Kev," he said. "You should follow
me around here for a whole day sometime and see how many pans of
oil I step into," he said.

I've never been nervous around Jerry since.

But he did make me clean up the oil.

Now, this job also has some *pret-tee* darn nice personal perks. My transportation these days is a Honda 90 Scrambler motorcycle because I don't have a driver license yet. I can ride this Honda with only a learner permit, which I got at fifteen-and-a-half. Turns out that this little critter needs some gas from time to time. Always the observant one, I've figured out that after I've pumped gas there's a little bit left in the hose that can be drained out into my motorcycle gas tank at no apparent cost to anyone. It's actually pretty amazing just how much gas you can get out of four gas pump hoses in the course of a six-hour shift. Regular or ethyl or mixed, my little Scrambler just doesn't care. It loves the mixture. In fact, I like to think that someone unbeknownst to me watches me mix these two grades of gas in my bike and comes up with the idea of a mid-range octane between regular and ethyl. Don't argue. I'm sure it's true.

It turns out that there's also a little oil left in the can after you've poured it into a car, and this leftover oil can be drained out, collected, and used. Also at no cost to anyone. More on that in just a minute.

Nice perks for a dirt-poor high school student.

Moving from the physical to the social-slash-spiritual perks, I even learn a couple of usable principles from Bill and Jerry. Different things like, be a man and don't back down from trouble. And like, if you make a mistake, have the guts to fess up and take your medicine if it's coming. And like, be a good person and give as good as you get.

And like, you get what you pay for.

Now, every once in a while some gas stations—for who knows what reason—lower their gas prices. Then other stations, not to be outdone, lower theirs. Before you can say, "You're a quart low," everyone's followed suit and the price of gas has dropped to nineteen or maybe even seventeen cents a gallon. This is called a *gas war*.

When I say *everyone* follows suit, I'm lying just a little. See, Bill and Jerry don't. They keep their prices steady no matter what the other stations are doing. They say they don't really understand the whole gas war thing because when they're charging full price for their gas, they only make about a nickel a gallon, anyway.

Here's what happens during a gas war. Customers leave whatever station they usually buy gas from and go to wherever the prices are lower. Then, when they find another station with prices lower than *that*, they go there. And so on, and so forth. But—again—the exception to this rule is Bill and Jerry's Union 76 Station. Their customers keep coming in to buy the thirty-something-cents-a-gallon gas even when just across the street they *could* buy Mobil gas for nineteen cents a gallon, and I'll bet you're asking yourself why.

Simple. Bill and Jerry use a tactic that, after all's said and done, keeps them in business with a loyal customer base that won't desert them during a gas war. Or any other time, for that matter.

Here's the simplicity of it. Bill and Jerry understand that the usual profit at the gas pump's minimal at best. They know that the *real* way to make money is to keep a strong customer base in the lube bay where the profit margin's greater. They also understand that the greater profit margin for *them* means that there's a greater cost to the *customer* for work done in the lube bay. And because the customer also recognizes this, what he *really* appreciates—even more than a temporary drop in prices at the pump—is any break he can get on work done in the bay. So when a regular, loyal customer drives in with a small mechanical problem of some kind, there's a better-than-even chance it'll get fixed for free. Or if Bill and Jerry can't fix it for free, once they get the car on the rack, they'll manage to do something extra along with what they started out to do—you know, just throw in stuff that they know the customer will appreciate. A new radiator cap. An extra squirt of grease into the chassis's lube fittings. Maybe a windshield wiper or a pint of STP oil treatment. Stuff that *would* cost money but *doesn't* because Bill and Jerry appreciate Mr. Loyal Customer for sticking with them during a gas war instead of hauling his buns over to the nearest station that'll serve up its gas cheaper but gouge him in the lube bay.

It's a win-win kind of deal.

You get what you pay for.

So. Bill and Jerry may have grown up tough in a tough neighborhood, and they may not have any college degrees behind their names, but I guaran-dang-*tee* you they know what's up. And they know how to be people. The right kind of people.

OK. So back to what I've learned about the nuts and bolts, so to speak, of this here job. Let's just try to name them, one by one.

For starters, I'm just *pret-tee* darn comfortable at the pumps. No dipstick can hide from me. Gas caps are at my mercy too. I even know when the little rascal's lurking behind a fold-down license plate, and

I can handle it—even got the two gazillion broken watch crystals to prove it. In fact, even though I'm right-handed, I've been wearing my watch on my right arm—where it'll stay for the rest of my life—since I started working here because nearly every time I hold down that dang license plate with my left arm so I can insert the pump nozzle with my right hand, the spring-held license plate manages to snap up or down or over and break my watch.

I also know how to wash windshields using just the right number of squirts of windshield cleaner and an effective pattern of washing—across, down, up, down, up, down, up, across, across, across. Right hand, left hand—makes no difference to me. I'm an experienced and ambidextrous gas rat now.

I know how to use my spiffy new tire gauge to check the air in the tires and how to air them—and I can easily pull off the fancy *s-n-n-n-a-p* of the air hose to whip it clear of the tires when I take it around to air the tires on the far side of the car.

I can drop a quart of oil neatly into a motor in what must certainly be some kind of record time, and still make sure I leave a little in the can to be drained later for my little Honda. [*Morals Note:* This isn't as dishonest as it sounds when you know that the manufacturer deliberately overfills the cans to make sure the customer gets a full quart measure without having to wait for every drop to drain from the can into the crankcase. A "baker's dozen" kind of deal.]

I know how to release the pressure on an overheated radiator by cracking the cap just a little before popping it completely off so the boiling water doesn't spew out of the radiator and all over me. [*Medical Note:* I learned this particular trick the hard way.] I even know how to cool off an overheated radiator with water before I open the cap and to never, *ever* put cold water into an overheated radiator—especially without the motor running to keep the fan working—because before you can say, "Overhaul my engine, please," you've got a cracked block. [*Mechanical Note:* I learned *this* little trick the hard way too.]

I know how to put a car up on the lube rack. I don't generally do it when I'm the only one working, but I know how. That means I can direct the driver into the bay so that his car sits centered over the "H" of the hydraulic rack and then position the four adjustable steel blocks on the "H" so that they hit the car's frame just right—and can I just point out that nothing, *nothing* good comes from failing to get those blocks under the car's frame—and then push the little control arm to make the hydraulic lift rise, taking the car along with it.

I can give directions to on-ramps of at least three different nearby freeways, all the local major intersections, and sometimes even a local neighborhood street or two that are too obscure to even be found on the maps that we give away for free to anybody who wants them.

I know how to handle gas cards and cash—and I say *no* to quick-change artists with a capital N.

Quick-change artists. Oh, boy. And I'm not talking about changing clothes quickly. I'm talking about money. If you've never been the victim of a quick change artist, you haven't lived. Here's roughly how it works. Some guy—often teaming with another social leper—hands you a fifty to pay for a pack of gum, for example. Then when you give him his change, he says, "Well, I don't want these big bills you gave me, so why don't you give me two fives instead of this ten?" So you hand him the fives, but as he's giving you the ten back, he says real quick, "Oh wait. Lemme give you this five and five ones, and you give me a ten," but he doesn't give you the five and five ones until you've forked over the ten. And then his pal steps up and starts distracting you with questions while you're trying to figure out what you've just done, and before you can say, "Well, *that's* not Dick Clark," your till's twenty or thirty bucks lighter and you've collected only a five and five ones.

Sounds confusing, I know. That's why it works.

But if you see the quick change coming and know what to do, you'll be OK. You've just gotta stay focused on making sure you collect *his* money before you hand him *yours*, and returning correct change every time he asks for a different configuration of change. Before you can say, "Hit the road, Jack," the jerk's frustrated and out of there, on his way to find easier pickings.

OK. So there you have a list of Kevin's duties, responsibilities, and skills—from finding a Chevy's dipstick to discouraging organized crime.

And now you're thinking, "Well, holy cow, it sounds like this guy pretty much knows everything there is to know about working at a service station," and you're wondering what in the *world* there could possibly be that I haven't mastered yet.

Oh, boy.

It turns out that there's a whole big *bunch* of other things I haven't learned yet and I'm about to be confronted by pretty much every single one of them.

All on the same night.

And all at the same time.

Orange County's currently in the middle of a rainstorm to beat all rainstorms. If Noah were here, even *he'd* be headed north by now. It's been raining uninterrupted for what seems like forever but turns out to be about two weeks. Water's running deep along the streets everywhere, and the drains can't handle it, so it's spilling up over the curbs and pooling in the intersections. I mean, as my father's wont to say, it's clear-over cloudy and raining straight down. Everybody with at least the IQ of an ice cube's learned to drive no faster than about twenty-five down State College Boulevard because if you drive faster than that, you'll rooster-tail big time and douse every car around you, blind the drivers, and cause a wreck maybe.

And it turns out that driving fast through deep, pooled water can do bad things to your car.

That's what happens to this one guy on this one night. This one night, with rain coming down in buckets. This one night, when Ron has the night off and I'm all alone at the job. This one night, right before closing time. This one night, when the Portals of Hell are about to open. This one, horrific night.

The Night.

So this guy rolls in and says, "Boy, I hit that water pretty hard and now my car sounds funny, so I think the water may have separated my tailpipe from my muffler. But if I could just get it up on your rack for a minute, I could reconnect it and be on my way."

Like I said before, I know how to lift the car, but I don't generally do it alone—make that, I've *never* done it alone—and at the moment, I'm alone. And here's this guy who seems to be in a *pret-tee* big hurry and confident that he can do this thing himself—which, even though he doesn't know it yet, will actually be *mandatory* if I agree to raise the car because yes, I can get the car onto the lift and into the air but no, I don't know the first thing about reconnectin' no tailpipe to no muffler. But despite this guy's oozing confidence, I haven't convinced myself quite yet to cooperate with him on his proposed project.

Ding-ding.

Saved by the bell. I tell the guy to hold on for just a sec while I take care of the car at the pump. Be right back.

The guy at the pump will just need some gas, I guess, so I hit him with the standard, "Good evening, sir. What'll it be, regular or ethyl?"

But this guy's not wanting gas tonight. "I need to rent one of your trailers," he says.

Uh-oh.

Now, I've actually known from the first day I started working here that we rent these little six-foot trailers that are lined up along the south side of the building, but no one's taken the time to tell me how to rent them or shown me how to hook them up. But I figure, how hard can this be. "Fine," I say to the guy. "Bring your car around to the other side where the trailers are, and I'll be right with you," I say.

So while he's doing that, I reconsider Tailpipe Guy's request and decide to let him use the bay to fix his problem. I tell him to bring his car around to the bay, and I'll be right with him. While he's doing that, I start walking over to the trailers to help the guy waiting there.

Ding-ding.

I tell Trailer Guy to hang on a sec while I catch this car at the pumps, and I'll be right there.

So I figure for sure *this* guy rolling up to the pumps is just gonna want a little gas and then I'll get back to the two projects awaiting my personal attention, so I hit him with "Good evening, sir. Fill 'er up?" "No thanks," he says. "Just need to buy a tire," he says.

Geez.

Now, I know we've got tires stacked along this big ol' rack that runs high along the wall inside the lube bay, but no one's ever told me how to sell one or shown me how to put one on the rim after I sell it. Or even how much to charge for one, for that matter.

But I figure, how hard can it be to find a tire and put it on? After all, I know where the price list is. So I think to myself, *I can do this thing.* As a plus factor, I think I once heard Ron say that we get a commission if we sell a tire or anything big like that. Extra money. That's a good thing.

So I tell this guy to bring his '63 VW bus around back with the other car waiting to come into the bay, and I'll be right with him as soon as I take care of Tailpipe Guy and Trailer Guy.

Now it seems the rain's coming down harder, if that's possible—and

I'm just as soaked as a guy can be, short of being in a swimming pool or a bathtub. But, undaunted, I forge on.

First, gotta get Tailpipe Guy up on the rack. I direct him into the bay with fancy arm signals—picture the guy with the orange ear muffs directing planes on the airport tarmac—and he finally comes in for a nice smooth landing over the "H" of the lift with the left front tire resting nicely on the bumpy metal plate attached to the floor that tells you you've gone far enough and you should think about stopping now before you go through the front wall. I adjust the lift plates on the "H" underneath his car so that each one's hitting the frame of the car because—well, remember what I said about nothing good coming of failing to center these little doohickeys on the car's frame. I mean, a lovely sedan hanging by one tire from a rising hydraulic lift just isn't what the owner typically wants to see. Then after I check it all out and find everything in order, I hit a little lever on the wall to engage the hydraulics and send the car slowly into the air. The hydraulic lift sings me a lovely *whoosh* as the car starts to climb. Just before it reaches head-level, I lay off the lever, and the lift coasts about twelve inches more before sliding silently to a stop at just the right height for us to get under the car without bashing our brains out or getting a crick in our necks.

Smooth. Kevin, you're a natural.

The two of us step underneath the car to look around. Sure enough, the tailpipe and the muffler are divorced. So Tailpipe Guy asks, "What tools do you have?" and I say, "I don't know 'cause I never use anything but an oil spout." So he asks, "Mind if I look around?" and I say, "I guess it'll be OK," and while he's nicely occupied with that, I tell him I'll be right back after I help Trailer Guy who just came in to remind me that he's still waiting and wonders when I will be out to help.

Meanwhile, Tire Guy's sitting in his car in front of the lube bay with his windshield wipers slurp-slurp-slurping a lovely rhythm, and as I walk past him, he reminds me that he, too, is still waiting and when will I be able to get the tire for him. "Just a minute," I say. "As soon as I get this guy's trailer hooked up," I say.

I swim on out to find that Trailer Guy's already backed his '65 Chevy Impala up close to a little six-foot trailer in anticipation of a successful union. Obviously, he doesn't have a trailer ball attached to his Chevy because—duh—it's a sedan. But even if it were a truck or some other kind of utility vehicle it probably *still* wouldn't have a trailer ball attached. It's 1967, for crying out loud. We're still some years away from the day when every car you see's a dang SUV and has a flippin' trailer hitch and ball attached to it.

The first thing I've gotta do is pick out one of the thousand-pound trailer hitches leaning against the wall of the building and drag it on over. Now, these are not small things. No-siree, Bob. They're big ol' honkin' steel critters that attach to your bumper—and they're almost as long as your bumper—by means of these metal hook thingies at the ends of two chains—one on each end—that look like they could moor the Queen Mary. Then the hook thingies slip in over the inside edge of your bumper to secure the whole unit to the bumper and can I just tell you that's it's not as easy as you think it is to get those hook thingies into that little gap between the inside edge of your bumper and the body of the car. I soon discover that your knuckles pay an awful price for your success.

So I select one of these monsters and drag it on over to the car. The *whole stinking thing* I drag, with its chains and big ol' bolts and nuts and trailer ball. By the time I get it to the car I've got a strangulated hernia and at least two broken fingers, and the hitch is an unrecognizable heaping mess of chains and bolts and balls, all tangled together. Amazingly not yet bothered by the chaos of the moment, though, I take to that pile of metal just like I know what I'm doing when, in fact, I don't have the slightest clue about which chain goes where and what nut screws down onto what bolt. So after a minute or so of just flipping pieces around, hoping for written instructions to flash across the heavens, Trailer Guy sorta figures out that I'm an idiot and says, "Here, let me help. I believe this goes here."

Obviously, he's fallen for my plan. I've suckered him into doing my work for me. Which is good because I think he actually knows how to do this. And I don't. So while Trailer Guy grunts and strains and wipes the rain out of his eyes—at least he's wearing a lovely rain slicker—and sorts out the various pieces of the pile, I say, "I'll be right back. I've just gotta help a guy with a tire."

With his car securely on the rack, Tailpipe Guy's moving busily around the lube bay. As I ricochet by, I ask him how it's going and he says he's hunting for a crescent wrench and a screwdriver, and I tell him, "Good luck with that." I mean, they must be there somewhere.

I trot on over to Tire Guy and ask him what kind of tire he needs. He says, "A five-sixty-fifteen," and I wonder what lock *that* combination opens—but he explains that it's the size of the tire. I say, "Fine, let's look in our little book over here that's hanging on the little chain below the tire rack," and before you can say, "rubber meets the road," we've found a listing for that tire in a bias ply. Now I've just gotta climb up on the ladder that slides back and forth along the tire rack to see if we've got one.

I shinny up the ladder and take a look around. And there it is. I see the 5.60-15 written on a rectangular sticker on the front of the tire, so right away, I figure it's a match. Dang. I'm getting better at this service station stuff by the minute. I grab the tire and start climbing down with it, but the little sucker's heavier than it looks, and when I'm about halfway down the ladder the tire slips right out of my little mitts and drops to the floor. It bounces once or twice, tries to roll but doesn't get far, and then—exactly as I'm gonna do in just a few minutes from now—collapses to its side, wobbles up and down and around a couple of times, and finally comes to rest on the lube bay floor that I haven't mopped yet and it's already past closing time.

Tire Guy tells me, yep, that's the tire he needs, and I figure I did *pret-tee* darn good finding the right one the very first time out, and I'm feeling just a little proud of myself. My plan's to toss this bias-ply puppy into Tire Guy's bus, make my best guess at what it costs, collect the coin, and bid the gentleman a good evening.

"Can I get that put on the rim?" he asks.

Dadgummit.

Now I'm starting to feel a little edgy because patience has never been my long suit, anyway, and what little I do have's now been stretched to its official limits. But in a rare—make that *unprecedented*—moment of mature and reasoned thinking, I decide to try to get through this, and I turn my attention back to the tire. That's when I notice that the tire isn't rubber.

It's paper.

Well . . . now that I look closer, I see that it's actually just covered by some kind of wrapping paper wound around it in an overlapping kind of deal—like the leather on the handle of a tennis racket. No problem. I'll just remove it.

Right.

I find the end of the who-knows-how-long-it-is paper wrap and start unwinding it from around the tire, kinda like I was unwrapping the red from a candy cane. Pull it over, pull it under, over, under, over, under. Now, personally I think I'm making pretty good time here. I've already got about five or six overlaps unwound and, heck, I've only been working on it for about, oh, say, like, an *eternity*, and there are only about five million or so—I'm rounding up—overlaps left to unwind. I figure I'll be done by morning at the outside and . . . well, now that I think about it, maybe it *is* taking just a little too long.

I don't have time to think about this anymore right now, though, because I'm hearing unfriendly noises out by the trailers, so I guess I'd better get out there ASAP and check it out. I tell Tire Guy, "Hang on, sir, I'll be right back."

On my way out, I hear Tailpipe Guy gleefully announce that he's found a screwdriver and "that, by darn, oughta take care of it," he says.

I'm happy for him.

Outside, Trailer Guy's already got the hitch installed on his bumper and it's just a minute's work for me to drag the trailer over and set its tongue on the ball. Now he wants me to hook up the trailer wires to the wires from his car so that on the way home the guy driving behind him doesn't do a Hollywood car-roll off the trailer when it stops with no brake lights showing. I figure it's the least I can do for the guy since he did, after all, install the hitch all by himself. He's even got the wires from his car's taillights detached and ready so I don't have to get out my hammer.

If I could even *imagine* a four-pole trailer end connector plug, I'd be wishing right now for a time machine to catapult me a few years ahead so I could pick me up one of 'em along with a matching female connector. You can bet I'd make quick work of this spaghetti mess I'm looking at right now. Brake lights, taillights, signal lights, ground—all in one simple connector. Land o' Goshen. Wouldn't it be sweet.

But I don't have such a plug, and I also don't have a clue about all these wires I'm staring at. I did study colors in kindergarten, though, and I'm pretty sure about this red-to-red and black-to-black and white-to-white and green-to-green matching thing, so I figure that's a good way to start, and I take a stab at it. Trailer Guy isn't yanking the wires out of my hand in a fit of panic, and he doesn't look like he's about to have a heart attack, so I'm encouraged, figuring I must be on the right track with this match-the-colors plan.

"Have you got any electrician's tape?" Trailer Guy asks, and I say, "Well, I guess there must be some around here somewhere 'cause this is, after all, a service station even if we can't find a crescent wrench or a screwdriver, so just hang on for a minute and I'll go get it."

On my way to find the tape, I pass Tire Guy and see right away that he's a lot smarter than I am and probably oughta have my job because he's figured out to just take a knife—I guess he got it out of his pocket because if it had been on the work counter or visible anywhere else in the work area, Tailpipe Guy would've snapped it up—and cut the paper all around the inside of the tire. And there's the conquered paper wrap, all peeled back from the tire in two easy steps and lying neatly on the floor. Tire Guy doesn't seem bothered that, instead of helping him, I'm just standing here watching him like he's the star of a floor show at a supper club. In fact, he's got one of our oil rags in his back pocket, and I think he's enjoying the work and probably even figuring he's on the payroll—which, by the way, would be fine with me.

I pass Tailpipe Guy, who's grunting and twisting on the tailpipe. Like Tire Guy, he *also* seems to be enjoying his work. I think we've got a good thing going on here. Ensemble acting, as it were. I wonder what time all these guys can start work tomorrow.

As long as we're all working so nicely together here, I figure what the heck. Maybe Tailpipe Guy can help me. So I just haul off and ask him if he happened to see any electrician's tape while he was searching for tools. He says, "Yeah, take a look in the first drawer on the right over by the bulk oil." I take a look and, by George, there it is. Geez. This guy knows the station better than I do. I pluck the tape out of the drawer, check to see that Tire Guy's still smiling, and start out toward the trailers.

Ding-ding.

There's a blue Ford Galaxie at the pump, and I'm not even wanting to *think* what *this* guy's gonna want.

But with courage screwed to the sticking-place and resignation, if not enthusiasm, I approach the driver-side window and say, "Yes, sir, how can I help you?"

"Fill 'er up with regular and check under the hood," he says.

Finally. Something I can do.

So I hustle around to the regular pump—noticing the gas cap on the rear left side of the Galaxie as I go—and in a flash I clear the pump, pop the gas cap, and stick the nozzle in. *Bing-bing-bing-bing* goes the pump as gasoline flows, and I head for the hood to check the oil.

Dipstick's right where I knew it would be. I yank it out, wipe it off, stick it back in, pull it out, and check. Sure enough. About a quart low.

I go back to the window and show the driver the dipstick resting on my oil rag. "Looks like you're about a quart low," I tell him, and, of course, on *this* night the guy actually *wants* the oil, so on the dead run I head inside to get it. See, I already put the oil display racks inside the lube bay because I was actually getting ready to close down when all these guys bushwhacked me.

It takes only a minute to fetch the can, punch the spout, and pour the oil where it needs to be. No time to worry about left-over oil—just toss the empty can in the trash can, finish off the gas, collect the guy's money, give him change, and get back to the lovely chaos.

As I turn to head back to my new friends and colleagues—all working happily at their tasks—I see two cars on State College Boulevard signaling to turn in to the pumps. This is trouble. It means that I'm about to have a problem because it's after eleven o'clock now and all my Chevron, Mobil, and Texaco neighbors are closed or have at least turned off their signs and lights. Now every car driving by on State College that needs gas or oil or a map or a restroom's gonna stop here now because my lights are still on.

Gotta get to the switch. Gotta turn off the sign and the island lights. Gotta do it before these guys *ding-ding-ding-ding* onto the island.

Gotta close the Portals of Hell.

It's a race. See Kevin run. Run, Kevin, run. Past the gas pumps. Through the door and into the lube room. Past Tailpipe Guy still grunting and twisting on his muffler. On to the back corner of the room by the sink. Stretch like you're trying to touch the side of the pool before the guy in the next lane touches. Hit the switch.

Ding-ding.

I win.

I go to the door, smile, and wave the guy on. He flashes an understanding smile and *ding-dings* his way on out with the second car right behind him.

Now it officially hits me. I'm wet. I'm tired. I'm frustrated. I'm hungry. On top of all that, my eyeballs are floating because I haven't been to the bathroom since Methuselah was in knickers. I should've been closed an hour ago and already sitting comfortably at home, enjoying the spaghetti or the steak my mom will have cooked for me. Instead, I've got smiley Tire Guy waiting for me to install his new tire on the rim, Tailpipe Guy trying to get his muffler and tailpipe together with a screwdriver, and Trailer Guy waiting for electrician's tape.

I just wanna go home.

But I've gotta see this through. Just like eating an elephant—one bite at a time.

First, out to Trailer Guy with the tape. I splice and tape the wires, check that all the lights are working, roughly fill out a rental contract, collect a deposit, and send him on his way.

Next, on to Tire Guy. I tell him that I'm just not gonna be able to get that tire installed tonight, but if he'd like to bring it back in tomorrow, I'm sure Bill or Jerry or whatever guy they've hired to replace me will be glad to help him with it. Behind a patient smile, he says, "Don't worry about it" and pops the tire into the bus. I charge him the lowest amount on the price range for the tire—which is gonna cost me tomorrow when I tell Bill and Jerry because I just gave this guy a tire at cost, and that's a no-no—collect the coin, and wave good-bye.

Finally, I note that Tailpipe Guy's stopped grunting and seems to have everything reconnected. He asks me to bring his car down, so I hit the hydraulics switch and down comes the car. Nice and easy. I kick the arms of the hydraulic lift out of the way so his car doesn't run over them as he backs out. I'm getting ready to arm-signal him out of the bay when he says, "What do I owe you?" and I say, "For what?" and he says, "Heck, for letting me use your rack to fix this thing." I say, "Oh, don't worry about it," so he climbs in the car and starts to back out, but before he leaves he reaches through the window and hands me a ten-dollar bill.

It won't pay for even half the hour of therapy I'm gonna need after tonight, but it's more than I'll earn for my entire six-hour shift, so I appreciate it a lot.

As Tailpipe Guy backs out, I begin closing the steel accordion door to the bay. Once his car's cleared the bay, I close the door all the way, thread the chain through a grid on each side, secure the chain with the lock, and head to the island to close everything down and retrieve the money box. The bay floors aren't gonna get mopped tonight, that's for sure. 'Cause I'm done for the day. And when I say *done* I mean *done*. As in *finished*. As in *exhausted*. As in *dead*.

Done.

Lights off. Display racks and cans and equipment and cash box locked away in the lube bay. All doors locked. On my bike, ready to crank 'er up and head for home.

But before I can hit the kick start and finally escape The Night, a blue Ford Galaxie drives in and stops in front of me. After I wipe the rain out of my eyes, I recognize the car as the last gas pump customer of the night. Don't remember the wrinkles and crinkles in that hood, though.

"Hey," the driver says.

"Hey," I say.

"Maybe you remember filling me up tonight," the driver says.

"Yes, sir," I say.

"Then you probably remember putting in a quart of oil," he says.

"Yes, sir," I say.

"Maybe you also remember closing the hood," he says.

"Yes, sir," I say.

"Betcha don't remember hearing the hood latch catch," he says.

Gulp.

And that would explain the wrinkles and crinkles in the hood that weren't there earlier. From a rather masochistic point of view, I guess there's a certain symmetry to this. The perfect ending, as it were, to an incredible night of anything goes. When I think about it, maybe there's even some advantage in having the entire world collapse around you all at once. Yeah, it's tough on you while it's happening, that's true enough. But after it's all done, there's one thing you know for sure: Pretty much everything bad that *can* happen *has* happened, so nothing else bad *will* happen. At least, not for a while. I mean, if you believe in averages, after a night like tonight, you can be *pret-tee* darn sure you've just *gotta* be in for a nice, long stretch of ain't-nothin'-bad-gonna-happen-to-you-today-bub.

Oh, how I look forward to that stretch.

5

I give my best friend a heart attack

I'm not a big fan of Audrey Hepburn.

There aren't many others like me in this regard. I know that. In 1967, pretty much the whole world thinks Miss Hepburn's the cat's meow. But I happen to think she's the greatest over-actor in the history of cinema—if only just slightly ahead of Charlton Heston. I guess such grandiosity works nicely on the stage where audibility and visibility are issues. But in movies, where audio and video can be controlled for every circumstance, it seems such a waste. And it actually kinda aggravates me.

Despite the irritation of her magniloquence, I do occasionally see one of Miss Hepburn's movies. And, if the scuttlebutt has it right, one just came out that should be right up my alley.

Wait Until Dark.

Now, *this* sounds like a *movie*. One for those who love—no, *crave*—suspense. One for any strong-of-heart movie cowboy who loves to be scared to within an inch of his life. One for those marvelous masochists who in just a few short years will flock in great, long lines to get the first glimpse of the monster shark in Steven Spielberg's *Jaws* and gladly submit to an awesome, clinging fear of the water in simple exchange for the scare of a lifetime.

One for me, on every count. I just love this kind of stuff. I love it *all*.

Take Alfred Hitchcock, for example. I love his collections of short stories. I watched *Alfred Hitchcock Presents* and *The Alfred Hitchcock Hour* when they were on TV. I've seen his movies. I *love* his movies. One night in 1960, I sat inside the little bring-your-own-chair—I'm exaggerating only slightly here—Ritz Theatre in my fifteen-hundred-resident hometown of Baldwyn, Mississippi, watching *Psycho* pretty much all by my eight-year-old self because nearly every other living resident of Baldwyn was outside in the town streets—make that *street*—enjoying a once-in-a-lifetime centennial commemorating the Civil War.

Once-in-a-lifetime, schmonce-in-a-lifetime. This was Hitchcock.

And Edgar Allen Poe. Forget about it. He's absolutely awesome. I've never read a Poe sentence that I didn't like. His poems. His short stories. Ho-o-o-o-l-e-e-e *cow*. "The Tell-Tale Heart" or "The Pit and the Pendulum" or "The Cask of Amontillado" can do as much to foster a phobia as any movie that could ever be made. More, in fact.

Well, there you have it. I love suspense. I love the macabre. I love to have the whazzit scared out of me.

So after I see the previews and promos for this *Wait Until Dark* movie that everyone's talking about, I know one thing for certain.

This one's for me. I'm there.

I'm not going by myself, though. I'm taking Jim along. My best friend.

Jim and I hooked up not long after my family moved here to Southern California, and we've been best friends since. Together, we've sampled and survived pretty much everything you can imagine. Even though we're Mormons—more about that in a minute—we sometimes fall just a tad short of what we know we should be. Don't always toe the line, as it were, with what one might call *high precision*. Give us a break here. We're youngsters. And we *could* be doing a lot worse, that's for sure. But we choose to be generally conservative in our occasional departures from the values we claim.

Therefore, dear Reader, read on with compassion.

Jim and I have fought over girls, challenged authority, and collaborated to destroy his sister's expensive art brushes by drawing peace signs and flowers on our jeans with bleach. We've cut school, hitchhiked, and tried—well, we've talked about it, anyway—to sneak into movie theaters. We've discovered Newport Beach and Balboa Island

and Corona del Mar, and together we've chosen those locations over the high school classroom on more than one occasion. We've shared Jack in the Box cheeseburgers and music and motorcycles—if a Yamaha 55 trail bike and a Honda 90 Scrambler are motorcycles. We've even been kicked out of Disneyland together.

And we've destroyed church plumbing together.

See, as I mentioned, Jim and I are members of The Church of Jesus Christ of Latter-day Saints, more commonly known as Mormons. Which means we get to attend an inordinate—compared with most other churches—number of meetings.

Let's see now. There's the usual Sunday worship meetings: priesthood meeting at six a.m., Sunday School at eleven a.m., and sacrament meeting at six p.m. During the week, we enjoy religious instruction in seminary classes at six o'clock every single, sleepy, bleary-eyed morning. And just to make sure we don't get out of touch with things, we also attend a weekly meeting of the Young Men's Mutual Improvement Association—commonly referred to as MIA or mutual—every Tuesday at seven p.m. For most young men, mutual's pretty much a night for Boy Scout activities, but—if we're just not all that hot on campfires and merit badges or if we've just plain outgrown the whole Scouting scene—we might choose to do other things. For example, it's a great time to hook up with the lovely young ladies who are enjoying the coincidental Young *Women's* Mutual Improvement Association. How sweet is that. Or we might choose up sides for a heated game of basketball on the full-sized court in the cultural hall and just impress the diddlywhozit out of the girls with our manly sweat.

Usually, we opt for the basketball game—whether our sweat, in fact, impresses or not.

Now, this full-sized basketball court's an amenity that nearly every LDS church building has. It comes in handy for large social gatherings, and the men and young men use it in preparation for the annual church-wide basketball competition that starts out in various age brackets on the ward (local congregation) level, advances to the stake (a wider local congregation) level, then to the regional (yep, you guessed it: an even wider local congregation) level. Regional winners move on to the All-Church Tournament held in Salt Lake City, Utah.

Which, by the by, is just no small thing. No, indeed. This All-Church Tournament championship's become so coveted that it's spawned competition just short of actual manslaughter. Not to mention the lovely methods of subterfuge it's inspired at the ward and stake levels, such as "drafting" seven-foot-tall, blood-thirsty ringers from Brigham Young University and other top-level athletic programs in order to improve a team's chances of advancing to Salt Lake. Which, of course, prompts someone else to "draft" someone even bigger and meaner, and then it all starts to get nasty and bloody, and refs who make unpopular calls begin to drop like flies amid the fists and fury of overheated competition, and church members in general start thinking, "Hey, maybe those less-violent protestant churches are just looking *pret-tee* darn attractive." Things will eventually get so bad, in fact, that the Church leadership headquartered in Salt Lake City will say, "Hey, what the heck's this whole thing turning into?" and in a stroke of collective wisdom—not to mention self-defense against the wounding and/or death of too large a portion of the male Church membership nationwide—will do away with the All-Church Tournament and leave the competition at the ward and stake levels only.

Even then it'll still be fun. And it'll endure at that level for decades to come.

But I digress.

Now, in addition to the Sunday worship meetings, the daily seminary classes, and the weekly mutual, Jim and I get to attend the semi-annual stake conference. Here's the deal. The local congregation is, as I mentioned, called a ward. A ward's presided over by a bishop. Then a few neighboring wards—maybe six or eight or so—are grouped together to form a stake, which is presided over by a stake president. Every six months, the stake president's responsible to organize a stake conference to be attended by all the members of all the wards in that stake. Although the conference consists of several meetings, Jim and I only have to worry about attending one. That would be the general session that's usually held between ten o'clock a.m. and noon on a Sunday. All members of the stake are expected to attend this meeting, and the usual Sunday meetings are canceled on this day.

Now, pay attention. I'm about to fess up to something here. Bare my soul, as it were. And I understand fully the repercussions that may follow this courageous act. In effect, it'll sound like I'm admitting that in my youth I'm falling short of the mark—failing spiritually, as it were. Like I don't fully understand the significance of religious training and spiritual worship. Or, at least, like I'm choosing to ignore it for the moment.

Risky. Very risky, what I'm about to say.

See, the harsh truth is that I really hate going to this particular meeting. Sorry 'bout that. I just do. So does Jim. And I'm even gonna be brave enough to suggest that maybe we're not the only two male adolescents in the LDS Church who feel this way in 1967. I mean, come on. We're teenagers. We've got the attention span of a rat running an electrified maze and the interest level of Tarzan at the opera. We're being asked to sit for two full hours—one hundred twenty minutes—seven thousand two hundred seconds—listening to men and women go on and on and on about you oughta be doing this thing and you oughta *not* be doing *that* thing.

Not that it's all bad stuff, mind you. In fact, I'll even admit that when occasionally, in some unexpected and unpredictable moment of spiritual and emotional maturity, I manage to sit still and quiet long enough to actually hear what's being said, I find that some of what I hear's pretty good stuff. And in years to come, when I look back at these times, I'll even regret that I didn't listen a little more closely a little more often than I did, realizing that I'd probably have turned out to be a much better old person.

Still, none of that changes the fact that at this particular moment in time, I'm just *pret-tee* darn bored by two hours of preaching. Out of my gourd, as it were.

So's Jim.

And when Jim and I get bored, Jim and I figure a way around whatever's boring us.

In this case, escape's the way.

The first essential part of escape is to ditch the parents. This isn't really all that hard to do. We've only gotta make sure that *my* parents think *I'm* with *Jim's* family, and that *Jim's* parents think *he's* with *my* family.

Don't you judge me on this, now. This isn't a lie. Nope, it isn't. Not when you look at it from our point of view, anyway. See, from our point of view, it's self-defense. Self-preservation, as it were. Personal survival, even. And if ever an end justified a means, well . . . then personal survival's that end.

So while everybody else is sitting quietly in the filled-to-capacity chapel pews and on the two billion additional folding chairs that are always set up in the adjoining cultural hall to catch the overflow, Jim and I are on the lam.

The church house where we meet for stake conference is on Raymond Avenue here in Fullerton. Just a good stretch of the legs down Raymond to the south is Chapman Avenue. On the corner of Raymond and Chapman's a shopping center. In the shopping center are an Alpha Beta grocery store, a toy store, and a lovely little ice cream and soda shop called Brookdale's.

Brookdale's sells cherry freezes.

Jim and I love cherry freezes.

And guess what. Two hours is plenty of time to make it to Brookdale's and back before the end of the meeting. Heck, we don't even have to hurry. We can walk leisurely and even stop off at Raymond Elementary to practice a few imaginary dunks on the six-foot-tall baskets that are there for the shrimpy grade-schoolers. When we're done with that, there's still plenty of time to hop on up to the shopping center, roam the aisles of Alpha Beta, make fun of the new Duncan Yo-Yos at the toy store, then stroll over to Brookdale's to collect the cherry freezes.

Doing it all again in reverse order, casually sipping our cherry freezes as we go, we'll arrive back at the church right on time. And this timing thing's *really* important. See, you've gotta get back on premises *just* before the meeting lets out. If you're late and the exodus has already started, and you're seen coming in from the parking lot—well, then you're just in trouble, bub. Busted. Sure as baby rabbits, word's gonna get back to your folks and then you'll be grounded for life, or longer, probably.

On the other hand, you can't get back too *soon* either. If the meeting's still underway and some mother's stepped out with a crying baby, or a suspicious parent happens to be roaming the halls in search of an errant youngster and you're spotted . . . well, there's that problem with word of mouth again. Such a nasty, nasty thing. Again, grounded for life, or longer, probably.

So timing's everything.

At this one stake conference, it turns out that Jimbo and I miss the timing just a tad. We get back from our jaunt to Brookdale's just *that much* too early. If we're gonna save ourselves from a fate worse than horrible, we've got one choice.

Hide out for the next ten minutes.

But where to hide.

Hmmm.

Got it. The bathroom. Of course. Perfectly sensible. Stands to reason that no one would go to the bathroom just minutes before the end of the meeting. I mean, if someone's been holding it for nearly two hours already, you can be *pret-tee* darn sure he can stand it for another minute or two. But if even that one more minute's one minute too long and he *does* come to the bathroom . . . well, we can defend our presence in the toilet stalls.

There's just one *leet-tle* tiny problem. From inside the bathroom, we can't see when the congregation's begun to spill out from the meeting and into the open quad area. If we're to mingle properly and invisibly with the exiting mob, some kind of reconnaissance is essential.

Now, there *are* windows in this here bathroom—but there's a problem. See, these particular windows—awning windows, I think they're called—are long, narrow, opaque critters positioned high along the top of the wall. High enough, in fact, that you'd pretty much have to be Paul Bunyan or the Jolly Green Giant to stand flat-footed and have them at eye level. And even if you *could* stand flat-footed and have them at eye level, it'd still be *pret-tee* darn hard to see out because these rascals tilt open only just so far—and at an angle that keeps you from seeing outside unless you're right up there at 'em.

How to get right up there at 'em. Aye, there's the rub.

Just thought I'd throw in a little Shakespeare to class this up a little.

But back to the windows.

OK. Notice the lovely sink. Notice that the lovely sink's just an inch or two away from the lovely tile wall adjacent to it. Notice that the lovely window's at the top of the lovely tile wall adjacent to the lovely sink.

Hmmm.

If I plant my knee on the lovely sink, I should be able to raise myself sufficiently to look out the lovely window.

A lovely idea. And Jim's in agreement.

So I plant my right knee on the edge of the sink and raise myself toward the window as my left knee joins my right knee on the porcelain sink. I reach to grasp the ledge just below the windows, then

I straighten my body so that I can gaze through the partially open window.

This is working great. I can see the quad outside. I can see that no one's leaving the chapel yet. I can see that—

C-r-u-n-c-h. *R-i-i-i-p.* S-q-u-e-a-k. *C-R-A-S-H.*

I'm doing my best to describe the noise, but mere words can't accurately convey the multiplicity of creaking, scratching, crashing, crunching, and scraping sounds you hear when a lovely porcelain sink tears loose from a lovely tiled wall and—amid the bending of pipes and the shattering of tile—heads toward the lovely floor.

With me kneeling on it.

Now, I'm not exactly what you'd call the brightest star in the heavens. Not the sharpest pencil in the box. I may even be one french fry short of a Happy Meal or a lamb chop short of a mixed grill.

Still, I know it's not a good thing when you rip a porcelain sink from the wall in the church bathroom, which is what I just did. Just look at it. Hanging there pathetically.

And here Jim and I stand, also pathetically, wondering what in the world's just happened and what in the world are we gonna do about it.

There's no communication going on between us except for some nonverbal stuff like gaping mouths, wide-opened eyes, and shallow breathing. But as we gather a bit of composure, it comes clear to us that in the midst of this disaster, there's some good news.

There's no water spraying from the pipes. By some good fortune—which must be attributed to the kindness of a simple, random fate because it's hard to imagine that this particular blessing would come from heaven, under the circumstances—the sink's remained connected to the pipes, allowing it to just hang there.

Pathetically, as I said.

So Jim says, "You're dead now, Morris," and I say, "Tell me about it. I think we gotta get out of this place." (Apologies to Eric Burdon and the Animals.) And Jim says, "I think you're right." So we open the door just a crack to see if any type of human critter's close enough to have heard the ruckus. Luckily, the hall's clear in both directions. We know we don't have any choice now but to roll the dice and leave the safe haven of the bathroom even though the meeting hasn't turned out yet. In a moment of unspoken agreement, we instinctively know that we'd rather get in trouble for ditching conference than for destroying church plumbing. So out we go.

With a luck for which we absolutely do not qualify, we make a clean getaway to reunite with our families, having suffered no consequences of our unintended—but nevertheless destructive—stupidity.

Unless you count the next forty or so years of unquenchable guilt as a consequence.

Anyway. Perhaps you can see my point, which is this:

Whether you're talking about being kicked out of Disneyland, ditching stake conference, destroying church plumbing, or having the bejeebers scared out of us while watching *Wait Until Dark*, Jim and I are together.

So we make a date of it. Friday night it is.

Jim swings by my house on his little yellow Yamaha. It's a 55cc step-through trail bike with no fenders and a single, well-worn seat in front of a flat, shelf-like carrier that a guy can strap his books or whatever to. And may I just say that sitting on this rack while riding double is an interesting sensation, to say the least. This bad boy's got three speeds and probably tops out at about 35 or 40 mph. It smokes like a chimney when it's running—only partly because of the oil/gas mixture the two-stroke motor needs—and Jim's gotta replace the piston in it about every month. But let me just say that this is one cool bike that'll make hills a grander bike wouldn't even try. And it's been our accomplice in many a wonderful adventure—with more to come.

It also creates a slight problem for Jim.

See, in California, it's legal to ride a motorcycle solo with just the learner permit that you qualify for at fifteen-and-a-half years, but riding double's a no-no until you get your driver license at sixteen. But Jim ain't a-skeert o' no law, and he don't pay it no never-mind. He rides double *pret-tee* much whenever he feels like it. And for this chronic envelope-pushing, my rebel friend gets so many tickets that when he finally qualifies for his driver license and opens the envelope from the DMV that contains that long-anticipated two-by-three-ish passport to personal independence, he finds a notice that it's been suspended. At the same time it's issued.

If that's not some kind of record, I'd sure like to hear what beats it.

But that's to come later. Right now, Jim's flying solo on his screamin' Yamaha 55, and I join him on my Honda 90 Scrambler that Dad bought recently on an impulse one cloudy summer day in Costa

Mesa. "Let's stop and look," he said—"just *look*," he said. But we did more than just look. To my surprise and absolute delight, Dad actually bought that little puppy. And is it ever sweet. Completely cool. Sport handlebars, silver fuel tank, chrome fenders and exhaust, four-speed transmission and manual clutch, exhaust pipe rising sleekly above the crankcase, sporty candy red frame. When you lose the baffle out of the exhaust pipe, it even *sounds* cool. Illegal, but cool. A deep, guttural roar. Kinda like a Harley Davidson puppy. And I can take it on the road, as I said, with only a learner permit.

Yeah, I know what you're thinking, and you're right. There's nothing fancy about these bikes, and they're pathetically small. Almost too small to even be called motorcycles, by bikers' standards. But they represent our independence, and we love 'em. And on this Friday night, they get us to the Titan movie theater on the Cal State Fullerton campus with no trouble at all.

Park. Pay. Enter. Popcorn. Sit. Watch.

Wow. This is one heck of a movie. Audrey Hepburn's Susie, a woman who very recently lost her vision. Efrem Zimbalist Jr. is Sam, her husband. As Sam gets off an airplane one day, an unfamiliar woman persuades him to hold a doll for her and then disappears, leaving Sam with the doll that'll make him the target for a trio of miscreants who are searching for said doll. Mike (Richard Crenna), Carlino (Jack Westin), and Harry Roat (Alan Arkin) suspect that the doll, containing illegal drugs, is in Susie's apartment. Together, the crooks devise a byzantine scheme to convince Susie that her husband will be in deep, deep trouble unless she can produce the doll. Roat, the leader, is a particularly sadistic and dastardly killer, and his stalking of Susie becomes more and more intense as the story unfolds. We viewers soon find ourselves anxiously wondering how in the world this blind woman will defend herself.

Granted, some things are just a little odd here. Like, it's strange that Susie's apartment lights are always on even though she's blind, and you'd think she'd just go to a neighbor for some help when the trouble starts, and just how in the world does she put on all that makeup so beautifully. It gets your attention, too, that Susie maneuvers just *prettee* darn well for being only recently blinded. And how about all those exotic disguises Roat uses when he meets with Susie even though she doesn't have a clue what he's wearing, anyway.

Hmmm.

OK. Raising these little questions is simply picking nits. And I'm gonna stop it now because the overall effect of this movie's beautiful. It's got suspense and to spare. Even the movie theater environment encourages nervous tension. As the plot thickens and the suspense crescendos into her final confrontation with Roat, Susie's on-screen apartment lights are extinguished. As those lights go out, the theater lighting's gradually lowered, too, until it reaches—as advertised—*the legal limit*. Whatever *that* is. By the time everything's nice and dark, you can only hear limited on-screen dialog and movements and noises behind the total blackness of the screen—with your imagination defining each little noise you hear. The sound volume's turned up and up and up again until you can hear every breath, every sigh, every anguished groan of the heroine as she does whatever she's doing in the darkness.

As the movie builds to climax, Susie douses Roat in flammable photographic developer fluid and then holds him at bay with a lighted match. At threat of lighting him up like the Fourth of July, she insists that he tap the floor with her cane so that she knows where he is. But by the dim light of each burning match, the audience can see Roat moving closer and closer to the refrigerator—while continuing to tap the cane in the same spot (it's a *long* cane)—and the lighted advantage its open door will give him. We see him finally reach the fridge, open its door, and lodge a kitchen towel at the hinge of the door so it can't be closed. Now able to see by refrigerator's light that Susie's made it to the front door but can't open it because he chained it shut, the madman makes his villainous move toward the heroine.

But the tables turn, and Susie manages to stab Roat with a kitchen knife. And as she makes her way carefully away from his body on the floor, we're convinced that Roat's dead. But he isn't. He *isn't*. And then . . . And then . . . And then . . .

The Leap.

From out of the darkness, Roat *springs* forward into view, maniacally grabbing Susie by the ankle. Screaming like a banshee and overacting to beat the band, she breaks free and finds the fridge, trying frantically to close its door and kill the light as the wounded but determined Roat uses the knife to pull himself rhythmically along the floor toward her. Unable to close the refrigerator—remember the towel Mr.

Roat wedged in its door—Susie searches desperately for the fridge's electrical plug. Roat draws closer . . . closer . . . closer . . .

Try Netflix if you wanna know the ending.

But I'll tell you about The Leap.

When Roat lurches from the darkness, accompanied by the soundtrack's deafening, shrieking, orchestral accent, the audience explodes in a communal scream to end all screams. And you get this double dose of fright because after you get the bejeebers scared out of you by The Leap, you get the added value of the terrorized audience's frightful scream that fuels your own scream to another level of intensity. If you're able to keep your eyes open through this terror, there's a bonus. You get to see people jumping clear out of their seats and grabbing serious air as they shriek in horror, with popcorn and soda and all manner of stuff flying into the air. And people aren't only jumping—they're actually injuring themselves and each other. Scratches, sprains, and even broken fingers for some who are holding hands at the crucial moment.

This is terror at its best.

And there's Jim, *w-a-a-a-y* out of his seat and flying high into the air right along with the rest of them. Screaming. Totally, *totally* frightened and pulling off some marvelous, gymnastic, mid-air contortion of the body that, as we'll learn tomorrow, costs him his forty-dollar-filled wallet when it falls out of his pocket at some point between liftoff and landing.

I sure am glad we weren't holding hands.

So. You know how *Jim* handles the fright, but maybe you're wondering to yourself, "What about *Kevin*? How does *Kevin* handle this?"

Well, I'm in total and complete control, not bothered at all by this foolishness. A tower of strength, a pillar of courage, fully able to rise above the childish, embarrassing, cowardly shock rolling like a wave over a gullible audience clearly lacking any semblance of emotional bravery.

At least, that's the way I'll remember it. You just shut up.

When the movie ends, Jim and I make our way out through the chattering, crying, cowering crowd, completely exhausted by the most wonderful terror currently available on the big screen. As we walk through the parking lot toward our screamin' machines, we laugh about the silliness of our—I mean, of the *audience's*—terrific response to The Leap. We chuckle about the mass fright and how could anyone get so scared by a movie and what a bunch of wimps. But the two of *us* are fine. We are. We *are*. Honest. I *swear*.

It just happens to occur to us, though, that we haven't had a sleepover for quite a while. Tonight's as good as any, we guess. Neither of us really *needs* to have company tonight as we sleep . . . alone . . . in the dark. It's just that we haven't had a sleepover for some time, like I said. So why not tonight? Fine. Let's do. We'll go to my house.

Well, first we'll need to swing by Jim's and pick up some stuff. Toothbrush. Underwear. Zit cream. Whatever. Maybe leave a note for the folks.

Now, Jim lives in a beautiful upscale Southern California neighborhood with lovely rolling hills where backyards oughta be, and his house is situated high above street level. After you park at the curb or in the driveway, you have to walk up this stairway-to-heaven kind of deal to get to the front door. All along the winding concrete stairway, there's lovely landscaping, including masses of ferns, bushes, and other pieces of lovely flora, some of which are tall enough and broad enough and thick enough for a guy to hide behind if he wanted to.

Hmmm.

So I tell Jim to go ahead on in and get his stuff, and I'll just wait here. Don't wanna wake up the parents. You know. I'll just wait here. On the sidewalk. By the bikes.

He goes up the stairs and in.

But I don't wait *here*. On the sidewalk. By the bikes.

I climb partway up the stairway and nestle in quietly behind a lovely juniper.

I'll wait *here*.

Inside, Jim gathers his clothes and other goodies into a big ball that he can either sit on or hold between his legs as he rides, leaves a note so the folks don't think he's run away to join the circus, and comes out the big front door. It's dark, for sure. There's no porch light. There's no moon. There's only blackness. Quiet. Still of the night.

And me behind a bush.

As Jimbo cruises past me, I leap with perfect timing from behind the juniper like a Harry Roat Jr. wannabe, reaching menacingly toward my best friend as I scream in the darkness.

Once, when I was a little boy, my father killed a rattlesnake. In later years, he'd probably be jailed for animal cruelty, but it seemed like a smart thing to do at the time. And as long as the thing was dead, anyway, we cut off the rattle, and Kevin had a nifty toy. It made a swell noise.

Wouldn't it be funny, I thought, if I rattled this little toy in Mama's ear while she's napping.

I've had some bad ideas in my life, but this one—did I mention that Mama has a paralyzing fear of all snake critters of any type—stands head and shoulders above the rest in its badness.

In a strange sort of way, I welcomed every swat Daddy delivered to my little seven-year-old butt and even hoped for more, thinking that each swat would in some measure reduce this unspeakable, eclectic feeling—consisting mostly of guilt and regret—and enough swats would make it totally disappear. But I was disappointed. After the spanking was over, the sting of unrelieved pain continued because I could still see in my mind's eye the terror on my mother's face after I rattled that thing in her ear.

Lurching from the darkness toward Jim's a close second to the stupidity of the snake thing.

Mind you, I don't mean to suggest that it isn't *funny* to see him completely unravel at just about every emotional level imaginable.

It is.

And, with all due humility, I claim that there's even a *leet-tle* touch of genius in the way I've helped my best friend relive the lovely, energizing, almost inspirational terror that he enjoyed earlier tonight, courtesy of Alan Arkin and Audrey Hepburn.

But somehow I feel a twinge of regret, less intense than but similar to what I felt when I almost killed Mama. Perhaps I've scarred Jim somehow. Wounded him. Even damaged him, as it were. Maybe he'll swallow and repress a bunch of complex, unresolved feelings of anger and resentment about me having stopped his heart, and, despite the fact that he's my best friend, maybe now he'll hate me in some silent, unspoken way for the rest of our lives.

Nah.

But if there's anything at all to the notions of conditioned response and discriminative stimulus, after tonight, Jim won't be any greater a fan of Audrey Hepburn than I am.

6

I fight a tow truck driver

In rural Mississippi during the fifties and early sixties, there just wasn't that much in the way of fast food. Not in our neck of the woods, anyway.

Yeah, you'd see the odd BBQ drive-in. And yeah, there were the local Dairy Bar in Baldwyn and the Tastee-Freez in Booneville that we passed on the way to church, but we stopped there mostly for soft vanilla ice cream cones or the occasional chocolate-dipped soft vanilla ice cream cone that leaked melting ice cream from beneath the warm chocolate while it was cooling off and setting up, and you were doing your best to eat the chocolate fast enough to not be completely covered in ice cream before you got it eaten but slow enough to enjoy it.

In Baldwyn, you could also find soda fountains at Tom's and Houston's drug stores and even a couple of cafés, like Christine's and Ozele's. But I didn't count these as fast food places.

So, really, just not that much in the way of fast food.

But when we moved away from Baldwyn and arrived in Southern California just as the calendar ran out on 1962, I soon learned that fast food in *this* neck of the woods was an altogether different story.

Along with the high-rise buildings and the palm trees and the beaches and the million other things that up until now I'd only seen in schoolbook pictures, I was just *pret-tee* darn impressed by the hamburger, taco, and chicken joints in this New Land. They were great. They were all over the place—and getting more and more plentiful and diverse as the sixties rolled along.

I discovered local favorites like Mi Ranchito and Buddy's Burgers, and franchise chains like McDonald's, Burger King, Taco Bell, Del Taco, Carl's Jr., and Kentucky Fried Chicken—each special in its own way and something an eleven-year-old kid from small-town Mississippi could never have even *imagined* because up until then I'd never had any idea that such things *exist*.

And The One. The first of the new fast food places I got to eat at because it was just right up the street from our house. The best of 'em all. The most fun of 'em all.

Jack in the Box.

I loved this place. I mean, I *loved* this place. I'd never seen anything like it before.

At Jack's I found these incredible, yummy hamburgers that left the greatest grease spots on the paper they were wrapped in, and they were nice and flat and easy to eat. The only downside—and it was manageable—was that they came with some stuff I'd just as soon not have. Stuff like pickles and onions and tomatoes. But once I tossed those offending ingredients, I was left with a burger that just almost made me cry for joy. I'd never tasted anything like it.

And the french fries. Mmmm. Not those big ol' fat things like you'd get at home, with too much squish and not enough brown. Nope. They were these nice skinny fries that—just like the burgers— soaked the little paper bag they came in with grease. They were long and skinny and a nice combination of crispy and limp. And just salty enough. And boy, did they taste good.

Now, Jack also had these newfangled things called onion rings, but my young palate just wasn't up to those right off. It'd be a few years yet before I'd discover what a treat an onion ring is. For the time being, the greasy, limp-but-crispy fries did just fine, thank you.

You could even get dessert here. Like turnovers. Apple turnovers at first, but soon Jack would also be serving up cherry turnovers. Now, you can call 'em whatever you want. As far as I'm concerned, these turnovers were just little rectangular apple pies in a paper sleeve. I generally like apple pie OK, but these critters had a tad too much filling for my taste and not enough crust, so they weren't my cup of tea . . . at first. As with onion rings, it'd be a few years before my taste buds matured enough to know just how good these crispy little pies really are.

And the soda pop. Oh, boy. In waxy cold cups with plastic covers and fat straws that made drinking soda more fun than is legal in several states. No Dr. Pepper—which is what I was weaned on and if you cut me I'd bleed it—but I could chug down the root beer or the Seven-Up.

If I wasn't in the mood for plain old soda pop, I could order a Big Shake. Vanilla, chocolate, strawberry. I found that Jack had all three flavors and every one was nummy—but I generally leaned toward the chocolate.

As if all this innovative, tasty food weren't enough, I discovered that the whole *ordering* thing at Jack in the Box was just terrific. In fact, for an eleven-year-old from small-town Mississippi who'd never seen anything like it, the ordering was the best part of the Jack in the Box experience. I mean, you didn't just walk up to some guy in a white shirt and white paper hat and say, "I'll have a burger." Instead, you got to drive your car around to this big ol' box with a clown's head springing up from it that actually talked to you and said, "Yes sir, what can I get for you?" and you'd tell the talking head just what you wanted and then in just a few minutes it was all ready for you at the window that you drove to after you'd finished talking with Jack.

This just *had* to be how food's ordered, served, and eaten in heaven.

I don't know how many times over the next few years my family and I will eat at this Jack in the Box, but what I do know is that every single time will be like a journal entry for me. And as for that *first* visit to Jack—well, I'll remember *that* feeling till the day I die.

So it stands to reason that on one fateful night in 1968 when my best friend, Jim, and I are driving around looking for trouble or food, whichever comes first, and decide that food sounds better than trouble at the moment—it is, of course, Jack in the Box that gets our patronage.

As it turns out, we discover that trouble and food aren't necessarily mutually exclusive.

Now, the inside of a car's an interesting place. A private place, typically—or at least *perceived* as private. If you don't believe me, just check out the Beatles wannabes in the cars next to you at stoplights, belting out "Nowhere Man" at the top of their lungs. Or count how many drivers' noses you can spy that have fingers shoved up into them.

Yep. We think of our car as a very private place.

However private it may or may not be, for a teenager, the inside of a car's an exciting and liberating place. When Jim and I find ourselves alone in his parents' blue '66 VW bug or my parents' white '66 Chrysler Newport, we can laugh and talk and cuss and spin yarns— all while piloting an enclosed, private world through unassigned space and unplanned time, creating for ourselves whatever experience we want. Nobody telling us where to go. Nobody telling us who to be or what to say. Listening to music we wanna hear, without a parent complaining that "that thumpety-thump bass is annoying" or "why don't they ever sing about anything but sex and drugs?"

Alone in the car, we are our own. We can be as we choose to be.

We're sixteen years old.

And silly's what we normally choose to be.

So on this one night, we're driving aimlessly around Fullerton and find ourselves headed west on Commonwealth Avenue. Before you can say, "Did you want cheese on that," we find the talking head at Jack in the Box and strike up a conversation with it.

Now, the talking head sounds different from visit to visit. Tonight it's got the lovely voice of a young lady. And that's all it takes to send the two of us sky-high on the silly meter that we've already been inching up all night. The softness of The Voice reminds us that tonight, as always, we're in search of The Perfect Girl who, as we imagine the scenario, hooks up with us spontaneously without needing so much as a proper introduction. In fact, in this particular fantasy, it's likely that we never even bother to imagine a name for this fantastic girl. Doesn't matter, though, because whether or not The Fantasy has a name isn't essential to the creation of another in a long line of memories to be called up and enjoyed from time to time—not only now, but deep in the autumns of our lives too.

At the moment, we're not interested in the autumns of our lives, though. We're interested in the today of our lives. We want The Fantasy to become real. To become The Girl. Flesh and blood. Yep, we wanna *find* her. If not today, then certainly by next Thursday.

But Thursdays just seem to come and go without us having found The Girl.

And even when we *do* find her, we *still* don't find her.

Take that one day, for example. On the beach at Corona Del Mar. Jim and I spend a lot of time, by the way, at Corona and Little

Corona. To be accurate, we actually spend *more* time just up the shore from there at Newport Beach—but Corona's a close second. Once in a while we might even spend a day Huntington Beach, but we don't like it there so much unless we're with family or a large group. See, there are about eight gazillion public fire rings on that beach, and where there are fire rings, there are parents and kids and family cookouts—things that just get in our way when we're looking for The Girl. On the other hand, Corona and Newport cater to the more serious surf crowd, so you find fewer kids kicking up sand, better waves to be body-surfed, and lots of pretty girls baking in the sun. So we mostly go there.

No matter which beach Jim and I are at, we love it. We love the sun and the sand and the surf, and we're pretty much all the time tan and sun-bleached—and that's cool because, after all, we *do* live in Southern California where some connection to the sun and beach and surf's mandatory. To be frank and truthful, though, the *real* reason why we're there so much is that there's no place better to hunt for The Girl than at the beach, where you get such a nice preview of the whole package to further inspire the imagination and motivate the dream.

On this one particular day, Jim and I are cruising up and down the Corona Del Mar shore, checking out what's lying around in the sand and making our way toward a stand of rocks that surrounds a lovely little secluded strip of sand that looks almost like a private beach but isn't. As usual, we're expecting—or at least hoping—that beyond those rocks we'll find what we're always searching in vain for.

And this time we *almost* get it right.

When we reach the rocks that you've gotta conquer to get to the strip of secluded beach, we notice two babes standing at the rocks, each holding a large, cold cup filled with some kind of tasty soda from the snack bar. They're eying a smaller stand of rocks, trying to figure out their next move. See, there's gonna be a little coordination required here for them to negotiate this stand of rocks and position themselves to climb on down to the beach below while holding the cups. [*Discrimination Note:* If you think I'm setting up a blonde joke here, you're gonna be disappointed.]

But then they see us. *Here are two totally outasight dudes,* these young ladies think to themselves, *and if we're clever enough, we can hook up with them,* they think to themselves. *Yep, two groovy dudes,* they're thinking, *and if we act like damsels in distress, they'll save us, and then we can get together and work things out.*

Yes, this *is* what they're thinking to themselves. I'm sure of it. Don't argue and don't contradict.

So the girl in the white bikini says to me—with an inviting smile—"Can you hold these cups for us just a sec?" and I say, "Of course I can," and then I prove it by holding the cups for them just like I said I could. Over the rocks they climb, smiling and playing eye-tag with us the whole time they're climbing, which climbing they *could've* done with the cups in their hands, but then they wouldn't get to meet these dudes. They're sure that once they've broken the ice by asking Jim and me to hold their cups, we'll get the hint and then something will develop and we'll all have a nice day here at Corona and who knows what'll happen after that.

So I hold the cups while the two dream-girls step up onto the rocks and over. When they're safely over, I hand them the cups. They thank us. Then they just stand there, looking at us and smiling. Waiting. Expecting.

In about thirty-six years, there'll be this great movie called *Dumb and Dumber*, written by Peter and Bobby Farrelly and Bennett Yellin and starring Jim Carrey and Jeff Daniels as the totally inept Lloyd Christmas and Harry Dunne. In the final scene, a bus carrying the Hawaiian Tropic Bikini Team stops next to Lloyd and Harry rambling lazily along the highway. Three beautiful girls appear at the opened bus door and explain to these dolts that they—the bikini team— are looking for a couple of guys to oil them down before shows and generally attend to their every need. Then these gorgeous creatures stand there, looking at the guys and smiling. Waiting. Expecting. But, oblivious to the heaven-sent opportunity, Lloyd and Harry glee-fully inform the bikini-clad beauties that they're in luck because there happens to be a town just two miles *that* way, where they'll be able to find someone to help them. Surprised that the two men haven't jumped at a once-in-a-lifetime opportunity, the beauties shrug their shoulders, withdraw into the bus, and drive on, leaving Lloyd and Harry to walk an empty highway, wondering why life's luck always seems to pass them by.

Now, I can't prove it, but I'm just absolutely convinced that the Farrelly brothers and Mr. Yellin are standing somewhere near enough to see me hand the cups back to those bikini-clad girls, tell them they're welcome, ignore their smiles and their expectant stares, and walk right away from what Jim and I've been searching for ever since the day we discovered that people with names like Jane and Mary are wonderfully different from people with names like Tom and Sam—with Jim punching me on the arm as we walk and calling me stupid or some other sadly accurate name.

And forty years from now, Jim will *still* be punching me on the arm and calling me stupid or some other sadly accurate name whenever the memory comes to mind.

But that's forty years from now. Today, hope springs eternal and I'm undaunted by the failure.

So. Here we are at Jack in the Box on this California summer night, facing another possibility of landing The Girl. It's true that we don't yet know what the face on the other end of the sexy voice flowing so beautifully from the talking head looks like, but we're brave. We're confident. We know for sure it's a girl on the other end of that voice and that's all we really need to know right now.

When The Voice says, "How can I help you?" we come back with some wonderfully funny double entendre that makes The Voice laugh even though it'll be forgotten through the years, and then we follow it up with our order.

"We'll have a couple of Jumbo Jacks," I say.

"Without onions," Jim says. Jim never eats onions.

"A couple of large fries," I say.

"Without onions," Jim says.

We laugh. The Voice laughs.

"A couple of cherry turnovers," I say.

"Without onions," Jim says.

We laugh. The Voice laughs.

"And a couple of chocolate shakes," I say. Momentarily focused on pushing radio buttons, trying to find a station that's playing the Lemon Pipers singing "Green Tambourine"—which pretty much *always* plays on the radio when Jim and I are in the car together—Jim's silent.

"Did you want onions in those shakes?" The Voice asks. Just to be sure, I guess.

A little surprised by the question but understanding The Voice's obvious agenda to give us every opportunity to be even more impressively funny, Jim and I look knowingly at each other, relish the opportunity The Voice is giving us, and say, "Yeah, we'll have onions in those shakes."

We laugh. The Voice laughs.

"Will that be all?" The Voice asks, and we say, "Yep, that's it," and as pretty and friendly and sexy as you please, The Voice says, "Just drive on up to the window, please."

We're gripped by anticipation.

At the window, we see The Voice personified—and, oh my gosh, this just isn't bad. Not bad at all. In fact, you could make a case for gorgeous and persuade a jury in your favor, probably. And it looks like she's thinking the same about us. She doesn't stay at the window to talk with us, true. Obviously, this would be her first choice, but heck, she's got work to do in there. But she smiled at us when we pulled up to the window, and now we see her sneaking smiling glances back at us while she's helping prepare our order. We even see her whisper something to another girl and a guy working in there with her, and we figure she's telling them about how she's fallen in love with these two clever and handsome boys as she prepares our shakes and then—grinning broadly—snaps the plastic covers securely on the cups.

Meanwhile, Jim's actually found "Green Tambourine" on the radio, and while we wait for our order, we enjoy our favorite song on 93 KHJ.

Now, in this neck of the woods, you just *gotta* listen to 93 KHJ with its totally boss DJs. Charlie Tuna, Humble Harve, Machine Gun Kelly, Sam Riddle, Robert W. Morgan, and—of course—The Real Don Steele with his signature "Tina Delgado is alive, alive!" If you're a teenager, you just plain don't listen to other stations—or if you do, you'd better not mention it to anyone. To be fair, though, KFWB Channel 98 was also OK to listen to—with the likes of Jack Hayes, Wink Martindale, Gene Weed, Don MacKinnon, and B. Mitchell Reed—until recently. I say "until recently" because KFWB just changed its format from Top 40 to all-news in March and adopted the slogan, "You give us twenty-two minutes, we'll give you the world." Hooey. What's the point of listening to news? *News.* I mean, *really.* Of course, KRLA—The Big Eleven-Ten—plays Top 40 tunes too and has a pretty cool cast of characters including Dave Hull, Dick Biondi, Casey Kasem, and Bob Eubanks. There's also KWIZ, but that's an oldies station. So for the best Top 40 format of all time, Boss Radio 93 KHJ's the *only* station to tune in to.

But I digress.

The Voice returns to the window and hands me a lovely bag filled with Jumbo Jacks, fries, and turnovers. I pass the bag to Jim and then return to the window to receive the two chocolate shakes and two fat straws. Failing to settle on anything more to say that's clever enough to persuade this young lady out from behind that sliding glass window and into the night with two dudes in a Chrysler, I pay for the goodies and then roll slowly forward toward Commonwealth and the continuation of our night's adventure, having failed once again to seal the deal.

Geez.

Oh, well. Eternal's eternal and, as I said before, that's how hope springs.

In the meantime, I've got this yummy chocolate Big Shake in my hand, so I use my knee to steer the car for a sec—I can't for the life of me understand why insurance rates for teenagers are so high—while I stick the fat shake straw through the plastic lid and into the creamy, ice-cold shake and *s-s-s-l-u-r-r-p* my first taste of chocolatey goodness through the straw.

Hack. Yuk. Cough. Hack. Ick.

What the . . .

I don't remember Jack's chocolate Big Shakes having chunks in them.

But this one does, in fact, have chunks in it.

What in the world's *that* all about.

I tell Jim, "Hey there's chunks of something in this shake," and then I pull the car over to a parking space so I don't have to worry about taking out a parked car or creaming some unsuspecting pedestrian while I focus on popping the plastic lid off the cup to check out what these lovely chunks might be. In just a moment I've got it figured out.

Onions.

Jim checks his shake. Onions in his too.

Hmmm.

Now *this* is funny. The Voice has a really good sense of humor. One to rival ours, even. She asks if we want onions in those shakes and we say, "Yeah, let's have onions in those shakes," so by darn she *puts* onions in those shakes.

We laugh out loud. This is really funny.

What's more, when we go back inside to return these onion shakes and get our *real* shakes, we'll have another chance to talk to The Voice and, who knows, maybe even think of the right thing to say this time to get her to give it all up and escape with us.

Park the car. Pop the car doors open. Cross over a couple of empty parking spots and on through the front door. Up to the counter, catch the eye of The Voice who's fiddling with cups and lids, hold up the shakes, smile, and here she comes.

"Can I help you?" she asks. We laugh, and Jim says, "That was a good one. You really got us with that one."

"Yeah," she says. Just yeah. No smile.

We keep smiling, though, and I say, "Yeah, that's a really good one, but can we have our shakes now? You know, the ones without the onions."

"You ordered onions in the shakes, so you got onions in the shakes," the girl says.

"'Scuse me?"

She repeats flatly, "You ordered onions in the shakes so you *got* onions in the shakes."

Wow.

Our first revelation that sometimes a pretty face can be attached to a not-so-pretty girl.

It takes a second or two for this thing to really sink in, and Jim and I have to glance back and forth at each other a couple of times, trying to read each other's response. Trying to understand what we've got here. Now suddenly we get it. We may be slow, but we're eventual. It's clear to us now that this chick's not kidding. Nope, not kidding at all. And what fragment of hope we were holding out that she'd give it all up and escape with us tonight has now been officially dashed. Worse than that, there'll be no edible shakes for the guys tonight.

Unless we wanna cough up another forty cents each.

Once, when I was about twelve or so, my dad was in an orange tree in our backyard, and I was on the ground catching oranges as he picked them and threw them down to me. It was a Valencia tree, so the oranges weren't very good to eat, but they sure made good juice. Who knows now what it was, but Dad did something or said something or teased me or somehow aggravated me, and I lost my temper and went right up that tree to get him. Now, Dad had used a ladder to get to the top of the tree, but I didn't need no stinkin' ladder. I flew up the branches without, I guess, even touching one of them. There was some new and undiscovered law of physics involved here, I'm sure. Just don't ask me what I was planning to do once I got up to him because I was about two-foot-nothin' and Dad's probably the world's toughest living human being who on his worst day could whip any selected platoon of special forces operatives without working up so much as a light sweat. So it boggles the mind to imagine what I could possibly have been thinking when I flew up that tree, headed for him.

What I was *not* thinking is more the truth of it—and the good news for me is that I stopped midway up the tree before I got to Dad, thus enabling me to live to see puberty.

Understated, when I got mad in my younger days, I didn't always use what you'd call good judgment.

And apparently nothing's changed in the four years since I flew up the orange tree.

In the moment when it occurs to me what's really happening here at this Jack in the Box counter, facing this hard-hearted girl-type-thing that will never—and I mean *never*—be invited into any fantasy of mine *ever* again, I instinctively know that the time for talk's passed. It's now time that—to quote a Tim Matheson line from that frat house comedy *Animal House* that I'll enjoy a few years from now—some really futile and stupid gesture be done on somebody's part. Having no problem being that someone, I turn from the counter. And as I take my first step toward the exit, I raise the onion-laced milkshake high above my head—but slightly to the right so I don't douse myself—and pour it slowly to the floor as I walk.

If they'd make their shakes a little thicker, there wouldn't be so much lovely splatter.

But they don't, so there is. And as the chilly, chunky, chocolatey concoction lands on the floor and fountains up in a magnificent volca-nic-eruption-of-a-splash that covers a great deal of the floor and even some of the adjacent wall, a hush falls over the people dining inside this lovely establishment. Like they've never seen a sixteen-year-old pour a chocolate shake onto the floor of a Jack in the Box restaurant before.

But as quickly as it settles over the onlookers, the hush is shattered by a blood-chilling shriek.

"Hey!"

A sound unlike anything I've heard before. A gruff, guttural, vibrating, echo of a sound with the timbre of a bull's bellow and the resonance of a lion's roar, held together by a near-tangible mixture of anger and threat.

It freezes me in my tracks.

Even though I'm afraid to, I know I need to look over and see what person or creature or thing made this noise. But it's a ubiquitous noise that seems to echo at once from every quarter of the restaurant, so I don't really know which direction to look, even if I could get my head and my eyes to move so that I *could* look.

I'm not sure what's happening to Jim at the moment because I'm only just this side of unconscious, and what tiny part of my psyche's still functional is *pret-tee* darn occupied with fear. So for all I know, Jimbo could be behind the counter making out with the girl dipping the fries in the hot grease—but I kinda doubt it. It's more likely that he's found a seat somewhere to blend safely into the background, dissociated from the death scene that's about to play out.

"Hey! Kid!"

And there goes the final piece of functional psyche.

Using the last vestiges of residual brainstem function, I manage to move my head to the left only because the stroke I just had makes it impossible for me to turn it to the right—which is a lucky coincidence, I guess, because when I turn to the left and focus my sweat-and-tear-filled eyes, I see him.

I see *it*, to be more accurate.

If I were writing a story about the meanest-looking man that could ever be, and if I needed a picture to illustrate him, I'd draw a man about six-and-a-half feet tall with a neck so thick you can't tell where head ends and shoulders begin. He'd be nearly bald, with a three-day stubble of beard, and his face would be square, wrinkled, and weathered—and generally look like it's never smiled for fear of revealing the several gaps left by lost or prematurely removed teeth. And what teeth remain would be kinda yellow and brown and sharp and pointy and would draw your attention away from the drool trickling down his chin. His face would be almost perfectly asymmetric, with one eye, just a tiny slit of a thing, almost entirely closed, and the other, a wide-open, gaping, colorless, grey hole. He'd be wearing a shirt that fits tightly over rippling chest muscles and bulging biceps, with sleeves rolled up clear to the shoulders, so tight that they look to split at the seams at any moment—and buttoned only halfway up a chest that's so hairy it would put James Bond to shame. In the shirt pocket, you'd see a pack of unfiltered cigarettes—Camels, let's say—and over the pocket would be a patch that reads "RJ Brody Towing." On his left biceps would be a lovely tattoo that says, oh . . . how about, "Ride Free or Die." His grey Dickey work pants would stop short of the tops of scuffed and dingy steel-toed work boots that have seen better days, showing a generous hint of yellowing white socks between boots and pants. I'd throw in some dirt and smudges on his face and slip some grime and oil beneath his yellowing, broken fingernails. And if it were possible for a drawing to stink, this one would.

Or I could just take a picture of the Thing stamping toward me and call it good.

Now, if I could move my feet, I would, but I can't, so I don't. Instead, I just stand like I'm nailed to the tile floor and watch Mr. Brody's employee of the month come closer and closer to me, picking up speed as he thumps one steel-toed boot in front of the other. He's manifesting clear purpose on his furrowed and menacing brow—and I'm thinking that this purpose is gonna cost my folks a lot, what with the expert facial reconstruction that'll be required to return me to my normal handsome self and then for general follow-up medical care and possibly rehabilitation.

I wish Jim were a little tougher so he could save me. For that matter, I wish I could *find* Jim.

But it doesn't matter, anyway, because the Thing's in front of me now and has me by the arm, and I'm *pret-tee* darn sure arms aren't supposed to remain for any length of time at the angle mine's just discovered. Fortunately, I'm too scared to feel any pain. For the moment, anyway.

"Whut do ya thank yore a-doin', ya little punk?" the critter says to me as he lifts my fear-stiffened body about, oh, say, fifteen or so feet above the floor, and I don't say anything in the way of protest because full paralysis of the tongue's a really strange feeling and makes it hard to talk. So I just listen to the demon howl at me even though by now my hearing's pretty much gone too and I'm only able to make out certain words like "beat" and "kill" and "notchere, ya don't" and "why I oughta" and "get a mop" and "ever' speck of it."

In a surprisingly lucid micro-moment, the thought ricochets across my mind that if this guy ever loses his current excellent employment that probably has a wonderful career path and ample opportunity for advancement, he could be a really good security guard at Disneyland.

But before I can offer any kind of career suggestion, the Thing slams me back down onto the floor. I'm glad to be back to earth even though my buckling knees make it hard for me to stay upright. Still hearing what seem to be unrelated words splattering all about me, I slowly begin to understand that this guy's actually asking me a question and may even be expecting some kind of answer to that question, which is—paraphrasing, of course—"Young man, why did you so rudely empty the contents of that large cold cup onto the floor of this fine establishment wherein work several individuals with whom I feel a particularly close kinship almost rivaling actual familial ties?"

Or something like that.

Well, now, let me just quickly consider some optional responses, select and organize one into some kind of clear and lucid phrasing, and answer this gentleman's inquiry.

"Shake. Onions. She put."

OK, so I need a little more considering and maybe the return of another ounce or two of psyche.

"Wh-u-u-u-t?" Oh, dear. Now I've confused him, I fear. I'd better try to clarify.

"Put. Onions. Shake. She did."

I, for one, think it was a little better that time.

"Boy," he says, "I ain't got the tiniest notion 'bout what yore a-sayin' tuh me, but whut I do know is yore jes' about to do sum serious moppin' 'cause these here's friends o' mine and you ain't a-leavin' till ever' speck of this here stuff's mopped clean up."

I'm convinced that what we have here, to quote Strother Martin's warden character in the movie *Cool Hand Luke*, is failure to communicate—so I ain't givin' up yet. I figure if only I can explain this all a little more clearly to Sasquatch, then he'll understand just why I did what I did and maybe then he'll go over there and grab Miss Personified Voice like he did me and flop her around like a rag doll like he did me. So I take one last crack at it.

"Shakes. She put onions. Shakes."

I don't care what you say. Under the circumstances, this is some fine oration.

But it doesn't help.

Because already standing in front of me is the girl who got me into this mess, holding a lovely mop in one hand and pulling a wheeled bucket full of grey water along with the other. She gives me this look that's half a gritted-teeth smile and half a sticking-her-tongue-out-at-me, and if you think I was mad before I saw that look, you should try to get your head around what I'm feeling now that I've seen it.

Now, if I had at least half a brain and knew now what I'll know forty or so years from now, I'd let Quasimodo take a poke at me and then I'd pretty much own Mr. Brody's towing service and the pretty boys at San Quentin would have a new shower buddy. But I'm just not that smart, and there's no way I can know now what I'll know in forty years, so I swallow back the anger and embarrassment the best I can, take the mop that Miss Kiss-a-Pig shoved in my face, and—with no risk of being described as energetic—begin to move the mop around, slowly smearing the icky mess back and forth and around on the floor.

Jim's visible at the counter now and seems to be encouraging me.

Godzilla stands over me for a moment or two to make sure my mop's moving, then serenades me once again with that singularly spectacular speech that's so incredibly lyrical and downright poetic that it nearly has me hypnotized.

"I'm a-leavin' now," he says, "but you jes' better keep on a-moppin' and I better not hear no smart remarks nur see no fingers in th' air nur nothin' like 'at when I leave or I'm a-comin' back here, and I guaran-dang-tee yore a-gonna be sorry I did when I do."

Well, I keep mopping—more like *pretend* to keep mopping—and watch the Beast push through the door and head for his truck. As he walks among the parked cars, I see him look back over his shoulder every step or two till he opens the truck door. Not seeing fingers or hearing any smart remarks from us, I guess he figures he's properly tamed the sixteen-year-olds. He bravely steps up into his tow truck, fires 'er up, and fades heroically into history.

For the next forty years, I'll often think of this gentle, loving man and hope life turned out just perfectly for him.

But he's gone now, and I'm finished with this indentured servitude. One last swirling push of the mop across the floor and against the wall smears the chocolatey mess sweetly about before I throw the mop handle to the floor. I look past the counter to find the girl who could've had the boys of her dreams tonight but instead fell from grace. Certain that I have her eye, I sing a four-letter serenade to explain to her just how much fun I hope she and Larry and Moe have while they're mopping up the rest of this mess tonight 'cause I ain't *about* to finish it. Then Jim and I swash through the door and head toward the Chrysler.

So tonight—once again—we didn't find The Girl. Well, we actually did find another *candidate*, only to see her snatched from our eager hands by the perplexing winds of adolescent fate. And we did get to know a lovely tow truck driver, so we've got that going for us. We also learned that we don't, in fact, prefer onion in our shakes, and determine never to order it again. All in all, I guess it's been a fulfilling night for Jim and me, rich in lessons about girls and shakes and onions and tow truck drivers that should certainly pay strong dividends in years to come.

But what I'll treasure most for the next however-many years is the knowledge that I didn't actually finish mopping the floor as instructed, and when he was out of earshot, I called the guy a dirty name.

Who's your daddy.

7

I become a Flat Tortilla

In 1968, I suppose just about every young man you run into would give the same answer if asked whether he'd like to play in a rock 'n roll band.

You betcha.

That's what every one of 'em would say.

And every single one would feel qualified to do it, too, even if all he can do is play three key-of-G guitar chords or knock out Chopsticks on the piano or blow trumpet or trombone or flute in junior high band. See, there's this *You-Too-Can-Be-in-a-Group* virus floating around, and it's reached epidemic proportions right now among young people, great numbers of whom are at this very moment planning—and fully expecting—to be the sound behind the next number-forty-with-a-bullet record debuting on 93 KHJ Boss Radio.

And why not? I mean, there's plenty of evidence around to support the notion that any four or five guys with a musical itch can get into the business of rock 'n roll simply by calling a quick meeting in somebody's garage, grabbing a couple of borrowed guitars and some kind of amp to plug them into, deciding who'll play what, and then recording a mega-hit on the first take.

Without *talent* necessarily entering into it.

Still, some aspiring musicians have actively pursued the dream and put together cover groups that make a *pret-tee* darn good showing, at least on the local scene. After all, there are dances around here. Oh, yeah. There *are* dances.

Take high schools, for example. If yours isn't hosting some kind of dance tonight, just try the next school down the road. Homecoming, stag, prom, girl's choice, sock-hop, post-game victory, post-game pity, Christmas, Valentine's, New Year's. Whatever. Some high school within driving distance has *gotta* be having a dance this weekend. I mean, here in our neck of the Southern California woods, you can't swing a dead cat without hitting a weekend dance *some*where.

And that's just schools. Other folks sponsor dances too. For example, even the LDS Church—I remind you that I'm a Mormon and know whereof I speak in this matter—rocks out pretty good. That's for sure.

See, ever since Church-founder Joseph Smith organized the Young Gentlemen's and Young Ladies' Relief Society way back in 1843, the LDS Church has maintained a strong tradition of providing activities for its youth—activities that are contemporary but nevertheless in line with tenets of the faith.

One such activity for youth these days is a stake dance. No, you don't throw filet mignon on the floor and boogie around it. It's a dance that's attended by young LDS men and women between fourteen and eighteen years, called a *stake* dance because it's hosted and organized by a *stake*, or group of several local LDS wards, or congregations. But there's no discrimination here. No-siree, Bob. Young LDS people from other nearby stakes are welcome to attend. The more, the merrier. Youth from the non-LDS community are welcome too, as long as they're not long-haired hippie freaks and are willing to abide by the conservative dress and behavior standards expected of participants, which basically means they'll agree to stay at least ostensibly sober and won't try to make out with my girlfriend when I'm not looking. And many non-LDS youngsters do attend, either under their own social power or as a guest of LDS friends.

The upshot of all this is that there are lots and lots of us at stake dances—often up into the triple digits, in fact. Depending, of course, on *who's playing* at the dance.

See, at a Southern California stake dance in '68, you'll find no record players. No radios. No DJs spinning vinyl, dispensing witty repartee, and taking requests. No canned music of any kind. Nope, not here.

What you'll find instead's a real live group playing Top 40 hits.

Yep, real live people with genuine musical instruments, playing songs for you to dance to—in fact, playing the very songs that you heard on your car radio as you were driving to the dance. Oh, sure, some older stuff might occasionally get thrown in. I mean, you may hear a hit or two from last year or the year before. Or maybe even from back in '65. Heck, if it's got the collective talent to do it, a really ambitious group might go so far as to give you a lively rendition of "Johnny B. Goode" or some other rock-out oldie from the archives. But mostly you're gonna be dancing to current Top 40 stuff at a stake dance. Don't expect to step into any kind of time machine here.

And, generally speaking, the groups are pretty cookie-cutter when it comes to personnel.

First, you've got the lead guitar. If you've gotta bet on who's the *serious* musician in the group, bet on this guy. See, lead's gotta do a little more with his fingers than just slide barre chords up and down the guitar's neck. He's gotta nail those eighth and sixteenth and maybe the odd thirty-second notes, and maybe even bend a string or two in the occasional solo riff that's mandatory for a good lead. Which means he probably even reads music. Likes to move around on stage too. Flashy. Passionate.

Then you've got your rhythm guitar. If he isn't also the lead singer, the rhythm guitar's usually pretty stoic. Just lays down the chords in a pretty businesslike way. If the drummer weren't there, this guy could set the tempo. Rhythm guitar's the bit most of us wannabes figure *we* could play if given the chance—and sometimes we might even boast to the girls we're with that we're just gonna hop up on stage, grab the instruments, and knock out a number or two while the band's on a break.

See, to be cool, the band's gotta abandon instruments every half hour or so and disappear offstage somewhere for a break. Just before they leave the stage, the lead shoves the mic about halfway down his throat and kinda speaks-slash-moans an announcement that they'll be right back in a minute or two and that we shouldn't go anywhere. Or something like that. In any case, whatever he says is gonna make the girls swoon a little bit. Bet on it.

Now, who knows what these rascally musicians are up to while they're out of sight during these breaks. Hittin' the head, checking out the female possibilities, doing crossword puzzles, writing memoirs, back-checking an algorithm for the solution of some problem to be expressed as a finite sequence of instructions, knockin' back a brewski, or plotting the takeover of the free world. No one really knows. It's one of the great unexplained mysteries of our time.

But I digress.

Getting back to the makeup of the group, you've got the bass guitar. The guy that handles this duty's often even less animated than the rhythm guitar. He just *thump-thump-thumps* out the bottom end without making any serious to-do about it. This cat may not be the best-looking of the bunch, but it doesn't much matter because he mostly just hides out near the drums and lets the music happen. No big deal.

And the drummer. Oh, yeah. The drummer. This guy's usually a freak. Talks hip, man. Longest hair, usually. Scrungiest-looking too. If anybody in the group does drugs, it's probably this guy. Or if he doesn't actually *do* drugs, he *looks* like he does. This guy's hard to ignore. He likes to take the occasional solo and just paradiddle and rimshot away till he gets all sweaty and out-of-breath. Boy, do the girls love it. Most of the time if a guy gets sweaty and tries to cozy up to a girl, he's gonna hear "get away from me, you sweaty slob." But if you're the drummer in a band, your sweat's completely acceptable to females. Sexy, even. It's just not fair.

Can't forget the lead singer, of course. This might be one of the guitar players, but it could be someone who just fronts the group and doesn't play any instrument, except maybe a tambourine some-times, just to look like he knows something about music. If one of the guitar players doubles as lead singer, it'll probably be the rhythm because it's easier to sing and play chords than to sing and play lead. Although you see it once in a while, it's least likely that the drummer would sing lead because that's kinda like chewing bubble gum and walking at the same time. But whether the singer's one of the four instruments or a fifth front-man, he's always the one the chicks dig. And he knows it.

I certainly don't mean to imply that every single group on the local scene's made up of these four instruments and no other. Nope, that's just not true. You'll run into groups that use keyboards, har-monicas, brass—even woodwinds. Yep, you can find 'em. But pretty much every group with an ounce of self-respect avoids the accordion.

And the ones who *fail* to avoid the accordion usually pay a *pret-tee* steep social price and have a short shelf-life.

Now, if you've been paying attention, perhaps you'll have surmised that there are enough local garage bands—whatever their makeup— to go around. Enough, anyway, to guarantee that every LDS stake dance, no matter when or where it's held, has a live band.

Some of which are crummy.

Some of which are OK.

Some of which are good.

And one of which is *really* good.

The Emperors.

Whenever Steve Watts and the boys play at a local Southern California LDS stake dance, you can barely find enough space on the dance floor to move your feet, let alone pull off any fancy spins or gyrations. And you can just forget about any splits or cartwheels.

People know the Emperors. Great rep. This band plays not only at local stake dances but also at clubs like Isadore's, Big Daddy's, St. George and the Dragon, and The Rain Tree. What's more, you can hear the band on wax too. It cut one 45—*Great Balls of Fire* b/w *The Breeze and I*—as Steve and The Emperors. As The Emperors, the band will record *Blue Day* b/w *Laughin Linda* and one other 45 on the Wickwire label, and *I Want My Woman* b/w *And Then* on the Sabra label. One more 45—*You Make Me Feel So Good* b/w *Love Pill*—will be released on the Two + Two label. Seven or eight years from now and with slightly different personnel, the band will release an LP album on the Private Stock label that'll produce *Dreamer* as a single, as well as *Woman*, *Time That It Takes*, and *I'm Alive*.

Despite its relative success, The Emperors will never really make it to The Show, so to speak. In retrospect, one of the band members will attribute this limited success to a label promotion failure—nice big production budget but skimpy marketing. Still, the group will survive in various forms and continue making music into the next millennium as Emperor.

Unlike The Emperors, though, a lot of garage—or pseudo-garage—bands across the country have actually made it to the Big Time. A ton of 'em, in fact. I mean, it's the sixties, you know. If it were possible to ferret out the name of every single one and if I weren't imposing on myself a page limit to this tale, I'd list them all. But it's not, and I am, so I can't, so I won't. I can give you just a taste, though, of what's happening out there right now.

Castaways, Gentrys, Count Five, Swingin' Medallions, Standells, Every Mother's Son, Them, Vanilla Fudge, Human Beinz, Cyrkle, Troggs.

Shadows of Knight, John Fred and His Playboy Band, Lemon Pipers, People!, Electric Prunes, Status Quo, Parade, Sopwith Camel, Outsiders, Question Mark and The Mysterians.

American Breed, Strawberry Alarm Clock, Blues Magoos, Yellow Balloon, Rose Garden, Blue Cheer, Four Jacks and a Jill, Kingsmen, Five Americans.

Sunrays, Fortunes, Jay and The Techniques, New Colony Six, Unit 4 + 2, Sam the Sham and The Pharoahs, Foundations, Beau Brummels, Trade Winds.

Don't get me wrong. I absolutely love every single one of these groups, and they actually do have talent. Well . . . *most* do, anyway. And every one of 'em, with or without talent, has a hit getting air play on the radio at the moment or has had one—with *one* being the operative word here. The future will remember most of these bands as One-Hit Wonders—even the ones that have released or will yet release multiple singles and albums. Because, after all's said and done and the Swingin' Sixties takes its assigned place in history, these bands will be remembered for one big ol' smash hit and pretty much nothing else.

Let me be clear here. Not every group that convened its first meeting in somebody's garage will turn out to be only a One-Hit Wonder. Nope, not by a long shot. I can name a bunch of bands that probably started out just like the One-Hit Wonders did but had a bit more talent that allowed them to move beyond the one hit. In some cases, *w-a-a-a-y* beyond the one hit.

Check it out. On the more successful end of things, you've got Buckinghams, Box Tops, Lovin' Spoonful, and Turtles. You've got Byrds, Association, Spanky and Our Gang, and Classics IV. Animals, Doors, Yardbirds, Kinks, and Buffalo Springfield. Grass Roots. Jefferson Airplane. Steppenwolf. Tommy James and The Shondells. Creedence Clearwater Revival. Gary Lewis and The Playboys. Paul Revere and The Raiders.

Paul Revere and The Raiders. Hmmm. Brings to mind an interesting moment back in early '66.

See, KRLA 1110 AM radio—The Big Eleven-Ten—had a disc jockey named Dick Biondi. Mr. Biondi was a pretty big deal as far as DJs go. He came to LA by way of New York and Chicago, where he was credited for being the first US DJ to spin a Beatles record when he played *Love Me Do* in February 1963 at Chicago's WSL 890 AM. Arriving in LA, Mr. Biondi worked at KRLA from 1963 to 1967, minus a little stint during 1964–65 when he hosted a nationally syndicated show called *Dick Biondi's Young America*.

While he was spinning platters at KRLA, the Wild I-Tralian and self-proclaimed World's Skinniest DJ also fronted a portable music show called *The Dick Biondi Road Show*. He'd pick up a couple of acts with current Top 40 hits—like Dick and DeeDee, Jan and Dean, Paul Revere and The Raiders, and the like—and haul 'em around to high schools where excitable, screaming, teenyboppers would fawn over 'em and paw at 'em and scream and yell and generally cause a scene. The bunch staged a pretty cool—if relatively unpolished—show and promoted The Big Eleven-Ten *pret-tee* darn well.

Well enough, anyway, to help KRLA 1110 nudge KFWB Channel 98 out of LA's number one spot—but not well enough to keep 93 KHJ Boss Radio from turning around and doing the same to KRLA.

I guess we Troy Warriors were just about as excited as Casper at the resurrection when our school newspaper, *The Troy Oracle*, reported that Mr. Biondi's show would be coming to spend a little time with us in our glorious gym. At the time of the report, we didn't know which artists would be tagging along with him, but it didn't really matter, anyway—we just thought how cool it would be to have the *Road Show* at an assembly in our house in March.

So much the better when we learned that Paul Revere and The Raiders would be the main attraction in Mr. Biondi's show. *Paul Revere and The Raiders*. Nice. I mean, it's true that this group's music's always been pretty pop, pretty tame—and probably their minuteman outfits didn't help them *serious up* their image, either. But these guys were really high-profile in 1966 because they had a lot of hit records and were regulars on Dick Clark's *Where the Action Is* on ABC. Pop or not, the Raiders had enough beat in their music and kick in their step to cut a pretty broad demographic. If it's true that not everybody loved The Raiders, it's equally true that nobody didn't like them at least a little.

Well, until they bumped up against Troy High's dress and deportment standards, that is.

The sixties is an interesting time—on several levels, a self-contradiction. Take dress standards for example.

On the one hand, you've got this counter-culture thing going on that requires pathetically little of its followers in the way of dress, appearance, or behavior. Pretty much anything and everything that regresses toward the mean's OK. Long, shaggy hair. Facial hair as you will. Grubby, distressed clothing that may or may not cover all the essentials. Sandals, moccasins, flip-flops, boots, tattered tennis shoes, or no shoes at all. Laid back, man. Cool. Groovy.

At the same time—in Orange County high schools, anyway—you've got just about the strictest and most conservative dress standards this side of the Middle Ages and the chastity belt.

For example, if you're a young lady wearing a dress at Troy High, you've gotta be very careful of its length. And a dress or skirt it must be, because pants aren't allowed except on field day or when there's some kind of special assembly or dance or something like that. [*Believe-It-Or-Not Note:* It's such a foregone conclusion that young ladies won't wear pants to school that the written dress code in the 1968 *Warrior Handbook* doesn't even *mention* pants in connection to the girls, one way or the other.] Anyway, if the principal or hall monitor spies your bare knees and suspects that the hemline may be just *that much* too far up your leg, you'll find yourself kneeling right there in front of heaven and everybody to see if the hemline reaches the floor. If it touches, you'll probably get off with a preliminary *you'd-better-watch-it-because-you're-just-about-to-have-a-problem-young-lady.* But if it doesn't touch, forget about it. You're outta there. On your way home with a note from the office explaining that you've been excused from school to go home and change clothes because your dress is an embarrassment to civilized society and may actually precipitate its downfall and if you return to school without having changed out of said dress you'll be sorry with a capital S, hon.

You may not need to actually go home, though, if you're wearing a *skirt* instead of a *dress* and have figured out that a skirt can be folded and tucked at the top to make it shorter at the bottom. This allows you to keep your skirt short and be totally cool as long as no teacher calls you out on it. And if you *do* get caught . . . well, then you just slip around the corner, drop the skirt a fold or two, and then head on down to Mr. Koch's biology class and the pithed frog that awaits your scalpel.

Short really isn't an issue for guys. In fact, if the legs of your Levi's—or even the twenty-five-bucks-a-pop Corbin or A-One Taper slacks, for that matter—hover about six inches above your shoes, well . . . that's beyond acceptable. It's totally boss. As for other appropriate attire for boys . . . well, you can wear either a casual buttoned shirt or a T-shirt—but whichever you opt for, it'd better be tucked into your pants, mister. If it's not, then that's just sloppy. And we can't have sloppy around here, can we? Unless you're in PE, of course, where slightly more flexibility's allowed. But if we talk about PE, then a jock strap's gotta enter into the conversation, and we don't want that.

Perhaps you can imagine, then, the mental conflict that weighs on teenagers from day to day. Take pity on us. It's just not all that easy. I mean, most of us kinda fall into the middle-of-the-road category of rebellious, but we've got these high-profile role-model-wannabes yelling at us to "loosen up and do your thing, man," and at the same time we've got teachers in cotton dresses and sharkskin suits and skinny ties hollering on us to "watch your step and your hemlines and your shirt tails and don't be lookin' like some kind of weirdo, commie, long-haired, hippie freak, for cryin' out loud."

Such was the backdrop to the unavoidable explosion that happened when the irresistible force of Mr. Biondi and the liberal, long-haired Paul Revere and The Raiders slammed into the immovable object of the conservative, short-haired Troy High dress and deportment standards.

Who knows what *really* happened. Puzzling to think that the school would've taken the trouble to book the *Road Show* just to turn around and tell KRLA that it was only kidding. "Nope, sorry about that, Mr. Biondi, but those Raiders characters just aren't in line with our dress and deportment standards here at Troy." Like the administration didn't know who The Raiders were and what they looked like *before* booking them.

I suppose it's just as likely, if not as romantic, that there was some kind of booking conflict. Or that Mr. Revere suddenly remembered that he needed time off to visit a long-lost niece on Grand Cayman. Or that the janitors griped because they'd planned to strip and refinish the gym floor that day.

Whatever the true dynamics, the deal went south. With or without details, the fact that there'd been a problem with the *Road Show* couldn't be kept from students for long. Nope. Keeping this kind of controversy from an active student rumor mill was a whole lot like trying to hold back the ocean with a pitchfork. Just wasn't gonna happen. So before you could say, "burn, baby, burn," word hit the halls that the Troy administration had caught The Raiders goofing off in the parking lot, misbehaving generally and spewing forth words that just hadn't oughta be said in or around our unspoiled campus, and had decided that these guitar-totin', beach-hangin', rock 'n rollin' boys were after all just a bunch of long-haired, hippie freaks and unsuitable for public consumption at Troy High.

The upshot of it all was the announcement that there'd be no Paul Revere and The Raiders playing for us Troy Warriors in our humble gym.

Geez.

No "Louie, Go Home." No "Steppin' Out." No "Just Like Me." Not a single Raiders hit. Not one. And this piece of news went over about as well as an announcement of Viet Nam escalation.

The Warriors were ticked, and someone was gonna hear about it.

This was the day of riot and revolt, by darn, and this mini-clash between our rock heroes and the Establishment could very well be Troy's one and only shot at a reason somewhere near good enough to justify a little social upheaval on campus. *So let's just get on with the upheaving*, we thought, *before someone figures out that this just isn't that big of a deal*.

Cue the fire alarms.

Pass out the matches. You take that trash can, I'll take this trash can. Light 'em up, baby.

Raise fists in common brotherhood of purpose. Cut classes. Storm the cafeteria. Leave your library books—*unstacked*, goshdarnit—on the tables.

Oh, *baby*. Revolt is where it's at.

OK. The pitiful truth is, the best we could manage was just a bit of a chaotic day on campus with some of the big-shot athletes posting themselves in front of the school, telling the escaping-under-cover-of-trash-can-smoke Warriors to just settle down and get back to class. But we weren't having it. Nope, we were outta there. This was our way of throwing our hat into the adult ring of raze and ruin, and we weren't about to back down just so some self-aggrandized jock could go home feeling like Lord Protector of the Realm.

Fun and contemporary as it all was, none of what we did made an ounce of difference. We never got the *Road Show* after all, and to this day, Mr. Revere and his Raiders don't know what a groovy gym we've got at Troy.

But after the smoke settled and everyone came back to school, we did get an assembly. You betcha. We got two singers. *Two*, mind you. We got crooner Mike Clifford—he of the perfect Fabian hair and gorgeous chiseled face that most certainly never had a zit anywhere on it *ever*—singing all his hits. Make that *hit*. From the 1962 archives, "Close to Cathy." We also got some talent show contest winner from Hackensack or beyond singing John Duffey's "Big Bad Bruce," a take-off on Jimmy Dean's "Big Bad John." The story line centered on a hairdresser courageously saving everyone from a salon fire. The lisp made it worth hearing.

So don't tell *me* that the Troy High Warriors don't know how to effectively engineer a riot for maximum results.

Well. I've just realized how far around the block I've gone in my rambling. Sorry about that. Please allow me to get back to my listing of groups on the more successful end of things—because I have one more to mention. One that I can't *not* mention.

My personal favorite.

A group clad in colorful civil war uniforms. A group first heard by producer-songwriter Jerry Fuller a year or so ago amid the sounds of rolling balls and falling pins at a San Diego bowling alley. A group led by a man with a soaring, crystal-clear baritone voice that shines singularly amid countless drab others that would pretend to this king's throne. A group that will release six consecutive gold records this year, selling more vinyl than any other recording act—yep, even more than those Liverpool guys.

I'm talking about Dwight Bement, Kerry Chater, Paul Wheatbread, Gary "Mutha" Withem, and Gary Puckett.

Gary Puckett and The Union Gap.

Make fun of their Civil War uniforms, if you will. Criticize their choice of songs, if you must. Call their chart hits smarmy, if you like. Your gripes don't make me no never mind. The sound produced by

Gary and The Gap's exquisite. Of course, to be convinced of that, you've gotta hear their complete albums, not just the singles that get air play. I mean, their singles are great, for sure. "Woman, Woman" is a masterpiece. "Young Girl" can never be forgotten, once heard. "Lady Willpower" and "Over You" are special. But some of the best music you'll ever hear are Union Gap deep album tracks that'll never get air play. And in a way, I'm kinda glad they won't. This music's just too special to cherish.

[*Vocabulary Note: Cherish* is the word I use to describe what happens to a song that gets so much air play that you can hardly stand the thought of even *accidentally* hearing it again sometime. As in, "The radio has cherished that song to death." My coining of the phrase was inspired by the twelve gazillion air plays of The Association's "Cherish" since it debuted in 1966, making it number one on my list of songs that I've heard so often I get sick whenever I hear 'em and I'll do anything I can to avoid hearing 'em again because if I hear 'em just once more I'm gonna grab somebody's butt and twist.]

Now, you can believe me when I tell you Mr. Puckett can sing. Oh, yeah. *Sing.* While other front men are trying their hardest just to find the tune and stay on key—sometimes managing it only through the help of some *pret-tee* creative recording technology—Gary's voice paints audio masterpieces that should be hanging in some kind of Soundwave Louvre.

As a group, the Union Gap will make personnel changes in 1969 and then disband altogether in 1971. But Gary will sing on and on. And on. In fact, unlike almost every one of the recording artists I've named, Mr. Puckett will still be releasing new records and touring more than forty years from now, continuing to entertain old fans and convert new fans.

Oh, I know. The more-successful-end-of-things groups I've named aren't the ones *you'd* have listed. That's what you're thinking. You're accusing me of leaving out this one or that one or the other one. I can *hear* you. You're whining and complaining about it right this very minute. But don't you worry. Let your hypercritical mind rest. I haven't forgotten the three originals. No way I'd do that. I could never overlook the greatest of them all.

I've just given them their own lines.

Beach Boys.

Beatles.

Rolling Stones.

The bands that set the standard for talent. For creativity. For uniqueness. For greatness, trendsetting, durability.

These three are not—I repeat *not*—One-Hit Wonders.

But then you knew that.

When these three bands go away—if they ever really do—the world will never see their likes again. You get one shot at genius like this. Yep, just one shot. What they've given us was never here before. It'll never be here again. Like Beethoven, Mozart, Tchaikovsky, and Buddy Holly, each of these bands is a unique bolt of cloth, not simply a piece cut from some common bolt that produced a hundred clones. It's almost as if the hand of heaven itself reached down and set them intentionally and carefully in place. And in time.

Well, I've drawn some *pret-tee* darn broad strokes here. I know that. I mean, hey . . . *volumes* have been written on what I just reduced to a few short paragraphs. But perhaps it's enough for you to understand that right now we're in a musical time and place that stokes the fire of imagination in each and every one of us who rocks out to the car radio or sits captivated in front of the TV during *American Bandstand* or *Where the Action Is*. We *wanna* be like these music-makers that we see springing up all around us or we imagine that we *could* be like them or we're trying like the devil to *be* like them. More to the point, everybody's *in* a band, trying to *start* a band, or convinced that he *could* start a band if only the right opportunity would knock.

And, heaven help us, that includes Jim, Scott, and me.

I've loved the guitar ever since Santa brought me one in 1965. A lovely little—and when I say little, I mean *little*—Rodeo-brand guitar. To be perfectly truthful, it was maybe just a *leet-tle* tiny bit less guitar than I'd had in mind when I imagined owning one, but it was a guitar and it was mine and I loved it. With three nylon and three wrapped nylon strings, this acoustic critter sounded a little tamer than I wanted it to sound, but I had no idea why it sounded that way or what to do to make it sound hipper.

Then one day I was at Gary's house and discovered that he, too, owned a guitar. It was a little bigger than mine—a big, black, single cutaway jumbo country-type critter—but that wasn't so important to me as was the thing I discovered when I strummed it. Its sound wasn't the subdued, plastic-like sound that my Rodeo produced. Nope. It was a sharp, crisp, metallic sound that exploded gingerly in my ears like an unexpected but oddly pleasant firecracker burst.

That's what a guitar's supposed to sound like.

Checking out Gary's guitar a little more closely, I realized that there weren't any nylon strings on this baby. Nope, not one. All six were of lovely steel, and this must certainly be what was making that sound that drew me to it like Tarzan to a vine.

Cue lightbulb over head.

I'd pick up a little coin by taking a few empty Dr. Pepper bottles to Thriftimart for the two-cents-per refund, and then I'd haul my little hiney down to Fullerton Music Store and pick up a new set of strings. A new set of *steel* strings. Before you could say, "Long live rock 'n roll," I'd be sounding like the Beatles.

Bottles. Cash. Strings. Cookin' with gas.

Now, up to this point, I hadn't really tried in earnest to learn to play this guitar, but now that I had the right strings and the right sound, I happily and eagerly hunkered down to the challenge. I pulled out the *Alfred Music Basic Guitar Method Book One* that Santa had thoughtfully packaged with my Rodeo, and, sitting on the edge of my bed and using the pillow as a music stand, I started learning the names and notes of all six strings. Having played the trumpet for a couple of years, I could easily read the music—so it was just a matter of learning how to make the guitar do what I wanted.

It didn't take long to get through the lessons on the individual strings, so I just slid right on into the more complex world of chords. Now, this beginner's guitar book took a nice, simple approach to chording. It taught me first to use only the number of fingers required to fret a selected chord on the first three strings. Then on the first four strings. Then five. It was sort of a building-blocks kind of deal. The idea was that, by the time I got to the point of using all the fingers required to fret a six-string chord, I'd be able to do it without thinking.

I'd like to tell you that it was that easy, but it wasn't, so I can't, so I won't. Even after I'd begun fretting complete six-string chords, I still had to consciously reset my fingers one at a time on the frets when I changed from one chord to another. It was a little like running barefoot through molasses in January. Kinda hard to play a song when I had to stop after every strum or two to reset my fingers on the frets.

That's when I discovered the reason why there'd been nylon strings on my little Rodeo in the first place: a very high bridge. The original nylon strings had fretted pretty easily, but not these steel strings. This high bridge forced me to *r-e-a-l-l-y* press the steel strings against the neck so they'd make sufficient contact to fret a clear chord. In fact, I had to press so hard on these rascals that my fingers bled when I played. I mean, these thin steel strings were just *pret-tee* darn sharp when you got right down to it. Sliced the tips of my fingers up like sticks of salami. Didn't stop me, though. I just kept right on fretting and ouching and bleeding and fretting and ouching and bleeding, trying to get those chords to sound crisp and clear. At the end of every practice session, I'd just wipe the blood from the strings and the guitar's neck.

Things improved, though. I eventually developed calluses on the ends of my fingers, and that stopped the bleeding. But I still couldn't fret chords without taking like a day and a half to reset my fingers each time. If I'd tried to serenade a girlfriend, she'd have thought I stuttered.

But then, to quote Peter, Paul, and Mary's "Puff the Magic Dragon," one gray night, it happened. I sat down to practice and set my fingers on a G chord, strummed it, then prepared to reset my fingers one at a time on the frets of a D chord. But this time it was different. All at once, my fingers just went to the right frets of that D chord like they knew exactly what they were doing. I just about fell off the bed, I was so surprised and excited. *Might've just been a freak thing, though,* I thought to myself, so I just hauled off and tried it again. G to D. Buttah. *One more time, please, just to be sure.* G to D . . . to G. Whoa. Where'd *that* come from? *OK. This is just flat cool. So now let's just try a C to a D. Nice.* To quote *M*A*S*H*'s Colonel Henry Potter in about ten or so years from now, there aren't enough o's in *smooth* to describe it. C to D to C. G to D to G. A to E to A. C to G to D to A.

This is where Professor Henry Higgins would've happily exclaimed "By George, he's got it! I think he's got it."

From here, it was just a matter of learning additional chords and putting them together to build songs. A handy chord chart at the end of the instruction book helped a lot. Before you could say, "Rock 'n roll will never die," I was barring my F chords at the first fret, my G chords at the third fret, and my A chords at the fifth fret. Added a few strum variations and a few picking patterns to the repertoire, and within a relatively short time, *voilà*. A guitar player I'd become.

Umm, loosely speaking, of course. I didn't headline at any major venue that weekend.

Still, I'd at last reached a point where I could actually perform a song—but with just this little Rodeo acoustic doing the work for me, I couldn't really show off my skills or even really take my playing seriously. Nope, I needed something else. Something grown-up-sized. Something cool. Something *electric*, dang it.

Time to hit Santa up again.

I've mentioned elsewhere that Mom and Dad have always supported my interest in music. When I had the chance to take piano lessons, they didn't let a little thing like a fragile family budget hold me back. When I had the trumpet on my mind, there they were again, shelling out the jingle to get me into that little game. And then the guitar. "You betcha, son. Here ya go."

But now *this*. *This* might just be the limit, I supposed. I mean, I did, after all, have a guitar. Perhaps it wasn't The Perfect Guitar, but it was a nice guitar. And I wasn't exactly what you'd call a professional musician needing to upgrade the tools of his trade. Nope, this was something else. This bordered on greed and ingratitude. I hardly dared even *think* of asking them for this, let alone actually broaching the subject.

But, oh, how I wanted an electric guitar. That overpowering desire put a little starch in my loincloth, and I managed to scrape together the audacity to ask.

Less than a month later, I was opening two packages from the Spiegel Catalog showroom. Inside the first was a small, tube-powered, thirty-three-amp, triple-input Kay Model 703 amplifier. Inside the second was a two-pick-up, double cutaway electric guitar in a lovely sunburst finish to make your mouth water.

At least, that's what was *supposed* to have been in the second box. What I actually found, though, was a triple-pick-up, double cutaway, candy-apple red Teisco Del Ray ET-312 with a tremolo arm and a note from Mr. and/or Mrs. Spiegel explaining that a substitution at the time of shipping had been necessitated by the regrettable unavailability—forevermore—of the brand I'd originally ordered.

Well, fine. Not what I ordered, true. But if you think for one single second that I was gonna let this little red beauty out of my claws and wait for another to arrive, well . . . well . . . I wasn't.

So now I was electrified. And whenever I played songs from my Beatles or Beach Boys or Raiders song books, I actually created the right kind of sound. Totally cool.

It turns out that my friends Jim and Scott are also into the guitar. At different levels.

Jim's a serious student of the guitar. He's worked and worked—ever since I've known him he's had a job of some kind, and I believe if you researched it, you'd find that he worked a part-time job in the hospital nursery while he was waiting for his parents to take him home—and saved up enough coin to buy a serious guitar to go along with his serious interest.

It wasn't electric, that's true. But a Martin D-18 doesn't have to be electric. It's a Martin D-18. And that's all it has to be.

Now, not everyone's allowed to play a guitar like this. In several states, it's actually illegal to own and play a Martin guitar if you're not at least so good. If you aren't very good and you try to own a Martin, you'll be tracked down by the Guitar Police and possibly killed. At the very least, that Martin guitar will be confiscated and donated to some poor-but-serious guitar student because you just by darn can't run around playing a Martin guitar if you don't qualify to play it.

Jim qualifies. If you know that he loves—and can keep up with—James Taylor and Paul Simon and Stephen Stills, then you'll know what you need to know to know how Jim plays the guitar.

Yep, Jim's a serious guitar player.

As for Scott . . . well, Scott tries. He's got an acoustic Goya G-12. It's not a cheap guitar, that's for sure, but rock 'n roll doesn't come off any better on this than it did on my little Rodeo before I changed out the strings.

Scott isn't completely unfortunate when it comes to guitar skills. It's true that he won't be headlining any sold-out gigs this week, just as I won't—but he can lay down a few chords and more or less keep a beat without a metronome. Some of the time, anyway.

Obviously, we're just a group waiting to happen. Just need to get organized, that's all.

Garage, here we come.

Granted. There are only three of us, and we only play six-string guitars. This presents a slight challenge. It means we've got no bass and no drums.

We don't have an accordion, either, but we're not looking for one.

Our unfortunate shortage of personnel means we've gotta get creative and adjust the traditional model just a tad. What we've got on our side is that we have no plans to play at stake dances. Nope, we won't be a dance band. We'll be a performing group—complete with songs, a little chatter, maybe even a little humor. Think Smothers Brothers meet Peter, Paul, and Mary.

Heck. Even if we *wanted* to add bass to our sound, we couldn't afford it. I've already pointed up that Jim almost always has a job that puts a little change in his pocket, but there can be sizable distance between the points of having a little change in your pocket and having enough disposable cash to buy a Fender Precision bass guitar.

Scott doesn't have a job. True, he does have a drawer full of solid silver half dollars that he figures oughta be worth about a trillion or so, when the sandwich coin finally forces all the solids out of circulation and he's the only living person left with about a gazillion solids. But you can bet he's not about to part with *those* babies.

As for me, it's true that I have a part-time job at Bill and Jerry's Union 76 service station, but with my money management skills—or lack thereof—it's a rare day when I can scrape together twenty-seven cents all at once.

So unless Fullerton Music Store's owner's suddenly overcome by an urgent, irresistible sense of community compassion that leads to the speedy development of a 501(c)(3) program with a mission statement centered on the donation of bass guitars to struggling young music artist wannabes, we're just in deep water here, bass guitar-wise.

So what? It's just one of several adjustments we're having to make to get our band off the ground. I mean, we're just not looking at all like The Rolling Stones here, but we understand quite clearly that we're not gonna. But we just ain't a-skeert. We find inspiration in The Kingston Trio. The New Christy Minstrels. The Chad Mitchell Trio. The Limeliters. The Rooftop Singers. Peter, Paul, and Mary. We Five. Even The Lettermen and The Vogues.

Basically, we find shelter in any folk rock or vocal group that relies on instrumentation similar to ours or uses no instrumentation at all. I mean, yeah, most of these groups got started in the folk era and more or less evolved into the folk rock genre, that's true enough. But however you wanna pigeonhole them, it's still true that they're making hit records without following basic garage band rules.

This gives us hope.

Which is a good thing because that's just about all we have.

Now let's talk about the music.

Pretty much anything that's relatively uncomplicated, chords-wise, is what we're looking for. This is quite important to us because *we're* relatively uncomplicated, chords-wise. I mean, our repertoire of chords is limited, but if we stick with basic key-of-G stuff, we should be pretty much OK.

On top of our restricted capacity for chording, there's just a whole big lot of music theory we don't understand.

Like, we don't know that each diatonic scale has seven different notes, allowing seven possible triads for each key. It's embarrassing enough that we don't know *that* without openly admitting that we *also* don't know that a triad's the first, third, and fifth notes of a scale played simultaneously to form a chord. Even worse, we don't know that all chords are formed based on their respective major diatonic scale, like in the key of C, for example. We don't know that you can form seven basic chords, or triads, from the notes in the key of C, with each different note being the root of a different chord. Or that the first chord in the key of C's the C chord—because C's the first scale degree, of course. So certainly, then, we don't know that the second chord's a D—because D's the second scale degree, of course—or that it's based on the D scale, of which the first, third, and fifth are D, F-sharp, and A. But this rascal F-sharp's a bit of a problem because it's not in the key of C and has to be flatted down to F-natural, giving us D, F, and A, which are scale degrees 1, 3, and 5 of the D major scale. If we weren't so stupid, we'd also know that we could continue in this way to identify every chord in the key of C.

But we are, so we don't, so we can't.

Well, the stuff that we don't know just goes on and on.

But we can play the song "Green, Green," by darn. This lovely little ditty was made famous by The New Christy Minstrels and requires only your basic G, C, A7, D7, and Em chords. We're up to that. No sweat. The song's got a nice upbeat feel, and the lyrics even provide a nice straight line or two for the humor we intend to infuse into our stage act.

I'll get to that later.

We've got some Peter, Paul, and Mary in our repertoire too. How 'bout "Don't Think Twice, It's All Right," a lovely little Bob Dylan tune. Or "Blowin' in the Wind," also a little Dylan ditty. Or "Five Hundred Miles." Not hard. We can handle these little numbers. At least, we can handle the *Made-Easy* versions of these little numbers.

We've even discovered that some of the music of The Great Ones can be adapted to our little ragtag group.

Take The Beach Boys, for example. Some pretty nice stuff here for us. We particularly enjoy "Sloop John B." Truth be told, this is anything but an original Beach Boys song. It seems to be a folk song, originally entitled "The John B. Sails," that was included in the 1917 American novel "Pieces of Eight" by Richard Le Gallienne. The "secret" narrator of that story describes the song as "one of the quaint Nassau ditties," but whether it's a genuine old-timey folk song or something written just for the novel's a little unclear. With a few slight variations in Mr. Le Gallienne's version, American poet extraordinaire Carl Sandburg included the song in his 1927 collection of folk songs, *The American Songbag*. As for contemporary efforts, the song's been recorded in one version or another and by one name or another by The Weavers, The Kingston Trio, Johnny Cash, Lonnie Donegan, Jimmie Rodgers, and The Brothers Four. If all these artists felt free to do their own versions of "John B," and if The Beach Boys could turn it into a Top 40 hit in 1966 and include it on arguably the greatest LP ever recorded, *Pet Sounds*, well . . . then . . . we believe we should certainly feel welcome to put *our* stamp on it.

OK. So maybe that's more than you wanted to know about The Beach Boys's "Sloop John B." But now you can be the Phone-a-Friend lifeline for someone you love on *Who Wants to Be a Millionaire* some-time in the future.

And then there's The Beatles. "I've Just Seen a Face" is a great little number on the *Rubber Soul* LP. It suits us *pret-tee* darn nicely with its guitar/vocal mix and a country feel that makes it warm and cozy, and it just kinda screams "You don't need drums or even bass for this one, boys." Plus, it's got room for a little harmony.

Speaking of harmony, it turns out that we've actually got the capacity for it. Jim's got a nice lead baritone voice that just lays right out there, all nice and comfortable. My baritone voice isn't all that bad, either, and I've always had a bit of a knack for finding a nice harmony line. Scott has a second baritone voice with a pretty nice timbre. When our voices get together in three parts, you wouldn't barf if you heard it. It's just not all that bad.

When we can *find* the three parts, that is.

See, we've got this *leet-tle* tiny problem. Scott tends to sing whatever part the person closest to him's singing. If he's standing on the end by Jim, Scott sings lead. If he's standing on the end by me, Scott sings my harmony. If he's standing *between* Jim and me, Scott could be singing lead at one moment and then my harmony line in the next, with maybe a measure or two of *his* part thrown in here and there without prior notice, just for flavoring.

We either have to settle for mostly-two-part-but-every-once-in-a-while-three-part harmony, or else Jim and I have to make Scott stand about, oh, say . . . five *hundred* yards away from us. This strategy may sharpen our three-part harmony, but the distance between us makes for poor cohesion in performance. I mean, if Scott's standing way over *there* it's just *pret-tee* darn hard to pull off any interactive Smothers Brothers–like humor. Or even to know what song each other's singing, for that matter. It all has the potential for being not very pretty. Not very pretty, at all. Plus, it's sure to confuse the audience when two members of the group keep pushing the third one over into the corner.

Still, we're undaunted. And we're optimists. We just figure that this little problem'll work itself out, and we move faithfully forward.

And now we're set. Jim's got his Martin D-18, Scott's got his Goya G-12 classical, and I've got my Gibson B-15. Yep, I said Gibson, not Rodeo. That's what I'm playing now. But it's not *my* Gibson, per se. It actually belongs to a boyfriend of my oldest sister. He's one of her speech and drama buddies over at Cal State Fullerton. Plus, the two of them date a little—so my guess is that he figures if he's nice to the little brother, it'll pay some sweet dividends with the sister. A tried-and-true strategy, for sure. Be that as it may, Deb's friend's generous enough to give me a fairly open-ended loan of this nice little mahogany-finish Gibson that plays like a dream and fits into our sound better than my electric Teisco Del Ray would because . . . well, hey. We're just not set up to be electric.

Again, we understand that it's a little unusual for a group these days to consist of three guys on acoustic six-strings, but we've learned to live with the limitation and actually make it work. More or less. I mean, we haven't played any professional gigs. That's true enough. Heck, we haven't even played any *nonprofessional* gigs. In fact, to be completely truthful, our only public performances so far have been from the stage in the cultural hall of our church house as we practice for that gig that we just *know* is coming. Sooner or later. Never mind that our audiences are only the eight or ten Boy Scouts playing skins-shirts basketball on the court below us and whatever teenybopper girls may be wandering aimlessly around after our Tuesday night church meeting.

Speaking of gigs, it all at once occurs to us that if we do actually land one, we'll certainly need to have a name. I mean, what kind of group can you possibly be without a name? It's arguably even the most important part of who you are, in some ways, because if you've got a totally cool name, *some*body's gonna show up when you play. At least *once*, anyway, just to see what a group with such a cool name looks and sounds like.

If you don't believe there's anything in a name, try to imagine The Beatles as The Quarrymen. The Beach Boys as The Pendletones. The Byrds as The Beefeaters. Creedence Clearwater Revival as The Golliwogs. The Outsiders as The Starfires. The Box Tops as The Devilles. The Buckinghams as The Pulsations. The Vogues as The ValAirs. Steppenwolf as Sparrow. The Turtles as The Crossfires.

Yeah, it's a good thing they changed their names, huh?

So we've not only gotta find *a* name, we've gotta find *the* name. The name that will sum us up. Tell the people who we are, what we stand for. Attract them, in the first place, and bring them back, in the second place.

Or, in a worst-case scenario, mercifully let every brave soul who comes to see us know who they'll be wanting to avoid at all costs in the future.

We use a flood of collective creativity to pool a variety of possible names ranging in quality from "I don't think so" to "what the heck does that mean." Mostly, they're not any good—although, personally, I'm a little partial to Kevin and The Guys That Are Playing with Him. But Scott and Jim think it's a little too self-serving.

Heathens.

So we just keep throwing words around and brainstorming concepts that might translate into some kind of acceptable name for our little whatever-kind-of-music-act-it-is.

Now, Scott's a brainy cat. No getting around it. While Jim and I are out trying to impress chicks and hustle gas money for our Honda 90 and Yamaha 55 motorcycles, Scott's holed up in his room studying and reading and doing other pointless stuff like homework. And it turns out that he's just lately been reading the classic 1935 John Steinbeck novel, *Tortilla Flat*. He suggests that title as a possible name.

The Tortilla Flats.

Hmmm.

Well. With surprisingly little discussion—read *argument*—the three of us agree that this could actually be a serious possibility. No doubt about it. Nice ring to it. Balanced. Unpretentious. Blue-collar but classy. Highbrow with a dash of modesty.

This could work.

And then Jim just kinda off the cuff says, "If truth be told, we sound more like *flat tortillas*."

Flat tortillas.

The Flat Tortillas.

That's it, by George. That's it.

We know who we are and we've got a name to print on the contract when it comes to us.

Now, I wish I could tell you that the run of The Flat Tortillas turns out to be a successful one. I wish I could tell you that we eventually get signed by CBS as a summer replacement for *The Smothers Brothers Comedy Hour* or that we enjoy a rags-to-riches story involving random discovery and instant stardom after a record producer accidentally catches one of our performances and inks us tout de suite to a multirecord deal.

Wish like heck I could.

But the truth is that The Flat Tortillas's performance résumé will, after all's said and done, consist only of an almost-appearance at a Gold and Green Ball sponsored by our local LDS stake and a one-night-only gig at a fathers-and-sons campout. A pathetically far cry from success, for sure.

In our defense, I'll tell you that our fathers-and-sons campout gig has a thing or two to recommend it. In this first-last-and-only Flat Tortillas performance, before a massive crowd of twenty or so fathers and sons around a campfire in the great Southern California wilderness, we pull together three of our best numbers: "Sloop John B," "I've Just Seen a Face," and "Green, Green." And I think I could make a pretty good case before an objective—if slightly sympathetic—jury that things go *pret-tee* darn well right up until the last song of the triple play.

That's when we lay our comedy line on them during our "Green, Green" finale.

It goes like this.

The lyric line is "Well, I told my mama on the day I was born, don't cha cry when you see I'm gone."

We sing "Well, I told my mama on the day I was born . . ." at which point, Scott and Jim continue with "don't cha cry when you see I'm gone."

Or they ostensibly try to, anyway.

But their valiant effort's interrupted by my loud, "waahhhh, waahhhh."

Think about it.

Yeah, I got the punch line. It's all mine. Lucky me. And I'd give twenty-five cents for the sure knowledge that I won't carry the mental picture of this moment in my memory bank for the rest of my life.

But it's a futile wish.

This enthusiastic-if-less-than-well-thought-out impression of an infant trying to explain things to his mama breaks up the song, of course, and brings upon the sayer of the punch line—me—the comedic wrath and feigned verbal assault of the other two. It's supposed to be comedy, see. It's supposed to actually prompt a few chuckles, if not outright guffaws from the listening audience. In a best-case scenario, it's supposed to bring down the house—er . . . campsite.

But after I leak out that punch line and we try to drive the interactive Smothers Brothers–like comedy home, we get no guffaws. We get no chuckles.

Perhaps a pity smile or two, but that's about it.

Even the crickets under cover of a darkened wilderness interrupt their own concert to sit quiet, seemingly in silent mourning for another sixties group that'll never find its way into the radio or, for that matter, even into another public venue before it—mercifully—goes the way of so many other of the decade's No Hit Wonders.

Still, despite this abrupt conclusion to our ill-fated professional music career, Jim, Scott, and I have been Flat Tortillas.

No one else on this earth can say that.

8

I get robbed

In the summer of 1969, I'm still working at Bill and Jerry's Union 76 Service Station. I've been working here since late 1967, covering most of my junior year of high school and all of my senior year. Since surviving The Night—when the Portals of Hell opened—I've learned many lessons and even faced another challenge or two here at . . . well, here at this place that's kinda become my home away from home.

I'll get to one of those challenges in just a minute.

First, let me explain just how this particular service station's laid out. There are two basic elements: the building and the island.

Facing west, the building itself consists of two sections. Entering from the front, you can choose a door on the right or a door on the left. If you walk through the door on the left, you're in the lube bay. Here you'll find the hydraulic hoist, lots of new tires stacked side by side on a shelf along the top of the wall, a workbench with three manual pumps to draw bulk oil up from containers beneath the bench, and a wide assortment of tools scattered about in an interestingly organized chaos. Cars enter the lube bay from the back after a steel accordion door's opened. This door consists of two separate units, each of which is attached to a side of the lube bay entrance—then the two of them are pulled together toward the center where they meet. To secure it, you wrap a chain through a grid space on the end of each side, then slap a Master lock through the chain and lock it. Unless there's a special reason to do otherwise, I routinely keep this steel accordion door closed and locked during my solo shifts. That way I don't get surprised by someone wandering in through the back while I'm with a customer on the island.

Like just the other night. I was out on the island, pumping gas for this guy in a late-model Chevy who looked like he was late for a date or a church meeting or something that he needed to be dressed pretty for. Anyway, for whatever reason, Mr. West Coast Black Tie was in a big hurry and didn't want anything but gas, so that's just what he got. After I finished, I meandered on back into the lube room through the front door, figuring to take up right where I'd left off with a lovely ham and cheese sandwich my mom had made for me, and the refreshing Dr. Pepper that I need to sustain life itself. But I didn't make it to the grub. I ran smack dab into this . . . this . . . well, this sort of scroungy young man who looked like he probably had firsthand knowledge about the Summer of Love and a personal connection to any number of sleazy, run-down apartments in the Haight-Ashbury district of San Francisco. About my age, maybe a tad older. Just standing right there in the middle of the lube bay by the hydraulic lift. Scared the what-chamacallit outta me, for sure. But he was smiling, and I didn't see any traces of weaponry, so right after my stomach settled from my throat back down into its proper place, I said to the guy, "Hey, how's it going? Did you need something?"

"Hey man," he said back to me. "How's it goin' man," he said to me. "Just wonderin' if you had a buck or two you could let me have, man, 'cause I'm, like, on my way home from visiting my old lady, and I been like walkin' all day and ain't had nothin' to eat, man, so I was wonderin' if you had a buck or two for some eats," he said. "Pay you back later, man, and you can even give me your address, man," he said. "Here, just write it down on this matchbook, man," he said. "I swear, man, I'll send you the bread as soon as I get home, man," he said.

Now, if this guy'd known me at all, he'd have known I don't usually have even fifty cents in my pockets while I'm at work because I usually bring a sack dinner, snacks, and drinks with me—and what else am I gonna spend money on while I'm at work. But that particular night I happened to have three bucks in my jeans, and offhand I couldn't think of a good reason for not helping the guy. I mean, you *know* he wouldn't be lying to me. I mean, he looked so honest and in proper personal order. So I pulled out the bucks, peeled off two of the three, and handed them to him.

"Here man," he reminded me. "Write down your address, man, and I'll mail it back to you in two shakes, man."

So I figured, well, what the heck—and I wrote my address inside the cover of his matchbook. Never know. Miracles actually do happen once in a while. I might get the money back. Yeah. And monkeys could . . . Well, suffice it to say that, deep down, I was just *pret-tee* darn sure I was saying adios to those dollar bills. But it was actually OK, and I didn't mind. I didn't know if the guy really needed to eat, or if he wanted a beer or a bottle of Thunderbird or a pack of Marlboros, or if he needed the dough to make the ransom on his best friend who was being held hostage a block away by some group of crazed extremists, or if he needed only two dollars more to enable him to reach his childhood goal of traveling to India to see the Taj Mahal just once before he dies. But in the end, it didn't really matter to me one way or the other because, for some reason, it felt strangely good to give.

One of those lessons I was telling you about. A lesson in giving that I won't forget.

So the guy told me how grateful he was—"man"—and slipped out through the back of the lube bay that was open because I hadn't pulled the steel accordion door together earlier like I should've done. As soon as the visitor was through it and gone, I pulled the accordion sides together and slapped on the ol' chain and Master lock. Won't forget this again.

Continuing on with the guided tour of the building.

If you walk through the front door on the right, you're in the main office. Here you'll find a chest-high counter-kind-of-thing that we almost never use except to display an assortment of California and local street maps that we give out free to customers. Behind the counter-kind-of-thing, you'll see a restroom, and against the wall that separates the two are a Coca-Cola vending machine, a drinking fountain, and a pay telephone.

Now, about this phone. It's just like the pay phones at other service stations, grocery stores, and street corners. Its body's a big rectangle of black metal with a handset hanging on its left side, a flip-open coin return at the bottom, and a rotary dial at the top. Above the dial, at the top of the rectangular body, are three coin receptacle slots—one for a quarter, one for a dime, and one for a nickel. If you wanna make a call, you hold up a dime—flat-ways—to the middle slot and push-slash-drop it into the phone. This gives you a dial tone. If the phone isn't busted.

Not long ago, someone—some very *creative* one, I'd say—discovered that if you take a piece of stiff-but-flexible paper, like cardstock or the stuff a cereal box is made from, and you tear off a strip of it that's narrow enough to slip into the dime receptacle slot and long enough to extend down into the phone about three inches or so—and if you actually snake it down into the dime slot and then drop a penny down the nickel receptacle slot . . . well, then you get a dial tone and can complete your call for just a penny instead of a dime.

So I'm supposed to keep my eyes peeled for kids who wanna make such a discounted call. And I *do* try. Honest, I do. But these rascals are hard to . . . They're hard to . . . Well, they're just . . . I mean . . .

Rats.

The *complete* truth is, I can't say with any degree of conviction that I ever really try all that hard to catch 'em.

I've got a four-inch strip of cardstock in my wallet.

Sorry 'bout that.

But I digress. Back once again to the guided tour.

The other three walls of the office—the south wall, the west (or front) wall, and the north (or common) wall separating the office from the lube bay—are mostly of glass. On the common wall, we've taped up a map of the local area with a "you are here" mark for guys who don't *wanna* stop for directions but stop anyway because their wives are sick of driving around in circles and say, "Harv, if you don't stop and ask directions, I'm gonna get out of this car right this minute and walk to the first lawyer I see and divorce you." And, thanks to our map taped to the common wall between the office and the lube bay, these poor guys can find out where they are, see where they need to go, pacify their wives, and avoid the heartache of travel-related divorce without technically violating the age-old unwritten order of things that forbids any living male from asking for directions no matter how lost he gets.

Against that same wall, below and just to the left of the map, there's a vending machine that, for thirty-five cents, dispenses to the customer a pack of cigarettes as he chooses from a lovely variety of brands. Now, if you're as old as fifteen or sixteen and Bill or Jerry sees you using this vending machine, he may frown at you—but otherwise he won't do or say much about what you're doing. Bill and Jerry have been smoking since about that same age, and if there's one thing my bosses are *not*, it's hypocritical.

But if you're twelve or thirteen or even *look* like you're in that general age range, you're not gonna want to let Bill or Jerry see you using this vending machine. Trust me on this.

Now let's go outside.

Between the front of the building and State College Boulevard's what we call the island, where stand two pairs of gas pumps, with one pump in each pair dispensing regular gasoline and the other dispensing super, or ethyl—some old-timers still call it "high-test"—gasoline. If you're counting, you'll know this makes a total of four pumps. There's enough space between the two pairs of pumps to allow two cars to be serviced at the same time between them. The island's covered by a roof that's supposed to protect me and the customer from the elements—and does, most of the time. Except when there's wind. It doesn't protect against wind. If there's windy rain, we're wet while we work.

Two brick-veneer support columns, one between each of the two pairs of pumps, hold up the roof. Attached to the inside of the column nearest the building, you'll find the cash box. It's a simple black metal box, maybe fifteen inches long by twelve inches wide by twelve inches deep. Inside lies a plastic coin and bill holder tray that can be lifted out to expose a deeper storage area below it. On top of the box is a spring-loaded cover that pops open when I insert a key into the lock on the front of the box and turn it.

Which key I keep handy on my belt by means of a retractable key chain.

Now, at the moment I happen to think this retractable key chain's totally cool. Until I got this job, I'd never had a reason to wear one. In fact, I'd never even *seen* one. But now I've discovered just how great a thing a retractable key chain is. I mean, it's not only functional—nope, it also keeps my keys handy so that I don't have to stick a greasy, filthy hand down inside my pocket to fish 'em out. Plus, it's a lot of fun to use. Every time I need to use a key, I grab the bunch of 'em hanging playfully from my belt, pull the lot gingerly forward, select the one I need, do what business I need to do with it, then let the bunch pop majestically back to the shiny metal casing that has some kind of spring-loaded goodie inside that calls those keys crisply home.

It's a wonderful, magical, intriguing thing, this retractable key chain. But I've learned something else about it, and I share it now with you. Be advised: It's only cool to wear the thing while on the job. Or if you choose to wear one while you're *not* on the job, you'd better also be sporting a lovely pocket protector to complete the ensemble.

So the salient point here is that the cash box is not in the office, not in the lube bay, not in any protected area. Nope, it's right out there in the open, attached to one of the brick-veneer columns. Right there, in front of heaven and everybody.

So that's about it for the tour.

Now we can move on to that challenge I said I'd tell you about.

It happens not long before closing time, just a couple of days after the Flower Child sneaked up on me in the lube room and bummed a couple of dollars. And it starts with a carful of guys pulling into the station and driving up to the pumps.

Ding-ding goes the bell inside the lube bay as the car's wheels roll over the black rubber rope-like alarm strung across the island drive-way, letting me know I've got a customer. Before you can say, "It's three blocks that way," I shove the last bite of a Gaucho cookie into my face, set down my red thermos cup full of piping hot chocolate, and hop on out to the island to eagerly do my buck-twenty-an-hour job.

I only get through the door and a couple steps out onto the island, though, before one of the guys piles out of the car, rushes over to me with a great big smile on his face, and tells me they just need some directions and do I have a map in the office.

"You bet I do," I'm proud to report, and I lead the guy through the office door to the lovely map hanging on the common wall between the office and the lube bay. He's walking so close behind me that I'm *pret-tee* darn sure he really likes my cologne, or else his personal space parameters are just way narrower than mine are. For my money, he could back off a few paces.

But without regard to my need for greater personal space, the guy slides past me as we walk through the door—still sniffing my neck, I guess, as he goes—and insinuates himself to my right so that if I'm gonna look at the map with him and instruct him on the intricacies of his intended journey, I'll have to turn my back to the front door and to the island.

And to the cash box.

"So where're ya headed?" I ask, and the guy stammers out some-thing about Beach Boulevard and then something about Placentia

Avenue, and I think to myself, *Wow, those two streets aren't even in the same vicinity.* Either this guy's from Floyd's Knobs, Indiana, or Monkey's Eyebrow, Kentucky, or else his sense of direction's screwed up more than mine. And mine's just short of a diagnosable disability.

Thinking maybe it'll be clearer on the second take, I ask, "Where was that you said?" but as soon as I ask it, I kinda wish I'd left it alone. Sores just don't get better when you pick at 'em.

With a lovely smile and very nice direct eye contact—which he seems to be actually *insisting* on—the gentleman gives me more randomness about Orangethorpe to Chapman but did he cross Beach on the way to Euclid and where does the Riverside Freeway meet the San Diego, or something like that. I'm beginning to feel like I'm having an out-of-body experience.

Well, right away, I entertain a couple of suspicions about why this guy's having so much trouble communicating, but I'm not smelling anything funny emanating from this smiling mouth—although I can't say, either, that there's any kind of *pleasant* fragrance here—so I don't believe he's drunk. And even in '69 there's surprisingly not really all that much tokin' going on around this neck of the woods that I know of, so I guess we're OK on that point too. But if this guy ever enters a contest of oration, he's just not going to fare well at all.

I still don't have a clue about what the man needs in the way of directions, but now he's pointing to the map and asking me about this road here, and I tell him that's Orangethorpe, does he wanna get to Orangethorpe—but he ignores me and points to another street about half a city away and asks me about that one. I'm just not making heads nor tails of this thing. If this is a tourist trying to find a route through Orange County that'll hit all the historical highlights, I'm gonna have to break the bad news to him that I'm originally from the Deep South and don't know that route.

Then, just like a windstorm that starts without warning in the blink of an eye and ends the same way, the guy says, "Well, OK then, 'preciate your time, fella. Gotta run," and before I can give him the number of a good therapist—speech and/or psycho—he's out of the office, into the car, and laying down rubber that I'll have to try to hose off before I leave.

Sheesh.

I watch these enigmas drive away, then I head back to the lube bay to find my box of Gauchos and the thermos cup full of hot chocolate that isn't piping so much anymore. My kingdom for a microwave. I sit down to polish off one or two more of these lovely peanut butter treats before I've gotta get up and prepare to close down for the night.

The cookies, as always, are nummy.

And now to my nightly tasks. Mop the lube bay floor. Make sure the accordion door's secured and locked. Bring in the trash cans, aka empty oil drums. Bring in the STP, Bardahl, Pennzoil, and Quaker State product display racks. Roll in the display tires stacked in front of the office. Hose down the island. Make sure the rental trailers are OK and bring in the hitches. Hit the main switch to turn off the island lights and the Union 76 street sign.

And bring in the cash box.

When my family moved from Mississippi in 1962, we didn't bring much with us to California because we sold all our furniture and replaceable possessions before we left. What few things we did want at our new home, other than clothes, we packed in boxes and left in our otherwise empty house in Baldwyn, where they were to stay until we made arrangements to have them shipped out to us. Mostly, it was just boxes of books—Encyclopedia Britannica, Book of Knowledge, Childcraft, church books, novels, Dad's college textbooks, stuff like that. My grandmother, who lived next door just down the hill, was to watch over the place and keep everything safe.

But even a loving grandmother can be tricked and deceived. And so it was one night when some lovely, considerate person or persons managed somehow to talk their way past Mama Morris to get into our house. There went all the boxes that were waiting to be shipped.

She called to let us know that everything we'd left behind was lost.

If you've ever had something taken from you, you'll certainly understand the feeling of violation, knowing that someone was in your personal world in a way that they shouldn't have been and that something you prize highly, or something that you're responsible for, or something that can't be replaced is gone. And there's nothing you can do about it.

It's a sickening feeling.

And it's the same feeling I'm experiencing right now, looking at my cash box.

Although the box's cover's closed as usual, I figure out pretty quickly that there's a problem. Along the left side of the box and also toward the front of the box—right where the cover rests when it's shut—the metal's gouged and dented and twisted this way and that, in just the way you might expect metal to be gouged and dented and twisted by a screwdriver or a crowbar or a knife. Now, I don't hold myself to be the most observant kid in the world, and if she were asked outright, my mom would either have to lie or admit that I don't pay very close attention to things around the house most of the time. But I'm just *pret-tee* darn sure about my cash box at any given time, and at the moment what I'm sure of is that it wasn't gouged and dented and twisted when I came to work today.

Which could only mean it's been gouged and dented and twisted *since* I came to work today.

The truth is, I'm not so worried about the *condition* of the box as I am about the *contents* of the box. So I guess the thing to do—even though I don't wanna do it—is to pop open the cover and see just what I've got here.

Yank the wad of keys from my retractable key chain, pick the big fat brass one that opens the cash box, shove it into the lock, turn it, watch the cover pop up.

Watch the cover pop up.

Watch the cover . . .

Hmmm.

Now, the cover usually pops up rather snappy as soon as I turn the key, but this time it doesn't. It tries to, but because it's bent and twisted, all it can give me's a little burp—just moves a fraction of an inch, and that's all it can do. So I use my shaky fingers to urge it open, and with a little pressure applied just above the lock, the cover finally pops all the way open.

Uh-oh.

Immediately I can see the dealer copies of credit card receipts lying on the bottom of the box. And while this may sound like good news, it isn't. Because the reason why I can see the credit card receipts is that the removable black plastic bill-and-coin tray has, along with all the bills and coins it was holding, been removed just like it was designed to be. But at the wrong time and by the wrong person.

Like I said, I'm not the world's most highly observant person, and if you tried, you could probably drive home to a jury that I'm not even all that bright generally. It really doesn't take Sherlock Holmes or a rocket scientist, though, to figure out who it was that wasn't supposed to open the box tonight but did, anyway.

The map guy.

Well, the guys *with* the map guy while the map guy was keeping me occupied.

If I weren't nearly in shock, I'd be all screaming and yelling and out of control and probably running frantically to the road to flag down the first police car I see, but I am, so I'm not, so I don't. I just numbly grit my teeth and bite my tongue in a futile effort to muster some manner of self-dispensed therapy as I detach the cash box and tote it inside.

Now, I'm emotional inches away from being in total shock and headed for being angry, and I'm just so sick at my stomach that I figure I'm gonna barf, but somehow I manage not to. After I set the box down in its usual place inside the lube bay, I know I've gotta call Bill or Jerry and tell 'em what's up. Again, I feel like I'm gonna barf, but, again, I manage not to. I swear I'd just rather have my front teeth pulled with rusty pliers and no novocaine than to make that call, but I know it can't be avoided, so I decide to go ahead and call Jerry.

Or maybe I'll just save us all some time and just scribble out a quick letter of resignation that includes an admission of total incompetence and a plea for forgiveness, leave it on the cashbox, and disappear pathetically into the night.

But Jerry saw me step into a pan of bulk oil once and didn't kill me for it, so I figure with him maybe I've got a chance.

I screw my courage to the sticking-place and make the call.

"Are you OK?" Jerry says to me after I explain briefly what's happened, and it almost makes me cry to know that the first thing he'd think to ask me is am I OK.

Another of those lessons I mentioned. A lesson in compassion that I won't forget.

But then Jerry's gotta get down to the nitty gritty of details, and I tell him—with the best sentences I can manage to put together—just what I think happened tonight and what the situation is. Do I know how much money was in the box, he wants to know, and I'm sorry to say I don't, but he understands and says he'll call the police and take care of it from here. So I hang around the station for a while, figuring Jerry will show up with the police and they'll probably want to ask me some questions about what happened and maybe even get my description of the map guy. But after nearly an hour, nobody's shown up, and I figure if anyone was coming they'd be here by now. No *way* am I gonna call Jerry and disturb him again, so I just make sure everything's locked up tight and then head for home on my trusty Honda 90.

When I show up to work the next day, I find that the wounded cashbox has been replaced by a new one, standing bravely out on the island just like nothing had ever happened. Neither Jerry nor Bill ever discusses the incident with me again, and I never talk to any police officers about it, so I figure that my bosses just wrote off the whole thing and let it go.

Another imaginable scenario that teases my sense of retribution is that, in their spare time, Bill and Jerry hunted down the heathens that stole their money and embarrassed their young friend and dispensed a little East LA justice of their own.

It's a fantastic scenario, I know, and one I'll never be able to prove—but as a means of salving my feelings of injury and violation, it'll do.

And if my sense of humanity's been diminished tonight by the selfish, unkind, greedy act of one person, it's raised to new heights by another just a few days later when I open an envelope mailed to me with a return name and address that over the years will be erased from my memory a bit at a time until they become altogether lost. But the lesson its contents teach me—a lesson in integrity—will endure forever.

The envelope contains two one-dollar bills.

9

I assault my roommate

Oh, the joys of a Friday night when you're a freshman male student living in the dorms at Brigham Young University in 1969. Sky's the limit when it comes to interesting activities.

There are places to be seen. Things to be done. Envelopes to push. Flames to brush. Excitement to be had.

Well, you get the idea.

Just check out these exciting deals.

Just across the street, you've got the 7-Eleven where you can bag—ahem—all the Doritos you could want—read *afford*—and enough Dr. Pepper to keep you going right on into the wee hours.

You've got the main-floor dorm lounge with the piano and the community television set that's guaranteed to have only the most interesting programs playing at all times, as decided—through some complex, unspoken, communal dynamics—by the lively and popular souls gathered there to watch.

Across campus, you've got the Wilkinson Center, with its exciting Memorial Lounge, where you can sit and watch the luckless people who apparently have no place to go on a Friday night except here, to sit on the lovely over-stuffed furniture and listen to the piped-in music while they watch the other luckless people who are also here.

Also in the Wilkinson Center, you've got the Varsity Theatre, where for a quarter—if you've *got* a quarter—you can watch a relatively current movie if you're OK with BYU's method of censorship, which is to just turn off the sound altogether for some arbitrary length of time to make sure that an offending word's exorcized. Most of the time, you can hear enough of a movie to follow its plot, if not its nuances. But to be absolutely certain that a swear word is completely expunged, the censor allows himself a rather generous margin for error. So you may lose the audio through an entire scene.

That's what happened recently when *Planet of the Apes* played here. In the climactic scene, there was Charlton Heston on the beach, looking at the head and torch of what appeared to be a buried Statue of Liberty. You couldn't be sure, though, because Mr. Heston's screaming tirade had been muted. Although you could tell from his famous overacting that this man was upset about *some*thing, you didn't have a clue about *what*, so you left the theater not knowing what the movie was really all about because you missed the entire dialogue of the last scene that contained the punch line.

See, Chuck swore.

Lots of letters to the editor, but no changes in Varsity Theatre policy.

If you, in fact, *don't* have twenty-five cents but wanna see a movie, you're still covered. In the Karl G. Maeser Building auditorium across campus, you've got the free weekend movie that features films sometimes as recent as ten years old and to which you can gain admission simply by flashing a blue, credit card–sized punch card that proves you made at least one cash donation to your LDS (Mormon) branch budget. Which is why they call it the "Budget Movie."

Located in the Harold B. Lee library, the listening library's another attraction at your disposal. You discover this facility when you take Humanities 101 because this is where you have to go to hear—and memorize—pieces by Beethoven, Tchaikovsky, and other classical composers so you can identify snippets of their music played by Dr. Britsch in his interactive quizzes and exams. Here you can check out a headphone set, plug it into this switchboard-looking thing on the desk in front of you, turn a spiffy dial to select a channel number as instructed, and listen to whatever music you ask for. Well, *almost* whatever you ask for. No Top 40 hits, mind you, but you can hear more than just the long-hair stuff. Yep, you can. You can listen to selected easy listening crooners or really nice elevator music. Even show tunes. Personally, I highly recommend the soundtracks from *Camelot* (the movie version with Richard Harris, not the Broadway production with

Robert Goulet) and Barbra Streisand's *Funny Girl*. All you can stand, bro. Listen till you drop or the library closes, whichever comes first.

Well, I guess that gives you a pretty good idea about the excitement that stands ready to be enjoyed by the active male freshman dorm resident. I get tired just thinking about all the intensely exciting options a guy like me has.

Which makes Friday nights like this one a little difficult to understand. Just can't figure it. All these fun and exciting things available to us, but here we are. Scott, my roommate, sitting at his desk, with his nose shoved deep into a zoology text. Big Ed, our down-the-hall neighbor, sitting at my desk, making strange noises and doing something funny with his hands—shadow puppets, maybe. I'm just not sure. And I, Mr. Excitement himself, lying on Scott's bed, absentmindedly checking out a Simon and Garfunkel album cover but mostly just staring at Scott and Big Ed and wondering what this scene's all about.

OK. I can't take it anymore. I hop to my feet in an attempt to inspire energy, and suggest that maybe there's something else to be done on this Friday night besides sit and study and mumble and read LP covers and play with our fingers.

Big Ed's up for it. You bet. *He* knows there's gotta be something better than this. *I* know there's gotta be something better than this. Heck, everybody else in the dorm isn't even *in* the dorm. That right there should be telling us something.

So let's go find it and do it—whatever the *it* is.

That's what Big Ed and I tell Scott, trying hard to recruit him to the cause. He's really enjoying this zoology text, though, and has no interest whatever in any random excitement we might be able to drum up together. In fact, he seems downright put off with Big Ed and me and our sudden aspirations—and getting more irked by the minute. The two of us are getting louder, we've got Gary Puckett and the Union Gap blasting on the stereo, and the energy barometer in the room's climbed. Now we're officially interfering with Scott's academic concentration. He'd rather we weren't here.

See, generally speaking, Scott's a bit more . . . well, let's say *spiritually conservative* than I am. Not that I'm off-the-wall wacko, mind you, just slightly rowdier and a tad more mischievous than Scott a lot of the time. But don't get me wrong about Scott. *Conservative* doesn't mean *dead*. And, despite his apathy tonight, the two of us manage to have a number of *pret-tee* darn interesting adventures together at BYU.

Take this one night during finals week, for example. Scott and I are all studied out and bored, and somewhere out there we just *know* there's trouble to be found. Conservative or risky predispositions aside, we're both just a-hankerin' to find it.

And we've got these firecrackers. Firecrackers just *begging* to fulfill the purpose of their creation.

Wouldn't it be funny, we think, *if we lit the pack and threw it up on the ledge of one of the girls' dorms and gave some lovely coed the fright of her life?*

We're on it.

We agree on a target and make our way there, firecrackers and matches in hand. It's nice and dark, and pretty much everyone's indoors, either studying for finals or in bed with finals-induced depression, so we figure we'll be able to pull off this operation easily with minimal risk of casualty or capture.

We've got the building in sight. We've got the ledge in sight. We've cased the area well enough to know that we won't actually have to run all that far to get out of sight after we've tossed the firecrackers up on the ledge. All we've gotta do's just make it to that ditch-slash-culvert over there and roll to the bottom of it. There we'll be safely out of sight, free to drink in the chaos we've caused.

Light the fuse. Toss the pack up on the ledge. Dart toward the grassy knoll as our noisy little firecrackers begin to break the stifling silence of a night heavy with Cokes and No-Doz and Doritos and beta waves and anxious anticipation of final exams.

Roll down the hill to safety and invisibility below.

R-o-o-o-o-o-l-l-l-l-l-l down the hill to safety and invisi . . .

What the . . .

It takes just a moment for Scott and me to realize that we aren't alone in this here culvert as we find ourselves pretty much on top of these other bodies that have apparently beaten us to the bottom of the hill. Two of them. I think. Maybe it's one. No, it's two.

A guy and a girl.

And they're not hunting for night crawlers.

See, the two of them are . . . Well, he's . . . I mean, she's . . . They're . . .

Hmmm.

To put it carefully, they're busy. And we're certainly not welcome. We're outta here.

But now we've got this slight problem. See, the firecrackers have caused a slight ruckus, just as we'd hoped—a ruckus that we'd planned to enjoy invisibly from down here in this culvert. A change in plans has been forced on us. We've had to come out into open view sooner than we'd hoped and now we've gotta worry about being seen. About being caught. About being fined or expelled or executed as an enemy to the BYU State.

Disguise. We need a disguise. Yep, that's what we need. But there's nothing handy in the way of a change of clothes. I guess we could go back down to the bottom of the hill and borrow that guy's clothes because he's not actually using . . . Nah. That might be confrontational. Attention-getting. And we've gotta keep a low profile.

So if we can't put *on* anything new or different we'll just take *off* something. That should make us look as different and as unidentifiable as if we'd put *on* something different.

Off come the shirts.

Of course, there's nothing obvious or conspicuous or blatant about this. Just a couple of young men running across BYU dorm lawns in the dark of night—naked from the waist up.

Despite our terrible planning and poor disguises, Scott and I manage to make it back to our good ol' C-2119. Oh, sure. Along the way we had to duck behind a car or two and even climb under one of them as far as we physically could to avoid the sharp eyes of those uniformed men in that BYU security car. As if they were actually looking for us, anyway. But the brief hiding was just a minor inconvenience. After all's said and done, Scott and I have racked up another night of campus high jinks, without casualty or capture.

But that adventure's yet to come. Tonight, Scott's clearly not in the mood for raising a ruckus. Big Ed and I are, though, and until we figure out what we're gonna do, we aren't leaving the room. It's just tough beans for my studious roommate.

At last surrendering to our determination, Scott huffs and puffs a little and takes his book to Big Ed's room down the hall for some peace and quiet.

Now, you can be sure that Big Ed and I aren't discouraged by this mutiny. Heck, let Scott do what he wants. We don't have to follow suit. We're our own men, after all. You bet we are. And we're just gonna haul off and do something exciting.

But what?

Not twenty cents between us. That takes care of the 7-Eleven and the Varsity Theatre. No interest in adding ourselves to the luckless people at the Wilkinson Center, and not in the mood for Barbra Streisand or Richard Harris at the listening library. Watching TV downstairs with whatever party crowd's gathered there couldn't possibly be any more exciting than what we're doing now, so that idea doesn't blow our skirts up, either. As for the weekend budget movie . . . well, it's too late for that.

And any activity involving members of the other sex is, sadly and pathetically, out of the question for us. Sigh.

What shall we do? What *shall* we do?

We need an adrenalin burst, that's what we need. We need to push the limits. We need to feel the intensity of life rushing through our veins. We need danger. We need risk. We need mischief. We need . . .

The Ledge.

On the second and third floor levels of our Chipman Hall, just as on all the other dorms in the Helaman Halls complex, there's a four-feet-wide concrete ledge running the length of the building on both sides. To picture it in your mind, imagine that the floor of the room extends right through the outside wall and four feet beyond.

Now, there are strict rules about this ledge, the first and main one being that you do *not* go out onto it. If you're fairly slim, it's *possible* to go through the window and get out onto the ledge—but there's a twenty-five-dollar fine for anyone stupid enough to get caught in the adventure. I said *twenty-five dollars.* To a student that doesn't have a quarter to buy a ticket to the Varsity Theatre, that twenty-five bucks might as well be eleventy bazillion gadzillion trillion.

But we ain't a-skeert. Just a few weeks from now, Big Ed and I will share the adventure of thumbing to California on a moment's notice with no money, no coats, essentially no food, and absolutely no regard for the weather.

OK. So we're stupid. But we ain't a-skeert.

And tonight we're gonna prove it. We've got a plan. A plan that just *o-o-o-z-e-s* excitement.

We're gonna assault Scott.

Since it's a nice warm night, we figure ol' Scott's gonna have the
window open while he's reading. We don't know whether he'll be sitting on a chair in front of the window, leaning back with his hooves
parked on the desk, or sitting on the bed, leaning against the concrete
block wall with one leg stretched out and the other bent at the knee so
that he can almost rest his chin on his kneecap. Scott sits like that a
lot. But we'll need to know his exact position in order to plan a proper
strategy, so Big Ed wanders on down and goes into the room, pretending to need something from his desk.

From this advanced surveillance tactic, we learn that Scott is, in
fact, sitting on the bed in the classic position and that the window's
open.

That would've been my bet.

Just down the hall, in the direction opposite Scott's location, is a
closet. In the closet's a utility sink—a sink with which Scott recently
became intimately acquainted during a bout with food poisoning. I
swear, I've never seen *anyone* throw up that much and for that long. I
was standing there by him, waiting for both his socks to splatter suddenly into the sink. But only one of them ever did.

I digress.

Above that utility sink are two shelves on which is stored a limited variety of cleaning products to be used at the students' discretion.
Yeah. Like any of us would ever actually *use* a cleaning product. On
one of those shelves—here's the salient info—stands a spray bottle.
A spray bottle filled with a fluid. We've absolutely no idea what *kind*
of fluid it is, but that information's superfluous, anyway, because we
know we need a spray bottle, and that's a spray bottle, and that's all
there is to it.

So Big Ed and I skulk on down to the closet and take the spray
bottle right down off the shelf. We dump out whatever's in it into the
sink. Let's don't take the time to rinse the bottle out, though. Surely
whatever liquid we've dumped out's perfectly safe and noncaustic. If
we're wrong, the water we're filling it with will surely dilute the residue
sufficiently to make it less than deadly.

Done and done. Now we head on down to Benny's room, just
across the hall from my room and on the same side of the hall as Big
Ed's room, which is where Scott's sitting on the bed resting his chin on
his knee, ostensibly devouring that zoology textbook.

In Benny's room, we're quickly at the window and opening it. This is the kind of window—an awning window, I think it's called—that tilts outward to open. Whatever it's called, when it's opened as fully as it can be, the tilted pane's rather horizontal but not quite perpendicular to the window frame, leaving about fifteen inches of clearance below it. *Fifteen inches.*

Now, this is one of those moments at which I'll look back in years to come, fondly recalling that I was once skinny and agile enough to maneuver my body through this fifteen-inch clearance. I'm at maximum slimness. I'm at peak agility. When these things go, I'll miss 'em forever. But tonight I've got 'em, and that's what counts. I make quick work of that slit-of-an-opening and find myself balanced carefully on the other side of the window.

Big Ed, taller than I but no bulkier, is right behind me.

We're on The Ledge.

Taking a quick look around and sighting nothing that causes us indigestion, we walk on down The Ledge past Dale's window, past Dana's window, past Jon's window. Now we're just a step or two away from the window to Big Ed's room, so we stop walking and silently drop to all-fours. Neither of us being in the ROTC program and of no particular military bent, we don't know all the silent hand signals that an ROTC cadet would probably be using—you know, the fist in the air to signify *stop*, the two fingers pointed at your own eyes and then away from you to indicate *look around*—stuff like that. Even without those covert stalking skills, though, we somehow manage to make each other understand that Big Ed will wait on this side of the window while I crawl carefully beneath it to the other side and make myself ready.

Swift. Smooth. Stealthy. We should do this for a living.

In place, we know exactly what to do. Big Ed raises his head just enough to get a visual on the target while remaining out of sight. He raises the spray bottle to clear the edge of the window, points it at the mark, and squeezes the trigger.

Nothing.

We forgot to prime the spray bottle.

Big Ed points the sprayer downward and squeezes the trigger several times until a stream of water shoots out. Now he's ready, and he aims again just as he did before.

Spray and yank the bottle down, out of sight. Wait.

We *wanna* look to see whether we've drawn blood and what kind of reaction Scott's blessed us with, but we don't dare raise our heads right away. So we stay out of sight while Big Ed carefully tosses the spray bottle to me, as previously planned.

It's a crossfire kind of deal.

We wait a few seconds until we figure it's safe to try again, and then I raise my head just enough to see the target. There Scott still sits—on the bed, reading. No panic that I can see. No response of any kind, as far as I can tell.

Maybe Big Ed missed. I won't.

I raise the spray bottle with my left hand because I'm on the right side of the window and need the angle to fire in the proper direction. I squeeze off two quick bursts. Duck. Wait.

From inside the room, blessed words of confirmation.

"What . . . What the . . ."

Bull's-eye.

The snickers are welling up inside Big Ed and me, and it's even money that we won't be able to suppress them for long—or even for another three seconds—so we show ourselves unabashedly and fire away. The streams find the target again and again, and the snickers have turned to guffaws, and Scott's up on his feet and coming toward us.

Now, *this* is fun. *This* is what we came to the university for. We've somehow stumbled onto our destiny. To heck with all this education stuff. We know what it's really about.

We're Ninja Spraymaster Assassins.

And our Friday night's seen some excitement at last.

Scott sees the light before we do. The flashing blue light. It's on top of the blue and white BYU security car that's rolled silently into the parking lot, unnoticed by the assassins as we focused carefully on our mission. As Scott runs toward the window, he's pointing and yelling something—laughter, warning, Gettysburg Address, who knows what he's yelling at us. Then Big Ed and I see the light too, and panic rolls over us like some massive ocean wave, freezing us where we stand.

If you've ever been caught red-handed doing some forbidden thing, you may understand our response.

There are times in a young man's life when he finds himself

suddenly at a crossroads—a crossroads that he hasn't sought out but which has been thrust upon him—and discovers the unspeakable anxiety of not knowing which road to take and having too little time to consider his options. Time only to act, knowing intuitively that, finally, the odds are that both of the roads will end badly.

I'm talking about a frying-pan-and-fire kind of thing.

It's in just such a moment of ultimate perplexity that Big Ed and I decide—independently but simultaneously—that we can*not* remain on The Ledge. One story below us lies the ground, the medium that can save us from the baton-toting, fully-armed security guard who's exited his lighted car and is moving—jogging—in our direction, spraying a flashlight before him and shouting at us with an arm in the air as though he were hailing a taxi.

In only another few moments, we will—if we remain on The Ledge—owe twenty-five bucks to whatever kitty BYU student fines feed.

With one brief moment of eye contact, Big Ed and I turn and take the twelve-foot plunge to the ground. The legs give on impact, but they're young legs. It takes only a moment to regain our balance and put those young legs in motion.

The officer's still running, still shouting, still pointing the flashlight, still waving the arm. But we'll not be the hailed taxi tonight. We'll not feed the kitty tonight.

We will be The Wind.

Around the corner and to the south toward the main door, the two of us run, knowing that The Man isn't far behind—but with our backs to him now, we can't be sure how much ground he's gained or lost. We just run like Olympians chasing gold and leave it to the Fates to decide the outcome of this contest.

We figure a straight-line flight's no good because the longer we stay in sight, the more likely we are to be identified in some future lineup. So we pass the main door of Chipman and round the southwest corner, headed for Hinckley Hall. We duck in the southwest door on the first floor of Hinckley and fly down the hall at somewhere near the speed of sound. We know we're not clear yet because halfway down the hall we hear the door slam—the door we just came through—and we know who that is because we still hear the yelling. We're not about to take the time to look behind us, though—we just fly on toward the other wing and the northeast exit, hit the crash bar like a DEA officer bustin' in the door to a suspected drug pusher's den, and bolt through it. But instead of streaking toward another building, we just head right up the outside stairs to the second floor, bust through the door and barrel down that hall. By the time we get to the end of the hall, we still haven't heard the door slam behind us like last time, and we take that as a good sign—but we ain't *about* to slow down yet. Right on down the other wing we race.

I quickly calculate that we may now have enough lead to change our tactic from fleeing to hiding, so I begin shaking door knobs as I pass each door in the hall.

We get lucky. In an unthinking heartbeat, I open an unlocked door and fall through with Big Ed right after me, flopping to the floor and hoping against hope that The Man isn't right behind us. We don't know whose room we've just crashed into, but we don't fear being shot as intruders because we know that gun control at BYU's just *pret-tee* darn severe. And we've found some luck here—no one's home. For a moment or two, we just lie quietly on the floor, trying our hardest to manage our breathing, which is just about out of control and way louder than is helpful in this predicament. Then we look at each other, and with the help of some extrasensory perception kind of thing, we both know exactly what we need to do. Head for the closets. Big Ed in this one, I in that one. After we pull the doors closed as far as we can, there's nothing to do but wait to see what the Fates have in store for us.

Who knows how long we've been in these silly closets. It seems like forever, and it's at least long enough that my breathing's almost down to normal except for the residual effect of the panic, which isn't going away anytime soon, I fear.

Can't hear any yelling in the hall, and no one's crashing through the door, so I begin to take heart. I crack the closet door open just a tad to see Big Ed opening his too. He's wide-eyed and smiling, so I figure *he* figures we're in the clear, and that gives me a lift. We both come out of the closet—so to speak—and wonder out loud whether we dare open the door and look out. For all we know, The Man could be standing just outside the door, waiting for us to show ourselves so he can scare the whazzit out of us, slap on the cuffs, and take us on down to the pokey.

But it's clear to us that we can't stay here forever. I mean, whoever lives here's gonna eventually insist that we leave, so let's just go ahead and check out the situation now.

Open the door. Look this way. Look that way. No one. Clear as far as we can see.

Even though we see nobody, we take a cautious tack and don't head straight back to Chipman. Instead, we serpentine our way through the other Helaman Halls buildings just to make sure we're not being followed or tricked into showing ourselves. We stand out on the sidewalk by 1230 North Street for several minutes to watch the area from a safe vantage point, making sure all's quiet on the dorm front before we commit to going in.

All is, in fact, quiet. No security vehicles. No uniforms. No commotion.

Quiet. Safe. Back to my room.

And there's Scott, sitting on the bed, leaning against the concrete block wall with one leg stretched out and the other bent at the knee so that he can almost rest his chin on his kneecap, ostensibly devouring a *microbiology* text.

There's just no hope for some people.

10

I try to buy a moustache

Mom and Dad lived in Minnesota for a few years in the forties while Dad was on active duty in the army. In fact, the third and fourth of their five children were born in Brainerd. I can only imagine the ecological shock of such cold, snowy, northern weather after having spent nearly all of their lives in the semitropical environs of Mississippi. But somehow they managed not only to adjust to it, but even to love it. And sixty-some-odd years later, they'll still look back at their Minnesota years as something very special, often remembering those cherished experiences aloud.

Not long after Minnesota, Colorado became the military home for Mom and Dad. Anyone who's visited that lovely Rocky Mountain state knows that there's just not a whole big lot of difference between it and Minnesota with regard to climate. Well, maybe Minnesota gets a *little* colder than Colorado, but after it reaches a certain point, cold's cold. Anyway, there in the cold and snow and ice of Colorado's where the fifth of their children was born.

That would be me.

Although I didn't live in Colorado for very long after making my grand entrance, I'll be forever perplexed that I've never developed at least *some* affinity for cold weather. I mean, cold being the first temperature I experienced—well, to be accurate, it was the first temperature I experienced after leaving the military hospital at Camp Carson—it seems at least an *arguable* supposition that my body and its internal thermostat would have developed a kinship with that chilly clime, and that from that day on, I'd somehow feel more comfortable in cold than in heat.

If there's ever been a supposition further from the truth, I'd love to hear it.

I thrive in warmth. In heat. In sunshine. It could never be too hot or too sunny for me. Throughout my entire life, I'll do all that I can to make sure I enjoy every possible moment of that warm-me-clear-to-the-marrow-of-my-bones feeling that only clear, splashing sunshine can generate. In my youth, I enjoyed the heat and humidity of the deep South. In my high school years, I spent every possible summer moment on Southern California beaches. In my midlife years, I'll drive a little Honda Del Sol convertible, become SCUBA certified, and go on Caribbean cruises where I'll seek the sun while others around me complain of exposure and try to find shade from the very thing they've paid so dearly to experience.

I will be friends with the sun.

A commitment that seems to fly in the face of my decision to attend college in Utah.

I mean, in Utah there's just a whole *bunch* of cold and snow and ice and, for the boy who's committed himself to a lasting relationship with warmth and the sun, climatological misery. But that's where I find myself in 1969, attending Brigham Young University right smack in the heart of Winter Wonderland, where there are only three seasons: July, August, and winter. And the greatest irony of all is that I'll complete both my undergraduate and graduate university education in Utah and settle here to raise a family and live out my life, wondering each year from December to April why in the world I'm here.

Go figure.

So . . . at the moment, I'm in the middle of my first Utah winter of 1969–70, and I just pretty much can't find a single thing about it that I like. It's cold. It's messy. It's wet. It's miserable. It makes my nose itch and chaps my lips. But I'm learning to deal with it.

Allow me to emphasize the point that *dealing* with something isn't the same as *liking* something. In fact, in the very moment when you realize you're having to *deal* with something, you know that it is—by incontestable logical extension—something you don't *like*. Things that you *like* you don't have to *deal* with.

I keep waiting for the delayed expression of some recessive genetic predisposition to enjoying cold, but it hasn't come. Nor will it, ever. From this I conclude that a Colorado cold-climate birth contributes nothing toward the development of a gene that'll express as an affinity for cold and snow and ice.

At least it didn't foster the development of such a gene in me.

So I deal with winter.

And I deal with a whole bunch of other inconveniences while I'm a freshman living in the Helaman Halls dorms at BYU here in Provo.

For example, I deal with the fact that I've no motorized transportation. Nor does Scott, my roommate. Very few dorm rats do, these days. Mel, down the hall, has a brand spanking new Mercury—albeit with a totally lame three-on-the-tree and just how cool can a Mercury coupe be, anyway—that he paid cash for on the very day he arrived here, but on *principle* he never lets anyone borrow it. Whatever the spam *that* means. Another guy down the hall has a car too, but I don't know him at all and won't even remember his name in years to come, so you'll understand that I never ask him for the loan of his car.

Of course, Scott and I do have one connection to motorized transportation.

Val has a car.

Val's engaged to Scott's older sister, Renee. If he weren't such a cool head, I'd hate Val's guts and even the ground he walks on because he's removing Renee from the realm of "possible-if-not-probable" to the grand abyss of "never-in-this-life-bub." See, Renee's the most beautiful woman I've ever seen. I'm talking drop-dead, jaw-dropping, you-can't-believe-what-you're-seeing beautiful. And, with apologies to my sweet Dianne who'll assume the title in just a few short years from now, Renee's been the fantasy love of my life since I met her years ago. Even though I've actually accompanied—well, sort of—this most gorgeous of creatures to see *Far From the Madding Crowd* and *The Sterile Cuckoo* on the big screen and even hiked up Y Mountain with her (where, by the by, I hugged her without—ahem—my shirt on) I've always known I'd never *really* have a chance with her because she's a goddess, for one thing. And the older sister of my best friend, for another. And every time I see her I get so excited and agitated that I become a total saphead and fall over any nearby table or chair, for another.

But I'm getting distracted. Even just the thought of Renee always does that to me.

As I was saying, Val has a car. Boy, does Val have a car. A silver 1969 Porsche 911-S Targa that's so sweet to look at that you just wanna cry, and so sweet to ride in that it makes movement through space an absolute joy. One of these babies will set you back about nine grand—and although that's more money than I can imagine *having,* let alone spending on a *car,* it's nothing when you know that forty years from now a restored version of this automotive masterpiece will bring you many, many times that amount. At least partly because production won't keep up with demand, with only about six hundred of these little critters produced.

It's just not a bad thing for chicks to see Scott or me in this sleek, sporty, gorgeous creation, either. See, here's the deal. If you see a silver Porsche tooling around Provo, you can be sure that one of two people's driving it because as near as we can discover, there are only two of these silver beauties in this neck of the woods.

Val's, of course.

And Robert Redford's.

Yep. *That* Robert Redford.

Now, Mr. Redford's ride may actually be a 912 Targa that was produced between 1965 and 1969, a model intended to ease the transition between the 356 and the 911. I'm just not *sure* this is what he drives because ... well, I'm really not that good when it comes to identifying high performance vehicles. I'm a little better at identifying basic transportation cars like Chryslers, Volkswagens, Fords—like that. And I'm especially adept at recognizing my all-time favorite: the 1957 Chevy Bel Air Nomad station wagon.

Like the one Jim and I had a close encounter with last summer. We were just driving around, letting our Jack in the Box cheeseburgers digest, when we happened to see this white '57 Nomad wagon at that used car lot on Chapman. It was late in the evening, and the lot wasn't open for business, but we liked the car and felt the urge to check it out, so we promptly parked the ol' Chrysler to take a look-see.

The thing is, ever since I became aware of these sleek '57 beauties some years ago, I've imagined owning one—but I might as well imagine owning California because I seldom have two dimes to rub together, so just forget about owning a car like this. But anyway, *you can look,* I said to myself, so out we hopped to get a closer view of this gorgeous thing.

Nice shape. Clean, good paint, no dents. Good interior, no bumpers hanging to the ground or anything like that. This particular vehicle fit nicely into my Fantasy-Vehicles-That-Kevin-Will-Never-Own list.

Then I noticed something. Something just lying there on the car—right there between the edge of the hood and the left fender.

Keys.

Omigosh. The *keys*.

Lying right there on the hood. Attached to a key ring with a plastic fob labeled, *1957 Chevy Bel Air Nomad Wagon.*

Wow.

Now, several possible scenarios entered our minds, probably at just about the same time because that's the way Jim and I think. We're two peas in a pod. Cut from the same bolt of cloth. One's yin to the other's yang.

Well, you get the idea.

So what's it gonna be? we both wondered, but not with words out loud. With eye contact.

Options.

First of all, it was *pret-tee* darn obvious that we could just climb into this little puppy and head for the north forty, never to be seen again. *Never* to be seen again. Hmmm. Didn't actually sound that great when I thought about it in those terms, but that's how it'd have to be if we just outright swiped this little beauty, because we could never come home again, that's for sure. Yeah, we'd get a pretty cool car out of the deal, that's true—but we just didn't even wanna *imagine* how our parents would take the news of sons on the lam. Pictures in the post office, and all that. And if we ever got caught, it'd be highly doubtful that we'd have a lot of family support on visiting day at San Quentin.

Then there's the joy ride angle. Could just take a nice spin around the block and enjoy local sights for a few minutes before bringing the ol' Chev back to its parking space on the corner of the lot. That'd probably give us a nice little adrenaline high. But if we were to get pulled over by some hyperactive Johnny Law who loves to make sure teenagers driving a cool car aren't up to no good, then the adventure would end up pretty much the same as if we got caught just outright stealing the thing. See, the cop just wouldn't understand the difference.

Of course, there's the whole *conscience* thing, too, that got in our way just a tad, what with the two of us having been born of goodly parents who'd taught us somewhat in the manner of truth and right. So, in the final analysis, we knew without discussion that we weren't gonna take this thing, no matter whether we thought we could get away with it or not.

Just wouldn't be right, man.

So we settled on a safer, saner, middle-of-the-road solution. Just unlocked the doors and sat in the beast for a few minutes, imagining owning the thing and using it to attract every manner of outstanding young lady. Then stepped back out into the real world, laid the keys back on the fender, and hit the road.

So, yes. I know a 1957 Chevy Bel Air Nomad station wagon when I see it.

But I digress.

Back to the Porsches.

Now, even though Val's 911-S Targa and Mr. Redford's 912 Targa may not be *exactly* alike, they're both Porsches. And they're both silver. That's close enough kin that the average passerby isn't likely to notice the difference.

So. If someone happens to know that Robert Redford lives around here and that he drives a silver Porsche, and if that someone happens to see Scott or me driving around in Val's silver Porsche, and if that someone happens to be a girl . . . well, the thought that Scott or I might be mistaken for the Sundance Kid or even that some young lady might think we're hanging with him just helps us feel a big fat lot better about ourselves. In our fevered little post-adolescent minds, we imagine that our stock's gone way up.

Like there's any other direction it could possibly go.

There's just one little drawback here. See, even though he's a generous soul, Val's no bonehead. Which means he won't actually lend the car to Scott and me outright. He'll chauffeur us here and there, but that's as far as his good sense allows his generosity to go. And because that little silver bullet of his only has two seats, Val's chauffeur service isn't practicable when Scott and I need motorized transportation to the same place at the same time.

What all this means is that, when Scott and I need to go somewhere that requires something more than shoe leather, we've gotta find someone with a car that has sufficient seating for the two of us, and someone who's adopted no principles against the lending of said car. It's not so easy for us to find this combination. In fact, it can be just a *leet-tle* bit like trying to find subtlety in Don Rickles.

So we've just gotta thumb, usually. Hitch a ride.

Now, we'd generally prefer to bum a ride from someone we know. That's a little less time-consuming and a lot less tiresome than thumbing. But sometimes we've got no choice in the matter. That's when we throw out the ol' thumbs and—just like Blanche DuBois in *A Streetcar Named Desire*—depend on the kindness of strangers. Of course, in late '69 and early '70, it's still a relatively safe thing to crawl into a car with a stranger who stops to give you a ride. And since everyone else we know seems to do it too, we don't give it a second thought when we've gotta pull that *thumbing* arrow from our quiver of transportation options.

Plus, we've seen the movie *It Happened One Night* and, having carefully studied Clark Gable's wonderful instruction to Claudette Colbert on the art of hitchhiking, we're just *pret-tee* darn skilled at this mode of transportation. You can bet your sweet bippy on that.

So on this one day when Scott and I decide we've a mission to accomplish in Salt Lake City—forty-ish miles north of Provo—and nobody with a large enough car's interested in shuttling us, we know it's time to use the thumbs. Even though this method's gonna take a little more time, we're willing to endure the inconvenience.

Because it's an important mission.

See, it turns out that I was born *with* some things I wish I'd been born *without*. A temper that can explode in a heartbeat, spraying emotional shrapnel on just about everyone within visual or auditory range. Curly hair that won't conform to the styles of the sixties and seventies. A nose roughly the size of Rhode Island, as I learned during my childhood years when my big brother pinned my shoulders to the ground with his knees and flipped my proboscis back and forth while taunting me with, "ooooh, what a big nose you have." Fingers that are shorter and pointier than fingers should be, which I know to be true because of Aunt Agnes's frank observations. Big toes that point up and curl like Aladdin's shoes, poking premature holes in every sock I own and making my Keds deck shoes look like they're trying in vain to contain some let-me-out-of-here critter inside.

And I was born *without* some things I wish I'd been born *with*. Patience with pretty much anything. Six-and-a-half feet of body. Muscles. Female-magnetic looks and personality. A med school IQ. A trust fund.

And facial hair.

On balance, I guess it's true that what a person wants most is whatever he doesn't have. And of all the things I don't have, it seems that facial hair is, at this moment in my life, my most serious deficiency. I'm just flat sick and tired of being the only guy on the dorm floor that doesn't shave. Well . . . OK. I *do* shave—and I even have my very own Gillette Techmatic razor, just like Elvis uses—but only once in a blue moon, and then only so the two or three hairs on my chin don't get so long that if I braided them I'd look like some villainous despot from early Chinese literature.

Which brings me to the purpose of our mission in Salt Lake City. I'm gonna buy a moustache.

See, I've heard that some hair salons sell fake—but high quality, mind you—moustaches. I figure this could be just the thing for a hairless lip like mine. Now, when I say hairless, I mean *hairless*. Even if I don't shave for a month, I still have so few cylindrical keratinous filaments growing in the skin above my upper lip that I can't even cheat and use mascara. And don't think I wouldn't do it. I'd paint every single one of those puppies with that stuff if only there were some to paint. But there aren't, so I can't, so I don't. And I'm not greedy. I'm not asking for a full beard, which I couldn't enjoy anyway, what with BYU officially outlawing the full beard this year. No, I'm asking only for enough lip hair to support a nicely trimmed moustache. Nicely trimmed moustaches are acceptable—or at least defensible—at BYU.

Even if I decide not to wear my fake 'stache here, I can sure take it home with me to Southern Cal and impress the whazzit out of my friends there. At the very least, I can look at myself in the mirror when I'm wearing it and happily pretend that I've finally and at long last reached puberty's elusive end.

Now, I don't even know that any salons in Salt Lake City actually sell such a thing. But what I'm *pret-tee* darn sure about is that no business establishment of any type in *Provo* would carry such avant-garde accessories. So I'm gambling that in Salt Lake's at-least-pseudo-progressive atmosphere I'll find the lip wig of my dreams.

Being a supportive friend, Scott's always been interested in my social success and welfare, so he'll go with me, he says, and we can make a day of it. Not that Scott needs to find a salon that sells fake moustaches, mind you. He's had hair on his face since he tossed his Binky. I mean, even after he shaves, his face still looks like it's painted black. If you completely de-bearded Scott, I believe you'd find a whole other beard underneath that one.

So with no more planning than saying, "Hey, this looks like a good time to go," the two of us hoof it on out to the nearest I-15 on-ramp and stick out the trusty thumbs. It's a little cold outside today, but that doesn't matter. I'm wearing my sheepskin coat, and it's keeping me warm enough. And we're not really worried about the weather because even though it's cold, it's not snowing. All we're worried about is can we get a ride into Salt Lake.

Which turns out to be not such a hard thing to do. There's a car stopping for us now, and its friendly driver takes us right downtown Salt Lake City. Couldn't ask for more than that.

And now what?

The best next step seems to be to find a phone book. So we look here and we look there until we find a pay phone that's got one of those hard-plastic-covered phone books hanging below, attached to the booth by some kind of double-jointed-metal-swivel-thingy that defies written description but is supposed to allow easy access to the book. It doesn't. In fact, it's about as easy to manage as a cowlick without Brylcreem. You want it to turn this way, it turns that way. You finally get it turned up, the phone book inside's upside down. And once you get it turned right and the book's right side up, the whole flippin' thing's so slippery and heavy that you can't hold it, and it crashes downward, often breaking bones as it drops.

Whoever invented this little widget really needs to be hunted down and physically harmed. Better yet, there should be a law that requires him to install this mess in his house and live with the pain of his ill-conceived, devil-inspired invention every time he needs to make a call. I guess I could say *her* instead of *his,* but I suspect the correct possessive pronoun to be masculine because no self-respecting woman I know would be sadistic enough to invent such a thing.

So we find a pay phone with a phone book monster hanging threateningly below. While Scott distracts it, I sneak up and come down on it like a cowboy laying his body on a bolting steer, intent on wrestling it to the ground. This time I'm lucky. Within less than an hour, and sustaining only minor finger sprains and some light emotional bruising, I manage to tame the beast well enough to get the book open.

Now we've gotta decide do we look under the word *salon* or *hair* or *moustache* or *fake* or what. We're both students at one of the country's finest universities, so you'd think we could figure this thing out pretty fast, but . . . well, it's gonna require a little discussion first. And when Scott and I put our minds to it, we can *really* discuss. I mean, we can discuss the whazzit out of just about *anything*. This time it turns out to be a pointless discussion, though, because when we finally get around to looking up the debated words, it turns out that only *hair* and *salon* are even *in* the yellow pages, and there are precious few listings under either of those.

But there are at least *some* listings, so now it's time to throw the dart. Looks like the nearest one—and because we're on foot, location's crucial—is some place called The Hair Den or some such name that I'll not remember in years to come. We figure it's as good a place to start as any, so up the street we go. Past the luggage store with lovely Samsonite briefcases on display. Past a little greasy spoon café with a *Special of the Day* advertised in the window. Across the street and past the Centre movie theater and around the corner.

And there it is.

This little cubicle of an office or store or what*ever* it is doesn't have much of a store front to speak of, and there's nothing to alert a passerby to what product might be sold or what service might be offered here. As I push open the glass door, I see little in the way of furnishings other than an odd-looking reception desk-slash-counter with a glass display built into the middle of it, beneath a cash register that looks like it might have been bought at a garage sale. Thirty years ago. I *think* those are hair products on display through the glass, but you may not wanna take my word for it.

Anyway, Scott and I enter bravely. As I release the door, a little bell hanging from it tinkles behind me. We step deeper into the enigma of this place, toward the desk where sits a young lady sporting the most interesting facial make-up I've ever seen and a hairstyle not attributable to any decade *I've* lived through. To the left of said desk, a narrow hall slithers back into the darkness of who-knows-what's-back-there, and there's no perceptible sound of any kind until the young lady at the desk says, "Can I help you?"

Suddenly I feel an inexplicable urge to whisper a password that'll get me past this young lady and into whatever's down that hall. The old speakeasy or blind pig was way before my time, but I'm starting to get the feeling that I'm having my first experience at one or the other of them.

I look at Scott and Scott looks at me, and I guess we're each struggling to decide without the benefit of discussion whether or not this establishment's been listed improperly in the yellow pages. But I know I need to respond to the young lady's question, so I pull myself together and cognitively organize the appropriate response.

"Uhhhhhh . . ."

Perfect.

"Did you *need* something?" the young lady asks—now with a little attitude—and I'm pretty sure I did just a minute ago, but now I can't for the life of me think what it might have been.

"Uhhhhhh . . ."

Maybe I'll change my major to speech.

But Scott, ever cool and collected and capable, manages to explain that we're looking for moustaches, and before I can jump into the conversation with another well-thought-out "uhhhhhh," the young lady says, "Excuse me, you said you're looking for *what*?"

Scott's strength has inspired me. I'm back in the game now, and I take the baton to run the next verbal lap. "We're looking for moustaches," I say, and when the lady seems to need a little clarification, I explain that I've heard about moustaches that can be glued or taped or—for all I know—*stapled* to the upper lip so a guy who doesn't have a moustache but wants a moustache can have a moustache.

Behind a perplexing, patronizing smile and without perceptible movement of any kind, the young lady just stares at me and says flatly, "Well, I don't think we have any of those." I fight the impulse to ask, "Well then, just what in the name of Aunt Fannie's girdle *do* you have here *any*way?" and instead just say, "OK, thanks a lot. See ya."

Out Scott and I go, leaving the little bell on the door to tinkle it's heart out and the young lady to do whatever she was doing before we intruded.

Safely outside, Scott and I agree that we've just enjoyed a Twilight

Zone moment, but we can't allow it to discourage us because I need a moustache. So we're off to the next place.

A couple of blocks to the south and another to the west, we find what appears to be a more traditional hair salon. We can actually see female persons milling around inside and others coming out the door sporting elegant coiffures, so we confidently conclude that this place is doing at least *something* related to hair. We've got a chance.

In we go. No bell tinkles as the door closes behind us, so I guess these folks don't require any kind of auditory warning as we come in. Right on over we go to the lovely lady standing behind a cash register that's resting on a pretty normal looking counter. Through the counter's glass front and glass top you can see a display of various hair products. A short distance to the left of the lovely lady are two or three other women seated on stainless steel and vinyl chairs along the nearby wall, in turn reading magazines and chatting.

"Yes, young men, how may I help you today?" the lady behind the counter says, and even though the several eyes that are riveted on me make me feel like I'm in the wrong place, at least I don't feel like I've barged into a 1920s speakeasy—so I'm able to wrestle my tongue away from the cat this time and say, "We're wondering if you have a moustache."

Scott throws a weird glance my way, but even with that prompt, the beauty of the ambiguity I just laid on this lady escapes me.

She smiles, so I guess it didn't escape *her*, but she doesn't seem to be all that surprised by the pseudo-question and says, "As a matter of fact, we do have a small selection of moustaches, if you'll give me just a moment." She disappears around the corner and momentarily returns carrying a rather hairy cardboard display. Being possessed of *pret-tee* keen powers of observation, I quickly recognize the hairy parts of the cardboard as moustaches. I see only four, but at least there *are* some. Color me pleasantly surprised. The nice lady lays the display on the glass next to the cash register and says, "Would any of these look like what you had in mind?"

Hmmm. Moustaches. I'll be darned. And they actually look pretty cool. Three of them are quite thick and black. No doubt they'd look good on Scott, but I'm a whole lot fairer than he is— think Paul Newman versus Clark Gable—and in anyone's wildest imagination, I could never have sprouted such thick lip hair in just the few weeks I've been away at school. So I figure these three are a little much. The fourth one's in the running. It's a lighter color and doesn't look so much like a Fuller brush, so I say to the nice lady, "I'd like to see this one, please" and she lifts it from the display and hands it to me. It's got a kind of mesh netting on the back of it, and the lady explains that with a little glue, this material will adhere nicely to my lip and no one will know the moustache isn't one hundred percent me.

I hold the caterpillar up to my lip and glance at the mirror on the wall behind the lady. Gee. This looks right cool, if I do say so myself. I look over to see if Scott approves, and—although I don't think his excitement will register on any Richter scale—I believe he's OK with this look, so I say to the lady, "How much is this one?"

"That one's just fifteen dollars," she says, and I can't believe that the ladies sitting around me aren't at all startled by the noise of my jaw hitting the glass top of the display case. "Did you say *fifteen* dollars?" I say, and she says, "Yes, fifteen dollars, and then a dollar ninety-nine for the glue. Shall I ring them both up for you today?"

It's funny. In all my thinking about buying a moustache, I only ever thought about could I *find* one, not could I *afford* one.

She may as well have said a quadratrillion gadzillion dollars.

Oh you bet, I think to myself, *just go ahead and ring 'em right on up, but wait just a minute while I step around the corner and knock off Zions Bank, and I'll be right back to pay you.*

Behind an embarrassed smile and down-turned eyes, I say to the lady, "I didn't think it'd cost that much," and she says, "Well, you can get them cheaper, I suppose, but this one is of very high quality and looks so authentic, and, after all," she says, "you know you always get what you pay for."

Well, quality or not, at fifteen dollars, there's just no chance for me on this one. But I can't admit to having no money, so I keep my thoughts to myself, and to the lady I just say, "Thanks, I'll have to think about it."

And out we go.

As we walk away, Scott and I discuss the whole situation and agree on a number of reasons why it wasn't really such a good idea to buy the moustache right now, anyway, but among those reasons we don't include a lack of money. See, even though we both know it was The

Reason, it's just the unwritten order of things that we don't *admit* it. Not out loud, anyway.

No point, I guess, in looking at any of the other places, and anyway look at the time, for heaven's sake. It's nearly two o'clock.

It suddenly occurs to the two of us that we're starving to death and if we don't find some sustenance soon we may start playing Donner Party.

We can't see a McDonald's in the immediate vicinity, and that triggers a moment of panic. This could be serious. I mean, if we can't find a McDonald's, we may have to eat at a place that serves real food, and any place that serves real food's gonna charge real money for us to eat it. And we've just in the last few minutes come to discouraging but realistic terms with our poverty.

Scott and I haven't spent what you'd call a lot of time in downtown Salt Lake, so we have no idea about what eating establishments we might find here. But I remember that little greasy spoon café we passed just a while ago on the way to the opium den. So I say, "Hey, Scott, how 'bout that little café we passed a couple of blocks up the street?" I remind him about the sign in the window advertising a daily special. I don't remember how much the sign said the special costs, but it's probably not too much if they're *advertising* it, for Pete's sake, so why don't we try that? We agree, and back we go.

The sign on the window reads "Daily Special 89¢." With some quick arithmetic, we figure we can cover that and still have a little left over, so we scoot right on in. We don't have any trouble finding a seat because no one's in the joint except us and some guy behind the counter with a dirty white apron over a tee shirt with a stretched-out neck—the shirt's, not the guy's. We go ahead and sit down at a booth table, and after a minute or so, this guy waddles on over and asks can he help us. We tell him we'll have two specials. Now, if we had at least half a brain between us, we'd ask what *is* the special, but we don't, so we don't—and apparently the guy's not inclined to reveal such top-secret information unless he's forced to. Instead, he just dumbly scribbles a little note on a white pad in his left hand and then returns to the other side of the counter. He tears off the little note from the pad and sticks it up onto a stainless steel wheel that he then rotates a half-turn counterclockwise so some guy in the back room—a cook, I guess, but I'm not jumping to any conclusions at this point—can read what he wrote on it.

Within minutes, Scott and I are eating some of the worst . . . some of the worst . . . the worst . . .

Nouns fail me.

It's got some kind of a noodle in it, we're both agreed on that, so our first diagnosis is a casserole of some kind—but I doubt we could drive that home to a jury. The reddish tint suggests tomato sauce or ketchup or . . . geez. *Some*thing. And there's *leet-tle* brown specks scattered throughout the mixture, but even after extensive discussion and a little arguing, we can't be confident that we've identified them properly. The truth is, it really doesn't matter *what's* in this concoction because there's no flavor to it, anyway. Salt helps some, and I even add some pepper—which I never do, ordinarily. But in this case, *any* flavor's at least *some* flavor.

The only good thing about this . . . this . . . this *stuff* is that it's easily forked. In fact, if your mouth were big enough, you could eat the whole thing in one bite because it's completely stuck together. We suspect it didn't start out as a solid piece of merchandise—that there was actually some kind of liquid sauce or topping involved at the outset. But somewhere during the cooking of it or the serving of it there's been some coagulation. At least, that's our best guess.

As bad as it looks, the worst part comes after you swallow. See, the stuff doesn't go directly to the stomach. It wedges itself somewhere between the goozle and the stomach and just kinda perches there until we send down some water to lubricate it. Bite after courageous bite, we assault the enemy, lubricating with water as we go—and when we've heard the last piece of it finally hit bottom, we figure we're finished here and stand up to leave.

We decide we'd better not leave a tip because we should save a buck or two for any incidentals we might need as we make our way back down to Provo. Like Alka Seltzer. Or a stomach pump. Or an emergency room co-pay. Anyway, it's OK that we don't tip because Utah's currently like the worst place in the country for tipping, so no one really expects it, anyway. Plus, this guy's probably the owner, and somewhere in the back of my mind I seem to remember that it's an insult to tip the owner. So we better not tip . . . just to be safe. Pretty sure we don't wanna insult this particular guy. He might make us eat more special.

By the time we've paid the man at the counter and made our way out of the Den of Last Meals, it's about three o'clock, and we're feeling a little depressed about how the day's gone so far. I mean, we don't get to Salt Lake very often—read *never*—so it seems like the fair and just thing would be for us to have a little more success and fun than we've had up to now. What with scary salons and expensive moustaches and inedible edibles, Scott and I are beginning to feel like we're getting the royal slam dunk. So it shouldn't be a complete loss, we decide to hop back down to the movie theater we passed a little while back and catch an early showing of *Mackenna's Gold* starring Gregory Peck and Omar Sharif. Heaven knows we shouldn't spend the money, but what the heck? We're on vacation.

By the time the movie's over and we're ready to make our way to the freeway, it's gotten pretty dark. Worse than dark, it's gotten colder and has begun to snow. When we catch our first ride, the snow's coming down pretty hard, intensified by a stiffening wind. As our ride drops us off at the 45th South exit, we're feeling the slightest bit concerned because we've got a *pret-tee* good snowstorm going on here now—and we're still thirty or so miles from home.

Oh, how I love Utah winters. But I mentioned that already.

The good news is that we don't have to wait very long for another ride.

The bad news is that we don't have to wait very long for another ride.

This midsixties model sedan pulls over, and the front-seat passenger rolls down the window and asks where we're headed, and we say, "Provo," and he says, "Well, we're headed for Lehi, so hop on in and we'll take you that far." We climb in.

Of the original attractions available to Disneyland visitors when it opened in 1955, a few will remain into the new millennium. Among those is Mr. Toad's Wild Ride. Based on Disney's adaptation of *The Wind in the Willows*, the ride takes the guest on a sweeping adventure in a car that begins at Toad Hall and continues on through the countryside, passing Mr. Rat's house, aggravating policemen, and terrifying farmers and livestock along the way. Then the guest's car heads for the docks, where it appears to be doomed to a watery grave at dock's end but avoids that seemingly inevitable plunge into the river when it makes a sharp, last-moment turn into a warehouse that explodes as the car crashes through a brick wall and out onto the streets of London.

Here, it narrowly avoids a close collision with a delivery truck, shakes up Winky's Pub on the way through it, and terrorizes citizens as it plows across the town square. Following a daring escape from the police, the guest's car tries unsuccessfully to avoid an oncoming train, thus precipitating—finally—a journey through hell.

The differences between Mr. Toad's Wild Ride and our slide-on-the-snow-packed-freeway-with-crazy-and-or-drunk-teenagers ride to Lehi are so minimal as to not warrant mention.

Suffice it to say that when we finally arrive at the Lehi exit about twenty-or-so miles to the south and the satanic sedan slides down the off-ramp, Scott's wrapping up his third seizure and I'm prying my fingers one by one out of the back of the front seat and putting my shoes back on.

And I think I swallowed my gum.

The car never actually comes to a complete stop as it sleds down the exit lane, so we pile out when it slows to what we guess to be the slowest point it'll reach. As we try to find some footing in the deep snow, the car resumes its inane speed—doors still open—and the maniacal noise of Lehi teenagers fades around the corner on two wheels and disappears into the darkness down westbound Main Street, trailing a rooster tail of snow.

If I could, I'd describe what I'm sure our faces must look like as Scott and I stand at this unlighted off-ramp on this snowy Utah night and begin to realize that we're enjoying something that for the past forty-or-so minutes we thought would never be.

One more moment of life outside of that car.

As blood slowly begins to circulate once again through our bodies, Scott and I feel the lifting of that hazy film that somehow envelops the human psyche to prevent its total deterioration during moments of extreme terror. Our legs still wanna behave like Elvis's on stage at a county fair, but we manage to pull ourselves together enough to take stock of our surroundings and our circumstances. Get our bearings, so to speak.

It's not snowing quite so much now, so we've got that going for us. But it's still freezing cold, we're still about chin-deep in snow, and it's still dark and we're still not home. About a block to the west, we can see the twin silos of Lehi Roller Mills, a lovely little establishment that'll be immortalized in the 1984 movie *Footloose* starring Kevin

Bacon, but otherwise, nothing's visible. No cars coming. No cars going. No people. No lights.

Just the two of us, the dark, the cold, and the yellow *Scott* and *Kevin* written in the snow.

We know we're not all that far from home—maybe ten or so miles—and with a little luck, we could make it all the way back to our general neck of the woods with just one more ride. If only we could hook up with something resembling normal transportation captained by an unimpaired human being that hasn't been drinking anything stronger than diet Dr. Pepper and isn't driving to win his heat in the qualifying rounds of some imaginary snowy-road NASCAR event. It just doesn't seem like all that much to ask.

At first blush, the two lovely young ladies in that blue '67 Mustang coupe that's pulling over seem to fill the bill, but I guess I'll withhold judgment for just a sec, if you don't mind.

"Are you guys OK?" asks the smiling driver of the Mustang. "Looks like you could use a ride," she says. "Why don't you hop on in?" she asks.

With a coordinated shiver, Scott and I harmonize "thanks a lot" and climb into the car with as much agility as remains in our ham-mered bodies after surviving a twisted, psychotic version of *Route 66*. Even though the back seat of this Mustang isn't exactly what you'd call spacious or comfy and we're pretty much resting our chins on our knees, we're getting warm, and we don't smell anything funny, and the girls look more or less normal—in fact, you could even argue that they're pretty fine, if slightly redneck-ish—so my defensive posture begins to relax just a tad. *Scott seems to be OK with this scenario, and I trust Scott, so maybe this is gonna turn out fine after all*, I think to myself.

And believe it or not, it does turn out fine. But minus a little stu-pidity on my part, it might have turned out perfectly.

Up until we near the Provo Center Street exit, there's mostly just small talk, and a lot of the time the girls keep their chatting between themselves while Scott and I sit quietly in the back, glad to be warm and not covered in snow and not sliding toward oncoming traffic at supersonic speeds. Makes you think that maybe Dr. Maslow got it right with his hierarchy of human needs. I mean, ordinarily we manly men would be more than mildly interested in these lovely young chauffeurs of the opposite persuasion, but we've learned that it's tough to think about romance when all you really wanna do is keep warm enough to thaw out important body parts.

But by the time the Mustang exits I-15 onto Provo Center Street, I'm sufficiently thawed to think a level or two up the hierarchy, so I begin considering the possibilities for some romance here. Coincidentally, this is when the driver turns her attention to us and asks where exactly are we headed and in future years when I think of how easy it would've been to just tell her we're headed to Chipman Hall at BYU and she'd have dropped us at our door, I'll be forever astounded that I chose instead to chuckle and say, "Well, we're headed wherever you're headed."

Wink, wink.

If murder weren't illegal and immoral, I'm *pret-tee* darn sure I'd be taking my last breath right now in the throttling grip of Scott's vise-like hands.

"Cool," the driver says. "We're headed for McDonald's," she says. "So why don't you join us, and that'll be fun," she says. Scott and I look at each other a little like Steve Martin and John Candy will look at each other in the 1987 movie *Trains, Planes, and Automobiles* as they sit on a trunk in the middle of the Interstate and, glancing backward over their shoulders, realize that their car has just burst into flames.

I already explained about the unwritten order of things that forbids us to openly admit that The Reason for not doing things like buying a fifteen-dollar faux moustache is that we don't have enough money. Now let me explain that this rule generalizes just *pret-tee* darn universally. Like, say, if two lovely young ladies were to invite Scott and me to go to McDonald's with them and despite the aches and pains of a very long day we both think this would probably be a nice idea but we can't accept the invitation because our pockets are empty after a day of derring-do in Salt Lake except for a few cents that we managed to hang on to by stiffing some unfortunate waiter out of a pathetic little tip. In such a situation, we'd remain bound by the same unwritten order of things and be compelled to offer some alternative explanation for declining such a lovely invitation, thus avoiding the embarrassment of admitting poverty.

So as the life-saving Mustang rolls into the McDonald's parking lot, Scott and I know we're on the spot. Gotta talk fast. That's the key. Just splatter words all over, like when you're answering an essay question on a test, hoping that some of them stick. "Thanks a lot," we say at almost the same time, and then Scott stammers out something about homework, and I stammer out something about being tired, and between those excuses and the miscellaneous stammering in between—stammering that would hold its own with Chevy Chase's Clark W. Griswold character in the 1983 film *National Lampoon's Vacation* as he tries cunningly to gain entrance to a closed-for-repairs Walley World past John Candy's ever-vigilant Lasky—we manage to escape the premises with a small piece of our dignity intact.

As Scott and I engage the shoe leather and trudge the last few snowy blocks to our dorm, I'm left to deal with my stupid response to two lovely young ladies who, but for my misplaced attempt at flirting, would've gladly delivered us to our door, saving us this last mile of pain.

I'm left to deal with the fact that Scott and I still have no regularly available motorized transportation and won't have any tomorrow, either, and are thus doomed to relive this highly inconvenient experience again in the future.

I'm left to deal with the fact that I still have no lip hair and won't have, for years to come—and now I know I can't even cheat my way through puberty with a fake moustache.

And I'm left to deal with that Utah specialty that'll plague me from every December to every April for the rest of my natural life.

Winter.

11

I give my best friend another heart attack

When I think about it, I guess it's a modern-day miracle that I can still call Jim my best friend.

Considering I've done my best over the years to kill him.

And had fun doing it.

I really liked seeing *Wait Until Dark* with Jimbo a couple of years ago and scaring him to within an inch of his life outside his house after the movie.

Then there was, of course, the little tow truck driver incident a year or so ago at the Jack in the Box restaurant when my temper nearly led to the two of us being pummeled by a critter that could have been used in a court of law as evidence of evolution.

Both times, lots of fun.

But not enough to satisfy my voracious, rather perverse appetite for the thrill of my best friend's agony and suffering. Apparently.

In 1979, Dudley Moore will star in Blake Edwards' movie, *10*. Mr. Moore's character, George Webber, will express perfectly to a bartender then what I'm thinking now: "I think . . . uh . . . one more time, basically."

I'm seventeen and all grown up now—a lot older than Jim, by a week—and attending Brigham Young University while Jimbo's still back in Southern Cal at Troy High, arguing with his cross-country coach about everything under the sun and writing soul-searing editorials to the wannabe-radical *Troy Oracle*, exposing the school cafeteria's soggy french fries.

It's true that I've got my other best friend and roommate, Scott, for companionship here at the Y, and I've made a lot of new friends in the Chipman Hall dormitory. Somehow life's just not the same without good ol' Jim, though. I miss him. I'm not weird enough when he's not around to egg me on.

So, when the holiday season rolls around and I don't have enough money to buy my way home for both Thanksgiving *and* Christmas, I think, *wouldn't it be fun to have Jim haul his long-haired hiney up here to visit me during the Thanksgiving break?* Scott's stuck in the dorm for the holiday just as I am, but most all the other guys on the floor have plans to bug out for home-cooked turkey somewhere in the world—so there'll be plenty of empty rooms on the floor for Jim to stay in. What the heck? I'll ask. Maybe he's up for a road trip.

He is. For Jim, any road trip's good and accomplishes several purposes, not the least of which is just getting him out of the house for a minute.

So. Arrangements are made quickly. Jim decides to bring his friend, Chris, along for the ride. And to prove to him that Mormons generally—and BYU students in particular—do not, in fact, have hooves or horns or keep unfortunate, tragic maidens trapped in towers.

At least the ones I know don't.

Scott and I welcome Jim and Chris to the sophistication of life at BYU and the glorious wonders of the dorm rooms on the right wing of the second floor of Chipman Hall—CR2, for short. The room next to ours is empty, so our guests make themselves at home there. Getting permission for them to stay in this room was no problem because we didn't bother to get it. To tell the truth, no one living on CR2 has anything worth stealing. And if someone comes in and makes a mess of your room while you're gone, it's impossible to tell that mess from the mess your room's always in, anyway, so who cares.

The first night together, we all get pretty "into" just getting caught up on things. You know. Stuff. School, girls, coaches, sports, recent felonies, court dates and appearances . . . whatever trivial matters we can think to talk about. But after a minute or two, we're all caught up because our lives are so pathetic that we don't need more than a minute or two to get caught up. Now it's time to talk about something *serious.* Something *interesting.* Something *meaningful.*

Like music.

It turns out that I'm a big fan of Blood, Sweat & Tears. They just played the Salt Palace in Salt Lake City, and, of course, I was there. Third row, dead center, with good friend and fellow dorm rat, Big Ed. Opening for BS&T was another group, It's a Beautiful Day, and its female vocalist, Patti Santos, was wearing this incredibly short, sexy, groovy, leather skirt outfit. Complete with beads, of course—I mean, it *is* 1969. When she came out to help with sound cables and mics before the show opened, she walked up to the front of the stage— right smack in front of Big Ed and me—and hunkered down to fiddle with a cable connection. Now, this skirt she wore wasn't exactly made for hunkering down. It was immediately clear to us that Ms. Santos's wardrobe budget had been in no way diminished by the cost of underwear.

And whatever vestiges of puberty remained with Big Ed and me were gone in an instant.

But I digress.

Now, David Clayton-Thomas's voice is outasight. But I had no idea that he hasn't always been BS&T's lead singer but only just joined them for their self-titled album released last January. Or that Al Kooper formed the group in '67 and sang lead on their first—and only, with Kooper—album in February 1968. Then they had issues and Kooper left, making way for Mr. Clayton-Thomas. Hmmm. Didn't know any of that. Just learned it all from Chris, who's apparently a bigger BS&T fan than I thought I was. So I say to Chris, "Is their older music as good as what they're doing now?" and he says, "Of course, even better, and if you like brass and a hybrid rock/jazz sound, you'll like the old stuff anyway even if you like David Clayton-Thomas's vocals better than Al Kooper's. So let's just go find a store and buy the album *Child Is Father to the Man,* and you can decide for yourself."

Sounds like a fine idea to everyone, so we saddle up and hit the streets of Provo to find the record.

Provo.

At eleven p.m.

Good luck with that.

Now, all of us spent our adolescent years in Southern Cal, where time of day has little to do with whether or not you can get something you want. You get the urge for a late-night burrito run—no problem. You feel the need for some midnight shopping—no problem. You wanna buy a BS&T record at midnight—easy-peasy-lemon-squeezy. You want it, it's available. At nearly any time you might want it.

But *Provo*. Different story. Now, don't get me wrong. I love Provo. Mostly it's just a fine place to be living while I go to school. But in 1969, Southern California it's not.

I mean, just check this out. On the day Scott and I arrived in Provo and moved into the dorm, we hopped on down to McDonald's just around the corner for some sustenance. Ordered the standard Big Mac. A smartly uniformed guy behind the counter said, "You can't have one." So we said, "What do you mean, we can't have one?" and he said, "We don't have any hamburgers because we're out of beef, but you can have a nice Filet-o-Fish if you want," and we said, "Are you kidding me?" and left.

I'm willing to bet that no one else in this world ever went to McDonald's and ordered a Big Mac and got turned down.

Provo.

So after we discover that the one record store we know about's closed and so is JC Penney and Skagg's Drug, and grocery stores don't sell records and neither does 7-Eleven, we figure we're just not gonna find *Child Is Father to the Man* tonight. And because this is Provo, and this LP isn't exactly a current release, there's a better-than-even chance that we won't find it *tomorrow*, either.

Disappointed but not surprised, we make our way back to the dorm. It's only a little after midnight, so there's plenty of time to hang out, even if we've got no new BS&T music to enjoy on Scott's portable desktop stereo turntable with detachable speakers that make music sound a little like wind whistling off aluminum foil.

We do have a few records, though, so we pop on a little Dylan to enjoy while we sit around talking about who knows what. Then Jim has to excuse himself for a minute, and while he's gone, I get this great idea.

Same idea I got about two years ago in front of Jim's house while I was waiting for him to make his way down those long winding stairs from the house to the driveway.

Think I'll scare Jim into a heart attack.

Worked then. Oughta work now.

Of course, on that 1967 night, I had the advantage of help from Miss Hepburn, Mr. Arkin, and the rest of the cast of *Wait Until Dark* to inflict emotional, psychological, physical, and for all I know, even spiritual trauma on Jim. Tonight that cast of characters isn't here to help, but I've got my buddies—and with just a little prep, I believe I can make some magic happen. So I share The Plan with the guys.

Here's how it'll be.

After Jim returns, we'll encourage a conducive spirit by talking about any scary or spooky or terrifying thing we can think of. Evil's good. Macabre's good. Death, dismemberment, terror, fear. Whatever. Anything to set the mood for fright. Once we've created a properly eerie atmosphere, Jim and Chris will go next door to get ready for bed. Chris will tell Jim that he left something in our room and needs to go get it. "I'll be back in just a minute," he'll say. He'll leave, and Jim will be alone. And properly prepared.

Now, one day not long ago, I just happened to notice that my built-in closet drawers share a wall with the corresponding drawers in the adjoining room. Then I discovered that if you take out the drawers, you can see a very small hole in the wall behind each one—a hole just large enough to accommodate a straightened clothes hanger.

And if you push a straightened clothes hanger through that hole, you push out the drawer on the other side of the wall, in the neighboring room.

Observation logged. Never know when this info might come in handy.

It's about to come in handy.

Jim rejoins us and the bull session starts. It's first one thing and then another, but everything's pointed toward the eerie. The spooky. The inexplicable. The surreal.

The best subject of all, though—the one that'll definitely get us where we wanna be—*the* hot topic of the day:

Paul is dead.

In a nutshell, here's the deal.

A couple of months ago, the Drake University paper, *The Times-Delphic*, ran an article claiming that Paul McCartney of the Beatles had been killed in a car wreck and replaced by a look-alike. A little later, someone identifying himself as "Tom" telephoned DJ Russ Gibb at WKNR-FM in Dearborn, Michigan, announced that McCartney's dead, and challenged Gibb to play "Revolution 9" backward and he'd hear the words "turn me on, dead man." Which he did. And which he did. After that, lots of people across the country joined in an obsessive search for other clues that proved Paul was dead. As a doornail. Teats up. Pushing up daisies. Bereft of life. Kicked the bucket. Shuffled off this mortal coil.

Over the next forty years, this rumor will gain all kinds of momentum, especially when it gets the power of the Internet behind it.

Now, the four of us don't know all that much in the way of clues at the moment because this whole thing's just gotten good started—but we all have *some* notion of *some* of the clues in songs and on album covers that have been discovered. The 28-IF license plate and the closed eyes and Paul's out of step with the others and the burial clothes and the gravedigger clothes and the bare feet and the cigarette in the right hand. Phrases recorded backwards and car wreck sounds and Wednesday morning at five o'clock and the Walrus is Paul and I buried Paul and introducing Billy Shears.

Of course, once we've picked up some momentum talking about Paul, a discussion of the Beatles in general ensues. And no general discussion of The Beatles can be complete without reference to their pact with the devil. So now we've brought the occult into this thing too.

The more we talk, the spookier it gets. All's progressing very nicely, thank you.

Then it's time. Chris and Jim head for their room next door to hit the hay. As soon as they're out our door, I pull out the middle drawer and remove it from its track. Set it on the floor. Get the clothes hanger ready. Wait for Chris.

Shortly, I hear their door open and close, and now our door opens. There's Chris, smiling to beat the band and excited to witness what promises to be an epic event of great proportions.

On the other side of that wall, Jim's standing in front of the drawers so he can use the mirror above them to examine his very handsome face and other body areas, inspecting for the presence of exorcisable blemishes. Finding one, he works on it. With diligence. With focus. With concentration. Unaware. Unexpecting.

Insert the hanger. *P-u-u-u-u-sh!*

I consider myself a great fan of vintage movies—and of comedies, in particular. I love W.C. Fields and the Marx Brothers and Bob Hope and Jack Benny. Abbott and Costello, the Three Stooges, Cary Grant, the Bowery Boys . . . well, just pretty much any old golden-age cinema comedy has my devotion. The slapstickier, the better.

I pay *pret-tee* darn good attention too, which is how I've learned a few things over the years—by way of recognition if not performance—about acting and comedy and what evokes crowd response. For example, I know that timing's everything. And an essential part of good timing's the pause, that simple beat right before the punch line, that makes everything that follows it funnier than it would have been without it. Say it. Wait a beat. Punch it. Hilarity.

It turns out to be that *beat* that makes this a most perfect moment.

That beat right after Jim sees the drawer pop out and has no earthly explanation for it.

That beat that allows an ever-so-brief moment for his mind to struggle in vain to make some kind of sense out of something that's clearly nonsensical.

That beat right before we hear the shriek, the door slam, the footsteps, the door open.

And in Jim flies—half running, half falling forward. White face. Wide eyes that remind me of another day in '67 when the two of us were developing close personal relationships with a couple of Disneyland security guards. Breathing in short, shallow gasps like he's just stepped out of a movie at the Pussycat Garden Theater. Trying to speak but managing no more than machine gun bursts of syllables. Needing desperately to tell us something but the neurology simply won't cooperate.

Anyone old enough or keen enough on classic movies of the thirties and forties may be familiar with a couple of grand old African-American actors: Willie Best, known throughout much of his career as Sleep n Eat, and Mantan Moreland. Along with Stepin Fetchit—the screen name of Lincoln Theodore Monroe Andrew Perry, who at one time was among the highest paid actors working in Hollywood—these peerless actors typified Hollywood's rather unfortunate stereotypic views of African Americans during that era.

Ironically, though, these men were so good at what they did that they transcended those stereotypes and showed a genius that will never be replicated.

The character that Willie typically portrayed was an easily

frightened, lazy, simpleton. Anyone who ever saw Mr. Best act—in *The Ghost Chasers* with Bob Hope and Paulette Goddard, for example—will certainly know that this pioneering superstar could register fear and terror on his face in so unique a way as to never be forgotten once it's been experienced.

And Mantan Moreland. Unbelievable. Mr. Moreland may be remembered best as Birmingham Brown, the nervous chauffeur in the Charlie Chan series, but the haunted mansion or the haunted pawn shop or the zombie-occupied island was where he showed that most incredible talent for registering side-splitting terror on his most perfect face. He has *the* most magnificent eyes that can open, it seems, to the size of a half-dollar—and you expect them to pop out of his head at any moment. It's an absolute gift. And it's hilarious.

Not that Mantan's *verbal* delivery has ever been anything less than genius. Perhaps no line in the history of cinema was delivered any better than Mr. Moreland delivered this, in Jean Yarbrough's 1941 *King of the Zombies*: "If there's one thing that I wouldn't wanna be twice, zombies is both of 'em."

Genius. Oh, yeah.

In the thirties and forties, anyone casting a film comedy that had anything at all to do with ghosts or scary or weird would sooner or later be found knocking on the door of one of these men. If they wanted the best, that is. It had to be one of these two gentlemen and none other. Simple as that.

In all my years of enjoying classic comedies, it's never occurred to me that *anyone* could generate a more perfect look of terror than Willie or Mantan—or be funnier doing it.

Until now.

Looking at the terror on Jim's face, I know that this is everything I'd hoped for and more. Here's quintessential fright. Here's emotional shock at its almost unimaginable best. Here's a moment for the ages—one to be experienced, embraced, exaggerated, and enjoyed again and again and again over the next forty years.

But in my efforts to achieve the superior scare, the total terror, the double-dyed discombobulation, only heaven knows the true scope of the cumulative damage I've done to my best friend.

Or how much I've yet to do.

12

I get robbed again

My roommate and best friend, Scott, and I have just finished our freshman year at Brigham Young University, and we've come home to Southern Cal for the summer months of 1970. After two full semesters at BYU, Scott brings home with him a clear understanding of augmented matrices, combinatorics, inverse trigonometry, theoretical yields, and density compensation. And a transcript full of As.

I bring home with me a mediocre talent for juggling and basketball-spinning, guitar tabs for ten Creedence Clearwater Revival songs, and the fifty-yard-line marker from a nearby stadium. And a transcript full of grades just barely the other side of why-don't-you-try-a-nice-junior-college.

But that's all behind us now. The obvious priority goal for the next three months or so is to find a job that pays enough for us to take care of our summer needs—read *girls* and *cars*—and to save a little coin for our next semester of college.

At least it's true that *I* need some money for the next semester. Turns out that Scott won't be returning to BYU in the fall because he'll leave in September to serve a full-time, two-year mission for the Church of Jesus Christ of Latter-day Saints (Mormon). He doesn't know it yet, but he'll be serving in the Germany South Mission, where our mutual best friend, Dave, is already serving. Jeff, our other best friend, will follow right behind Scott to that same mission.

And next spring, I'll join the three of them there.

Four best friends serving in the same LDS mission at the same time. Wow. A stroke of coincidence pretty much unheard of. Roughly the statistical equivalent of being struck by lightning four times within twenty minutes of winning the lottery for the third time.

But I digress.

My first choice for work this summer was, of course, pumping gas again at Bill and Jerry's Union 76 service station, where I worked part-time from '67 to '69. The problem with that scenario's twofold. First, Bill and Jerry don't need any help right now. Second, even if they did, it'd only be part-time help—and I need full-time pay. Beyond covering my summer expenses, I'm gonna need a little extra coin to cover the increased cost of off-campus living next year. Plus, I'll be taking my trusty Honda 90 with me, and gas ain't free, buddy. So full-time pay's what I need.

After we returned from BYU, Scott and I immediately applied for a job at the Alpha Beta grocery store warehouse in nearby La Habra, just like we've done about a gazillion times since we first began as youngsters to even *imagine* that we might actually have a job one day. Now, the reason that we've kept applying again and again to work at this warehouse despite repeated rejection isn't that it's the coolest job in the world—no, *that* would be working at a service station job. Still, it's certainly not an altogether *uncool* job. After all, you do get to do a lot of manly physical labor—which makes muscles, you know—and you also get to mess around with forklifts and box cutters and get sweaty and dirty. Neat stuff like that. But the real reason why we've kept applying is that this job pays around five bucks an hour—about three times what we'd get working at any other local job we might land.

It's about the cash.

So as soon as we got home, the two of us went on down to the Alpha Beta warehouse—*again*—to fill out the forms—*again*—and give them our phone numbers—*again*—and take the little test—*again*—that asks marvelously irrelevant questions like, if two trains are traveling from Boston to Des Moines at exactly the same speed and then one slows down by fifty mph . . .

Well, you probably know the kind of question I'm talking about.

The two of us turned in the tests and written applications with our phone numbers on them to the lovely lady with bluish-grey hair sitting at the reception desk just across the room from a set of double swinging doors with heavy rubber sweeps at the bottom that brush noisily against the floor when the doors swing open or closed and if they'd just let us go through those doors we'd be smack-dab in the middle of the warehouse that we've dreamed of for years, but they won't, so we aren't, and they never will, so we never will be.

"Thank you, young men," the nice lady said. "We've got your phone numbers, and we'll call you if something opens up. Now you just have a great summer," the nice lady said.

Pie in the sky.

So I've kept on trying to find a job that I might actually, really get hired to do so I can earn a little bread to contribute to the cause. I'm not what you'd call well-networked in the local business or corporate world, though, so my prospects seem limited to pretty much nothing.

Scratch the *pretty much*.

But good ol' Dad comes through for the kid.

Now, Dad's been connected to the military in some way, shape, or form for nearly his whole life. When he was seventeen, he dreamed of attending West Point Military Academy and enjoying a wonderful military career as a commissioned officer. More than just the dream, he even had the promise of the congressional sponsorship required for admission. What he didn't have, unfortunately, was parent consent, which he needed because he was underage at the time. Apparently, my grandmother—we call her Mama Morris—didn't want her boy to spend his whole life dodging bullets in the military, so she withheld that permission in hopes that he'd pick some safe and sane job like farming or driving a milk truck or some other work considered acceptable for a young man in rural 1934 Mississippi who's just about to slip his hobbles.

So Dad joined the army, anyway, when he was of age—but instead of serving as a commissioned officer with all the perks and privileges of that lifestyle, he served instead as a noncommissioned officer. After doing his duty in World War II—in the tank corps—and then again in Korea—this time in artillery—Dad retired from active duty as a six-stripe E-7 master sergeant, continuing his military service in the Army National Guard and Air Force Reserves for another hundred or so years before fully and finally retiring as an E-9 command sergeant major.

Good strategy, Mama Morris.

Reminds me a little of the University of the Pacific at Stockton.

See, after I applied and was accepted for admission to Brigham Young University back in my senior year of high school, I got a letter from the University of the Pacific at Stockton that almost made me feel a little impressed with myself. It seemed that this university, boasting a highly respected music conservatory, was interested in my music skills and had put its money where its mouth was by offering me a half scholarship in music.

Now, I carefully considered this attractive offer, but there were two immediate problems with it. First, only a *half* scholarship was offered, and the other half cost way more than tuition at BYU. Second, and equally important, I just wasn't interested in spending my professional life in education. Even though—I say humbly—I'd shown a little talent in music and played a pretty mean trumpet and a few other instruments, I'd long since realized that I don't have The Gift. And without The Gift, I figured the only thing I'd be able to do with a music degree is wave a baton in front of a high school or junior high school band or orchestra. I didn't wanna spend the next forty or fifty years in education, so I passed on a respectable scholarship offer.

But life will win out. As it turns out, I'll end up taking an undergraduate degree in psychology at BYU and then a master's in school psychology at the University of Utah. After a decade and a half of working in public schools as a psychologist, I'll give nearly another decade to education as an administrator. Then I'll give another couple of decades to a private sector nonprofit organization whose work looks so much like education that to the day I retire I won't be able to convince my folks that I'm *not* in education. In the final analysis, I'll have spent my entire professional career in education after all, in one way, shape, or form.

Good strategy, Kevin. Clearly you're no better than Mama Morris was at outguessing life.

Anyway, here in 1970, Dad's still serving Uncle Sam. In the Air Force Reserve this time. Serving along with him's this guy named Jack who owns a Shell service station in Garden Grove, just a short piece down the road. Jack needs some help, he tells Dad, and can pay a little better than the average bear. He needs help right away too, so he'd be glad to have me start immediately, he tells Dad—providing he likes me.

So it looks like I may get to work at a service station again, after all.

Of course, I'm older now, so the mystique of working at a service station's a bit faded—but I know how to do the work, and it still sounds fun to me, so I roll on down to Haster to meet Jack and see what we can work out.

As it turns out, Jack's a really nice guy. A little on the cocky side, some might say, but when all's said and done, this is a really bright, competent businessman who's been around the block a few times and knows what he's doing. Maybe because we've so much—ahem—in common, we hit it off. Whatever the reason, Jack likes me and agrees to hire me. I get to start the next day.

My shifts will be various. I'll work a couple of full days, a couple of evening shifts, and a graveyard shift from ten p.m. Saturday to six a.m. Sunday.

Graveyard shift. Hmmm.

It's pretty common knowledge among those who know me that I'm a night person and feel much more alive, awake, and invigorated at nine p.m. than at nine a.m. Occasionally, I even enjoy staying up all night reading or watching TV or playing Monopoly with my brother-in-law, Mike. But I've never had a *job* that *requires* me to stay awake all night. *This oughta be interesting*, I think to myself.

As it turns out, I'm right. Interesting it is. At *least*.

I'm pulling my very first solo graveyard shift. I'm coming in off the island. The phone rings. I pick it up.

"Jack's," I say. "Can I help you?" I ask.

Silence.

"Jack's," I say again. "Can I *help* you?" I ask again.

Weird noise. Kinda like a breathy grunt. I've heard something like it before, at the end of a wrestling match in high school when my opponent and I simultaneously released that desperate grip on each other at the final whistle.

"Ex*cuse* me," I say.

Silence.

"Hello," I say again. "*Hello.*"

Finally, the silence is broken. "Hey," says a voice. "Just wondering how you're doing tonight, man," it says.

The words are breathy, kinda playful. And puzzlingly masculine. A little spooky, actually.

I'm a little confused here.

"Yeah," the voice continues. "Just wondered how you're doing and if you're busy," it says. "What you're wearing. You know."

"OK, Jim, is that you? Scott, is that you? Who is this?"

"Oh, you don't know me, hon," the voice says, "but I'd like for you to know me," it says, "so how's about I drop by and we can . . . and then we can . . . and if you want you can . . ."

Gulp.

Better *not* be Jim or Scott.

What an unfortunate happenstance that the first time I hear such interesting suggestions, they come not from a lovely, soft, feminine voice but from a husky, unshaven, masculine voice.

Now, there aren't that many things about my personality that I can swear to with absolute certainty. Some may say I'm a little neurotic. I don't know. I don't *know*, I tell you. Some may say I'm spoiled and pretty much always get my way in life. Maybe. Some may say I've got the worst temper in the world, and that may or may not be true. I mean, yeah, I've got a bad temper. But whether it's the worst in the world or not, I'm not sure.

But I *am* certain of *one* thing, without question or hesitation or equivocation.

I like girls.

And while it may be true that, at the moment, I'm entertaining a fairly perplexing and eclectic feeling that strangely mixes *weirdly disgusting* with some odd sense of flattery, I'm just as sure as I can be that I don't want this guy dropping by tonight to entertain me.

My problem is, I don't know how big is the guy on the other end of this voice or how mean is he or what degree of kill-you-with-a-meat-cleaver attitude has he developed over the years. And while I don't know *his* whereabouts, since *he* called *me* I've gotta figure that *he* knows precisely where *I* am. So if I make him mad and he decides to inflict great personal harm on me, he can just walk right up anytime he wants and I won't even know it's him until it's too late and I'm dragging my bruised and broken body along the concrete floor, looking for a box of Band-Aids and trying to reach the phone to call an ambulance and the Coalition Against Obscene Callers Sneaking Up On People And Hurting Them.

Well, then, I'd better be nice, I think to myself. *Better not aggravate this gentleman,* I think to myself. Out loud I say, "Oh my, well, that certainly does sound interesting" and then he says, "yeah, well, you ain't heard nothin' yet 'cause after you . . . then I'll . . . and we can . . ."

Double gulp.

The guy's really got a creative imagination. Aimed at the proper gender at the proper time, some of his ideas may actually be winners. In fact, I kinda wish I had pencil and paper handy to make a note or two for future reference. But I don't, so I can't. Anyway, there's really no time to worry about notes or to ponder future use of the romantic techniques this guy's describing. Just now what I need most to do is get rid of this admirer without ending up in the morgue. And in this particular circumstance, I'm absolutely not above lying to make that happen.

So I say, "Thanks man, I appreciate your interest, and you're so very nice with your compliments, but I'm just really too busy here at work right now to talk, and the other fifteen r-e-e-e-a-l-l-y big guys working here with me tonight are hollerin' on me to get off the phone and help mop over there, so I guess I'd better be going now. But, hey, thanks for the call, and maybe I'll hear from you another time when it's not so busy and we can get caught up. But now you have a nice evening and thanks again for calling."

I pause for a beat to see if I hear anything like, "if you hang up the phone, man, I'll come over there and insert your face into the tire changing machine." Hearing nothing, I take it as a good-bye and hang up the phone.

So on my first solo graveyard shift, I've gotten an obscene phone call from a guy.

How can it get any better.

Well, I somehow manage to get through the shift. At six a.m., Jack rolls in on his Honda 350, brakes to a stop in front of the office door, yanks the blue-and-chrome beauty up onto its stand, and bounces on into the office to see how I'm doing.

"So, Mr. Morris, how was your first graveyard?" he says to me, and I notice this strange kind of smirky smile on his face.

"Not bad," I say. "Pretty quiet," I say. "Not all that many customers," I say.

Now Jack wants to know if I had any trouble during the night, and I say, "Trouble? No, I don't think so, but I did have a sorta goofy phone call. But no, I wouldn't say I had any trouble."

"Yeah, well, you're gonna see all kinds of weird stuff in the early morning hours," Jack says, "but I guess you didn't have any trouble with machines or money or anything like that."

"Nope," I say, and I'm getting *pret-tee* darn curious about his curiosity.

Now my boss just stares at me. A deep, introspective, intrusive, prying kind of stare that kinda makes me want to check to see if I've something hanging from my nose or a piece of broccoli stuck in my teeth, or if Raquel Welch has wandered into the station and is standing directly behind me. An intimidating stare that almost makes me feel compelled to admit to things I've done wrong in the past and maybe even to some things I *didn't* do wrong in the past.

If you've ever tried to outstare a non-alpha dog, perhaps you'll have observed that it'll hold eye contact with you for only so long before it's gotta look away. I've always wondered if the critter actually owns feelings like shyness or embarrassment or humility that erode his confidence and make it hard to hold eye contact with the master, or if maybe there's some kind of ocular or optical or neurological basis to the phenomenon.

Now I believe it's because he's confused about why you keep staring at him and convinces himself that he's about to meet his end without even knowing why, and he just can't bear to watch the slaughter.

Whether or not this is true for the non-alpha dog, it's why I finally have to break eye contact with Jack.

And then he shows mercy. With Jack, I guess breaking eye contact's equivalent to tapping out in professional wrestling.

"Good," he says. "Glad to hear it," he says. "Knew I could trust you," he says. "Remember that the true measure of a man's what he does when nobody's watching, so when you're alone, always act like you'd act if you knew someone was watching you and you'll always be trustworthy," he says.

Looks like my old bosses, Bill and Jerry, aren't the only automotive-types that can dispense life lessons from the office of a service station.

Then Jack says, "Well, Kev, it's Sunday morning, and I know you wanna go to church, so get on outta here, and I'll hold down the fort till Harold comes on shift."

Jack's right. It's important to me that I don't miss church services, so I've actually thought about this situation beforehand and considered what to do to get to church on time after my shift's over. I know it's gonna be tight because I get off at six a.m., and my first church meeting starts at six-thirty, so I've developed an efficient plan to get me from Garden Grove to Fullerton—presentably—in less than thirty minutes.

It's a simple plan, really. A quick-change deal. Since the brown work pants I'm wearing look kinda like slacks, I figure they should be passable at church. And my shoes are work oxfords, so they oughta pass without too much notice too. So I only brought along a white shirt and tie to change into.

All righty, then. Work shirt off. White shirt on. Tie tied and tucked into said white shirt so it doesn't beat me to death while I'm riding. And I'm off to the chapel on Raymond Avenue in Fullerton.

I arrive at church on time and enjoy the first meeting of the day, a bit proud of myself that my plan was so well thought out in advance. But after the meeting's finished and I'm walking to my car, my friend, Dave, comes up behind me and says, "Hey Morris, I love your hip pocket accessory." I say, "What the heck are you talking about?" and then I feel my right hip pocket.

There's a greasy red oil cloth hanging from it. Forgot to take it out when I left Jack's.

Rats.

Well, the weeks fly by, and it's just a lot of fun working for Jack. Before you know it, though, it's time to turn in my brown pants and red oil rag and get on back up to BYU in Provo to continue working on my juggling and basketball spinning.

And now I come to my final two shifts at Jack's.

What happens during these last shifts completes a circle of oddity that began with an obscene phone call during my first graveyard shift.

Here's how the system works at Jack's station. When I come on shift, Jack gives me a key to one of the four drawers in the cash register. This drawer's assigned to me when I start my shift, and only I can put money in and take money out of it. That way, if there's any problem with the money in the drawer after my shift, it'll only be *my* problem, and the other guy or guys working with me can't be blamed for any problems with the cash in my drawer.

But if I'm gonna be responsible for what's in this drawer at the *end* of my shift, it stands to reason that I've gotta know what's in it at the *beginning* of my shift. So when I come on shift, I open my drawer, count all the cash and coin, write the numbers down on a check-out slip that's kept in the drawer below the removable cash and coin tray, make sure everything in the drawer matches what the last guy said was in it when he closed it out, and then put everything back in the drawer, close it, and get to work.

At the end of my shift, I essentially repeat the procedure in reverse order. Count all the money to make sure the gives-and-takes of my drawer balance out right. Count out the right number of twenties, tens, fives, ones, and coins to be left in the drawer so the guy coming on after me will have what he needs. Take out all the credit card receipts, total them up using the ten-key, and write the numbers down on the check-out slip. Take the cash in excess of what needs to stay in the drawer, count it, and write the total on the check-out slip. Put the money, credit card receipts, and check-out slip into an envelope and seal it. Slide the sealed envelope into a slot on the front of the safe. Finally, slip the key to my cash drawer into said slot so no one can monkey with the drawer once it's been checked out.

At the close of my Thursday swing shift, I do it all just right, slip the sealed envelope and drawer key into the safe, and head for home, leaving the station to the graveyard guy.

Everything's fine and dandy.

Or not.

My Friday shift will be the last before I quit, and it's scheduled to be another two-to-ten swing shift. But at about ten a.m., I get a call at home from Jack, who says, "Kevin, I know you're not supposed to be here until two, but I need you to come on down a little early if you can." "How early?" I ask, and he says, "Right now if you can." I hop on my Honda and hustle down to the station without wasting time because Jack sounds a little troubled.

When I arrive at the station, I see lots of activity going on. Every employee's here, even the ones who aren't clocked in. Everyone's kinda wandering in and out of the office, where Jack stands in front of the cash register. I'm nearly to the office door when Jack catches my eye and says, "Kev, I need to talk with you for a sec, so just step over here with me," he says.

We walk to the far side of the lube bay doors, out of earshot of the other guys. With a serious look glued to his face, Jack says, "We've got a little problem here, Kev, and I think you were the last one on the job before it happened."

Gulp.

"Tell me what you did," he says, "when you checked out last night."

"I did it just like always," I say. "Counted the drawer, totaled the card receipts, counted the money, filled out the slip, and put everything in the safe," I say. I'm hoping I've said it all in the proper order with the right words, but I'm just a tad upset here, so it wouldn't surprise me to learn that I just told him how I got dressed this morning instead of how I checked out last night.

Jack seems to understand me, though, so maybe I said everything like I tried to say it. But he's still got a puzzled look on his face, as if I'd said the *words right* but not the *right words*. Of course, I'm dying to know what's going on here, but I bite my tongue and don't ask anything. Here I stand, probably looking like a deer in the headlights, and Jack says, "Thanks, Kev, hang on just a minute. I'll be right back." He walks back over to the office to talk with Harold. And then with Ted. And, finally, with the graveyard man.

Then he's back to me and wants to know did any of the other guys stop by during my shift.

"No."

Now he wants to know was anyone here at the station when I closed out to go home last night besides the graveyard man.

"No."

Now he wants to know am I sure the envelope and the key cleared and fell to the bottom of the safe when I dropped them in the slot.

"Yeah," I say. "Like always."

Jack falls silent and stares at me.

I've seen this stare before.

Then, while still looking directly into my eyes, Jack's face turns all of a sudden friendlier and his eyes light up a little and he says, "OK, Kev, you can go on home now if you want, and I'll see you at two."

Well, I'm just *pret-tee* darn glad nobody's slapped handcuffs on me. I probably should let well enough alone and just go on home like Jack says, but there's just no way I'm leaving here without knowing what's going on. So I screw my courage to the sticking-place and say, "Jack, what's going on? Did I do something wrong?"

Jack looks at me for a time without saying anything at all. Then, after what seems like an eternity, he speaks. "We're missing a few things this morning," he says. "Tires. Rims. And the drawer you used last night's empty but the key to it's in the safe," he says.

Jack turns and starts walking toward the office.

Wow.

Now this is a problem, I'm thinking. The only way my drawer could've been emptied is if someone had the key that opens it, but I put the key that opens it into the safe when I left. As far as we know, there's no way anyone could've gotten it out of the safe once I put it in. So guess who looks like the number one suspect.

Even though Jack's excused me to go home, I'm just suddenly scared out of my wits. I know I've gotta say *something* in the way of defending myself, but I feel about as emotionally flat and brain-dead as Pat Paulsen giving his weekly editorial on *The Smothers Brothers Comedy Hour*. What could I possibly say to convince my boss that I didn't do this thing when the only logical answer is that I'm the only one who *could* have done it? But I didn't, and Jack's gotta know that.

"I didn't do it, Jack."

Jack stops in his tracks, looks down at the concrete for a beat, then turns to me and smiles.

"I know you didn't, Kev," he says.

Then he turns and walks on toward the office.

I suppose there'll be times in the next forty or so years when I'm doubted, suspected, blamed—maybe even accused. If I remember those occasions at all, I won't remember them for long.

What I *will* remember, though, from today right on through to that day when I shuffle off this mortal coil, is that, late in the summer of 1970, on this one day, in this one moment, a man who had good reason to doubt me, to suspect me, to blame me, and even to accuse me . . . didn't.

A lesson in trust I'll take to my grave.

13

I get—are you kidding me— robbed again

coincidence > noun 1 a striking occurrence of two or more events at one time apparently by mere chance. 2 a sequence of events that although accidental seems to have been planned or arranged. 3 the noteworthy alignment of two or more events or circumstances.

Derivatives coincident > adjective, coincidental > adjective, coincidentally >adverb.

Synonyms accident > luck > fate > chance > fluke

Lightning never strikes twice in the same place.

An old adage suggesting that an unusual event never occurs twice under the same circumstances to the same person. Its origin may have been traced to 1857 in author P.H. Meyers's *Thrilling Adventures of the Prisoner of the Border.*

Ranger Roy C. Sullivan (1912–1983) of Shenandoah Park, Virginia, would've argued this adage with you. And he had some pretty compelling evidence to support his point of view. Between 1942 and 1977, Ranger Sullivan—aka Human Lightning Rod—was struck by lightning a world-record seven times. One strike blew off a toenail, another knocked him unconscious and burned off his eyebrows, and another sprained his ankle. He was burned on his left shoulder, chest, and stomach. His hair caught fire twice, prompting him to carry a pitcher of water around with him all the time. He lived to tell about each strike, though, and his scorched ranger hats were put on exhibit.

Lee Trevino, a renowned professional golfer, can also argue this adage. He's been struck on two different occasions while playing golf. He says that when he sees rain and lightning on the golf course now, he holds up his one-iron—because even God can't hit a one-iron.

But there are so many different kinds of lightning.

In August 1970, I left my home in Southern Cal to return once again to Brigham Young University for my third semester of education. I'd had a great time in the dorms during my freshman year, but I knew it had come time to get a little more serious about this education thing, so instead of returning to the dorms for more mirth and merriment, I took up residence in the Ream Apartments complex in Provo.

My third semester ended in January, and I returned to Fullerton to prepare for missionary service for the Church of Jesus Christ of Latter-day Saints. It's customary, you see, for nineteen-year-old young men to serve the Church full-time for two years, and since I'd just turned nineteen in December, I needed to go home and prepare for the call that would come within the next three months.

Waiting for my call, I find myself with a little time on my hands. Until March, anyway. So I'm figuring . . . well, why not see if I can pick up a few hours at Jack's service station while I wait. Kill the boredom and knock down some coin.

I've gotta confess that I'm just the slightest bit hesitant, though, to ask Jack for a job again, remembering my last shift of the summer when several tires and rims went missing and the money in my cash drawer disappeared, and I had to go back to BYU without knowing how the whole situation turned out. I still remember how trusting Jack was when he told me he knew I hadn't taken the stuff—but who knows what he's thinking now. Maybe he's rethought his position since then and, instead of giving me my job back, maybe he'll call the cops when I show up at the station and have me slapped in irons.

Then I think, *Well, maybe jail wouldn't really be all that bad. I mean, I'd get three squares a day, develop a strong social network, and maybe get in a little weight lifting. On balance, not such a bad way to spend one's time.*

So I muster up the nerve and drive on out to the station. When I arrive there, I find my fears unfounded—in fact, Jack actually seems happy to see me and gladly agrees to let me work for him again. I won't work as many hours as I did during the summer, but hey. Every hour I work's a couple of bucks I wouldn't otherwise have. So I sign on again, get my work schedule, and get ready to head on back home.

Wait just a doggone minute, though. I can't possibly leave without asking about last summer's missing tires and cash, so I do. Turns out that the next day after I'd left, Jack had announced to all the guys that they'd be taking a lie detector test. Even though he absolutely intended to carry out this plan because he's not the kind to bluff but he *is* the kind to do exactly what he says he'll do, Jack never actually had to go through with the deal because one of the guys—The One, apparently—read the writing on the wall and never came back to work. After a little more investigating, it was discovered that the register drawer key that I'd inserted into the drop safe before I closed out my shift that night could—with a clothes hanger and a little elbow grease—be fished back out through the drop slot.

It's nice that there's proof that I didn't take the wheels or the cash, that's for sure—but it's still the best thing of all to know that Jack believed I didn't do the deed even when it made sense for him to believe I did.

So there'll be no slapping the kid in irons today.

At work the next day, I find that Jack's still the same good ol' guy and the work's just like I remember it to be. The only real difference I notice is that his wife may be spending a little more time on premises now than she used to. I don't talk with her much, though, and I certainly don't expect—nor do I get—anything warm and cozy from her because . . . well, I'm just a peon and she's royalty. Anyway, she scares the diddlywhazzit out of me, so distance between us is a good thing, as far as I'm concerned.

I don't wonder now like I used to about why Jack spends such long hours at the station.

My job description's pretty much the same now as it was the first time I worked here. I mostly just pump gas and push oil, but once in a while I get to repair a hole in an inner tube or even plug a tubeless tire. And I've used the tire machine to break a tire off the rim a few times and I didn't even hurt myself all that seriously doing it. I also get to do an oil change from time to time, and maybe the occasional lube job. Plus, I've learned a little bit about adjusting brakes and bleeding brake lines. Really fun stuff.

No matter how much fun it may seem, though, this is, after all, still *work*—and certainly not as much fun as I was having up at BYU, enjoying playing intramural flag football with the Slippery Rock Eleven on the fields at Farrer Junior High and watching Big Ed get his cheek bone broken when a down-and-out pass play went bad. Not as much fun as going to the KEYY radio station on the outskirts of Provo with my friend Larson, who's a DJ there, and doing my John Wayne impression on the air. Not as much fun as the classes I've been taking for the last three months, but it's . . . No, wait. It *is* as fun as *that*.

But it's *absolutely* not as much fun as walking to the Paramount Theater in downtown Provo with Jody on a snowy night, holding hands and wondering about days to come. It's not as much fun as taking her to a Dennis Yost and the Classics IV concert to hear Dennis sing and English White wail on that soulful sax. And it's certainly not as much fun as hearing her tell me about this one really interesting day she'd experienced.

See, Jody cooked for the guys in the apartment next to me. By tomorrow's more liberated standards, the arrangement will seem odd, but at BYU in the sixties and seventies, it's not only common but just *pret-tee* much understood that guys living in an off-campus apartment will pay—and I use the term loosely—a young lady to cook for them.

But cooking isn't all they get from her.

What happens is, the guys pitch in a few dollars each week, all of which goes to the young lady who then plans dinner for each of the coming weekdays and creates a food budget based on the menu and the dollars available. Sometimes the money she collects is actually enough to buy all the food she needs to pull off her planned menu—but more often than not, she's gotta toss in a dollar or two of her own to cover for the cheap-o slugs who don't pony up the dough. Then she does the shopping. She's gotta hustle a ride from somebody with a car and a generous heart down to Ream's Grocery Store, where she grabs one of those black wax crayons to write the price on each item—this is how the market saves on overhead in order to pass discounts on to starving students—before she puts it into the cart, buys all the food her meager budget will allow, and then drags her exhausted-after-a-full-day-of-classes-not-to-mention-grocery-shopping body to the apartment each afternoon to do the Julia Child thing and serve a bunch of economical, delicious food to the guys. Now, this may sound like a lot of work. And I guess it is. But remember. She gets paid to do this.

Well, she doesn't actually get paid *money*, per se. Nope, not money.

See, somewhere in the creation of this time-honored tradition, they—whoever *they* were—decided that offering filthy lucre for these duties would somehow be an insult to a young lady. So the standard pay's not dollars but the privilege of being allowed to eat dinner with the guys each day. Now, think about it. This is saving her a lot of money on groceries. Well, maybe not a *lot* of money, when you deduct all the money she's gotta pay out of her own pocket at the grocery store to cover for the cheap-o slugs who don't pony up the . . . wait. I already insulted them once.

A great system.

If you're one of the guys.

So on this one day, I arrived home from classes, parked my little Honda 90 Scrambler on the sidewalk outside my apartment, and then trickled on over to the next-door apartment to see Jody. I figured she'd be cooking dinner there, and sure enough, there she was. Not really trying all that hard to be stealthy, I kinda half-heartedly sneaked up behind her to say hi—and what I got in return was this little wide-eyed, heart-warming "hey you," the most genuine sure-am-glad-to-see-you smile I've ever seen, and a light, comfortable kiss on the beak.

Could heaven be any better.

"So how's your day been?" I asked, and even though the perfect smile on Jody's perfect face didn't actually disappear altogether, my keen powers of observation told me that maybe it'd been a pretty rough day for my friend. Well . . . my keen powers of observation plus the fact that she said, "Kevin, it's been a pretty rough day."

"So what's wrong?" I asked, and she answered, "Well, not much has gone right today from the time I got up, so I'm not really feeling all that great when I get here today. Then the phone rings while I'm up to my neck in chili," she said, "and no one but me's here, so I have to drop everything I'm doing to answer it, and this deep kinda old voice on the other end asks to speak with Mark. Well, I've had about all I can take for one day," she said, "so I come back with 'No, you can't speak with Mark because he's not here, and before you ask, I'll tell you that I don't know when he'll be here and there's no one else here to ask where he is or when he'll be back.'"

Right about then, I was thinking that the gentleman on the phone should've sneaked up behind my good friend instead of telephoning. Maybe he'd have gotten a little kiss instead of a brow beating.

"So," Jody continued, "after I get done hollerin' on the guy, there's this pause, and then in a real sweet, patient tone, he says to me, 'I understand. Would you mind just telling Mark when he comes in that his grandfather called?'"

Now, there's a little something here I haven't mentioned. See, two of the young men living in this apartment that Jody cooked for were Clark Hinckley and Mark McConkie. If you're Mormon, you'll certainly recognize these surnames immediately. And, yes, their fathers would be Gordon B. and Bruce R., respectively.

If you don't happen to be LDS—and I can help you with that, if you'd like—it'll help you to know that Gordon B. Hinckley and Bruce R. McConkie are members of the Quorum of the Twelve Apostles, the second-highest governing body of The Church of Jesus Christ of Latter-day Saints, which, together with the First Presidency—consisting of a president and two counselors—oversees the entire Church worldwide. Mark is Bruce R.'s son. Bruce R.'s father-in-law is Joseph Fielding Smith. Joseph Fielding Smith is the President of the Church and a man accepted by its membership as a prophet. If you've paid attention, you'll see that he is also, of course, Mark's grandfather, to whom Jody just explained the facts of life so clearly.

And so, as Jody's smile dissipated even more, she set the capstone on her woes by saying, "So on top of everything else today, Kevin, I've hollered on a living prophet of God."

No, working at Jack's station isn't as much fun as enjoying moments like that, but it's still fun in its own way, so I like being here when I'm here. Sometimes I'm here even when I'm not getting *paid* to be here. Maybe I'm thinking that if I hang around enough, I'll be handy when last summer's obscene phone caller calls back and I can make sure everything's going OK with him.

That call never comes, but there's more than one way to enjoy coincidence here at Jack's.

This evening I'm working the swing shift with Ted, and we're coming to the end of the shift. I'm handling the gas pumps and a few other miscellaneous duties while Ted's in the lube bay under the hood of a car. When I say "under the hood of a car," I mean "under the hood of a car." Most of the engine of this particular car's been removed, and Ted's right down there in the space where the rest of the engine should be.

I'm in the office, having just finished servicing a car at the pump. I'm standing between the cash register and the candy vending machine, thinking about buying a Mars Almond Bar. I'm actually trying to decide between that and the Snickers, and I'm having a hard time making up my mind. See, Jack just recently added the Mars Bar to the vending machine, and I've only had it once, but it sure was tasty, and I love that you get a whole almond in each of the four bites it takes to eat the whole thing. But that Snickers bar's been a favorite for a long time.

This is really a hard choice. People underestimate just how much stress there can be in choosing the proper sweet for the proper occasion. Finally, I decide that I just can't decide, so I return the dime to my pocket and turn to leave the office to straighten up things at the pumps.

I don't make it to the door. In fact, I've taken only one step toward it when I see a young man—probably about my age—standing there, just inside the door. He's wearing a stocking cap pulled down over disheveled hair, jeans, T-shirt, a faded brown cloth jacket, and a serious look on his face.

Oh, yeah. And he's holding a gun in his right hand.

Pointed at me.

Now, I'm no genius, as I've mentioned before, but I know right away—call it intuition, if you will—that it'll probably be a good idea to just stand where I'm at for a moment or two. The guy with the gun reinforces my notion when he says something on the order of "Don't move or we've got a problem."

Not wanting the particular problem that I'm pretty sure he's referring to, I quickly decide that I won't move. And I don't. But then the guy says to me, "Hey, as long as you're standing there, why don't you go ahead and open that cash register and give me the money that's in it?" He waves the gun around a bit as he talks, sorta like what you might see in a George Raft gangster movie when a thug gets the drop on another thug.

Well, I hear what the young gentleman in the lovely stocking cap's saying to me. Don't think I don't. And, to be fair to his point of view, I can understand how opening the cash register and handing him all the money might seem like a good idea to *him*. But I wish he'd extend the same courtesy and understand how it might *not* seem like such a good idea to *me*.

Pay attention now, because I'm gonna show you just how stupid I can be when I set my mind to it.

First, I've gotta tell you about a conversation with Jack last summer, just before my first graveyard shift, when he sat me down and explained a couple of things to me.

"You may get robbed sometime," he told me.

Hmmm. Interesting start to the conversation. There are several directions this little tête-à-tête could've taken, and I'd hoped for a more upbeat conversation—but, as Mr. Jagger so aptly put it, you can't always get what you want.

"You may get robbed sometime," Jack told me. "So there's a couple of things you need to know," he said. "First of all, try to keep yourself safe," he said. "Usually a robber just wants money or stuff, and if you cooperate and give him what he wants, he'll usually just go away without hurting you or doing any other damage because that's the easiest thing for him to do, so whatever he tells you to give him, you should just give him," he said.

"B-u-u-u-t," he added, "if you can get him to open the cash register himself, that'll be good because then he'll leave fingerprints on the register buttons, and we'll nail the sucker."

The development of cognition in children's a most interesting process. For example, when you ask a small child whether he wants A or B, most of the time he'll say B, even if A would be the better choice—because B's the last thing he hears.

I guess I never progressed beyond that particular developmental level because apparently the only thing I heard Jack say was that if I'm ever robbed, I should get the robber to open the cash register himself.

OK. So I'm developmentally splintered. I'll give you that. But I'm also obedient and not too proud to do as Jack instructs. So, remembering that counsel, I say to the guy with the gun—and here's where you can have some fun estimating my general level of intelligence—"I'll give you the key, but if you want the cash register open, you're gonna have to open it yourself."

At this point, I don't know who's more surprised—the guy with the gun, because I've told him to open the register himself, or me, because I haven't been riddled with bullets yet. But after staring at me kinda funny for a few seconds, the guy apparently recovers from whatever level of incredulity his neurology has allowed and concludes that, well, the poor scared kid just didn't understand what I said to him so let's just try this again.

"I said open the register," he says. "Open the register *now*," he says.

Any therapist worth his or her salt will tell you that the really important part of any relationship—even, or maybe *especially*, a dysfunctional one such as this—is communication. So this is good, I think to myself. I mean, the guy's still talking and I'm not shot yet, so on balance this thing's actually going pretty well. All things considered, though, I'd still rather he lost the rod he's still waving at me, albeit with a little smoother action now. Rather more like James Cagney than George Raft.

Not wanting to be the one who retards the development of a relationship that started out somewhat shaky but seems to be gaining a little positive momentum, I decide I'd better reciprocate the guy's effort, so I repeat—

"I said if you want the register open, you're gonna have to open it yourself."

Now, if we had some kind of portable EEG unit and could hook young Mr. Stocking Cap up to it, I'm *pret-tee* darn sure we'd get some interesting readings as his uniquely organized brain struggles to accommodate the incompatibility of my repeated response to his instruction. Sadly, instead of promoting our relationship, my response seems rather to have brought it to its metaphorical knees. I see now that I've inadvertently set up an impenetrable wall between us.

Perhaps worse than that, I seem to have confused the young man.

"I said . . . well . . . I mean . . . you should . . . I mean . . . umm . . . you . . . well . . . then . . . well then just go and . . . umm . . . just go and stand over . . . go stand in the corner over there."

Stand in the corner. Hmmm. I'm actually OK with this. I believe a little time out would be beneficial for both of us just now.

So I walk carefully to the other side of the cash register, heading for the wall. I face it just like he told me to. Behind me I hear some grunting and some button pushing and some more button pushing and some more grunting and some silence and then some more button pushing.

He hasn't asked me how to open the register. Not that I'd tell him. Apparently this guy's a cut above your average idiot robber, though, and he's up to the challenge without any need for assistance. After just a little more button pushing and a tad more grunting, I finally hear a lovely *ding*, telling me he's got the drawer open.

I knew he could do it. In some strange way, I feel kinda proud of him. And now we've got all those lovely fingerprints on all those lovely register keys.

Now that Al Capone's got what he wants, I'm gonna hold him to what Jack said robbers usually do after they get what they want, which is to just go ahead and leave without killing anybody or doing any damage. I don't really know how to broach the subject, though, so I decide to just keep quiet for a minute and see what he's got in mind.

"I don't reckon you ain't got no key to the safe," the guy mumbles.

It takes me a moment to understand that this is more than just self-talk or rhetoric—he's actually wanting a response from me. Understanding at last, I say, "Nope, they don't give me a key to the safe."

"I don't reckon you can open these other drawers," he says.

Now, I already know from my experience with his last pseudo-question that the guy's actually expecting a response, so this time I just blurt out right away, "Nope, they don't give me keys to them either."

"Well then, I'm gonna go now," he says, "but you stay right over there against that wall till I'm gone 'cause if I see you comin' out the door too quick, we're still gonna have a problem," he says.

I don't want that problem any more now than I did at the beginning of this activity, so I'm happy to stand right still for the next few seconds. It doesn't really make any difference, though, because from where I'm standing I can see him and *another* guy—whose acquaintance I didn't get to make—running like out-of-the-medals Olympians around the corner and into the darkness along the avenue.

I guess the bandit's partner must've been just a little shy or else maybe they're students at the Rob and Threaten School of Theft and Robbery and the guy that stayed outside was just nonmatriculating the Armed Robbery 101 class and not allowed to participate but only to observe.

Whatever.

I step around to the cash register to see what kind of damage we've sustained. Now, the drawers in this register have a removable black plastic cash-and-coin tray inside that holds our working capital—and because the drawer's still open, I can see immediately that the cash-and-coin tray's nearly empty. I mean, the coins are all still in their little compartments, but all the paper money's gone. But underneath this removable tray's where we keep credit card receipts and bills larger than twenties. Wondering just how experienced this guy is at his work, I lift the tray to see what's under it.

He's not very experienced.

Some fifties are there, untouched. Even a couple of hundreds. So many large bills under the tray at one time's pretty rare—and if my new friend had bothered to lift it, he'd have enjoyed a much greater profit margin, but he didn't, so he didn't. I set the tray back down into the drawer, and as it clunks its way into place, it suddenly hits me.

Where the heck's Ted?

He was in the lube bay when this whole thing started, so maybe I'd better check to see if he's OK in there. I step into the lube bay and see that the car with the open hood's still there. And there's Ted, still under that hood, fussing around with some screw or nut or hose.

"Hey Ted, didn't you just hear what was going on in the office?" I ask, and he looks up at me kinda puzzled like and says, "I didn't hear nothin'. Whatcha talkin' about?" "Well, I just got robbed," I say. "Yeah, right," he says, "whaddaya mean you just got robbed?" and I say, "Well, I'm not sure how many meanings you can get from the words 'I just got robbed,' but if you'll climb out from under the hood, I'll show you what I'm talking about."

Out of the car's front end Ted climbs, a reddish-orange oil rag in each hand and a face so dirty I can see mostly just the whites of his eyes and the couple of teeth that are still good, and together we walk into the office.

As I explain to Ted all that happened, I find it's actually a little hard for me to talk because I'm feeling just a little shaky here. It's just occurred to me that there was a guy waving a gun at me and I argued with him and what the heck was I thinking.

I manage to keep it together well enough to explain the happening to Ted and then he says, "Well, we gotta call Jack and I guess the police too, but we'd better call Jack first and see what he wants to do."

Call the police is what Jack wants to do, so while we wait for our boss to arrive at the station, we call the police and report a two-eleven. "Be there as soon as we can," the dispatch officer tells us.

We don't hear anything else from anyone or see anyone for what seems like a really long time, and it's starting to get pretty late. Then suddenly everyone starts showing up—with really lovely timing. Jack and the police officers pull into the station at just about the same time, Jack on his motorcycle and the police officers in a couple of lighted squad cars. I'm not sure whom I should approach first—but after I remember whose name's on the check I get every week, I figure Jack oughta have first crack at me. So I walk in his direction. Cautiously.

Courage, Camille.

But just like my old boss Jerry did three years ago when I told him I'd just been robbed, Jack attends first to my welfare. "Kevin, are you OK? Are you sure you're OK?" he says as he's walking toward me.

"I guess so," I say. "I mean, I feel a little weird, but as far as I can tell, I'm OK," I say.

Interrupting our conversation, a police officer steps right in between us and says to me, "Are you the one that was here tonight when the robbery occurred?" and I say, "Yes, sir, I am," and he says, "So show me where you were when it happened and tell me everything you saw and heard."

I show the officer to the scene of the crime and start explaining about my dilemma in deciding between the Mars Almond Bar and the Snickers. He suggests that I can leave out those details. Like detective sergeant Jack Friday, he seems to want "the facts, ma'am, just the facts" so I skip the candy and move right to the subject of the bandit's weaponry—which this particular officer seems pretty interested in.

"Yes, sir, I'm sure it was a gun," I say. "Do you know what kind of gun?" he asks. "No, I can't say I'm all that familiar with firearms in general or handguns in particular," I say, "but I've seen enough movies and Sears Roebuck catalogs to know a gun when I see one."

"Can you describe the perpetrator?" he wants to know. "Of course I can," I say. "It was a guy, and he was . . . well, he was . . . you know . . . I mean, he . . ."

Crap.

At the moment, I can't for the life of me think of a single thing about the way the bandit looked even though I'm sure that just a few minutes ago I noticed everything there was to notice about him. Now it all seems to have run clean out of my head, like there's some kind of bizarre neurological leak and everything I knew thirty minutes ago has seeped out and evaporated.

Except that I remember that there was another guy with him that

I didn't meet but only saw as the two of them were hightailing it away from here—and that I did manage to get the gunman to open the cash register.

Now, when he hears me say, "I did manage to get the gunman to open the cash register," Jack, who's been listening in nearby, suddenly chimes in. "You did *what*?" he says. "You got him to open . . . You got him to . . . Whaddaya *mean* you got him to open the cash register?" he says, spitting out syllables like watermelon seeds.

I remind Jack that he'd told me once that if ever I was robbed I should get the guy to open the register so we could get fingerprints and nail the rascal, so when the robber told me to open the register, I gave him the key and told him to open it himself.

Jack does this really funny thing with his face, like he's just heard the weirdest thing ever and the news is giving him a facial seizure of some kind. Then he spins dramatically around a couple of times, muttering under his breath and looking toward the dark sky like he's expecting something to fall down from it at any moment. Then he turns back to me, his crimson face registering a look that's a little bit puzzled, a little bit angry, and a whole lot incredulous.

"I can't *believe* you did that," he says. "Don't you know you coulda been *shot*?" he says.

Well, I know I probably *shoulda* thought about that, but to tell you the truth, the idea, as good as it might have been, didn't occur to me until after Barney and Clyde had left because at the time I was too busy thinking that I should do what I'd been told to do.

That's what I'm *thinking*. What I say to Jack is "yeah." Just "yeah."

"I didn't tell you to *argue* with the guy, for cryin' out Pete's sake," Jack says, and wipes his hand across his forehead and then down over his face like he's trying to wipe away the whole night and everything that's happened in it, but when his hand gets to his chin he realizes it's all still here and looks real disappointed about it.

I'm just standing there quiet, thinking how lovely it would've been if last summer Jack had explained a little more clearly to me that getting the fingerprints wasn't so much an *expectation* as it was a pie-in-the-sky *hope*. Would've been really helpful info just a few minutes ago when I was sucking around for some unfriendly fire.

The police officers are having a bit of a conference, and then one of them walks over to me and says, "Why don't you go have a seat. You're not looking all that great." It kinda makes me happy that he says that because—to quote the wisdom of *M*A*S*H*'s Colonel Henry Potter just a few short years from now—I'd hate to feel this bad and have it be just my little secret. So I go ahead and sit down at the small desk on the other side of the cash register.

It feels really good to be off my feet. Sitting here, I hear the officers talking again. "I've called the prints guy," one says to the other, "and it'll be a while before he gets here, so why don't we talk to the guy who was in the lube bay when it happened." I watch as the two swagger over and chat with Ted for a minute. I guess it doesn't take Ted long to tell them he was inside the front end of a car and didn't hear or see a thing because they just scribble a couple of quick notes and then go on back over to their black-and-white to wait for the prints guy.

After a while, a little white car that doesn't look at all official swerves up to the lube bay pretty fast and screeches to a stop. A tall guy with a rumpled sport shirt, black slacks, loafers with no socks, and hair standing pretty much straight up opens the door and steps out of the car. My guess is that this guy's head was very recently squashed against a fluffy down pillow. And by the look on his face—sort of a combination of put out, ticked off, and half asleep—I can tell that this service station at this moment on this night's pretty much the last place this man would care to be.

But being the dedicated public servant he obviously is, he's here. The prints guy, I guess. He comes on into the office carrying a briefcase which, as I'll learn in just a moment or two, contains powders and brushes and tapes. When he gets to the cash register, he says, "So is this what I'm dusting?" and before I can decide whether he's talking to me or to somebody else, one of the other officers says, "Yeah, the perp touched these keys when he opened the register 'cause the kid over there told him he had to open it if he wanted it open."

Prints Guy's eyebrows climb practically to his hairline, and he says, "*which* kid," and the other officer points to me and says, "*that* kid," and the prints guy doesn't say anything else, but from the way he's looking at me I figure he either thinks I'm the bravest person he's met this week or is trying to figure out why there's no medical examiner bending over my tagged-and-bagged body. Then he shifts his gaze from my eyes to his briefcase as he prepares to consider which tools he'll need to do his job. That's when something about the cash register catches his attention, I guess, because I hear him mutter under his breath, "What the . . ."

"Get over here, Thompson," Prints Guy says, and the officer who must be Thompson trots on over to see what Prints Guy will have. I don't have to strain to hear what they're saying because Prints Guy's making no effort whatsoever to lower his voice when he asks Thompson whether he'd bothered to even *look* at the register keys before calling him out at this late hour.

"Well . . . yeah, I looked at the keys, but no, I guess I didn't really study the keys," Thompson admits, "but a register key's a register key, isn't it? And besides, what do I know from register keys anyway?" he says. "I'm just supposed to check out the scene and then call you if we need you, and I figured since we knew the guy touched the keys, you might wanna lift some prints," he says.

Personally, I think Thompson's offered a lovely explanation, but Prints Guy holds a slightly higher expectation, I guess, because he makes it clear to Thompson in *pret-tee* short order that his time's been wasted. It seems that these particular register keys have teensy weensy little grids cut into them. Kinda like *leet-tle* tiny tiles. I don't know, but I guess the texture of these little tiles is supposed to help keep a guy's fingertips from sliding off the keys when he's punching them. Seems a little overkill-ish to me, but then I've never really done any empirical research on tiny textured tiles, so what would I know? Whatever. In any case, it turns out that the keys' texture—whatever else it may or may not do—makes it impossible to lift a print.

All of a sudden, I find myself in the conversation because Prints Guy turns his attention to me and asks, "Son, did the perp . . . I mean, did the robber touch anything else?" and I say, "Well, I don't think so, at least not while I was talking to him, but after he sent me to face the wall over there, I couldn't see what he was doing," I say. "I guess he could've touched the drawer," I say, "but I kinda doubt it 'cause once you hit the right key, the drawer pops open on its own, and it was still open when he left, so I doubt he touched the drawer," I say.

"That wouldn't help anyway," Prints Guy says, "because the face of the drawer's got the same tiled texture on it that the keys have, so I guess we're just outta luck on this one."

"*Aren't* we, Thompson?" he says, smiling at Thompson. But his clenched teeth and red face kinda make me believe that this isn't a sincere smile.

So Prints Guy closes the briefcase that never got more than partly opened anyway and heads back to his little white car that doesn't look at all official. I can't hear what he says to Thompson's partner, who's standing by the little white car, but after he says whatever he says, he hops into his car and jets away.

Thompson and his partner step outside with Jack for a few minutes. When they get into their cars, turn off the lights on their squad cars, and start to drive away, I guess they've gotten everything worked out. Jack turns to come back into the office.

But before the two officers can exit the station and before Jack can get back into the office, here comes another lighted squad car.

The two squad cars that were leaving stop suddenly and back up to the lube bay door, and the officers get out of their cars. Seeing the third car turning in, Jack stops and turns back the other way to find out what's going on. I stand up and walk on over to the office door so I can see better. Things seem to be getting interesting again.

Everybody's walking toward the third squad car that's still got its lights flashing. And out of that car climbs another uniformed officer. He says, "Hey, I've got a guy here you may wanna meet." The officer opens the back door of his car, reaches in, grabs the arm of a young man, and kinda helps-slash-pulls him from the car.

"This guy and another guy," the officer explains, "was walkin' down the street just around the corner from here lookin' kinda suspicious-like, and when I slows down to take a look-see, the two of 'em dives into the bushes. The one got away," the officer continues, "but I got my hands on this'n here, and I heard the call come over about this two-eleven here, so I'm thinkin' maybe there's a connection, so I decides I'll bring him by and see if anybody here can ID him."

In about fifteen years from now, I'll be visiting my folks in Mississippi. My dad will have a beautiful little horse named Ginger, a barrel-racing Peruvian Paso that can stop on a dime and leave two cents change and can change direction from north to west in pretty much one step while running full speed ahead.

Which I learn the hard way the first time I ride her at a gallop and rein her left when I reach the corner of the house. Ginger plants her outside leg and makes the left turn at 90 degrees—and I continue on straight ahead.

On another day, I'll be riding Ginger in the woods behind Dad's house, exploring a little path and enjoying the beautiful, thick deciduous forest at a leisurely walk. On the way back in, I decide that a gallop would be fun, so I kick Ginger up into high gear. I'm keeping her on the path, and everything's just ducky until we round a little turn in the path and I see—directly ahead of us—a hole in the hard red Mississippi dirt. Such a hole's just not a good thing when you're galloping a Peruvian Paso down a path in the woods—but my opinion of the hole notwithstanding, I know I can't stop Ginger quickly enough to avoid it. All I can do is hope she steps over it.

She doesn't.

The right front hoof hits square in the hole, and the two of us go down hard, Ginger on her right shoulder and neck, and I, straight ahead with my arms stretched out in front of me like Superman trying to get air. We both skid along the path, although I've flown on a little ways ahead, and after I've slid to a rest with the breath knocked clear out of me, I lie there on my right-side shoulder and hip, hoping to breathe again soon. Then I see something that I immediately disapprove of.

Ginger's slid to a stop just short of my feet. Well, I'm fibbing just a little bit here because it's really only her *front* half that's slid to a stop. The *rear* half's still coming my way, flipping over her head and neck and aimed to fall square on me. In a heartbeat, I decide this isn't good, but there's nothing to be done but wait—literally breathless—to see how this story will end. If her butt's got the momentum to clear center and come on over onto my poor breathless body, my poor breathless body will probably be *permanently* breathless.

Good news. The butt stops just short of center and then plops back down to the ground behind Ginger, where it should be. She scrambles to her feet, and I stand up too—as soon as my winded body will move—and here stand the two of us, staring at each other. I still can't breathe at all, and Ginger's scared to death, huffing and puffing with red Mississippi dirt shoved up her nose and her eyes round and big as plates.

Except that he doesn't have any red Mississippi dirt shoved up his nose, the face of this young man cowering in front of the squad car looks just like Ginger's.

I'm still at the office door and can hear some of what's going on.

Jack turns toward me and waves me over, so I trot on out to join them by the squad car.

Jack tells me how the officer nabbed this kid and wants to know if the kid looks familiar to me. I look carefully at the guy shaking in his boots, but I know right away that I'm only gonna be able to give my best guess on this identification thing because, except for the stocking cap the robber was wearing, I really can't remember now just what he looked like—and *this* guy isn't *wearing* a stocking hat, so that's no help. I saw *two* guys running away, so it could be that I don't recognize this guy simply because maybe he's the one that waited outside while Butch Cassidy did the dirty work. Or maybe these two guys that jumped into the bushes had nothing to do with the robbery but were just scared because their parents had threatened to call the police if they stayed out too late just once more. Or maybe they were feeling guilty because they hadn't gone to the trouble to register their bicycles or maybe they were holding someone's pooch for a doggie ransom and figured they'd just been made. Who knows why two kids jump in the bushes late at night when a squad car passes by. In any case, I just can't say for sure that we've got a guilty kid here, and I'm not willing to pin something on someone unless I'm sure, so I tell Jack and the officers that I don't think I recognize this guy.

Clearly, this is good news for the captured kid, but I don't think it's done much to brighten the overall mood of Jack and the police officers. It seems they'd already made up their minds that this is one of the guys and are eager to find a conclusion to this story tonight.

But the conclusion to this story isn't gonna come tonight. It'll come, but not tonight.

"You sure?" one of the officers asks me, and I say, "No, I can't say that I'm sure, but I don't think I recognize him, and I'm not gonna say I do if I don't."

See, even though I don't say it aloud to the officer, I'm thinking I'd rather see this kid go home tonight and wonder for the rest of my life whether or not he's one of the guys who robbed me than to make a mistake and help nail an innocent guy.

The officer frowns at me and then gives the kid a real nasty look as he helps-slash-shoves him back into the squad car and closes the door. The three officers have another brief conference, then climb into their cars and drive away.

Now that the excitement's abated some, Jack observes aloud that it looks like a wrap for the night and tells me I should just run on home. I'm so thrilled with the prospect of going home, I can't begin to tell you. But Ted's already gone home, and the graveyard guy hasn't shown up yet, so I wonder out loud if maybe Jack wants me to stick around till graveyard gets here. "That'll be OK," he says. "I can manage till he gets here, so you just go on home and get some rest," he says.

I do.

Within a couple of weeks, I've left to serve as a missionary for the Church of Jesus Christ of Latter-day Saints, going first to Utah for language training and then to Munich two months later to serve in the Germany South Mission. I spend an incredible two years living among the wonderful German people, then return home to Southern Cal in March 1973. After getting reacquainted with friends and family, I find myself sitting around one day with not much to do, and I think maybe it's a good time to hop on down to Jack's station and say hey.

So off I go.

When I arrive at Jack's station, I find little changed. Even the gas prices have gone up only about three cents, to thirty-nine cents a gallon. And there's Jack, just like I remember him, sitting at the little desk in the office doing paperwork—and, by the way, can I just tell you that no human being anywhere in the world's got better speed on a ten-key than Jack does. Blinding.

But I digress.

So I park the blue Datsun 510 sedan that Dad's graciously allocated to me temporarily and hop on into the office. When Jack sees me, he smiles big and stands up to shake my hand. "How's it going, Kev?" he says to me, and I'm happy to report to him that everything's going just fine. Then we step out onto the island, where he listens politely as I give him a quick bulleted report on my two-year experience overseas.

Now here we are, standing outside the office door, gabbing and smiling and kidding around, when, at just about the same time, we both notice a man approaching us. He appears to be a clean-cut young man, probably about my age. He's got a smile on his face and seems pretty focused on making eye contact with both of us. Jack steps around just a tad so that now he and I are standing shoulder to shoulder and facing the man directly as he speaks to us.

"Excuse me, gentlemen."

"What can I do for you?" Jack asks rather curtly.

"Excuse me," the man says again and then explains how he doesn't want to interrupt, but if we've got a minute, he'd like to talk with us.

"What's on your mind?" Jack says without improving his tone much.

"Wondered if you guys got robbed here about two years ago," the guy says.

Well, if Jack wasn't interested in this guy a minute ago, he sure is now—and I have to say that my antenna just shot into the air too.

"What are you talking about?" Jack asks.

"Well," the guy explains, "a couple of years ago, me and my buddy robbed this station—at least I'm pretty sure it was this station—and I waited outside while my buddy went in and made some kid give him the money out of the cash drawer and then we took off."

I look at Jack and see his face turning redder by the second, and a few sparks are shooting from his teeth as he begins to grind them. Tiny beads of sweat are popping out on his forehead and upper lip, his body posture's coming to a nice military attention, and he looks like he wants to say something but it's just not time yet, so he just grunts a kind of *hmmm* and keeps listening.

"Yeah, that's what we did," the guy says. "I guess you probably remember that," the guy says.

Jack manages to tear his gaze away from this guy long enough to give me a look that tells me I should respond, so I tell the guy, "Yeah, I remember it because it was me that got robbed."

"Man, I'm sorry about that," the guy says and then explains that in the last little while, he's found Jesus and is trying to make restitution for everything he can remember doing wrong. This is something he remembers. "So I want to confess this to you," he says, "and ask for your forgiveness, and here's my half of the money we took from you, and you can have it back."

The guy hands two twenty-dollar bills to Jack. My first thought is, *Man, this guy had a pretty lousy partner because I know for a fact he got more than eighty bucks out of my drawer that night. Looks like it was divided just a tad unequally.*

Jack stands there, holding the two twenty-dollar bills in his open hand in total disbelief, looking first at the bills, then at the guy, then at me, and then doing the whole sequence again before looking at me and saying, "Kev, are you believing this?" and I say, "No, I guess I'm not."

The guy stands there quietly with a hmmm-wonder-what's-gonna-happen-now smile on his face, looking almost as if he's waiting for a thank you or a congratulations or a what-a-good-boy-you-are. To be honest, I feel inclined to give the guy what he seems to be waiting for, but then you've gotta remember that I've just returned from two years of missionary service, so my forgiveness muscles are pretty well developed at the moment.

But if Jack's forgiveness muscles ever were strong, they're *pret-tee* darn atrophied now—and it's a lead pipe cinch that this young man isn't gonna get a thank you or a congratulations or a what-a-good-boy-you-are from Jack.

Nope, not today.

But even though he doesn't have a thank you or a congratulations or a what-a-good-boy-you-are in mind, you can be sure Jack's got something in mind for this young man as he says, "Excuse me just a moment. I'll be right back. Wait here."

Jack turns and goes into the office and picks up the phone. Meanwhile, I realize that I'm in a rather awkward situation here that seems to be begging for someone to say something to break the weird silence that suddenly envelopes John Dillinger and me. Then it occurs to me that this is my chance—my chance to get an answer to the question that's been bugging me for over two years now. So I just flat-out ask the guy if he or his partner had been caught by a cop after robbing me that night and then brought here for me to identify.

"What're you talking about?" the guy says. "Nobody caught us," the guy says. "That's why I'm here now and trying to make good on what we did that night," the guy says.

And two years after the fact, my mind can finally rest.

But Jack's got no intention of letting anything find rest at this particular moment. Here he comes, storming out from the office. I don't know who he was talking with on the phone, and I won't know later today, either, or tomorrow or the next day, because he'll never tell me. Maybe he was checking on a late pizza delivery. Maybe he was getting an on-the-way-home-from-work shopping list from the missus. Or maybe he was learning that the statute of limitations has run on this crime and there's nothing anyone can do now to this converted criminal.

But whoever Jack was talking to and whatever he learned, that conversation's over now, and here he stands, red-faced and angry, in front of this seemingly repentant soul. He gets right up in the guy's grill and explains—with crystal clear magniloquence and in words a recently returned LDS missionary would mostly prefer not to hear—that he is, and I'm paraphrasing, persona non grata here at this particular facility and that he should remove immediately every single part of his body from the location or else suffer the indignant wrath and calculated punitive violence that will be inflicted post haste and without regret upon said body parts should he decide to ignore the warning and remain.

The repentant robber with an embezzling partner who'd clearly never heard the adage "honor among thieves" turns timidly and disappears, never to see Jack or this service station again.

And after a few short minutes, I, too, turn quietly and disappear, never to see Jack or this service station again.

Even though in just a few short years from now I'll have taken and passed several graduate-level statistics and research classes, I'll certainly never hold myself to be anything of a statistician. Still, I'll try many times throughout my life to imagine the odds against the sequence of events that played out around me at Bill and Jerry's Union 76 Station and Jack's Shell Station between 1967 and 1973. And I shall be persuaded that the odds against it all were essentially insurmountable.

Nevertheless, it all happened.

Although I've not called down literal lightning bolts from the heavens as Ranger Sullivan and Mr. Trevino did, it's nevertheless true—or at least defensible—that, as other kinds of lightning go, my name's entitled to hang right up there with the names of Roy C. Sullivan and Lee Trevino in the Hall of Coincidence, if it's ever created.

14

I play tennis with Howard Hughes

My preadolescent body was never mistaken for a prototypical athletic build. If there existed a book entitled *Mesomorphs I Have Known*, my name would be found neither in the text nor in the footnotes.

But being built more for butterfly collecting than for blitzing didn't stop me from enjoying sports as a youngster. I did. From the time I was old enough to know about big-league baseball and football, I've followed them to one extent or another. And will, for the rest of my life.

Those of us chosen by fate to spend our childhoods in rural Mississippi during the fifties had to deal with the reality that we had no *home* professional sports teams. I guess the St. Louis Cardinals were the closest thing to a local or home team we had, and they were four hundred or so miles away.

The good news was that this left us free to adopt as our home teams whichever ones we liked. For me, of course, that *had* to be baseball's New York Yankees and football's Green Bay Packers. Could there ever be any team greater than Lombardi's Packers with Hornung, Starr, Nitschke, Taylor, Gregg, Kramer, and others? And what about the Yankees teams captained by Stengel and Houk, with Mantle, Maris, Berra, Skowren, Ford, Kubek, Boyer, Richardson, and so many other greats? The greatest of all time, in fact. Argue if you will, but you'll never change my opinion.

Moving from Mississippi to California at eleven years old changed nothing with regard to my loyalties. The Rams could never unseat the Packers as my home team. And there'd be no replacing the Yankees with the Dodgers or the Angels. Bond in youth, fan for life.

Until the Steinbrenner era, anyway.

Still, nothing even so dire as George could ever change my childhood memories of the great Yankees. In fact, it's entirely possible that among the last thoughts to skitter across my consciousness at that moment when I transition from my journey in this world to my journey in the next will be the memory of those simple words that I heard time and time again throughout my youth. Those words that rang out from the living room every half hour or so during a Yankees game. Those words that stopped me in my childhood tracks and drew me in a flash to the television or the radio like steel to a magnet.

Those simple, wonderful, exciting words.

"Mantle's up."

But in the seventh grade, I discover that baseball and football aren't the only sports that are fun to watch and play.

There's tennis.

And for one of my meager physicality, there are advantages to this newly discovered game.

For starters, to play tennis you don't have to be physically imposing because there's no murder-minded, three-hundred-pound linebacker to worry about. And you don't need arm muscles strong enough to tame a killing-capable baseball traveling toward you and your head at somewhere near the speed of sound.

That said, tennis isn't without its challenges. There *is*, in fact, a ball involved, and it *does*, in fact, travel toward you—and *pret-tee* darn fast too. But it's a fuzzy, soft, bouncy ball, and how bad could it hurt? And there *is* an opponent on the other side of the net trying to win the game—but he's not looking to stop your travel from this spot to that spot by separating your head from your body, and there are no cleats on the bottoms of his shoes to be aimed maliciously at precious parts of your body. In fact, your opponent compliments your good shots during the match, and if he beats you, then he jumps over the net to shake your hand after the match is over. How friendly's that?

So tennis simply turns out to be a safer and saner sport that doesn't require great height or great weight or great muscle or great meanness.

Since at eleven years of age I've none of those things, I guess I'll just give this friendlier and saner game a try. But to do that, I'll need a tennis racket, and that brings me to how I get my first one.

No, I don't find my first tennis racket at Boege and Bean Sporting Goods on Commonwealth just past Harbor in downtown Fullerton. Or at any other sporting goods store. Or even at a department store, for that matter. All those places have tennis rackets for sale, true— but in a depressing flash of reality, I discover that they actually want money for them.

My money.

I don't have any money.

So.

I get my first splendid tennis racket from a place called the *Redemption Center*. With S&H Green Stamps.

I'm talking about those wonderful little trading stamps that you get for free—one for each dime you spend—when you buy groceries or gas or just about anything you need to buy. In different parts of the country, you'll find different kinds of stamps—blue, green, gold, orange, even plaid. But most stores in our area offer Blue Chip Stamps or S&H Green Stamps. And in *our* house, you'll usually find Green Stamps. You might run into a few of the blue ones scattered about here and there, but for the most part, my family seems to favor those stores that give away the green ones. Don't know why. Maybe we need a master's thesis or a doctoral dissertation to discover and describe the differences between families that save Green Stamps and families that save Blue Chip Stamps.

Personally, I believe that the families that save Green Stamps are the ones that have really good-looking kids.

But I can't back that up.

It happens one day that I discover while reading the S&H Green Stamps Ideabook—a catalog with a fancy schmancy name—that I can get a sweet little racket from their Redemption Center for the measly cost of two-and-one-half books of stamps. Deciding on this as the best approach for a kid in my financial condition—read *broke*—I make my mind up that this is the tennis racket I'll have. It's a lovely Pancho Gonzalez autograph model. It's what they call a *junior* size, so maybe I can actually swing it. And wooden, of course. Nothing but wooden rackets are available at the moment, and for several years yet.

So I need to find stamps.

I start by tearing through the cupboards above the kitchen counter, collecting a wad of Green Stamps from this Mason jar, another from that Tupperware, and then all the errant loose ones that have escaped the confines of their respective containers to rest in freedom all about the cupboard. And can I just mention that to do this, I've gotta kneel on that hard countertop surface for about, oh, say, *fifteen years* or so, all the while enduring a pain in my knees that's just *gotta* be akin to the most awful kind of interrogation torture ever devised.

Having cleaned out the cupboards, it's time to hit the drawers. Especially That One Drawer. You know the one. It's usually in the kitchen, but once in a while, you'll find it in an end table or coffee table in the living room. Wherever it is, it's got pieces of rubber bands and tacks and pens with dried-up ink that wouldn't write if your life depended on it and pieces of paper with scribbles on them that mean nothing to anyone except Mom. It's got dead batteries and small steel washers that belong with nuts that'll never be seen again and bite-marked pencils that haven't seen a sharpener in the last decade. It's got old keys to lost locks and pieces of erasers and lots of little tiny things that may or may not have been living organisms at one time, and without some kind of DNA testing it'll never be known.

Yep. That One Drawer.

In our house, it's in the kitchen. Among the other gazillion things stashed in it, you'll usually find a few trading stamps.

Now I've cleaned out the cupboards and That One Drawer. I dash out to the car to see if any stray stamps might have fallen out of overfilled grocery sacks or Mom's purse as she hurriedly searched for car keys or a lipstick or a half-stick of Wrigley's Doublemint chewing gum. This is reaching—I know that. And it turns out that I don't find many here, but a few—and every one counts.

Now I've collected a pretty nice batch of stamps, with special acknowledgment to That One Drawer for yielding up a jackpot: one saver book almost completely filled with stamps already. Even with that advantage, though, I still won't know whether or not I've got enough stamps until I start pasting them into saver books. I'll need to fill two and a half books, worth about three dollars each, putting the total cost for this high quality wooden tennis racket somewhere between seven and eight dollars. At that price, you just *know* the racket's *gotta* be a good one.

Now, about these little saver books. The rascals measure about four inches by six and have little template squares printed on *most* of each page but not completely *covering* each page, which I guess they do because they figure if you can match stamps to those squares on the edge of the page then all the other stamps—which are mostly in strips or small sheets except for the rebellious ones that are on their own—will have to step right in line behind them, and the page will end up properly and fully covered.

Now, you've *gotta* use these saver books. If you take a wad of not-pasted-into-a-book stamps into the Redemption Center, they'll just laugh and say, "Come back when you've got 'em pasted in a book, young man, 'cause we're not gonna count those puppies for you, that's for sure."

So now here I am, back on my knees again and feeling the hard countertop surface actually shoving my kneecaps into my throat. I'm just ignoring that pain as I hunt eagerly for empty saver books because I know that a tennis racket lies at the end of my search if I'm successful.

Now, sometimes you can find these saver books in the cabinet over the stove, amid scraps of paper with never-used recipes scribbled on them and pieces of tomato soup can labels that lie forlorn in the topless Tupperware container. The same topless Tupperware container that I believe—although I've nothing empirical to back it up—sits in some cupboard in every house in America. But I already looked in the one in our cupboard, and it didn't have any saver books in it. I also find none—zip, zilch, nada, nichts—jammed in between the thirty-year-old cookbooks that are partly standing and partly lying there in the cabinet, next to the Tupperware container.

So I've got stamps but no saver books to paste them into. Shoot. Not to worry, though. See, a Thriftimart grocery store isn't far away, and thanks to my spiffy Sears three-speed bike that I got last Christmas, it'll be no sweat at all to get there and back in a jiffy. I've just gotta round the corner of Santa Ysabel and San Carlos and then cross Commonwealth, then Balfour, then Clarke—and then just before I get to Chapman Avenue, I'll be at the back of a shopping center with a Sav-On Drug Store on one end, then Hales Jewelry, then TG&Y—a five-and-dime referred to by some as Turtles Girdles and Yo-Yos but more often by my crowd as They Gyp You—and then Thriftimart.

Mom usually shops there, so I know for sure that Thriftimart gives S&H Green Stamps. So it stands to reason that they'll have the saver books too—for free, of course.

Off I ride, and within a few short minutes, I'm home again with a fistful of saver books to paste my little stamps into. I'd have been back sooner, but whenever I've got any pocket change at all—and today I did—I've gotta stop at TG&Y for a dime's worth of malted milk balls—which'll last me a couple of days—or at Sav-On for a ten-cent double dip of Rocky Road ice cream. If you've ever tried to eat an ice cream cone while riding a bike on a warm Southern Cal afternoon, then you'll know why I opted for the malted milk balls today.

OK. I've got stamps, and I've got saver books. Now the work starts.

I wonder if you've ever licked about fifty-two million trading stamps at one sitting. It starts out OK and, in fact, the glue on the back of the stamps tastes a little minty at first. But after licking about twenty million or so, things change. What starts out as a zesty little mint flavor turns into a taste that falls somewhere between mud and the bottom of a Goodyear tire that's seen about sixty thousand miles. And that's just the flavor. There's also the problem of all that glue that makes your tongue stick to the roof of your mouth, and when you're able to pry it loose to lick a stamp, there's no moisture left on it at all, and the best you can do is kinda rake that poor thing over the back of the stamp without any moisturizing effect whatsoever—kinda like sandpaper over a piece of rough board. Right after that, you start to feel *leet-tle* tiny pieces of your tongue actually tearing away as you lick, and you'll swear you should see little taste buds stuck to the back of the stamp.

And sometimes you do.

This is where the wet washcloth comes in. I take a wash cloth, fold it into a square, soak it in water, set it on the table just in front of me, and press the dry stamps to it before pasting them into the book. This works really well, but I should've started using it sooner. Now it's too late to avoid short-term damage to my sense of taste, and at the moment, my speech is pathetically impaired. But, better late than never. Perhaps the use of the washcloth-slash-sponge will have prevented any permanent damage.

When the last stamp's sponged and stuck, I'm just thrilled beyond repair to discover that I've got three complete saver books. I only need two and a half, but that's OK—when I take them to the Redemption Center, the lovely lady at the counter will rip the third book in half and give me the leftover pages to be used another day.

All that's left now is to find a way to get to the Redemption Center. As always, Mom's happy to help and will gladly drive me on out there when she can peel off a few minutes from the merciless schedule that she follows to run a household, raise four children, support a hard-working husband, hold down a full-time job to augment the family income, and fulfill various church and civic responsibilities. Not to mention caring for Gavan, the neurotic poodle that we inherited from a good friend, and the five-hundred-pound, black-and-white, terror-of-the-neighborhood tomcat, Tiki, that I raised from a kitten. [*Stewardship Note:* Although I love Tiki dearly, I can't honestly say I'm as careful to feed and look after him as I promised to be when I was talking Mom and Dad into letting me bring him home from Jeff's house, where my friend's mama cat had just increased the critter population significantly.]

Now, Tiki loves me to death, but he just hates my big brother. *Hates* him. Dave just mercilessly torments the bejeebers out of Tiki, so he hates him. But Tiki doesn't get mad—he gets even. Once in a while, he'll stealthily hide himself behind the ceiling-to-floor drapes that cover the sliding glass door to the backyard and wait patiently for Dave to wander by. When the unsuspecting tormentor passes within reach, Tiki springs out from hiding and sinks teeth, claws, or some of one and some of the other into any part of Dave's body that's exposed. Usually it's a heel or an ankle, but sensitive—and more private—body parts have been targeted.

But I digress.

So Mom and I hop into our blue '61 Chevy Bel Air and roll on down to the S&H Green Stamps Redemption Center. Into the building and up to the counter we go. Using the demo copy of the Ideabook catalog that's chained to the counter as though its loss would mark the beginning of some horrific tragedy or plague of Biblical proportion, I point out to a friendly lady the picture of the Pancho Gonzalez tennis racquet I'll have. I flash the saver books in front of her so she doesn't think I'm bluffing. 'Cause I'm not, that's for sure. I'm down to some serious redemption here.

"Yes," she says. "I believe we have that racket available," she says.

"If you'll excuse me for a minute, I'll just go get it for you," she says. The nice lady disappears behind a wall of shelves and comes back in pretty short order—but, for a youngster excited to get on with this new athletic chapter of his pathetically dull life, her absence seems way too long.

When finally the lady returns, I note that she's carrying a tennis racket in one hand and some other *thing* in her other hand. When she plops them both down onto the counter, I can see that the unidentified thing's made of wood. It's kinda broad at the bottom and narrowing toward the top, like a triangle with the top cut off. It's in two matching pieces, separated with about an inch or so in between and connected by four bolts—one at each corner—that I guess can be tightened by means of the wing nuts on them.

Not a clue what this thing is.

"Here's your racket and your racket press," she says.

Aha. A racket press. Hmmm. *What in the name of Kenny Rosewall's inside-out forehand's a racket press?* I think to myself, but out loud I say to the nice lady, "What's a racket press and what do I do with it?"

"Oh," she says, "you slide your racket head in between these two pieces like this"—she demonstrates—"and then you tighten down these four wing nuts like this"—she demonstrates—"and then your racket won't warp from moisture or heat when you're not using it. But," she cautions, "you have to be careful not to overtighten the nuts or you could break your head."

Well, heaven knows I don't want a broken head or nuts that are too tight, so I agree to be careful. And before you can say, "love-fifteen-thirty-forty-game," I'm on my way out of the Redemption Center with a racket in one hand, a press in the other, and a half-book of leftover S&H Green Stamps stuffed in my pants pocket.

Now I can be a tennis player.

Through my junior high and high school years, my tennis game never reaches a level that you'd describe as *advanced*. Most of the time, I'm just running after the fuzzy little ball and swatting at it, hoping that when I actually do make contact with the thing, it clears the net. More often than not, it doesn't—and when occasionally it actually *does*, someone on the other side usually hits it back over to my side. To some place where I'm *not*.

In my post–high school years, my relationship with this Sport of

Kings changes. Gets stronger. More mature. First, I take tennis classes at Brigham Young University to learn better technique. Then, during a two-year visit to Germany from 1971 to 1973, I see the most beautiful red clay courts you can imagine. Even though the circumstances of that visit prevent me from ever playing even one single solitary game on one of those grand courts, even just the sight of them somehow deepens my love for the game. Then I return home from Germany to discover that professional tennis matches are actually being televised a lot more than they used to be, and one day I watch one of those matches. Rod Laver versus Stan Smith. Seeing these masters play, I begin to understand what really good tennis is supposed to look like.

As for the great Rod Laver, this is my first exposure to him, but not my last.

After watching this Laver-Smith match, I take up the game in earnest. In such earnest, in fact, that I marry the daughter of the man who sells me my next tennis racket.

OK. I know that doesn't sound good. For the record, I do *not* marry Dianne because her dad sells me a tennis racket. But that's all I'll say about it right now because to do justice to the whole story of how she and I end up marrying, I'd have to go into a lot of detail—interesting detail, to be sure, but just too much for the moment.

For now, suffice it to say that I meet a lovely young lady named Dianne shortly after I return from Germany. I can tell immediately that if this incredible nineteen-year-old were a Boy Scout, she'd be in full compliance with every adjective in the Scout Law: trustworthy, loyal, helpful, friendly, courteous, kind, obedient, cheerful, thrifty, brave, clean, and reverent. To those you could add a few more like beautiful, bright, lovely, wonderful, fun, happy, and athletic.

And Dianne just happens to play tennis. Well, I guess she sorta *has* to play tennis because everyone in her family plays. This coincidence is more than just *interesting* to me—it's also fodder for conversation during our first date, during which I happen to mention that I'm looking for a new racket. See, the S&H Green Stamps racquet I've had since '63 isn't only too small for me now, but it's finally just generally given up the ghost. I mean, I'm just *pret-tee* darn sure I'd play better using only my hand or even just trying to kick the ball over the net. I explain to Dianne that I'm leaning *pret-tee* seriously toward the Head Arthur Ashe Comp 2 composition racket at the moment and what does she think of that.

Well, she just doesn't happen to think *much* of that.

This is when I learn that Dianne's father doesn't just love to *play* tennis, the game actually represents a sizable part of his livelihood. See, he also happens to be a sales representative for a number of sporting goods lines, including Yoneyama—later to be Yonex—tennis rackets. "You really need to talk to Dad about rackets before you buy that Head," Dianne says. "He can tell you about the Yoneyama," she says. "I think he's even got one you can hit with to see if you like it," she says.

Well, one thing leads to another, and before you can say, "game-set-match," I find myself headed over to Dianne's house to see this here Yoneyama racket she's been bragging on. When I arrive at her beautiful home in Placentia—one that any kid would be proud to come home to every day—I notice that there's no longer just Dianne's orange 1971 BMW 2002 parked in front of it but now there are other BMWs too. More of them, in fact, than any one family oughta be allowed to own, and in some states it's probably actually illegal for one family to own so many BMWs.

So. Let's see now. Here's this lovely Dianne. She's gorgeous. She's smart. She lives in a big, beautiful house. There are BMWs in the driveway, one of which is hers. She plays tennis. Everyone in her family plays tennis. And her Dad sells tennis rackets.

This could be love.

Yep. Love it is. And don't think the double entendre's lost on me here.

So I meet the parents, Joanne and Dale, who turn out to be just the coolest people you could ever imagine. When we're introduced, this lovely mom says, "Hi, Kevin, how are you? We've heard lovely things about you," and then she chases me into the garage with a water hose because . . . well, just because at the moment it seemed like the right thing to do. And my clothes aren't even dry yet when it occurs to me that I'm instantly connected with this mom and this dad on several levels, among which connections is a mutual love for their daughter.

And for tennis.

And—in a minute—for the Yoneyama racket.

Now, when Dale removes the lovely green-white-blue cover from the racket and hands it to me, it's love at first grip—and I don't need to hit even one single ball with this aluminum beauty to recognize *serious* differences between it and my recently deceased junior-sized Pancho Gonzalez signature model S&H Green Stamps racket. It takes only a moment longer to become convinced that this Yoneyama 7500's what's *supposed* to be in my hand when I'm playing tennis. I've *gotta* have one, no doubt about it. And today's my lucky day because Dale's good enough to actually sell me his demo racket at the killer price of twenty bucks.

I now own the first of several Yoneyama rackets I'll enjoy over the years.

And the racket I'll be using when I'm seriously thumped in a doubles match with Howard Hughes.

Soon after I've scored this great racket, I head back up to BYU to continue my education. But within only a couple of weeks after arriving there, I realize that the love I feel for Dianne goes way beyond the fact that she helped me get this great racket. So I call her up—romantic devil that I am—and pop the question. Yep, I just haul off and ask her to marry me. And she, like a misguided little lamb and in a moment of some inexplicable gullibility, actually says yes.

I wonder how many times in the coming years she'll wonder what the heck was she thinking.

For the moment, though, I've got this lovely young lady fooled into thinking it could be a fun ride with me, and I'm not about to give her any time to actually *think* about what she's done—at least, not without me in the neighborhood to remind her of what a good selection I am. So I finish up fall semester at BYU and then roll on back down to Southern Cal to keep an eye on my sweet Dianne and our relationship.

To stay active toward my education goals, I enroll in a German class and a psychology class at California State University, Fullerton. The German class is *pret-tee* darn easy, though, I say humbly—because having lived for the past two years in Germany, I've gotten a pretty good handle on that lingo. And as for the psych class . . . well. *Well.* After an hour of watching this totally-hip-in-his-own-mind psych professor swiveling back in his puffy black chair, with hands laced behind his head and feet propped on his desk, puffing on a pipe, staring thoughtfully—ostensibly, at least—at the ceiling, and spewing forth this most laughable, perplexing, not-to-be-understood-by-any-reasonable-human-being interpretation of existentialism . . . well, I can see that it's just not gonna be as easy to stay focused on my education as I'd imagined it might be.

So I promptly drop both classes.

A decision, I might add, that just doesn't blow my dad's skirt up, as it were. See, he forked out the bucks for these classes, and now he's out all that cash because I've dropped too late to get a tuition refund. So what I get instead's a really nice lecture from Dad about the importance of money and how I need to respect it, and how I should be just a *leet-tle* more responsible—especially with other people's money. Even though I know he's absolutely right, I just figure I've reached a point in my life where my father shouldn't be telling me what to do—so I get all huffy and tell him I'll just pay for school myself from now on and then I won't get hollered on again if I drop a class or two, or even out of school altogether if I want.

Somehow, I'll manage to stick to that decision through undergraduate and graduate degrees, but I'll forever regret my childish response to a loving father who was trying to help me become a better person. For the rest of my life I'll wish I could have that moment back again.

But it'll never come back. They never do.

Anyway. Water under the bridge. Or over the dam. Or something.

Now that I don't have school to worry about, I'd happily spend every waking moment with my Dianne—but somehow I manage to scrape together enough maturity to see that I need to find a paying job because you can live on love just so long before some idiot wants his rent money. And I'm *pret-tee* darn sure there'll be other less romantic, more practical needs to be discovered after the rice has been swept up, so a job it must be.

Now, it turns out that Dianne's dad's connected with the Brunswick Corporation, which has just opened some retail stores nationwide to outlet pool tables and other billiards products to the general public. One of those stores is in the city of Orange, just a few short miles away from me here in Fullerton, and to my happy surprise, Dale tells me he thinks he can help get me a job there. Before you can say, "eight ball in the side pocket," I'm working for Lloyd at the Brunswick store in Orange, doing my best to sell pool tables, bumper pool tables, and even the odd air hockey table. Plus cues, cue racks, ivory and Aramith balls, chalk, and other miscellaneous supplies. I'm collecting a healthy three dollars an hour for my trouble and enjoying a few other little perks—like an employee discount that makes it possible for me to purchase some lovely future collectibles. Like a full set of ivory billiard balls and a two-piece Willie Hoppe cue with solid maple forearm, leather wrap, and four full-spliced hardwood points of four-colored, hand-inlaid veneers. Beauty and craftsmanship to make any true poolster drool. Plus a top-of-the-line, fully lined, leather carrying case. Unfortunately, because I don't have any place to keep one at the moment, I can't take advantage of my employee discount to buy a classic Brunswick table for a price that's so low it'd just about render you unconscious to think about it.

Once in a while, I also get to help out at "sister" retail stores in Torrance and Burbank. The manager of the Torrance store's Owen, a nice young man—not much older than myself—with John Denver hair, eyeglasses, and laid-back demeanor. Owen's store doesn't get a lot of customer traffic in the little strip mall it hides in, so most of the time I'm just *pret-tee* darn bored. But I do pick up a couple of clever marketing strategies from Owen, like how to put the only-slightly-warped Valley cues out in front of the store with a marked-down price of a dollar each. Owen explains that this'll bring in customers that we can talk to so our lives won't be so boring and maybe we'll even sell a table or two because anyone interested in discounted warped cues will surely wanna spend a couple thousand bucks on a new Brunswick table.

I'll never sell one single pool table at this store on account of those cues standing outside the front door, in a bucket with a hand-written sign that reads *Top Quality Cues Just a Dollar Each*. But I make note of the marketing strategy.

Now, the manager of the Burbank store's a whole different story. He's Lou Butera, aka "Machine Gun" Lou, a renowned professional billiards player who'll win the US Classic Pocket Billiard Championship and the All Japan Open this year. This man can flat *play* pool. Trust me on this. His nickname comes from his habit of moving at roughly the speed of sound from one shot to the next. And his one-hundred-fifty-and-out run in straight pool against Allen Hopkins last year certainly didn't hurt his rep or dent his nickname in any way.

It's true that "Machine Gun" Lou doesn't actually teach me all that much—read *nothing*—about managing a retail business, but he sure doesn't hurt my pool game any. He generously shares lots of pointers that'll help me win an occasional game on my own pool table against my sons and daughter and various other victims not too many years from now. Lou also has a great rep for trick shots. I get a glimpse of this one day when I ask him to "show me something" and he proceeds to break and run a rack cuing only with his left hand. He's right-handed.

Now, I really enjoy this Brunswick retail gig, and three bucks an hour's respectable pay. But when I find out from a friend that jobs at the GAF factory in La Habra pay a little better than that, I hustle on out and apply for a job there. Color me surprised when I actually get hired there and start earning nearly a dollar an hour more than I've been making selling pool tables. Plus the occasional overtime. Sweet.

But silver linings have clouds.

It turns out to be kinda fun to run these machines that fold and roll GAF photographic paper and, as I said, I'm making more money than I made working for Brunswick. But, as a downside, I've gotta work a shift that starts at five-thirty in the morning. Now, you could never use me as an eyewitness in a court of law as to the *existence* of five-thirty in the morning because up until now I've never seen it, if you don't count the five-thirty that I sometimes run into from the night before. I *hate* five-thirty in the morning. I *detest* five-thirty in the morning. If I had my way there'd *be* no five-thirty in the morning.

But I'm pathetically poor, and I need some money to rent a tux for the wedding—how would it look if the groom showed up in Levi's—so I just keep getting up at five-thirty in the morning again and again and again. And hating it.

To be fair, I guess five-thirty wouldn't be so horrible if I'd drag my worthless body away from Dianne's house sometime before two o'clock in the flippin' morning so I could get some sleep, and then I wouldn't be so drowsy at work every day. But I won't, and I don't, so I can't, so I'll keep being.

The good news is that I get really good at running a folding or spooling machine while sleeping on my feet, with nothing but theta waves pumping through my semiconscious brain.

Now, when I'm not working and can manage to slip away from other responsibilities, I play a little tennis. Actually, I play quite a bit of tennis. OK, let's just say it. I play a *lot* of tennis. Usually with Dianne or her brothers or her dad or her mom. And, by the way, playing with these tennis veterans has helped me learn to play a lot better than I used to.

But lots of times I play with my friend, Dave, with whom I served an LDS mission in Germany South . One of my best friends for life.

See, Dave and I've *pret-tee* much adopted tennis as a religion of sorts, and we look for every available moment for the free exercise thereof. Ricocheting between work and personal relationships, the two of us manage to find half-days and even the occasional full day that can be dedicated to the game. Whenever we manage to get together— either after work or instead of work—we usually stay on the court for as long as we can. Sometimes for hours and hours and hours, and right up to that very minute beyond which we'll be in life-or-death trouble if we stay another moment. So then we leave, but on the way home, we always seem—despite the risk—to eke out another few minutes to visit the local A&W Drive-In and enjoy a couple of frosty mugs of root beer. The first mug we kill in one continuous, stop-the-thirst gulp, and the second mug we enjoy by the sip as we process the good and bad of our play that day.

To be truthful, Dianne isn't always pleased about the time I spend with Dave on the courts or about the way I prioritize tennis into my schedule, so from time to time I have to pay a price for my obses-sion. "I guess your tennis is more important to you than I am," she says. "Sometimes I feel like I'm competing with another woman," she says—referring, of course, to my tennis.

But my sweetheart always finally comes around in her own patient, selfless way and lets me stray to the tennis court every now and again. Usually with Dave, but once in a while, I find an opportunity to hit with someone new.

Now, it turns out that Mike, who's married to my sister, Ricki, works for Summa Corporation. Summa's been Howard Hughes's holding company since the tool division of Howard Hughes Tool Company was sold off in 1972. He—Mike, not Howard—works in an office building at 17000 Ventura Boulevard in Encino and has regular contact in one way, shape, or form with The Big Guys of Summa, one of whom is Randy Clark, an executive assistant.

Mike knows that Mr. Clark loves to play tennis. Mike knows that I love to play tennis. So . . . knowing that we both love to play tennis, Mike sets up a date for me to hit with Mr. Clark at his—Mr.

Clark's—home. It'll be a doubles match, I'm told.

When in years to come I learn more about the men I'm about to play tennis with, I'll have a retroactive heart attack.

On the day appointed for the match—a little less than a week before my wedding date on June 15, 1974—I drive down to the corporate office building in Encino where I'm to meet Mike and get directions to Mr. Clark's house. Uncharacteristically—meaning I usually get lost in my own backyard because I've got the same sense of direction as a compass at the North Pole—I make it to the Encino office without any problem.

But then I've gotta get from the parking lot to Mike's office a couple of floors up.

Turns out, that's not as easy as it sounds.

When I try to enter the building, I find the front door locked. As I stand looking through the glass door and wondering what to do, I notice a bevy of cameras attached to the building high above my head on either side. On each camera, I see a red light *blink-blink-blinking*, so I presume they're all working and that I'm at this very moment on Candid Camera. Just for the briefest moment, the thought flitters across my mind that maybe it'd be funny to do a little soft shoe routine as I whistle "Carolina in the Morning." You know, maybe entertain whoever might be observing me. But—again, uncharacteristically— good sense prevails, and I decide the tap routine wouldn't be dignified, so I restrain my happy feet. Turns out to be a good decision.

Only a few moments pass before I see an armed security guard approaching the door from the other side. The uniformed, stern-faced gentleman stands opposite me, glaring through the glass door for what seems to be an hour but is probably more like a few seconds. When he's persuaded, I guess, that I'm not up to no good, the man slips a key into the door lock and turns it, then opens the door to allow me entry. Before I take the second step inside the door, the guard asks, "Yes, sir, how may I help you?" and I notice that the ostensible friendliness of his words isn't exactly compatible with the flat affect and granite face that seem more interrogating than accommodating. I brush the contradiction aside and paste a smile on my face as I say, "Yes, sir, I have an appointment to see Mr. Ericksen."

"Mr. Ericksen," the guard repeats thoughtfully, still giving me a visual grilling. "That would be the third floor," he says. "If you'll just step this way with me to the elevator," he says.

I side the alert and very armed officer to the elevator, fully confident that if I run into an ambush on the way, I'm in pretty good shape as long as this guy doesn't turn against me. As we walk, I notice more monitoring cameras positioned here and there at ceiling level, and each one's got a lovely little red light *blink-blink-blinking*. Still on Candid Camera, I guess.

At the elevator door, the guard lifts the handset of a telephone hanging on an adjacent wall and says, "I've got a Mr . . . what was your name, sir? A Mr. Morris here to see Mr. Ericksen." Then I guess someone on the other end says both okey and dokey because the guard hangs up the phone and presses the elevator's up button. The two of us stand together silent, waiting for the *ding ding* of an arriving elevator—I staring pie-eyed at the shiny steel elevator door wondering if today will be my last, and Mr. Smith and Wesson staring at me staring at the door.

Awkward.

Finally. The eagerly awaited *ding ding* of the arriving elevator. I'm excited to think that I might be able to lose Barney Fife now, but then the shiny door slides open and my hopes are dashed in an instant. There stands another armed guard, facing me with his hands resting on belt and attached weaponry, looking me over from head to toe, and then locking eyes with me as if just *daring* me to break into that dance routine I thought about when I was standing outside the front door. After eying me for several pregnant seconds, RoboCop turns his head slowly—but never breaking eye contact with me as his head moves—toward his twin standing at my left, who's explaining that he's got a Mr. Morris here to see Mr. Ericksen on the third floor.

I find myself feeling a bit like a baton in a relay race when Mr. Front Door Armed Guard takes me by the elbow and hands me off to Mr. Elevator Armed Guard, who then takes me by the other elbow and ushers me to the back of the elevator. Without turning his back to me and without breaking the icy gaze he's got me locked in, this new guard manages—using, I suppose, excellent peripheral vision—to press the button for the third floor, and the door slides closed with a *ding ding*. He's still eyeballing me pensively like a grade-schooler staring at the second hand of the classroom clock as it approaches the last second of the last minute of the last hour of the school day. Now the nerves are starting to kick in, and I'm beginning to feel just the *teeniest* bit violated here. If I don't get out of this pressured situation soon, I may start confessing things. Horrible, unspeakable things. Things I've never even done.

And all the while, the monitoring camera just above the elevator door keeps on *blink-blink-blinking* red at me.

Ding ding, second floor. *Ding ding*, third floor. Door slides open.

Now, I'm guessing you won't be all that surprised to learn that a *third* armed guard already has me locked in his sights as the door begins to slide open—and when it's completely open, Mr. Elevator Armed Guard hands me off to Mr. Third Floor Armed Guard.

If I look at this thing from a positive point of view, perhaps I can imagine myself as a VIP of some kind. Perhaps an entertainer. Perhaps a politician or other world figure. Perhaps the inventor of duct tape. Then if I imagined paparazzi swirling and pushing about me, maybe I'd feel important through all this man-handling.

But I'm not any of those things, and there are no paparazzi, and all I feel is scared.

As I'm handed off to Mr. Third Floor Guard, I'm hoping it's the last leg of the relay. I mean, I'm just not sure how much more of this personal attention I can stand. And the last leg's just what it turns out to be as the third of the guard trilogy takes me by the elbow and ushers me into an office area where sits my dear brother-in-law.

"You made it," Mike says. "Come 'ere and sit down," he says. "How 'bout something from McDonald's?" he says.

Well, I don't usually have anything for breakfast except a Dr. Pepper—but even if I *were* the kind of guy that had an appetite in the morning, I wouldn't have one this *particular* morning because one of the casualties of heart-stopping fear is said appetite. A good thing too because if I ate something right now, I doubt it would hit my stomach before it reversed direction and showed itself again.

Being scared nearly to death will do that to your digestive system.

But now I've got my buddy Mike at my side, so I know all's gonna be fine. I'm still not hungry, though, so I say, "No thanks, nothing for me right now."

Mike makes apologies for all the extra security, explaining that just a few days ago there'd been a major break-in at the main Summa office on Romaine Street in Los Angeles. Apparently, some money and a number of top secret documents had gone missing, documents that later would be allegedly linked to the Watergate political scandal. Mike explains that the whole sordid affair's got everybody just a little edgy, so they're being pretty careful at every office to make sure visitors are watched and accounted for.

Lucky me.

So while he waits for some flunky to hop on down to McDonald's and bring back his breakfast, Mike keeps on working, making a phone call or two and taking care of some odds and ends. It's not too long before breakfast shows up, and then he says, "We've got a car waiting outside to take you to Mr. Clark's house, and as soon as I finish a couple of things here and give proper attention to this Egg McMuffin, we'll get you on your way."

"A car waiting outside to take you." Hmmm. Well, *that* sounds kinda uptown, and I'm just *pret-tee* darn excited to think I'm gonna be chauffeured to my tennis date. I've always looked forward to the day when I'd be treated with the respect I deserve. I guess today's the day.

Mike finishes whatever pressing business he's wrestling with, scarfs down the Egg McMuffin, and walks me to the elevator. I guess the local militia figures that as long as Mr. Ericksen's with me, I'm no threat to company operations or world security, because we walk together onto the elevator and off again without any side-by-side accompaniment. Except for Mr. Elevator Armed Guard, of course, who enjoys the ride down with us.

When the elevator docks at the ground floor and the door *ding dings* open, Mike and I walk to the front door, exit the building, and ramble over to the parking lot. I quickly glance around, expecting to see a limousine of some sort—maybe a nice Cadillac Fleetwood, or something of that ilk—with a uniformed subordinate type standing at attention beside the car's door, a brimmed uniform cap tucked neatly under one arm and all ready to say to me, "Yes, sir, please allow me to get the door for you, sir." Maybe he'll even throw in a nice salute as he speaks.

Instead, I see in front of me a new but nondescript Chevrolet Impala sedan. Seafoam green. Mike explains that this is the car I'll be driving, gives me some quick verbal directions to Mr. Clark's house, and then tosses me a key on a chain with a rectangular plastic fob that identifies the car as Unit 27.

OK. To be perfectly honest, I've gotta admit that I'm just a *leet-tle* bit disappointed here. I mean, there's no limousine, and there's no chauffeur. But . . . well, it's still a company car, after all, and I think it's just *pret-tee* darn nice of them to provide me with company transportation.

"One other thing," Mike says. "Go *straight* there and come *straight* back," he says. "No sightseeing," he says. His tone's serious enough to convince me that it'll just be a *pret-tee* darn good idea for me to go *straight* there and come *straight* back.

I slide into the Chevy and, under Mike's watchful eye, ease the sedan out of the parking lot, heading toward the freeway that will—hopefully—take me to my destination. I say "hopefully" because with my impaired sense of direction and general navigation disability, there's no question in my faithless mind that I'm as likely to end up in Hatchechubbee, Alabama, as in Mr. Clark's driveway. And by now I'm so nervous and apprehensive as I negotiate the LA traffic that I dare not even turn on the car radio because that would be a distraction, and every distraction's just one more log on the fire of my directional ineptitude.

An old sententious saying holds that the Lord watches over drunks, children, and fools. I don't drink and I'm of legal age, so . . . presuming that I have, in fact, gotten some help from Him today on the road between Mike's office and Mr. Clark's house, one must conclude either that I'm a fool or that a fourth category's needed in the axiom—like, the Lord protects drunks, children, fools, and the directionally confused.

Whichever of the cases is true, I miraculously find my way to Mr. Clark's house without side trips or double-backs or any assistance from a gas station attendant. I park the Chevy and make my way through foliage and landscaping to the front door. The secluded house is beautiful and clearly not a small one, but neither is it something you'd *oooh* and *aaah* at too much as you drove past.

A lovely lady—Mrs. Clark, I presume—greets me at the door, invites me in, and then accompanies me through a lovely living room to a large sliding glass door that leads out onto a beautiful and spacious patio that, in turn, transitions cleanly to a beautiful swimming pool just beyond. Passing the pool, we wind our way along landscaped sidewalks and past umbrella-shaded patio tables and other casual lawn furniture to a lovely tennis court. It's enclosed by a chain-link fence that's covered on all sides by an opaque green windscreen.

Thirty-four years later, I'll learn that one of the reasons for this windscreen is to provide privacy for friends and fellow tennis players who visit and enjoy the Clarks' tennis court—friends such as legendary entertainer Johnny Carson, no less. Keeps them from being annoyed by rubberneckers or paparazzi.

Mrs. Clark stops walking just before we get to the enclosed court, points me on toward it, and tells me that Randy's just inside the gate there, so I should please just go on in. She smiles absently and turns to make her way back to the house.

I timidly step inside the enclosure and onto the court to see a forty-something man pulling a tennis racket out of a sports bag. Looking up with a smile, he says, "You must be Kevin," and I say, "Yes, sir, I am," and as he peels the cover off his racket, he introduces himself as Randy Clark and says, "Mike tells me you can play this game pretty well." I say, "Well, I don't know about that, but I sure like to play," and he says, "Well, let's just hit a few balls and see how it goes."

Mr. Clark grabs a can of Wilson tennis balls, pops the top, and pours two of the three balls into his left hand. He tosses one of them to the net, sticks the other in his left pocket, then pours the third ball out into his left hand. He drops the empty can into his sports bag, picks up his racket at the throat with the fingers of his left hand that's already holding the third ball, and walks over to me with his right hand outstretched. "Glad to meet you," he says as he shakes my hand. "Why don't you take this side, and I'll take that side, and let's hit it a little," he says.

Thanks to my sweet mom's employee discount, I'm sporting some *pret-tee* spiffy Catalina tennis wear—from the Arthur Ashe Collection—but I've got nothing fancy like Mr. Clark's sports bag to carry my gear in. I remove my Yoneyama racket's head cover and drop it next to the net post as I walk to the base line to wait for Mr. Clark to start the volley by hitting the ball over to me. Here it comes, and I get my racket on it without any trouble—but the sorry thing just heads right for the net, pops against the tape, and rolls down the net and back toward me.

"Sorry," I say. "I'll get this one back to you," I say. Mr. Clark says, "Don't worry about it. Here ya go," as he strokes another ball over the net to me. I get my racket on the little yellow critter, but again, it catches the tape and rolls down the net and back toward me. All three balls are now on my side of the net, and I'm feeling just a tad embarrassed about it, but I hustle toward the net, scrape up the balls one at a time, pop two of them into my pocket, bounce back to the baseline, and say "coming" as I stroke the third ball over the net to start the volley. Mr. Clark sends it back to me with a forehand, and I get my racket on it again—but this time the ball heads for the right sideline and on to the fence.

This just isn't going well at all.

"Sorry, Mr. Clark," I say, and he says, "Don't worry about it, Kevin, and by the way, my name's Randy, so just tap that thing over here and let's get a couple hits." I pull a ball from my left pocket, bounce it once, and stroke an easy forehand over the net to Randy. He gets a racket on the ball and sends it back to me. This time I *really* focus on making solid contact, and I actually manage to get a forehand back over to him. I guess he's thrilled by my success because he kinda shrieks out an "Attaboy, Kevin."

Terrific. He's gotta compliment me on starting a practice volley.

Making a great first impression here.

Well, in the next few minutes, we manage a few pretty good practice rallies. I wish I could say I don't make any more unforced errors, but I can't because I do. I manage to get a few balls back over the net, though, and we're both starting to feel pretty warmed up when the gate opens and a couple of gentlemen walk in.

Randy and I stop hitting, and I follow his lead over to greet the two gentlemen. When introductions are finished, I find myself standing on the court with Randy, Bill, and Chester. If anyone said Bill's and Chester's last names, I didn't hear them—but even if they *were* mentioned, they wouldn't mean anything to me today and won't until one day many years from now when I discover just who Bill and Chester are.

Which is when I'll have that retroactive heart attack I already mentioned.

Here it is in a nutshell.

Chester is Chester Davis, attorney. General counsel for Howard Hughes and his corporate interests. The man who in a couple of years will be described by Time Magazine as, "the pugnacious Wall Street lawyer who masterminded Hughes' long and ultimately successful legal battle against the Eastern financial Establishment regarding alleged antitrust violations at TWA."

Bill is Frank William Gay. Chairman of the board of directors of Hughes Air Corporation. Senior vice president and member of the board of directors of Hughes Tool Company. President and chief executive officer of Summa Corporation. Some go so far as to say that during these last few years of Mr. Hughes's total seclusion prior to his death, Bill is . . . well, in a variety of ways and for many intents and purposes, Bill is . . . well . . . he's . . . sort of . . . well, Bill is . . .

Howard Hughes.

Even as I'm playing tennis with them, these gentlemen are involved in circumstances and events that'll have far-reaching and—some say—national and international impact. Much is being written about them now and will yet be written about them—about things in which they've been involved, are involved, and will be involved. In fact and in speculation.

And can I just share that it's a dang good thing I don't know right now what I'll know in future years about the men I'm sharing a tennis court with. I mean, even *without* knowing who they are, I can't hit two strokes in a row worth talking about and apparently I'm trying to drill a hole through the net with the ball. I've tripped over my own shoe-laces more than once, fallen over the net, and run smack dab face-first into the fence. I've lobbed the ball over the fence, watched my racket sail from my hand to the other side of the net, and hit Bill Gay in the butt with the ball on my serve. I've got a bruise on my left ankle from hitting myself with my racket, a tennis ball's floating in the pool, and nobody's seen the cat for at least a half hour. Every time the ball comes to me—and by the second set it's only coming to me when someone accidentally fails to hit it *away* from me—the three amigos turn and run screaming for cover with their arms and rackets shielding their heads because they figure there's no way for them to know where the little round yellow sphere of death will go after I hit it and there could be injuries. So if I'm playing *this* rotten just thinking of these men as friends of my brother-in-law that he hooked me up with for a little tennis, imagine how I'd play if I really understood who they are. In that scenario, I'm pretty sure my feet would stop working, my hand would melt onto the grip of the racket handle, and after suffering a massive anxiety attack that'd stop a locomotive, I'd collapse and fall to my back at the net, wide eyes staring blankly toward the heavens.

Well, with me in that condition, at least Randy, Bill, and Chester would all be safer.

No matter what anyone today or in future years might think or guess or write or say or prove about these gentlemen, for my money, each and every one of them's a saint. A *saint*, I tell you. They've all stayed on the court with me for more than two hours, all the while complimenting my pathetic game and encouraging me on. They've smiled and said, "good shot" and, "my fault" and, "Kevin, I think your ball just caught the line" and in general just tried to compensate for the fact that the B-plus game I brought with me today turned out to be a D-minus game and pretty much ruined the day for these poor guys.

The courtesy of these gentlemen notwithstanding, I'd say the odds against my being invited back for a rematch are only slightly shorter than the odds against me hoisting a championship trophy on Centre Court at Wimbledon.

Well, I've done just about as much damage to Randy's tennis court and the surrounding landscape as I can do today, and all three of my tennis partners are sitting against the fence, making funny noises, and browsing golf equipment catalogs—so I guess it's time for me to say farewell and roll on back to the office.

The traffic gods are still smiling on me, it turns out, and I'm able to make it back to the Encino office without delay. I pull into the office parking lot and return the borrowed car to the same parking stall I took it from. I lock its doors and head on inside to play Duck-Duck-Goose with my three friendly armed guards. And with them at my side one at a time, I finally make it back to Mike's desk to find him chatting with someone on the phone. I catch my brother-in-law's eyes, and while he's staring wide-eyed at me, I hear him say into the telephone, "Yes, sir, he just walked in, and everything seems to be just fine."

Mike's speaking with Mr. Gay, who's called to make sure I've returned the company car to the office without delay. And his call's come with perfect timing, I might add.

"Go straight there and come straight back."

How glad am I that I didn't run into a wad of LA traffic, stop off at Taco Bell for a late lunch, or try to hock the company car at Joe's Pawn and Trophy. I've no idea what would've happened had I not done as I was told, but some things in this life are just better undiscovered.

I thank Mike for taking the trouble to set up today's Grand Slam event, bid a sorrowful farewell to my new armed guard friends, and climb into the orange 1971 BMW 2002 sedan that's part of Dianne's dowry.

As I make my way back to Orange County and the comfort and security of loved ones, I'm oblivious to the retroactive questions and what-ifs and wonders that will tease my imagination throughout the coming years whenever I remember this day. This exciting, frightening, sobering, incredible day.

The day I played tennis with Howard Hughes.

And hit him in the butt with a ball.

About the
Author

Born in 1951, J. Kevin Morris enjoyed a wondrous childhood in small-town Mississippi surrounded by woods, mud holes, and simple pleasures. His family removed to Southern California (Orange County) in 1962, where he experienced a teenage-years environment very much unlike that of his childhood.

After graduating from Troy High School in Fullerton, California, in 1969, he began his university studies at Brigham Young University in Provo, Utah. After three semesters, he received an assignment in 1971 to serve as a full-time missionary for The Church of Jesus Christ of Latter-day Saints. For the next two years, he enjoyed the great fortune of living and working among the wonderful German people.

He resumed his studies at BYU in the fall of 1973. Because he'd just met the woman he would marry, however, he completed only one semester before returning home to Southern California to prepare for a wedding and married life.

He married Dianne Raddatz in June of 1974, and the two of them returned to Provo in the fall to resume his BYU studies. English was his first major, and he enjoyed creative and technical writing classes; but the notion of writing as a career gave way to an interest in a more direct approach to helping people, and he took an undergraduate degree in psychology in 1976. He worked full-time as a psychologist at the Utah State Training School in American Fork while he pursued a master's degree in school psychology, which he received from the University of Utah in 1984.

Along the way, his little family grew by one daughter and two sons—Anne in 1975, Kristopher in 1978, and Jeremy in 1980.

Accepting an offer of employment as the school psychologist for Iron County School District, he left the employ of the Training School and moved his little family to Cedar City, Utah, in the fall of 1984. He missed "home," however, and returned to Utah County the following summer.

Home again, he accepted employment as a school psychologist in the Provo City School District. His assignment was at the Oakridge School, a "special placement" school that served students with multiple disabilities in a self-contained environment. In 1989, he accepted the assignment as the administrator of that school.

He served as the director of Oakridge School until 1996, when he accepted the position of executive director of DDI VANTAGE (then simply DDI), a nonprofit service agency in Salt Lake City, in which position he presently serves.

His interests include, first and foremost, his family, which has now grown to include children's spouses and eight grandchildren. He also enjoys church service, helping DDI VANTAGE fulfill its mission of service to Utah's babies and families, writing, listening to and playing music (sixties music, of course—is there any other?), collecting vinyl LP records and sheet music, boating, sports, and a little amateur video editing.